Ant Story

Jay Hosler

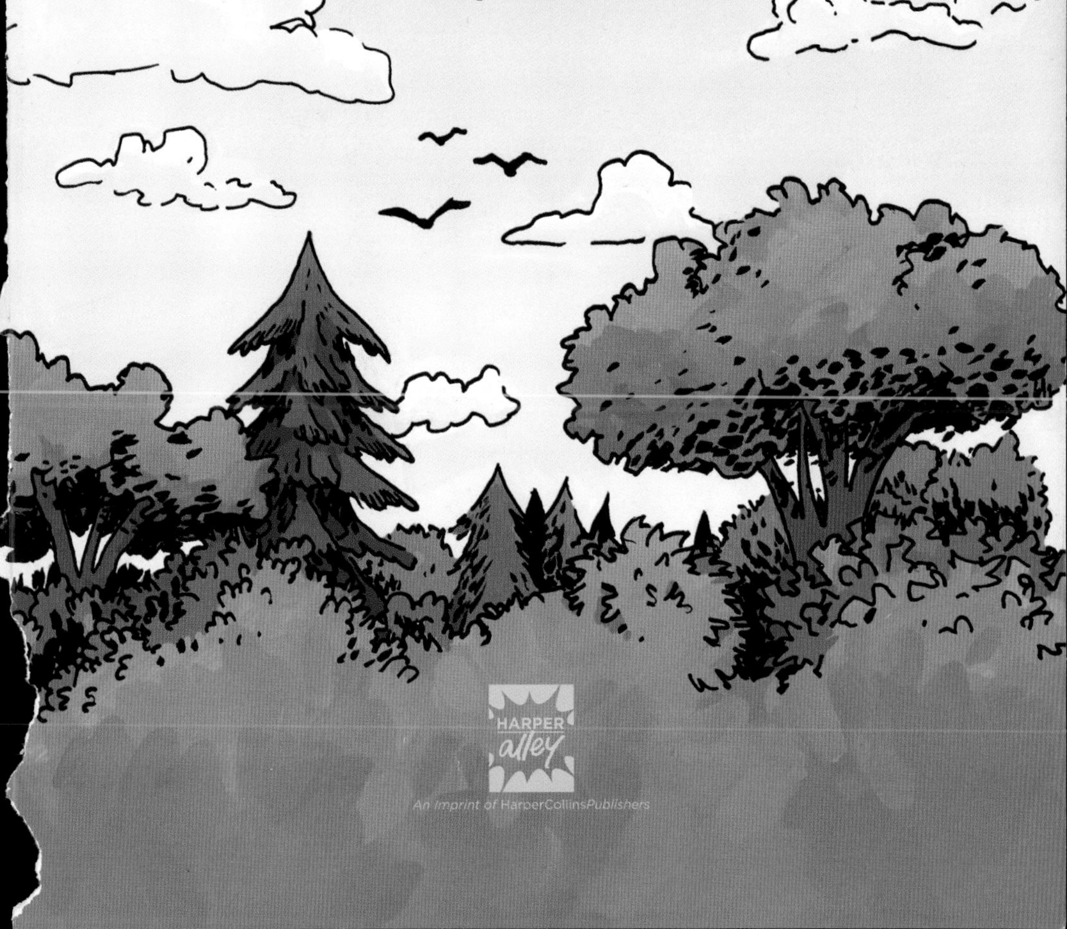

HARPER alley
An Imprint of HarperCollinsPublishers

For Lisa, Max, and Jack

HarperAlley is an imprint of HarperCollins Publishers.

Ant Story
Copyright © 2024 by Jay Hosler
All rights reserved. Manufactured in Malaysia.
No part of this book may be used or reproduced in any manner whatsoever without
written permission except in the case of brief quotations embodied in critical articles and
reviews. For information address HarperCollins Children's Books, a division of
HarperCollins Publishers, 195 Broadway, New York, NY 10007.
www.harperalley.com
Library of Congress Control Number: 2023937006
ISBN 978-0-06-329399-1 (pbk.) — ISBN 978-0-06-329400-4
The artist used a 0.7 mm color Eno mechanical pencil and soft blue graphite to draw the art on smooth Bristol
paper. The illustrations were inked using India ink in Koh-i-Noor Rapidograph technical pens (0.35 mm,
05 mm, 0.6 mm, 0.8 mm, and 1.2 mm) and a Kuretake fountain brush pen No. 40. A Staedtler Mars Plastic
eraser was used for analog corrections and the eraser tool in Photoshop was used to make corrections after the
pages had been digitized and resized.
Typography by Jay Hosler
23 24 25 26 27 COS 10 9 8 7 6 5 4 3 2 1
First Edition

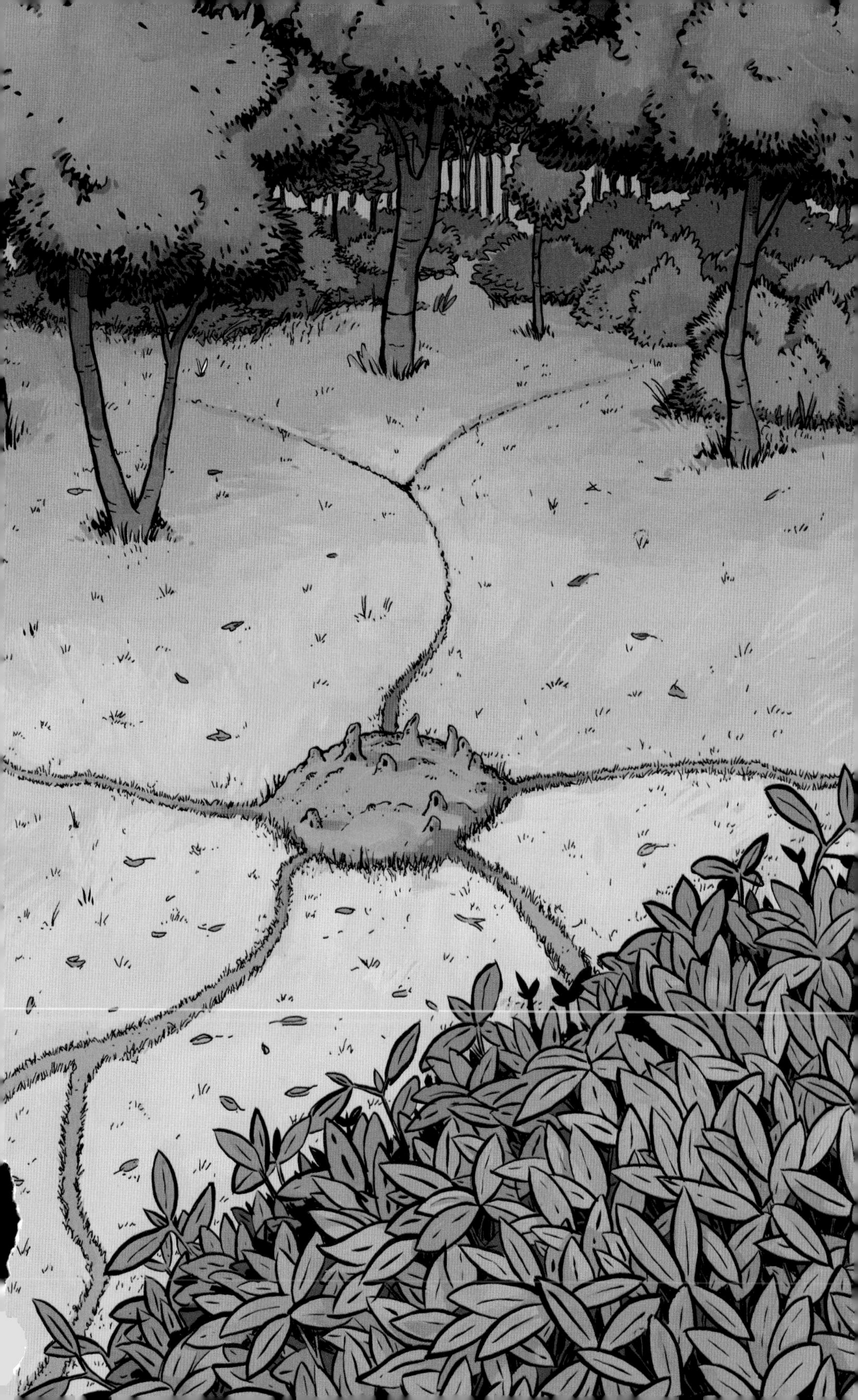

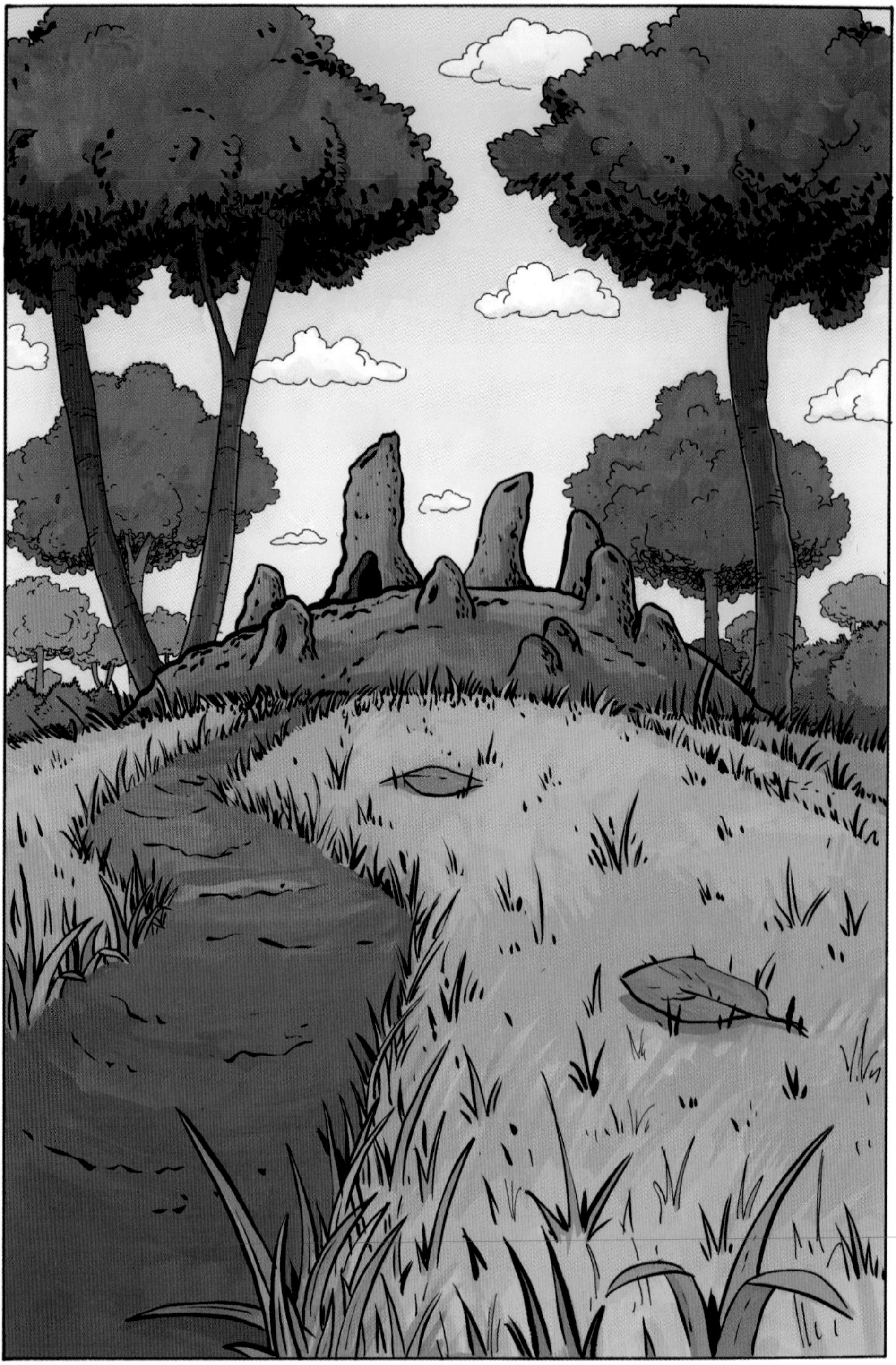

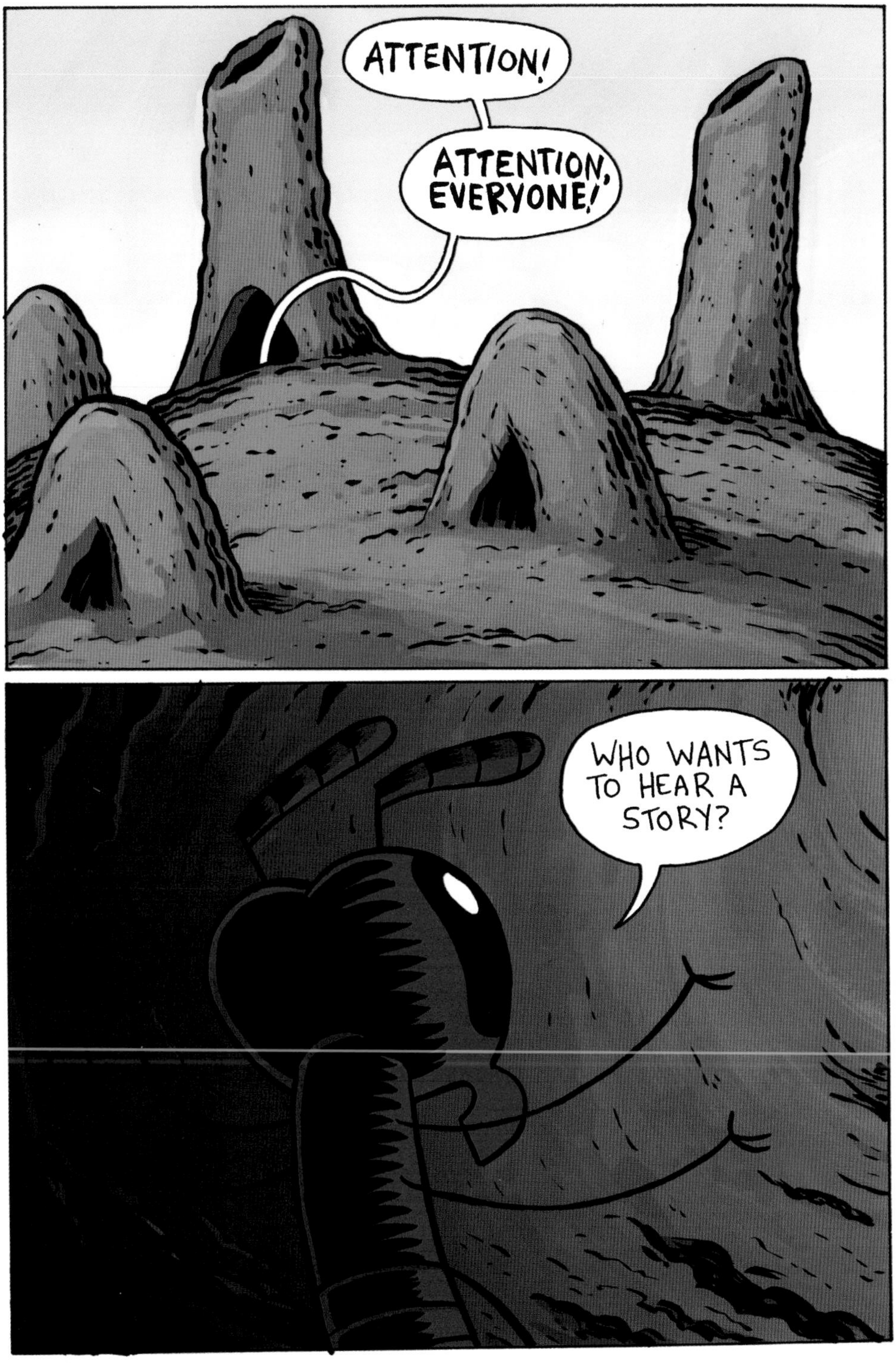
ATTENTION!
ATTENTION, EVERYONE!
WHO WANTS TO HEAR A STORY?

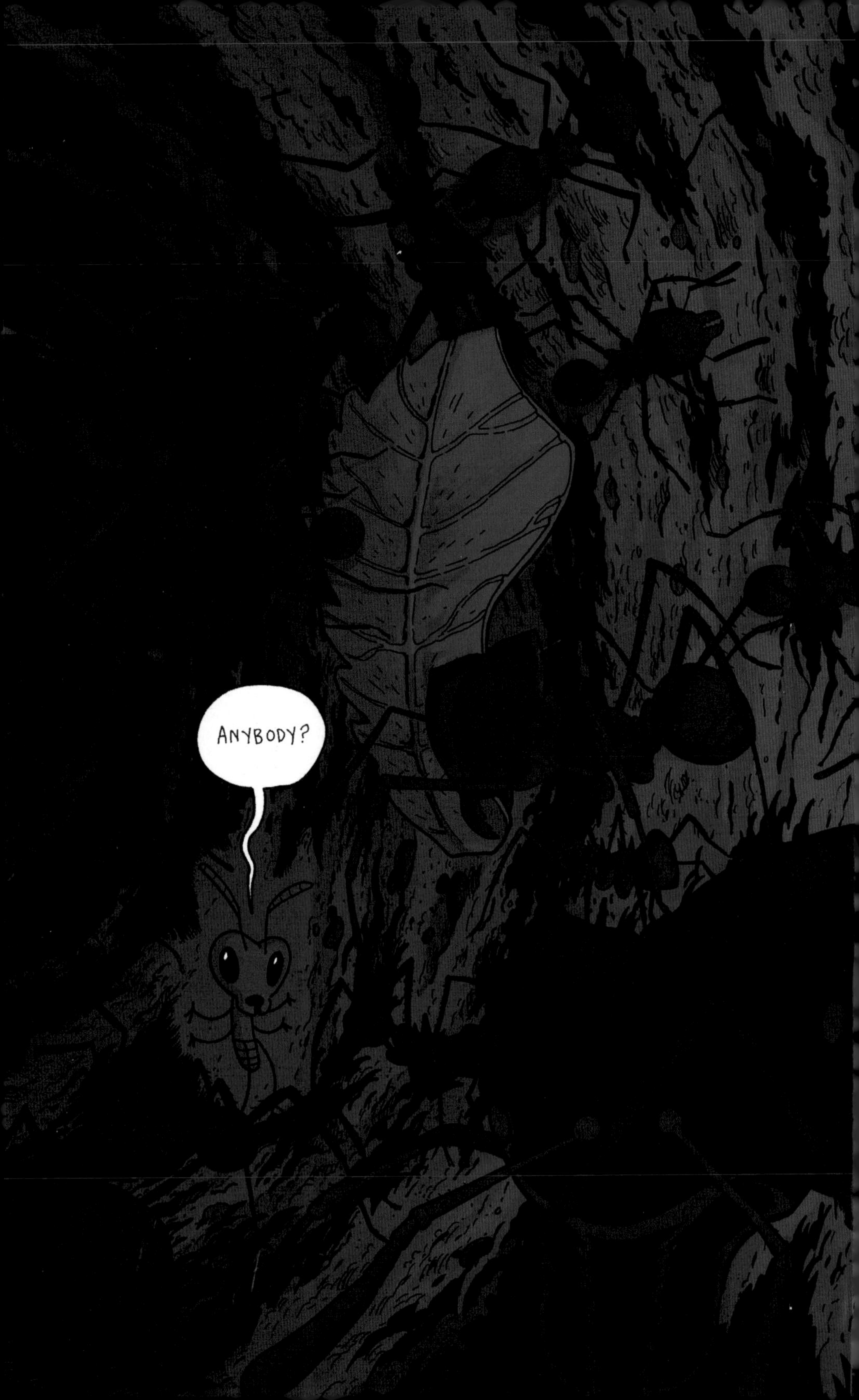
ANYBODY?

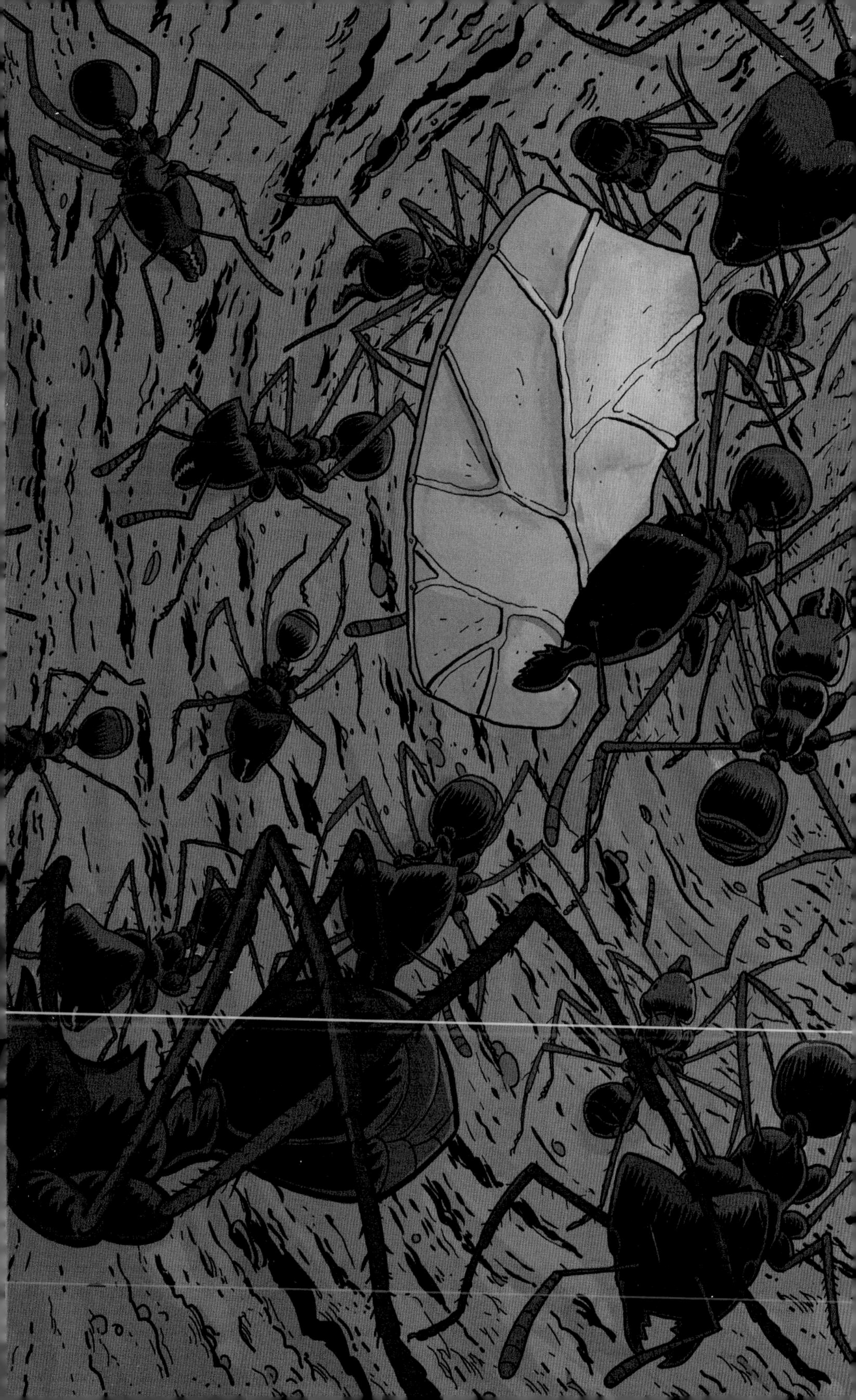

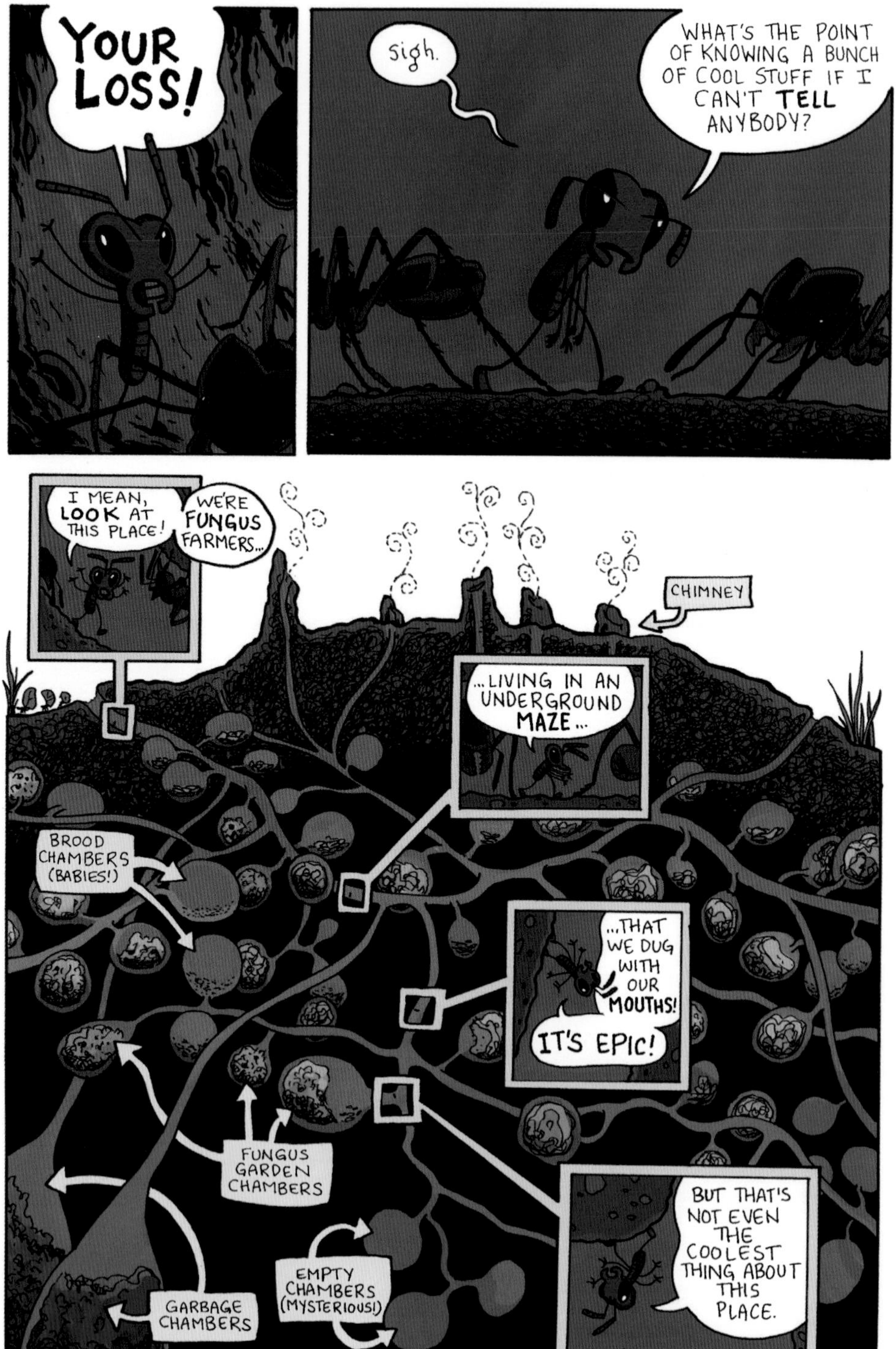
YOUR LOSS!
Sigh.
WHAT'S THE POINT OF KNOWING A BUNCH OF COOL STUFF IF I CAN'T TELL ANYBODY?
I MEAN, LOOK AT THIS PLACE!
WE'RE FUNGUS FARMERS...
CHIMNEY
...LIVING IN AN UNDERGROUND MAZE...
BROOD CHAMBERS (BABIES!)
...THAT WE DUG WITH OUR MOUTHS!
IT'S EPIC!
FUNGUS GARDEN CHAMBERS
BUT THAT'S NOT EVEN THE COOLEST THING ABOUT THIS PLACE.
EMPTY CHAMBERS (MYSTERIOUS!)
GARBAGE CHAMBERS

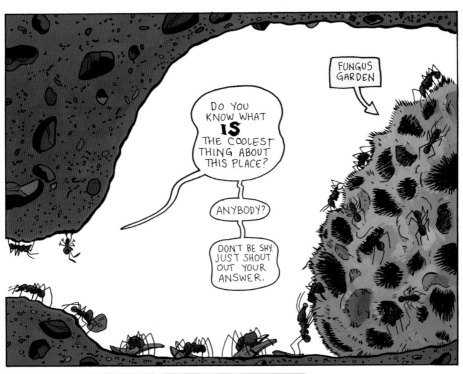

FUNGUS GARDEN

DO YOU KNOW WHAT **IS** THE COOLEST THING ABOUT THIS PLACE?

ANYBODY?

DON'T BE SHY. JUST SHOUT OUT YOUR ANSWER.

AND DON'T SAY "CUTTING LEAF FRAGMENTS INTO SMALLER PIECES FOR THE FUNGUS GARDEN."

although that is very cool.

good job cutting.

NO!

THE COOLEST THING IN THIS GINORMOUS, ASTOUNDING, SUBTERRANEAN AGRICULTURAL PALACE IS...

...ME.

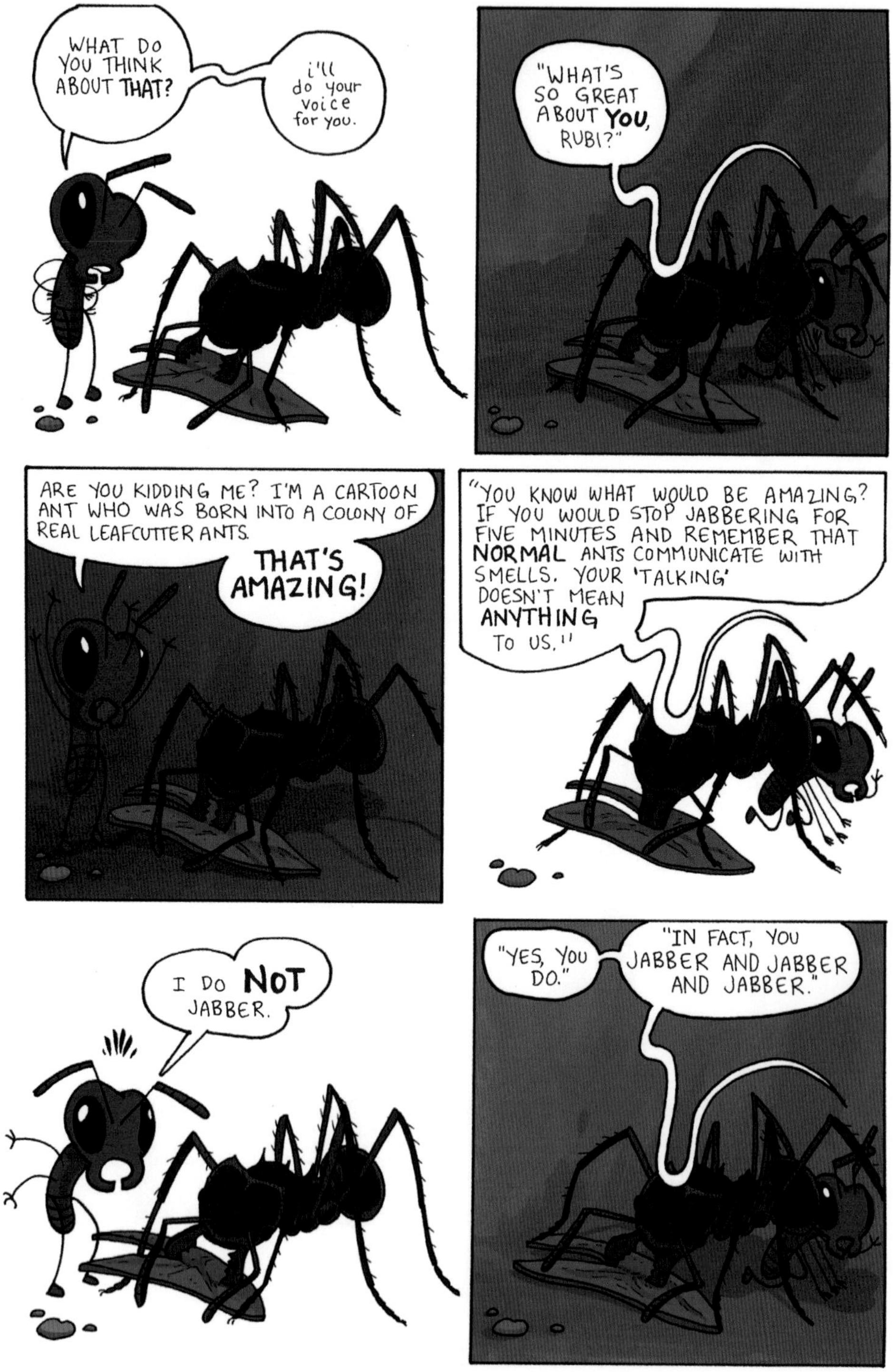
WHAT DO YOU THINK ABOUT THAT?
i'll do your voice for you.
"WHAT'S SO GREAT ABOUT YOU, RUBI?"
ARE YOU KIDDING ME? I'M A CARTOON ANT WHO WAS BORN INTO A COLONY OF REAL LEAFCUTTER ANTS.
THAT'S AMAZING!
"YOU KNOW WHAT WOULD BE AMAZING? IF YOU WOULD STOP JABBERING FOR FIVE MINUTES AND REMEMBER THAT NORMAL ANTS COMMUNICATE WITH SMELLS. YOUR 'TALKING' DOESN'T MEAN ANYTHING TO US."
I DO NOT JABBER.
"YES, YOU DO."
"IN FACT, YOU JABBER AND JABBER AND JABBER."

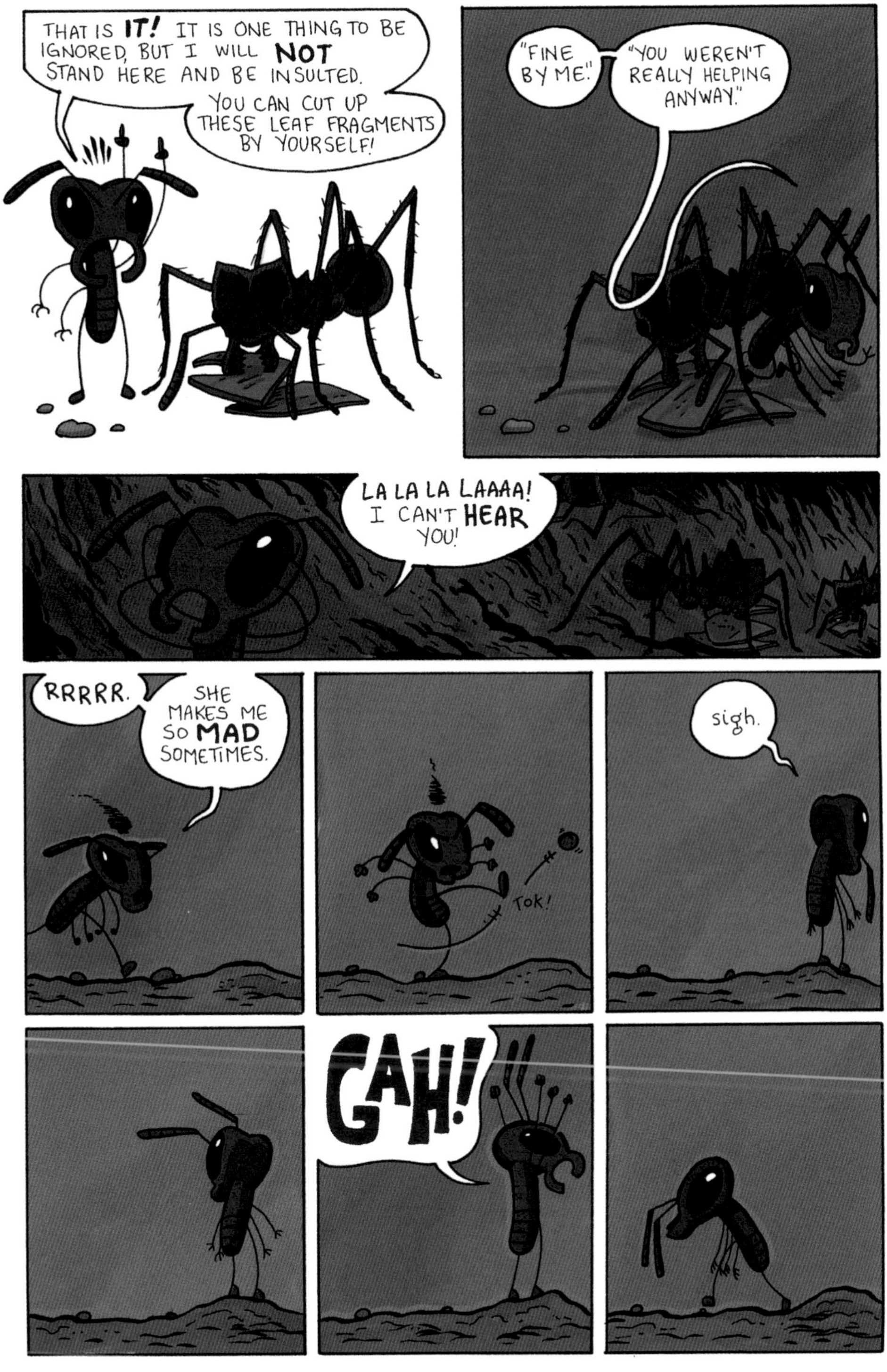
THAT IS IT! IT IS ONE THING TO BE IGNORED, BUT I WILL NOT STAND HERE AND BE INSULTED.
YOU CAN CUT UP THESE LEAF FRAGMENTS BY YOURSELF!
"FINE BY ME."
"YOU WEREN'T REALLY HELPING ANYWAY."
LA LA LA LAAAA! I CAN'T HEAR YOU!
RRRRR.
SHE MAKES ME SO MAD SOMETIMES.
TOK!
sigh.
GAH!

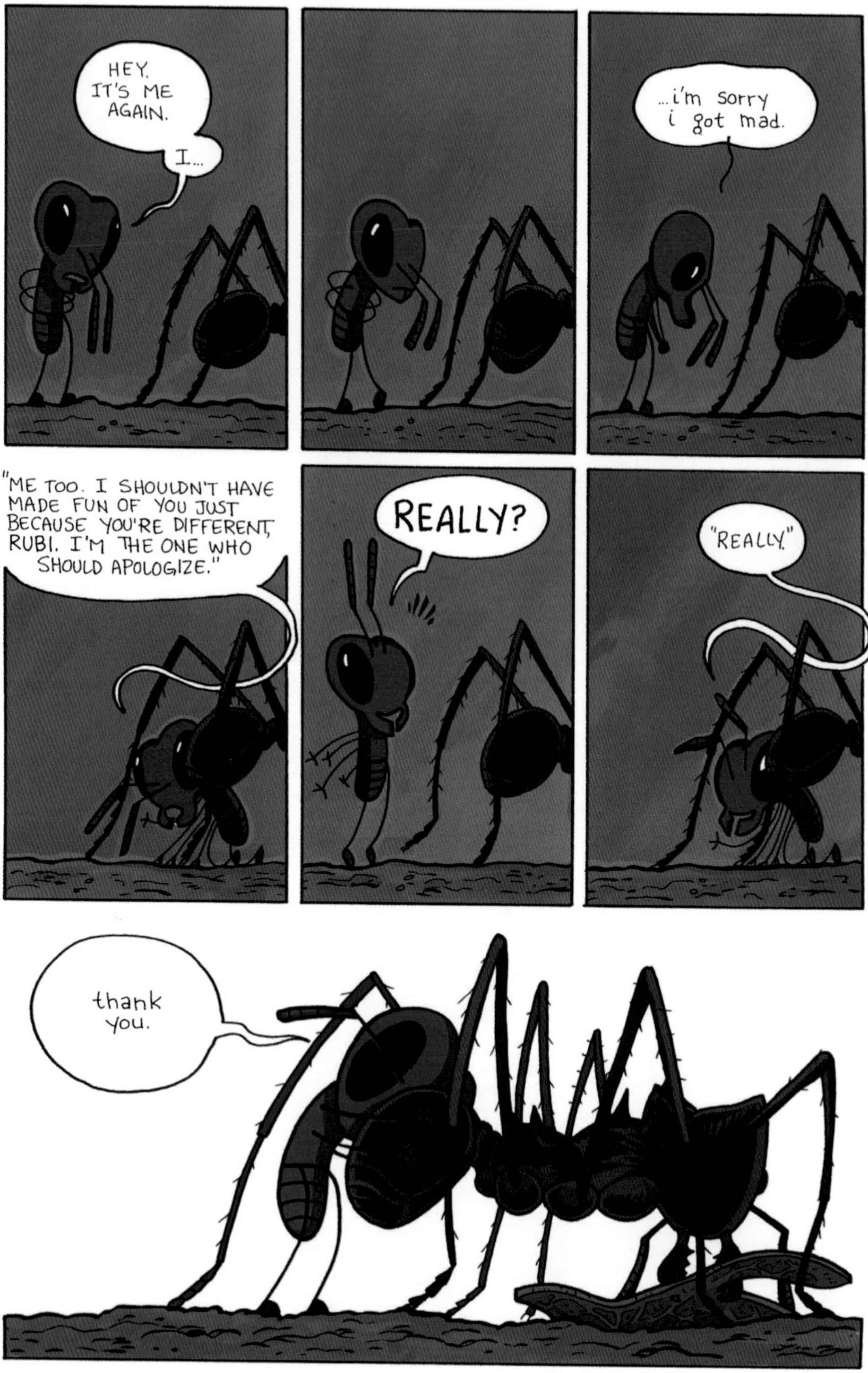
HEY. IT'S ME AGAIN.
I...
...i'm sorry i got mad.
"ME TOO. I SHOULDN'T HAVE MADE FUN OF YOU JUST BECAUSE YOU'RE DIFFERENT, RUBI. I'M THE ONE WHO SHOULD APOLOGIZE."
REALLY?
"REALLY."
thank you.

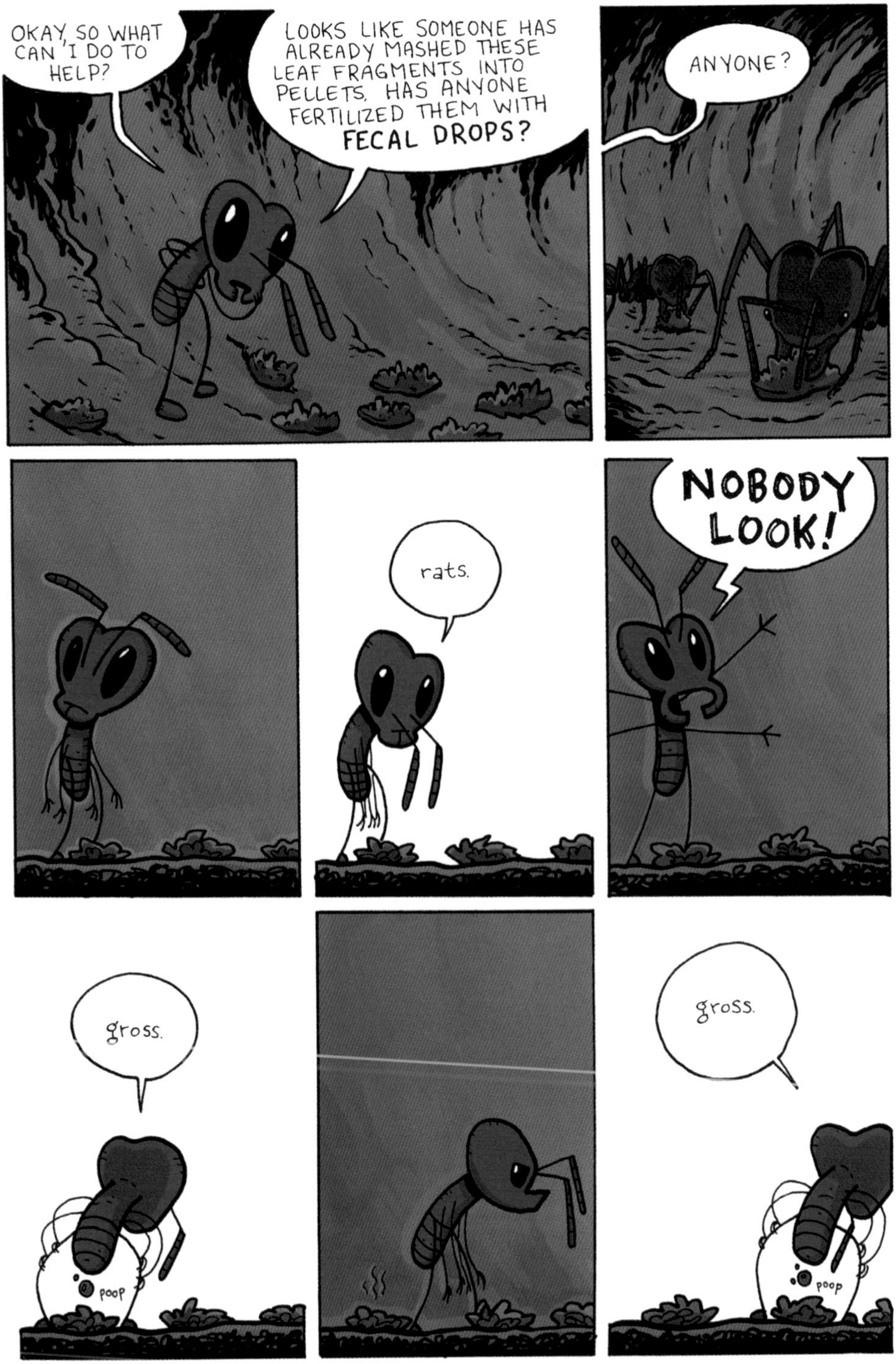
OKAY, SO WHAT CAN I DO TO HELP?
LOOKS LIKE SOMEONE HAS ALREADY MASHED THESE LEAF FRAGMENTS INTO PELLETS. HAS ANYONE FERTILIZED THEM WITH FECAL DROPS?
ANYONE?
rats.
NOBODY LOOK!
gross.
poop
gross.
poop

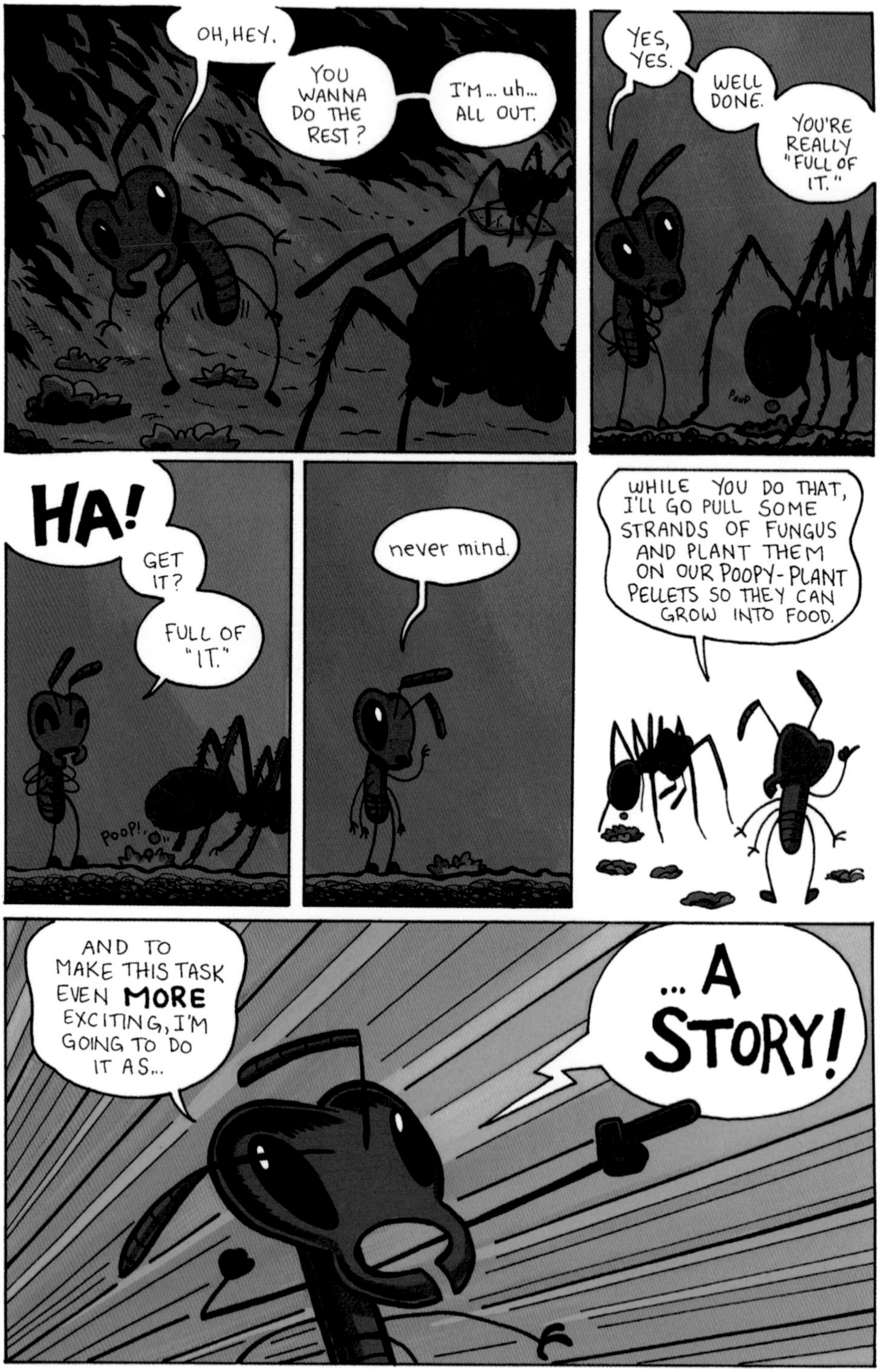
OH, HEY.
YOU WANNA DO THE REST?
I'M... uh... ALL OUT.
YES, YES.
WELL DONE.
YOU'RE REALLY "FULL OF IT."
POOP
HA!
GET IT?
FULL OF "IT."
POOP!
never mind.
WHILE YOU DO THAT, I'LL GO PULL SOME STRANDS OF FUNGUS AND PLANT THEM ON OUR POOPY-PLANT PELLETS SO THEY CAN GROW INTO FOOD.
AND TO MAKE THIS TASK EVEN **MORE** EXCITING, I'M GOING TO DO IT AS...
...A STORY!

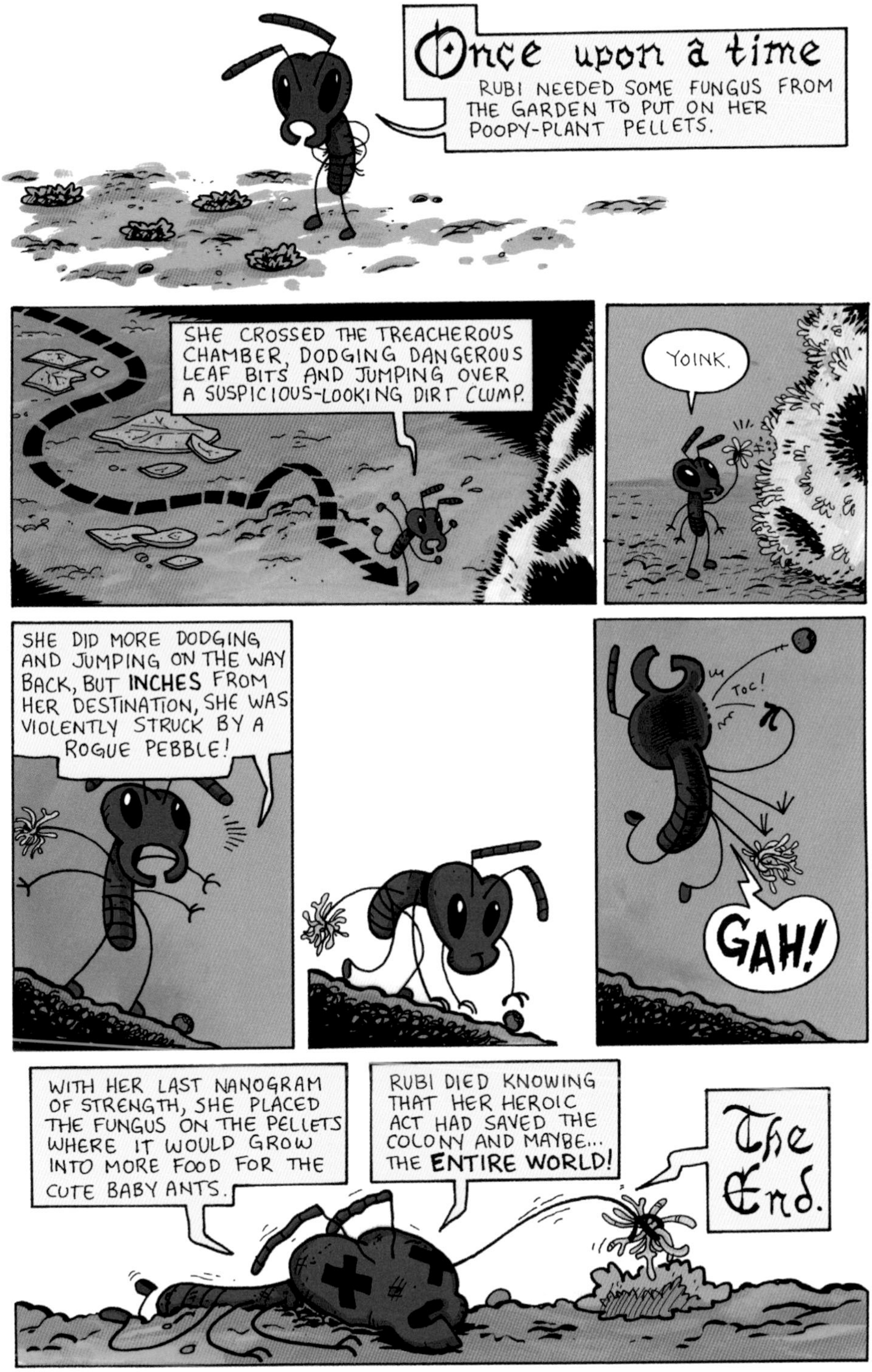
Once upon a time
RUBI NEEDED SOME FUNGUS FROM THE GARDEN TO PUT ON HER POOPY-PLANT PELLETS.
SHE CROSSED THE TREACHEROUS CHAMBER, DODGING DANGEROUS LEAF BITS AND JUMPING OVER A SUSPICIOUS-LOOKING DIRT CLUMP.
YOINK.
SHE DID MORE DODGING AND JUMPING ON THE WAY BACK, BUT INCHES FROM HER DESTINATION, SHE WAS VIOLENTLY STRUCK BY A ROGUE PEBBLE!
TOC!
GAH!
WITH HER LAST NANOGRAM OF STRENGTH, SHE PLACED THE FUNGUS ON THE PELLETS WHERE IT WOULD GROW INTO MORE FOOD FOR THE CUTE BABY ANTS.
RUBI DIED KNOWING THAT HER HEROIC ACT HAD SAVED THE COLONY AND MAYBE... THE ENTIRE WORLD!
The End.

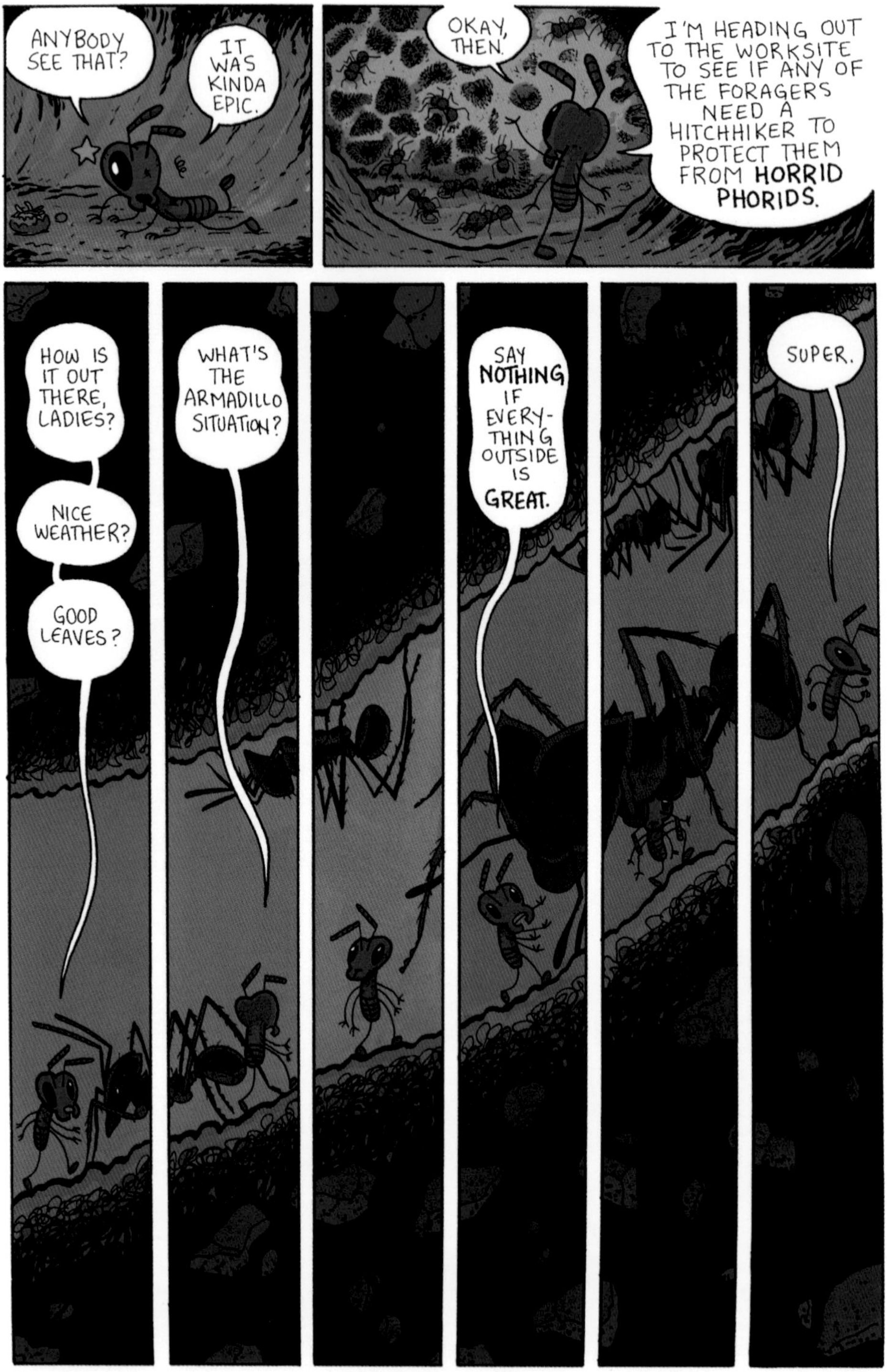
ANYBODY SEE THAT?
IT WAS KINDA EPIC.
OKAY, THEN.
I'M HEADING OUT TO THE WORKSITE TO SEE IF ANY OF THE FORAGERS NEED A HITCHHIKER TO PROTECT THEM FROM **HORRID PHORIDS**.
HOW IS IT OUT THERE, LADIES?
NICE WEATHER?
GOOD LEAVES?
WHAT'S THE ARMADILLO SITUATION?
SAY **NOTHING** IF EVERY-THING OUTSIDE IS **GREAT**.
SUPER.

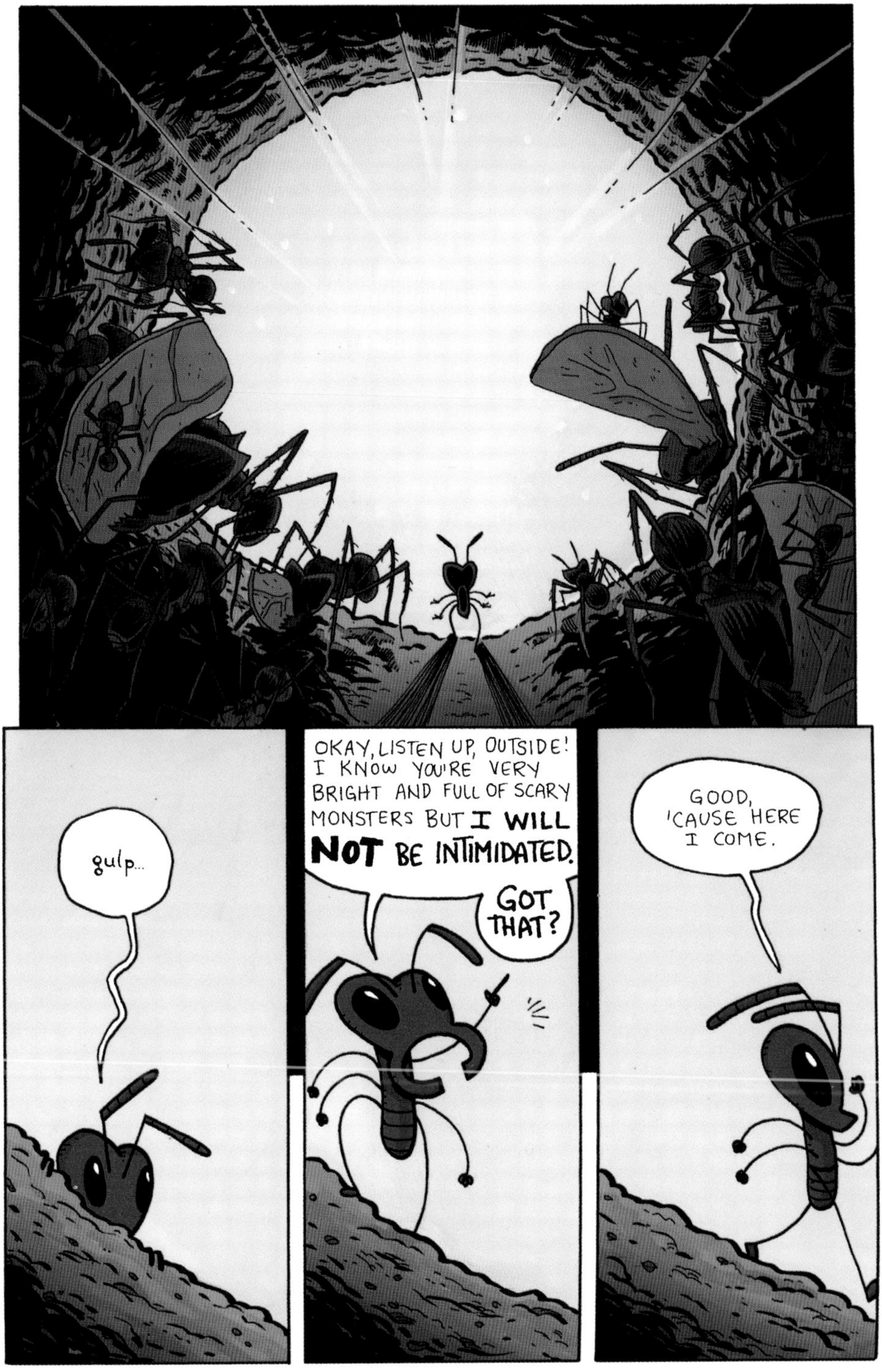
gulp...
OKAY, LISTEN UP, OUTSIDE! I KNOW YOU'RE VERY BRIGHT AND FULL OF SCARY MONSTERS BUT I WILL NOT BE INTIMIDATED.
GOT THAT?
GOOD, 'CAUSE HERE I COME.

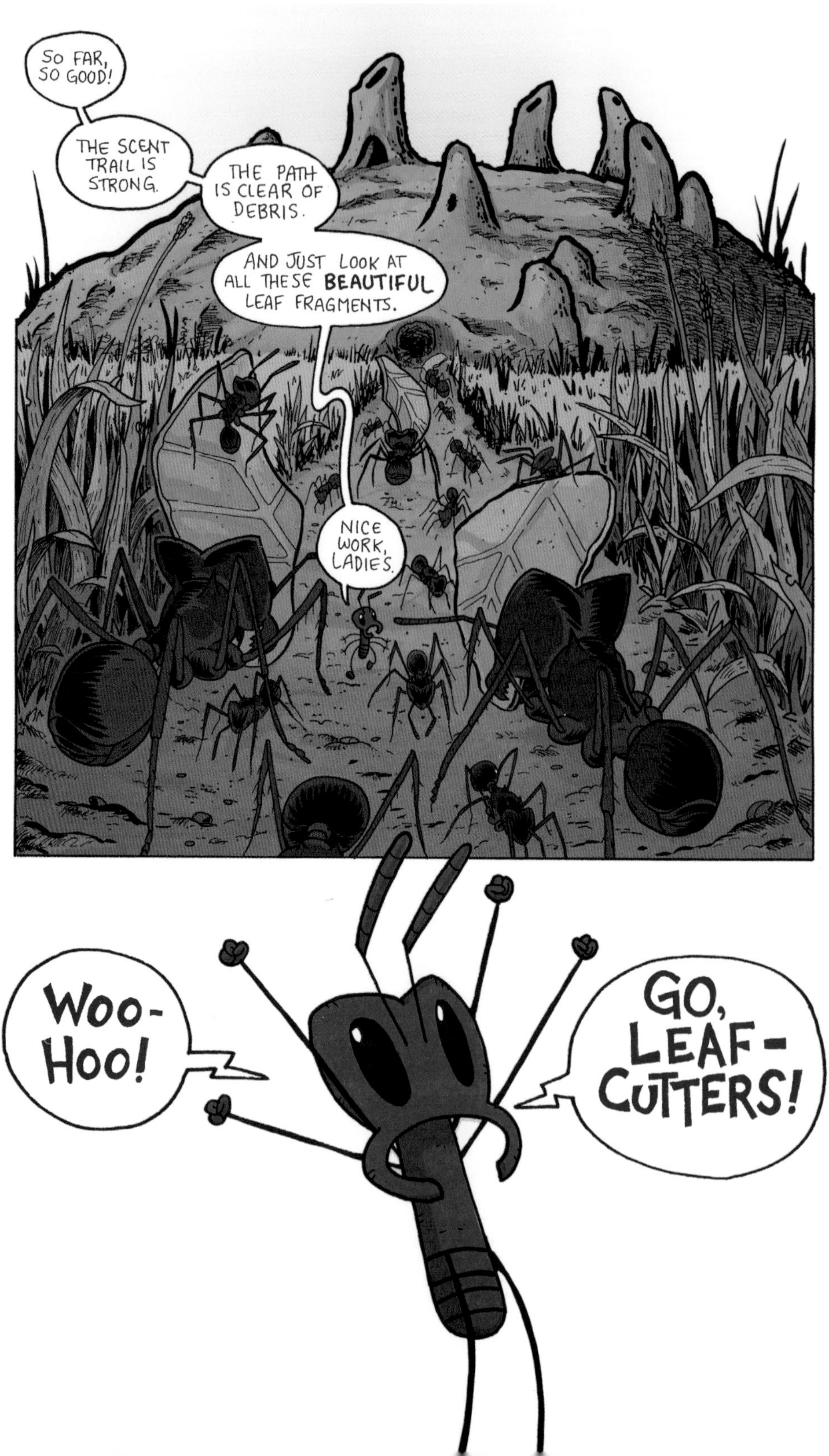
SO FAR, SO GOOD!
THE SCENT TRAIL IS STRONG.
THE PATH IS CLEAR OF DEBRIS.
AND JUST LOOK AT ALL THESE **BEAUTIFUL** LEAF FRAGMENTS.
NICE WORK, LADIES.
WOO-HOO!
GO, LEAF-CUTTERS!

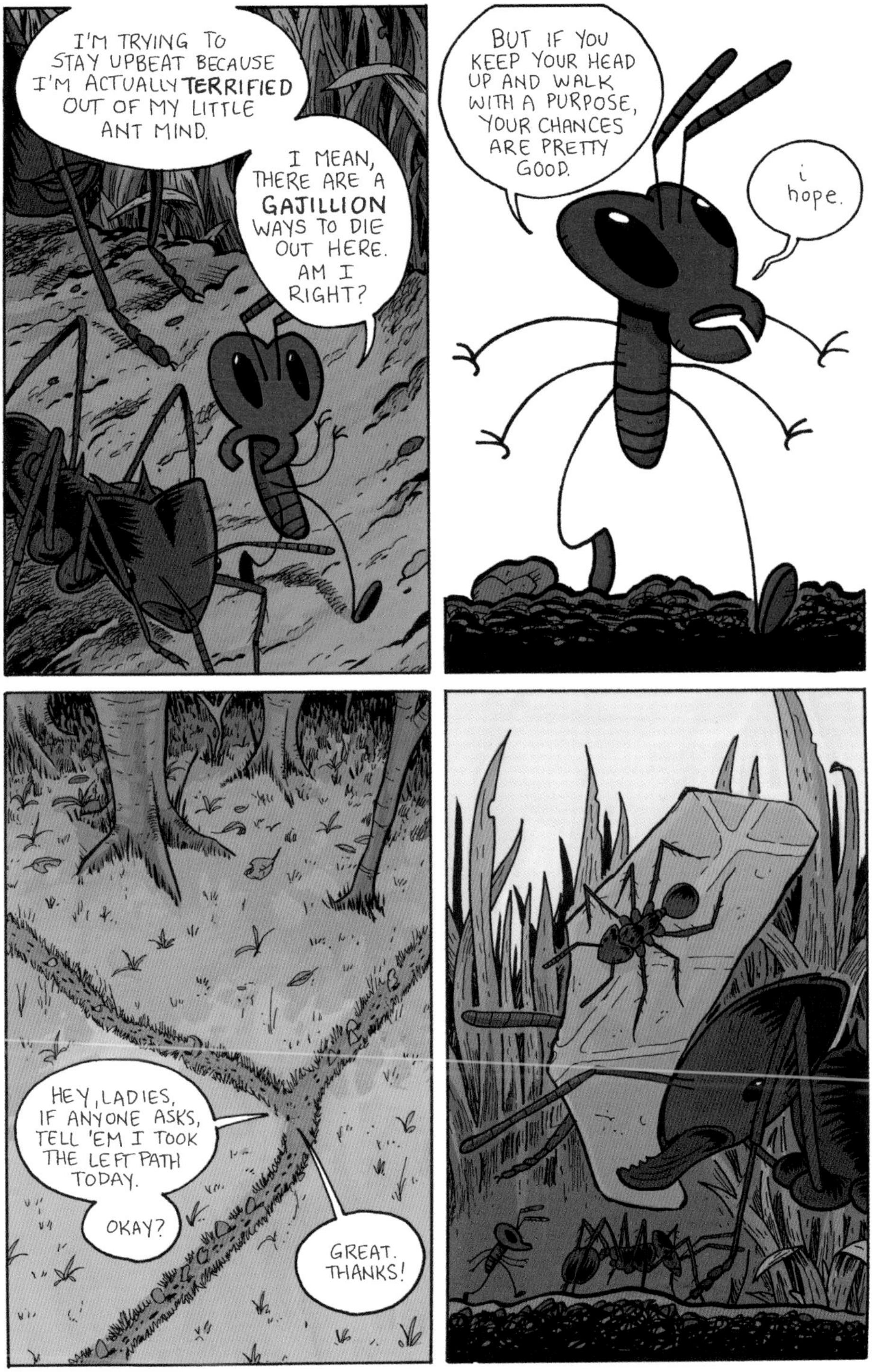
I'M TRYING TO STAY UPBEAT BECAUSE I'M ACTUALLY TERRIFIED OUT OF MY LITTLE ANT MIND.
I MEAN, THERE ARE A GAJILLION WAYS TO DIE OUT HERE. AM I RIGHT?
BUT IF YOU KEEP YOUR HEAD UP AND WALK WITH A PURPOSE, YOUR CHANCES ARE PRETTY GOOD.
i hope.
HEY, LADIES, IF ANYONE ASKS, TELL 'EM I TOOK THE LEFT PATH TODAY.
OKAY?
GREAT. THANKS!

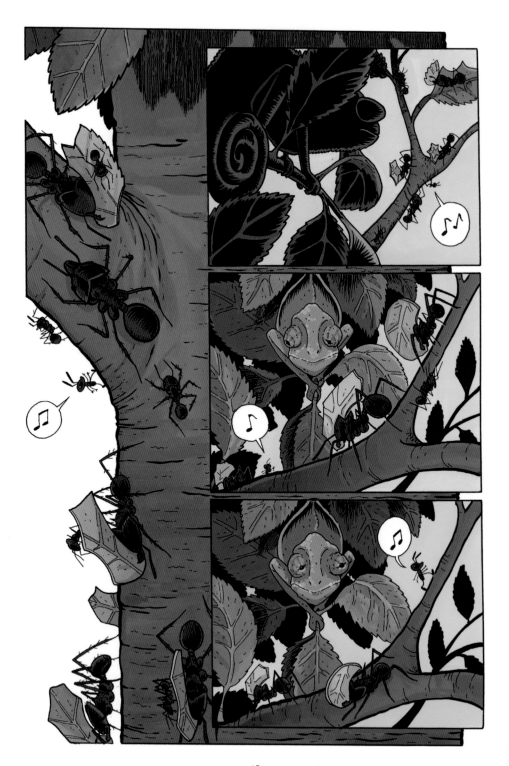

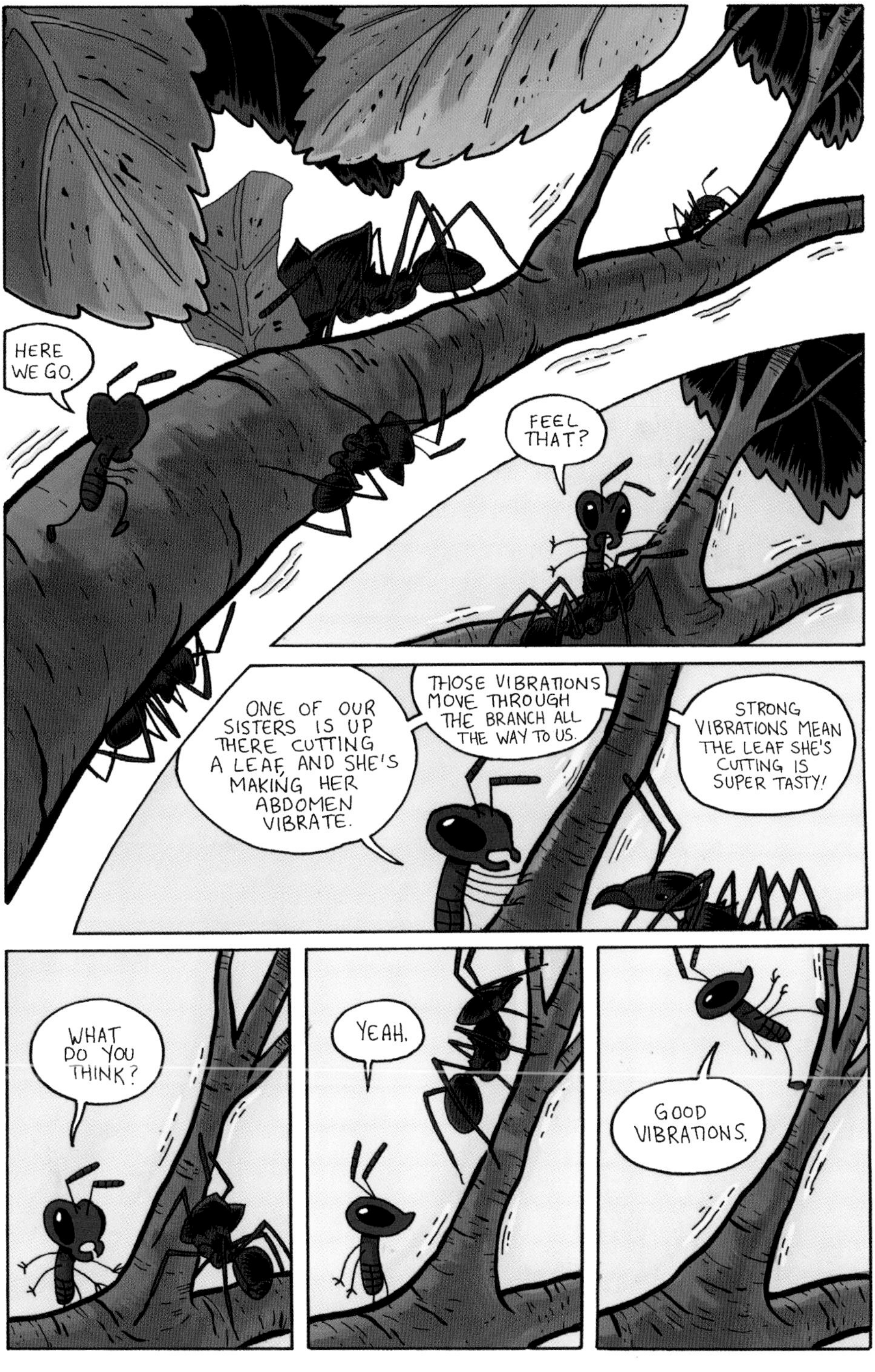
HERE WE GO.
FEEL THAT?
ONE OF OUR SISTERS IS UP THERE CUTTING A LEAF, AND SHE'S MAKING HER ABDOMEN VIBRATE.
THOSE VIBRATIONS MOVE THROUGH THE BRANCH ALL THE WAY TO US.
STRONG VIBRATIONS MEAN THE LEAF SHE'S CUTTING IS SUPER TASTY!
WHAT DO YOU THINK?
YEAH.
GOOD VIBRATIONS.

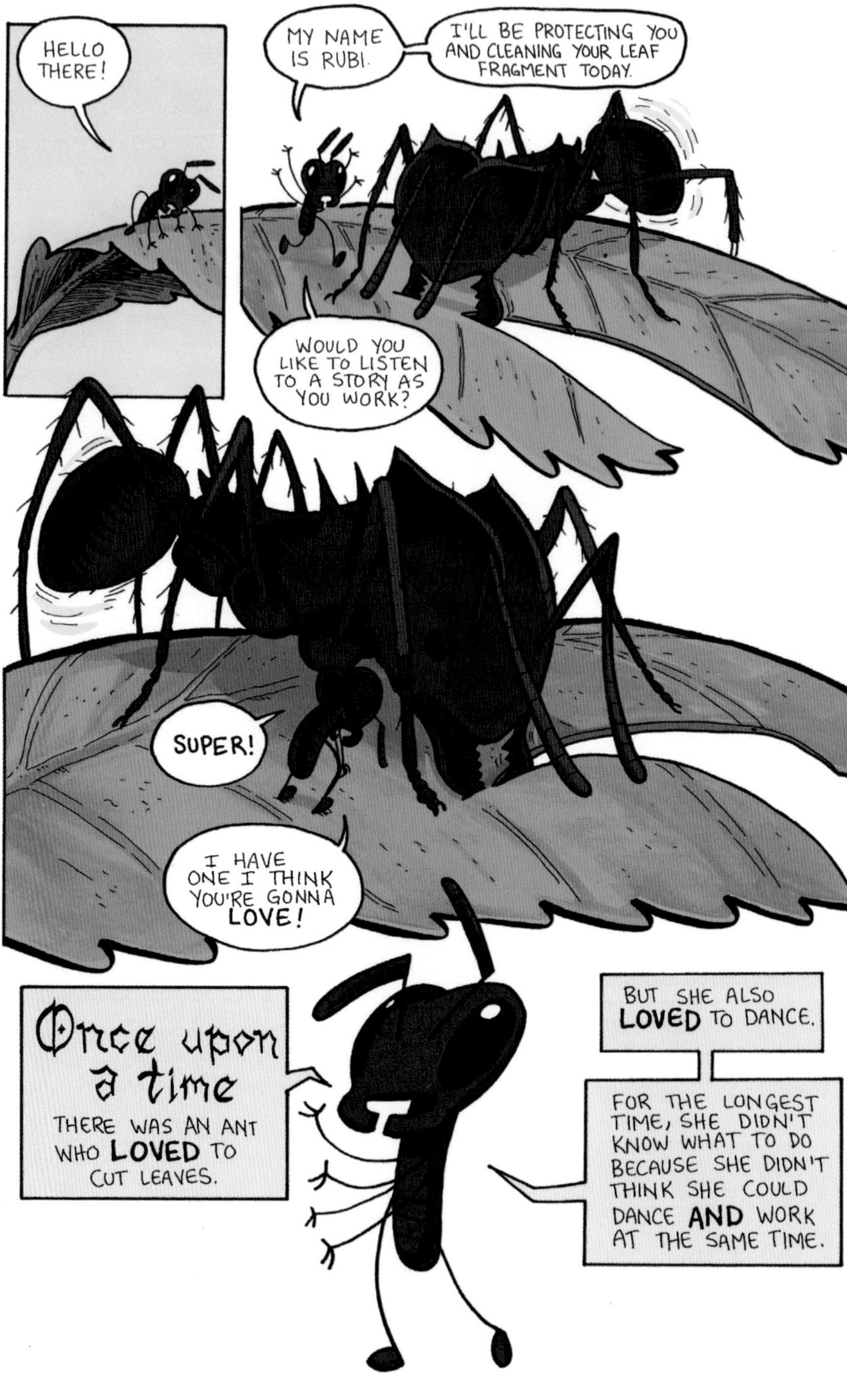

HELLO THERE!
MY NAME IS RUBI.
I'LL BE PROTECTING YOU AND CLEANING YOUR LEAF FRAGMENT TODAY.
WOULD YOU LIKE TO LISTEN TO A STORY AS YOU WORK?
SUPER!
I HAVE ONE I THINK YOU'RE GONNA LOVE!
Once upon a time THERE WAS AN ANT WHO LOVED TO CUT LEAVES.
BUT SHE ALSO LOVED TO DANCE.
FOR THE LONGEST TIME, SHE DIDN'T KNOW WHAT TO DO BECAUSE SHE DIDN'T THINK SHE COULD DANCE AND WORK AT THE SAME TIME.

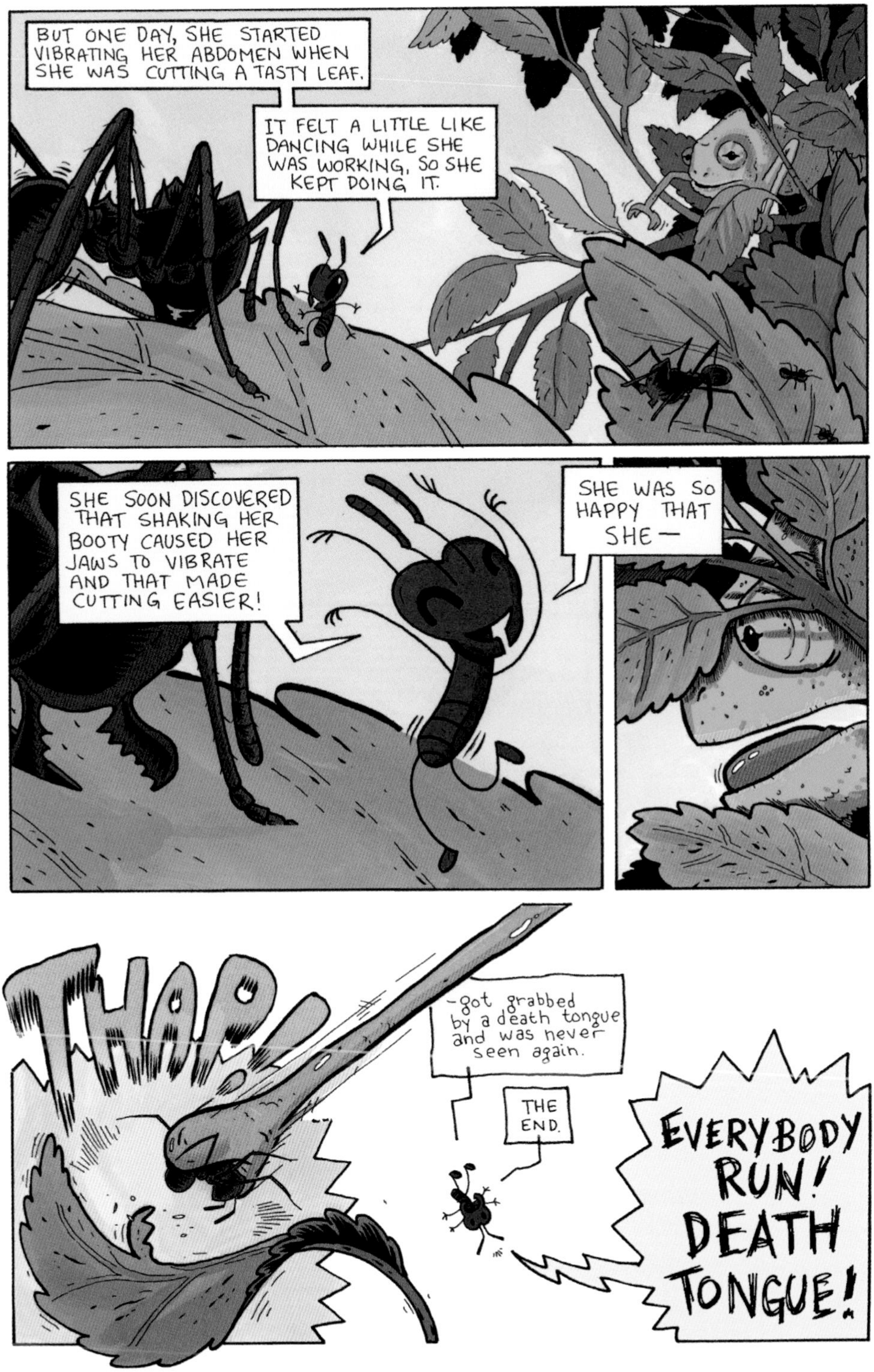
BUT ONE DAY, SHE STARTED VIBRATING HER ABDOMEN WHEN SHE WAS CUTTING A TASTY LEAF.
IT FELT A LITTLE LIKE DANCING WHILE SHE WAS WORKING, SO SHE KEPT DOING IT.
SHE SOON DISCOVERED THAT SHAKING HER BOOTY CAUSED HER JAWS TO VIBRATE AND THAT MADE CUTTING EASIER!
SHE WAS SO HAPPY THAT SHE—
THAP!
-got grabbed by a death tongue and was never seen again.
THE END.
EVERYBODY RUN! DEATH TONGUE!

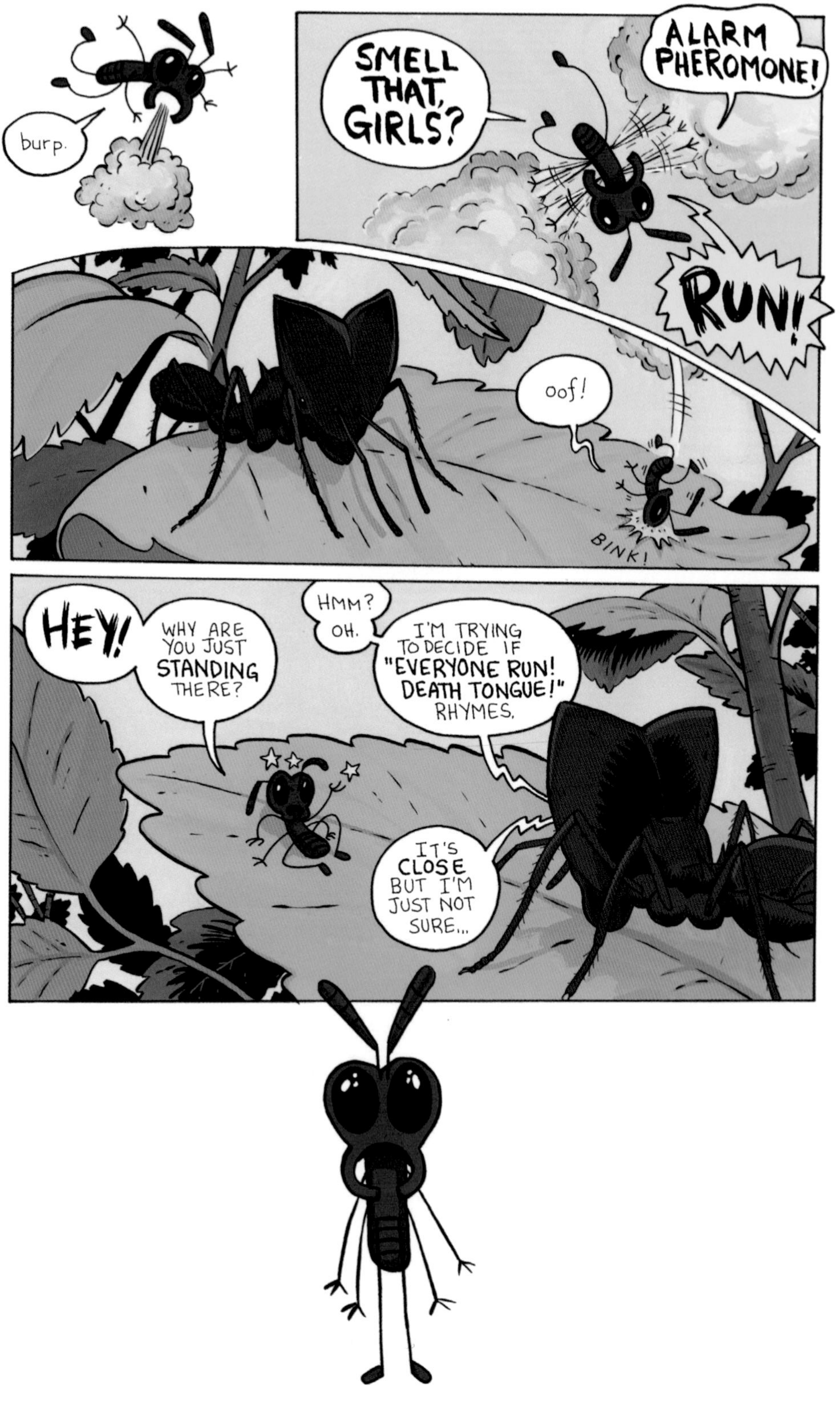
burp.
SMELL THAT, GIRLS?
ALARM PHEROMONE!
RUN!
oof!
BINK!
HEY!
WHY ARE YOU JUST STANDING THERE?
HMM? OH.
I'M TRYING TO DECIDE IF "EVERYONE RUN! DEATH TONGUE!" RHYMES.
IT'S CLOSE BUT I'M JUST NOT SURE...

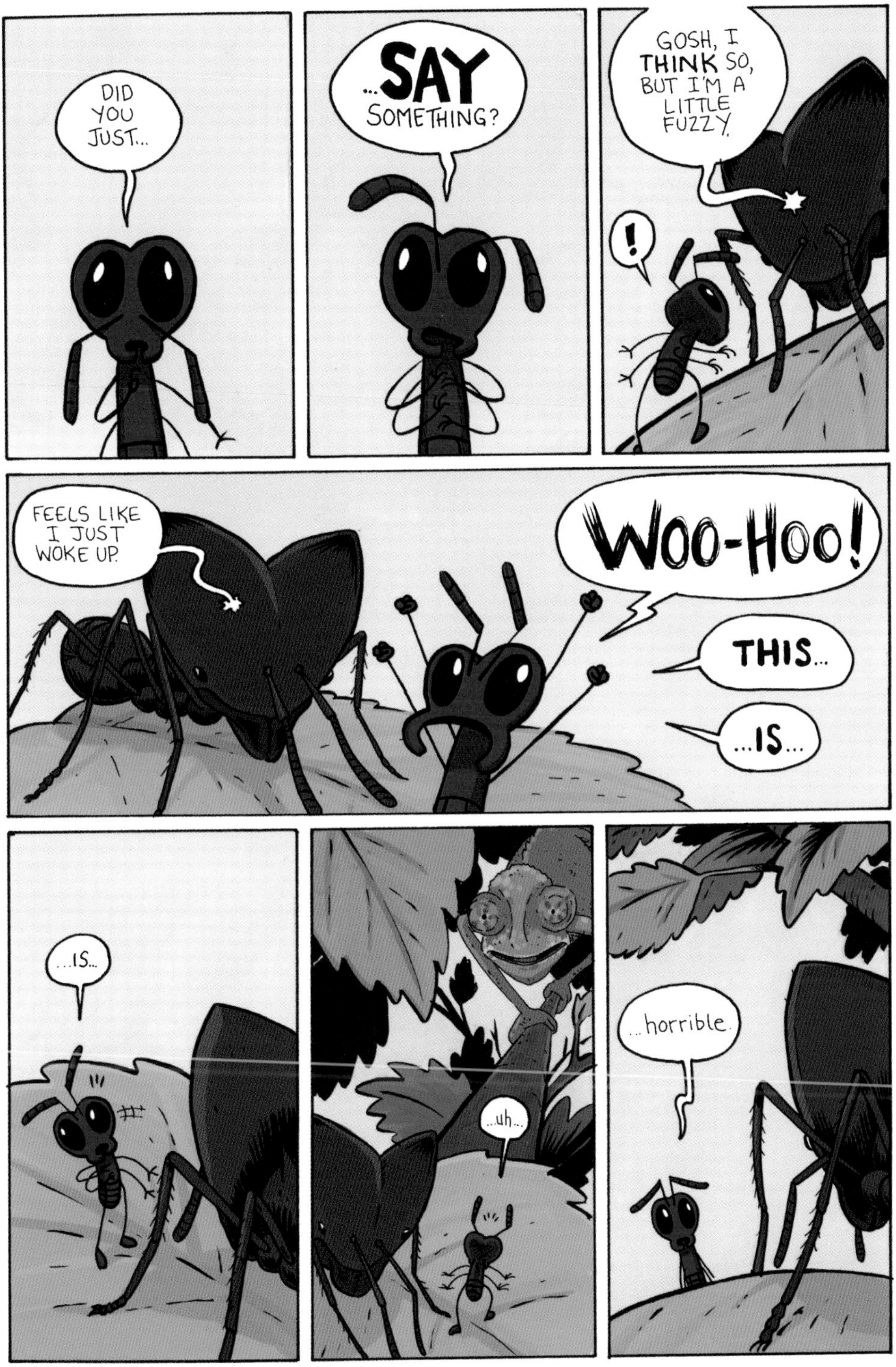
DID YOU JUST...
...SAY SOMETHING?
GOSH, I THINK SO, BUT I'M A LITTLE FUZZY.
!
FEELS LIKE I JUST WOKE UP.
WOO-HOO!
THIS...
...IS...
...IS...
...uh...
...horrible.

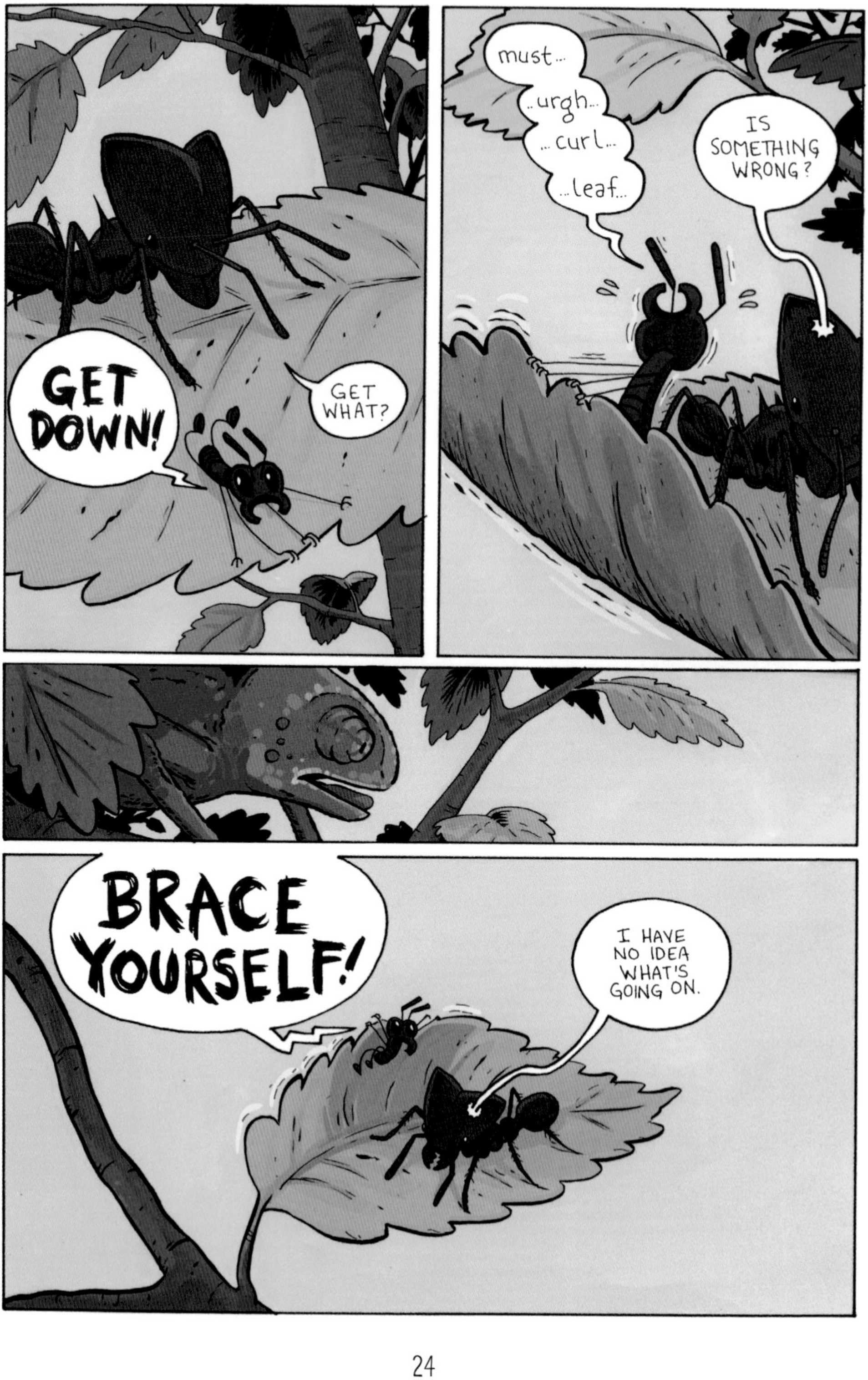
GET DOWN!
GET WHAT?
must... ...urgh... ...curl... ...leaf...
IS SOMETHING WRONG?
BRACE YOURSELF!
I HAVE NO IDEA WHAT'S GOING ON.

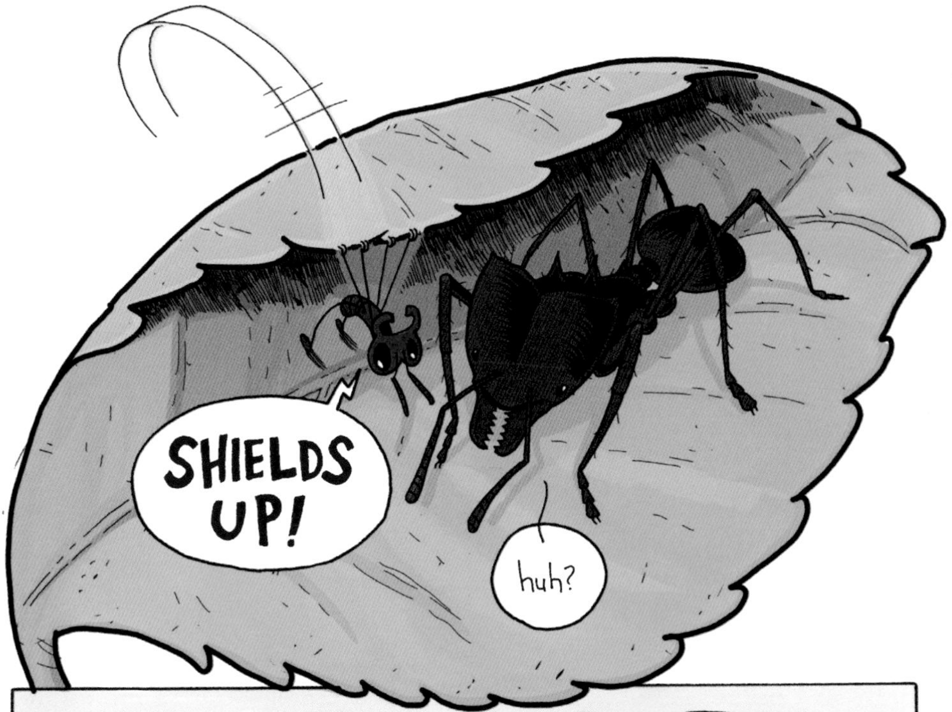
SHIELDS UP!
huh?

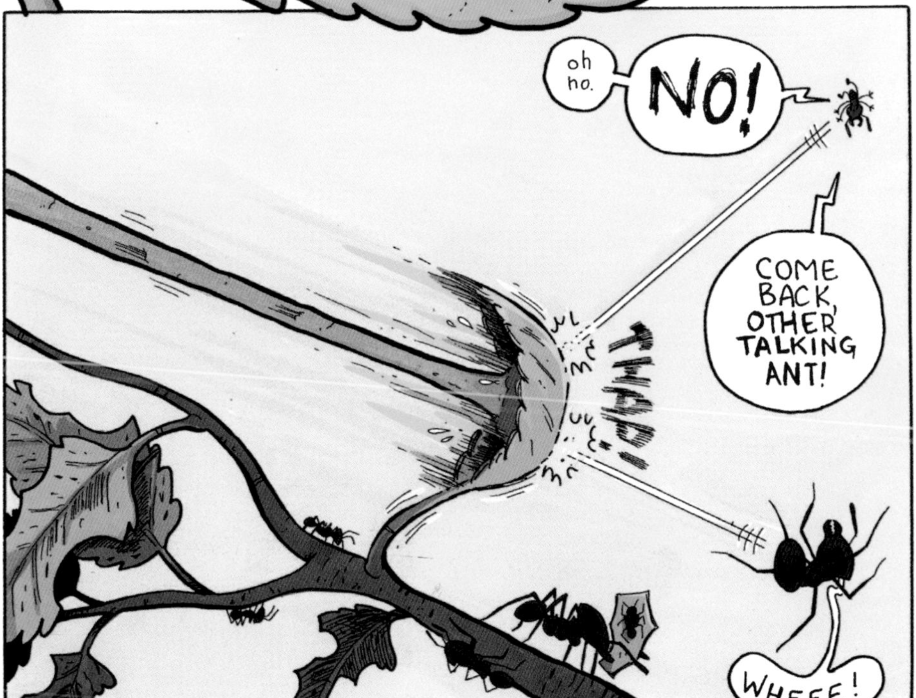
oh no.
NO!
COME BACK, OTHER TALKING ANT!
THAP!
WHEEE!

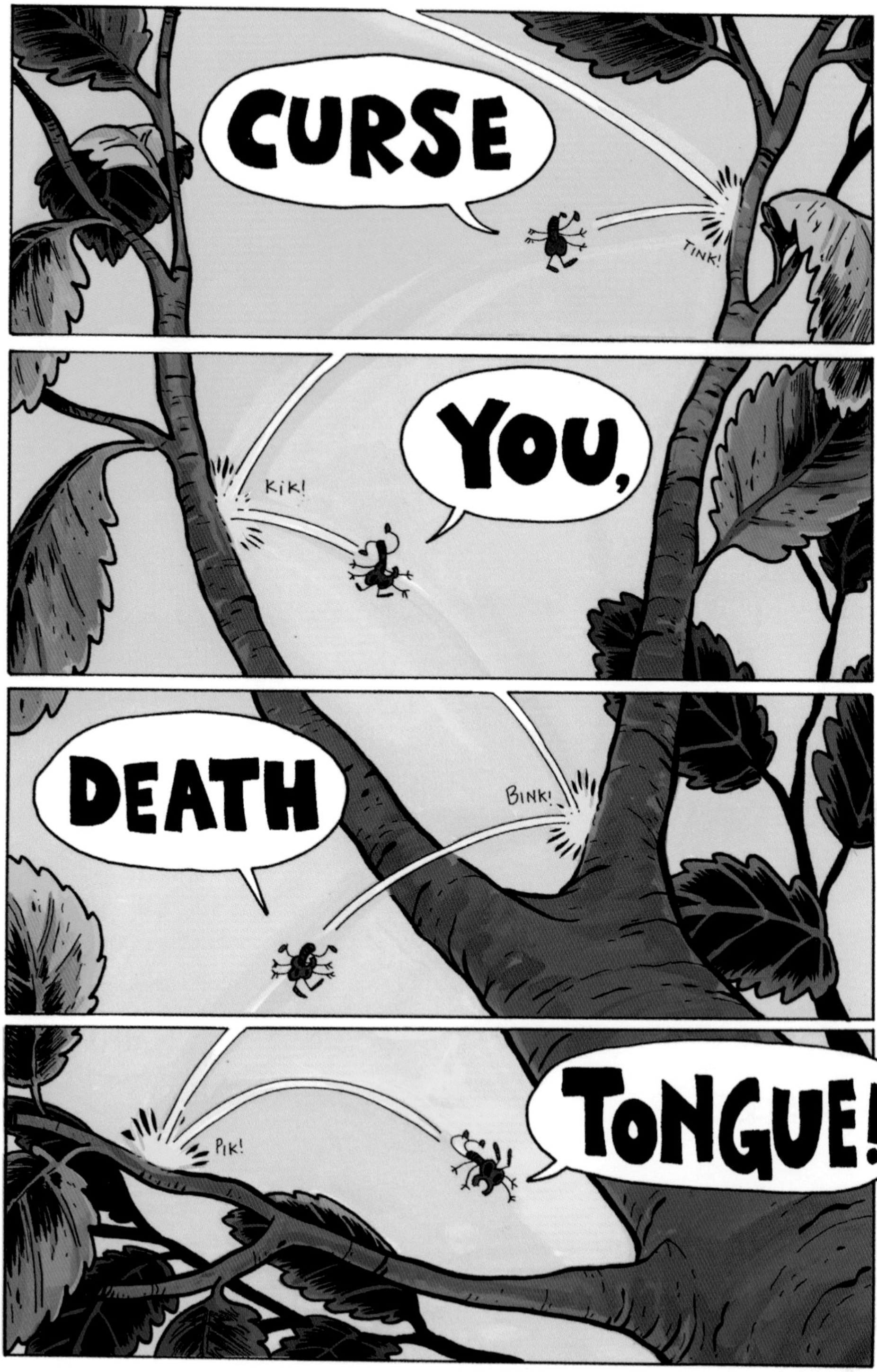
CURSE
TINK!
YOU,
KIK!
DEATH
BINK!
TONGUE!
PIK!

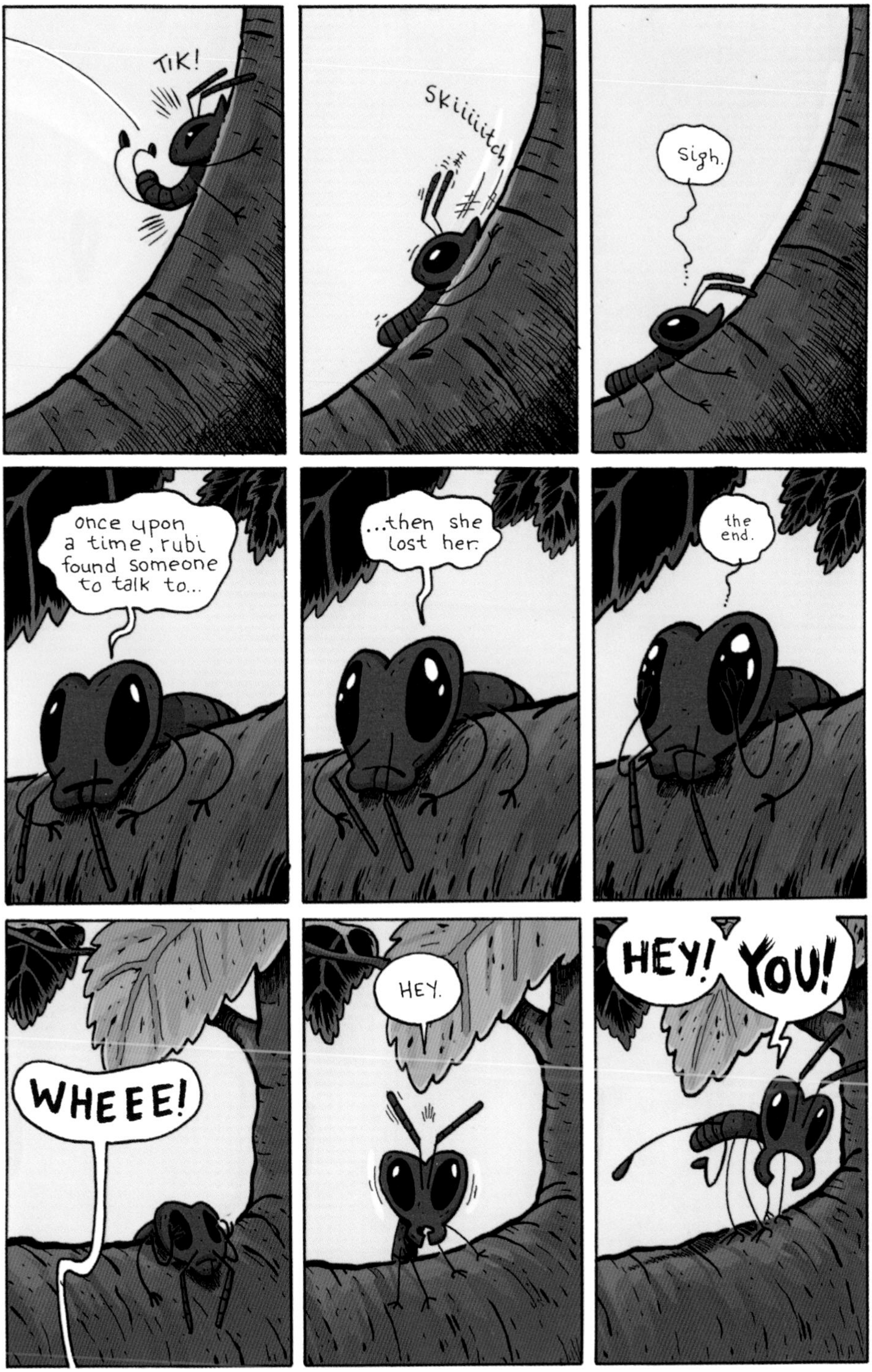
TIK!
Skiiiiitch
Sigh.
once upon a time, rubi found someone to talk to...
...then she lost her.
the end.
WHEEE!
HEY.
HEY!
YOU!

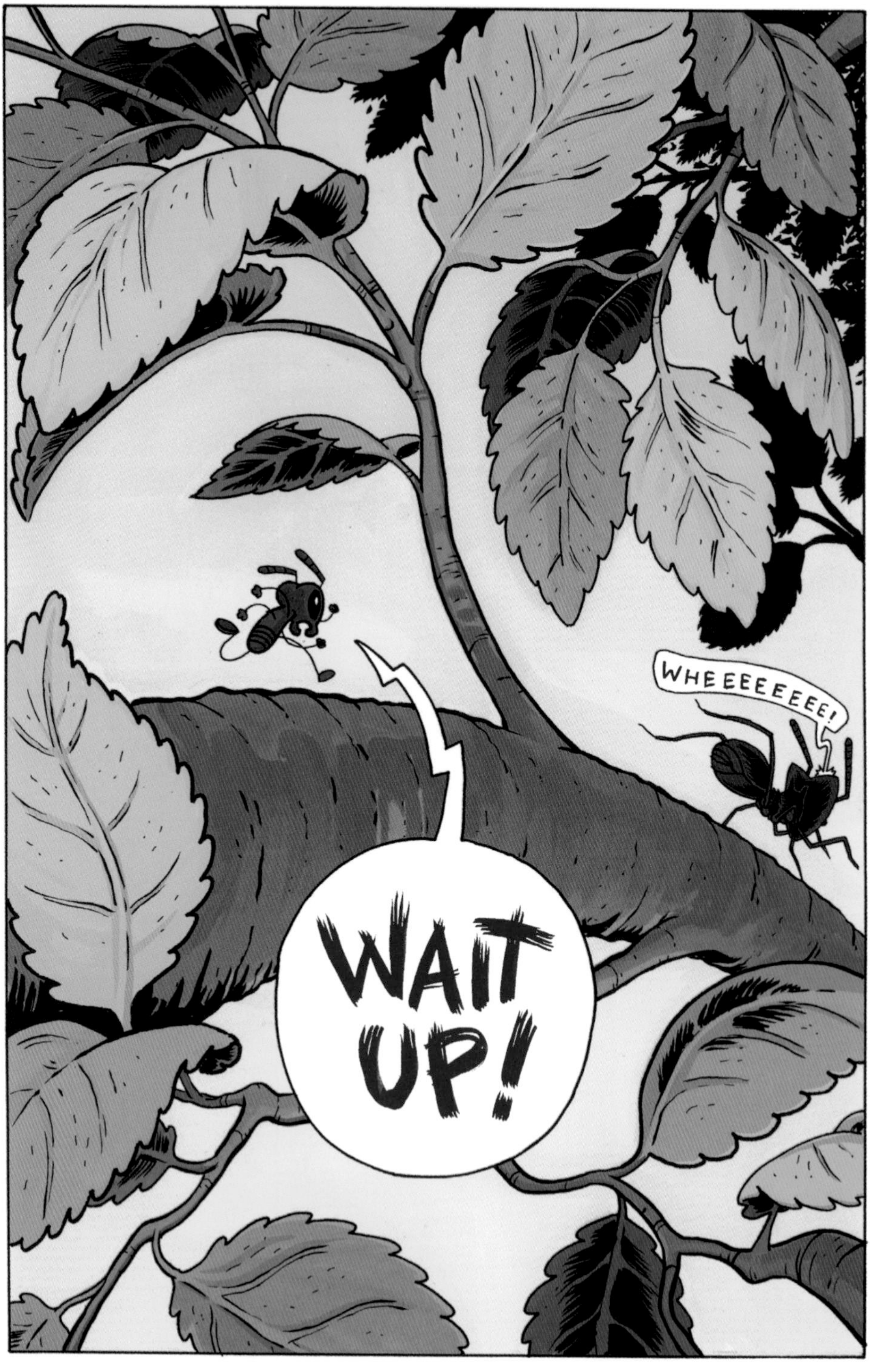
WHEEEEEEEEE!
WAIT UP!

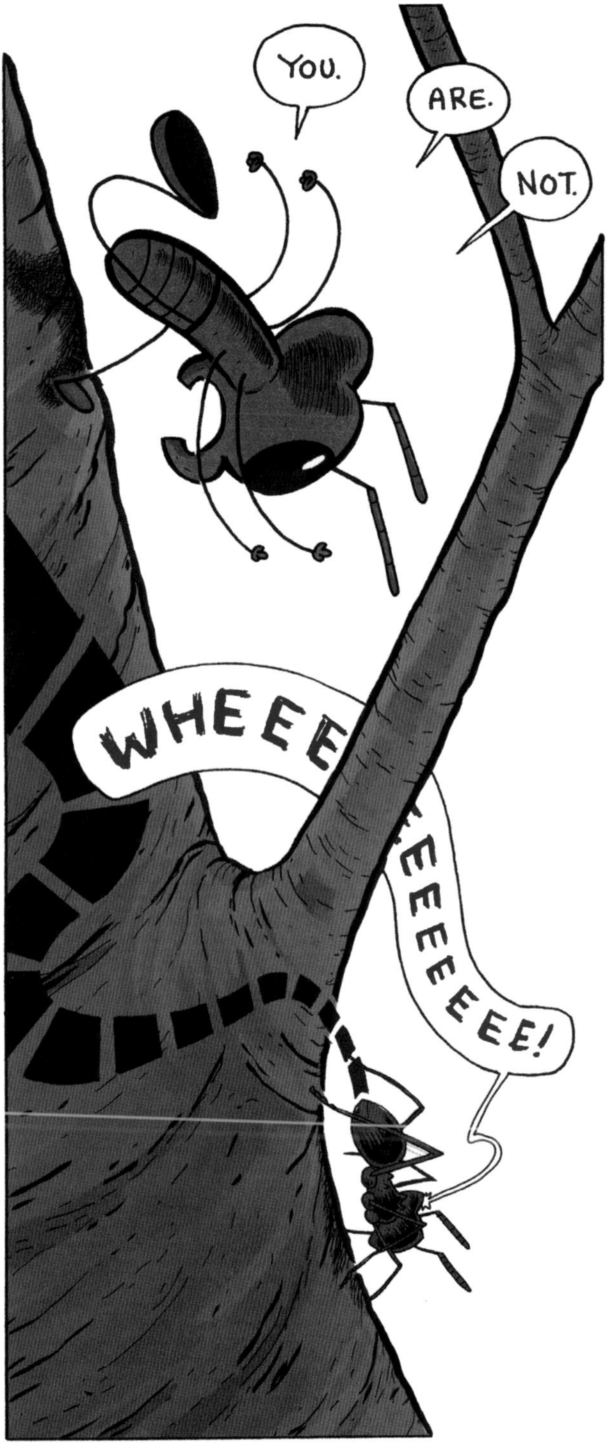
YOU.
ARE.
NOT.
WHEEEEEEEEEEEE!

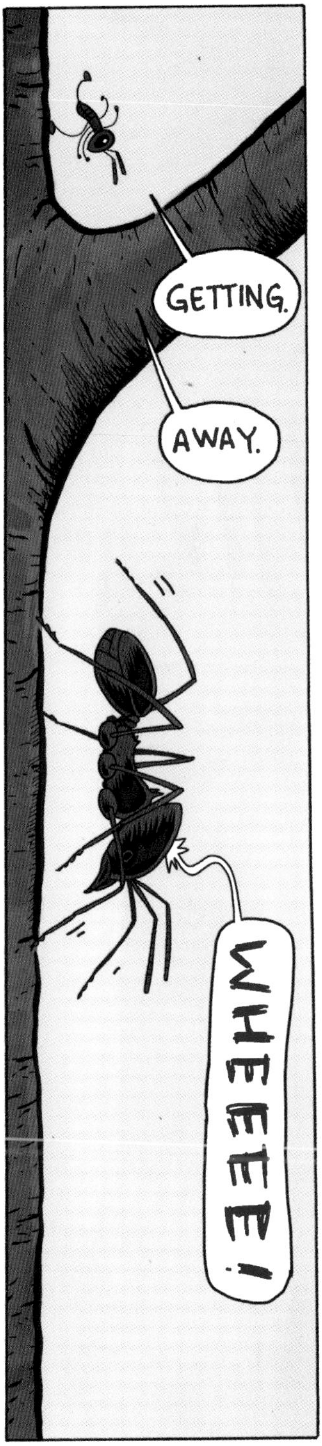
GETTING.
AWAY.
WHEEEEE!

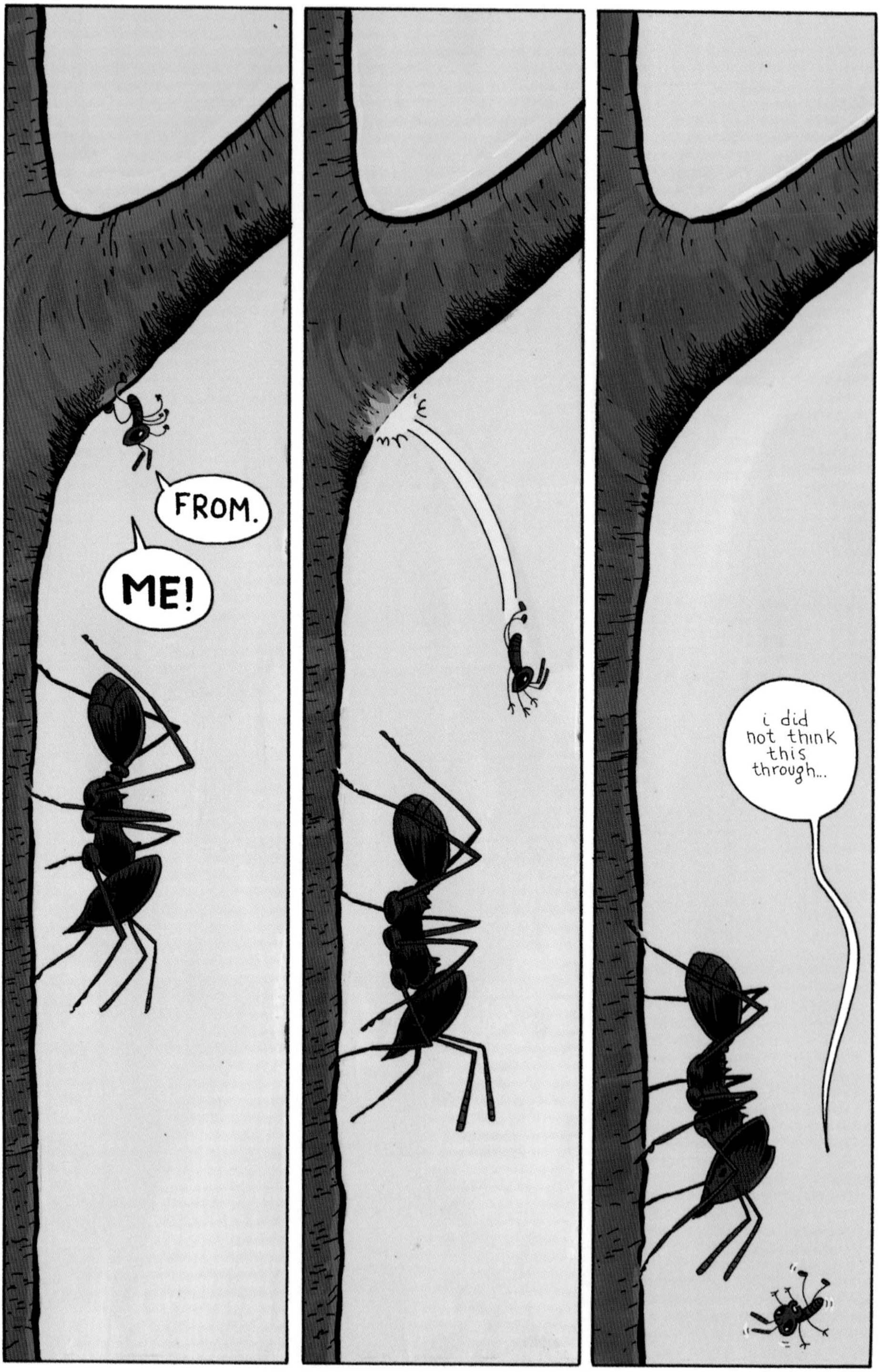
FROM.
ME!
i did not think this through...

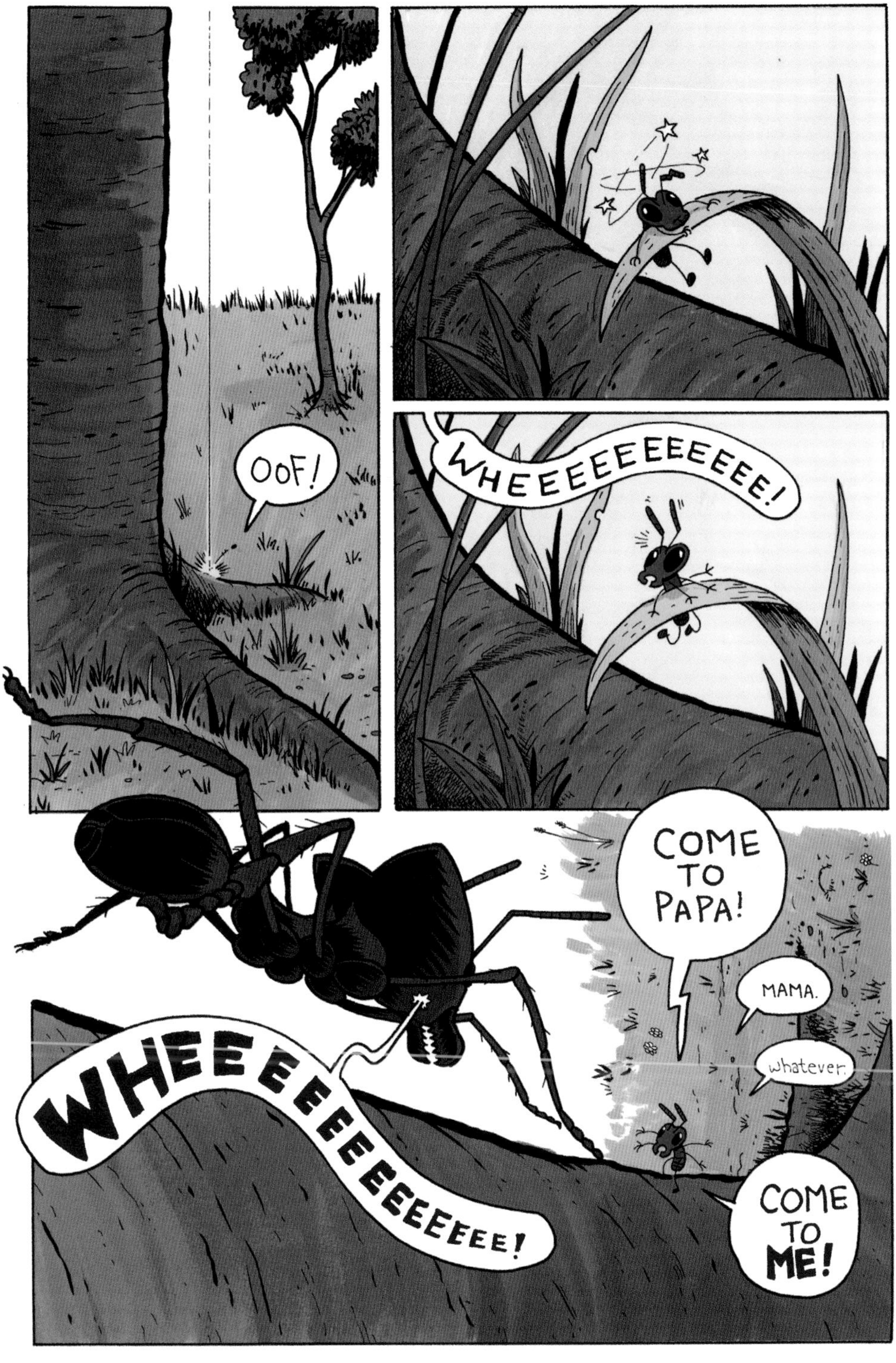
OOF!
WHEEEEEEEEEE!
COME TO PAPA!
MAMA.
whatever.
WHEEEEEEEEEEEEEE!
COME TO ME!

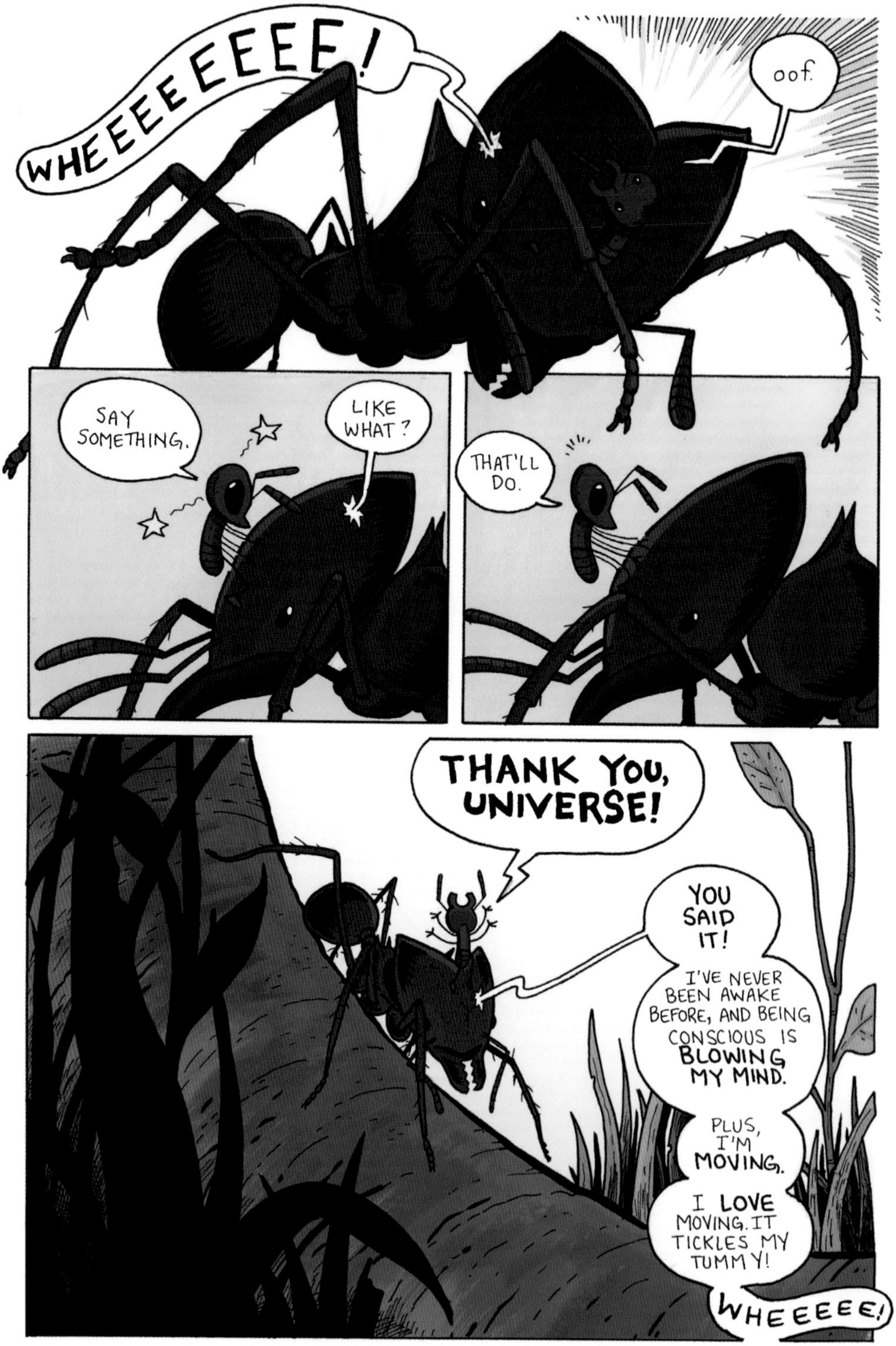
WHEEEEEEEE!
oof.
SAY SOMETHING.
LIKE WHAT?
THAT'LL DO.
THANK YOU, UNIVERSE!
YOU SAID IT!
I'VE NEVER BEEN AWAKE BEFORE, AND BEING CONSCIOUS IS BLOWING MY MIND.
PLUS, I'M MOVING.
I LOVE MOVING. IT TICKLES MY TUMMY!
WHEEEEE!

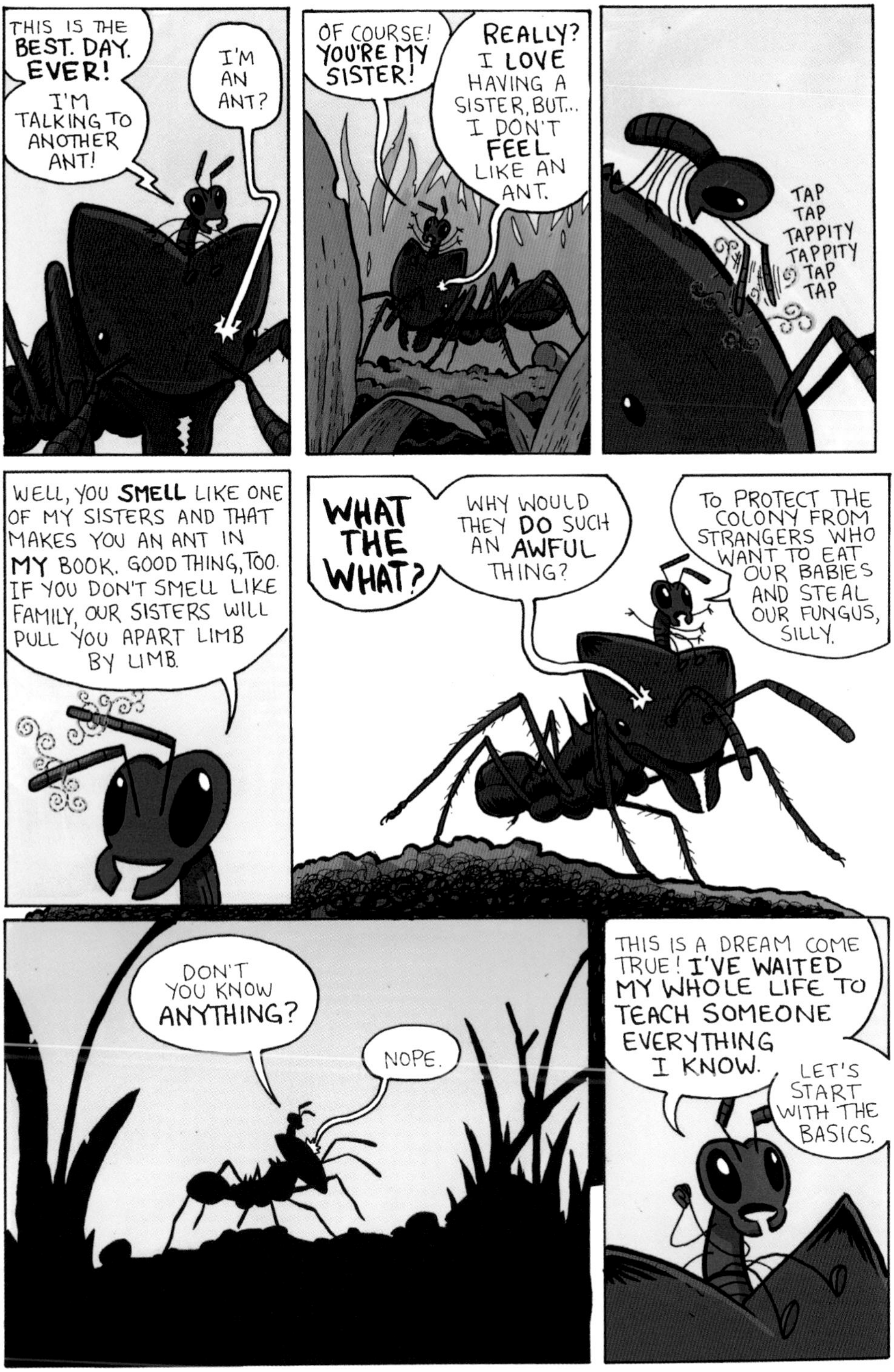
THIS IS THE BEST. DAY. EVER!
I'M TALKING TO ANOTHER ANT!
I'M AN ANT?
OF COURSE! YOU'RE MY SISTER!
REALLY? I LOVE HAVING A SISTER, BUT... I DON'T FEEL LIKE AN ANT.
TAP TAP TAPPITY TAPPITY TAP TAP
WELL, YOU SMELL LIKE ONE OF MY SISTERS AND THAT MAKES YOU AN ANT IN MY BOOK. GOOD THING, TOO. IF YOU DON'T SMELL LIKE FAMILY, OUR SISTERS WILL PULL YOU APART LIMB BY LIMB.
WHAT THE WHAT?
WHY WOULD THEY DO SUCH AN AWFUL THING?
TO PROTECT THE COLONY FROM STRANGERS WHO WANT TO EAT OUR BABIES AND STEAL OUR FUNGUS, SILLY.
DON'T YOU KNOW ANYTHING?
NOPE.
THIS IS A DREAM COME TRUE! I'VE WAITED MY WHOLE LIFE TO TEACH SOMEONE EVERYTHING I KNOW.
LET'S START WITH THE BASICS.

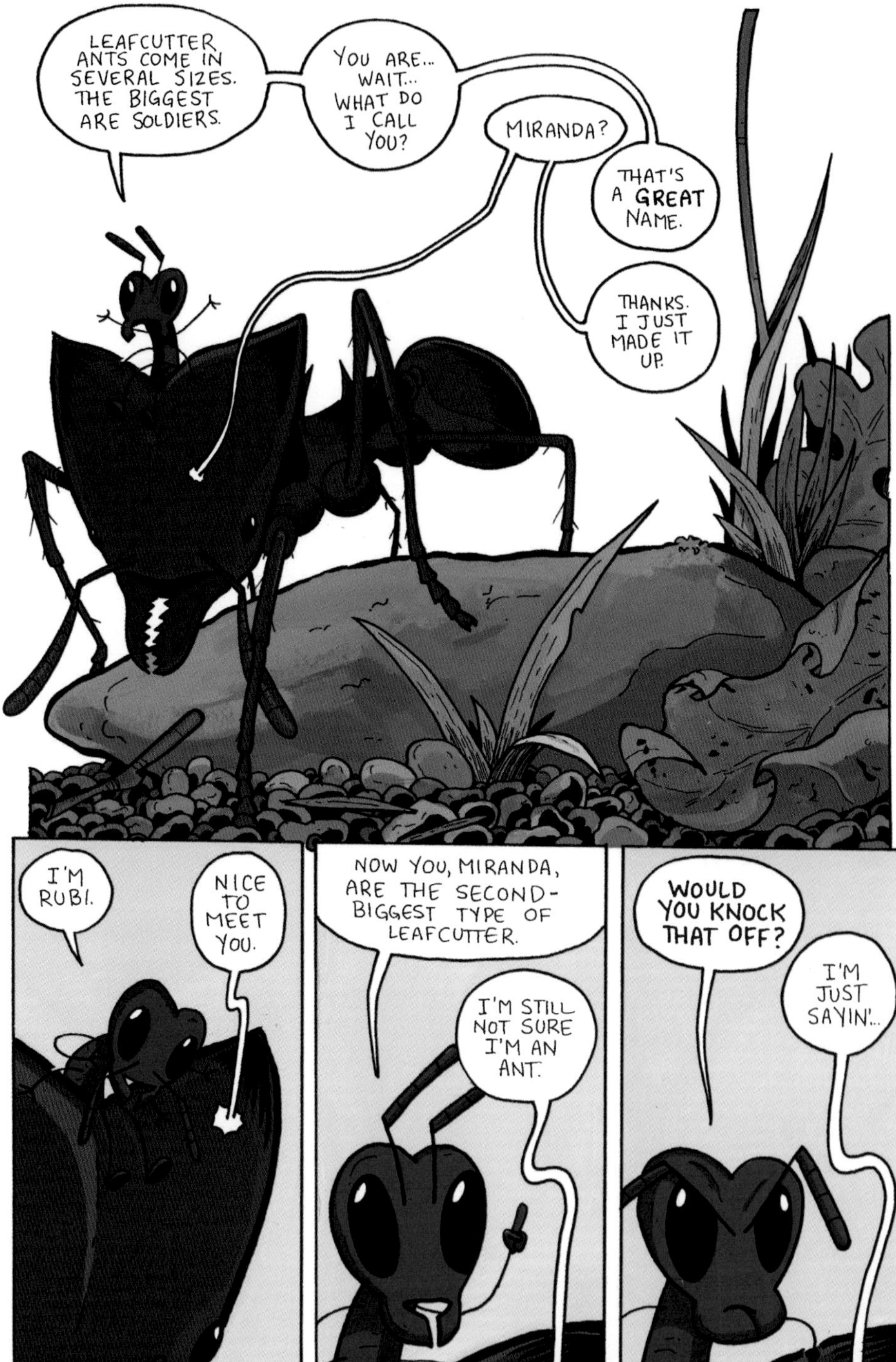
LEAFCUTTER ANTS COME IN SEVERAL SIZES. THE BIGGEST ARE SOLDIERS.
YOU ARE... WAIT... WHAT DO I CALL YOU?
MIRANDA?
THAT'S A **GREAT** NAME.
THANKS. I JUST MADE IT UP.
I'M RUBI.
NICE TO MEET YOU.
NOW YOU, MIRANDA, ARE THE SECOND-BIGGEST TYPE OF LEAFCUTTER.
I'M STILL NOT SURE I'M AN ANT.
WOULD YOU KNOCK THAT OFF?
I'M JUST SAYIN'...

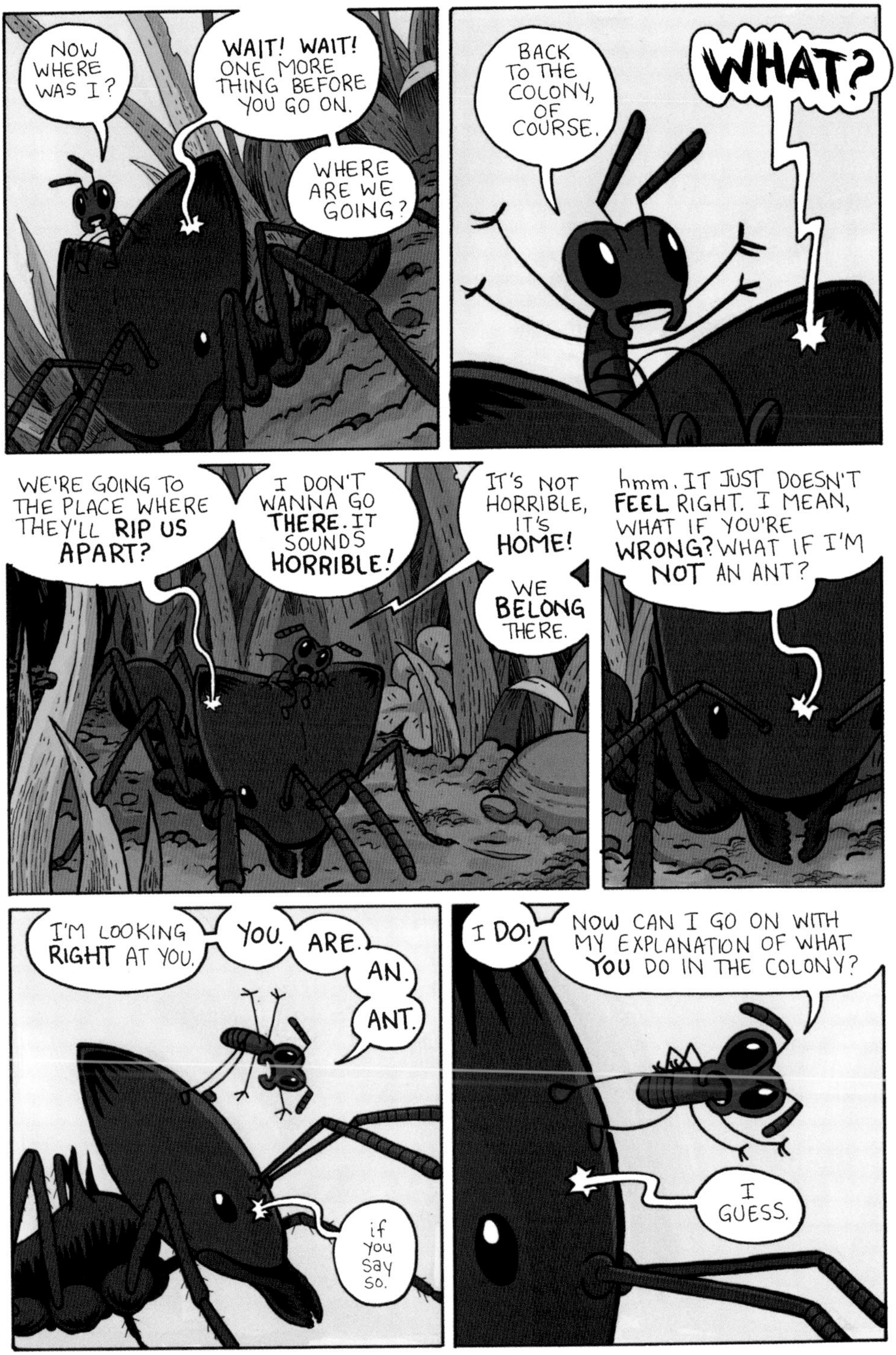
NOW WHERE WAS I?
WAIT! WAIT! ONE MORE THING BEFORE YOU GO ON.
WHERE ARE WE GOING?
BACK TO THE COLONY, OF COURSE.
WHAT?
WE'RE GOING TO THE PLACE WHERE THEY'LL RIP US APART?
I DON'T WANNA GO THERE. IT SOUNDS HORRIBLE!
IT'S NOT HORRIBLE, IT'S HOME!
WE BELONG THERE.
hmm. IT JUST DOESN'T FEEL RIGHT. I MEAN, WHAT IF YOU'RE WRONG? WHAT IF I'M NOT AN ANT?
I'M LOOKING RIGHT AT YOU.
YOU.
ARE.
AN.
ANT.
if you say so.
I DO!
NOW CAN I GO ON WITH MY EXPLANATION OF WHAT YOU DO IN THE COLONY?
I GUESS.

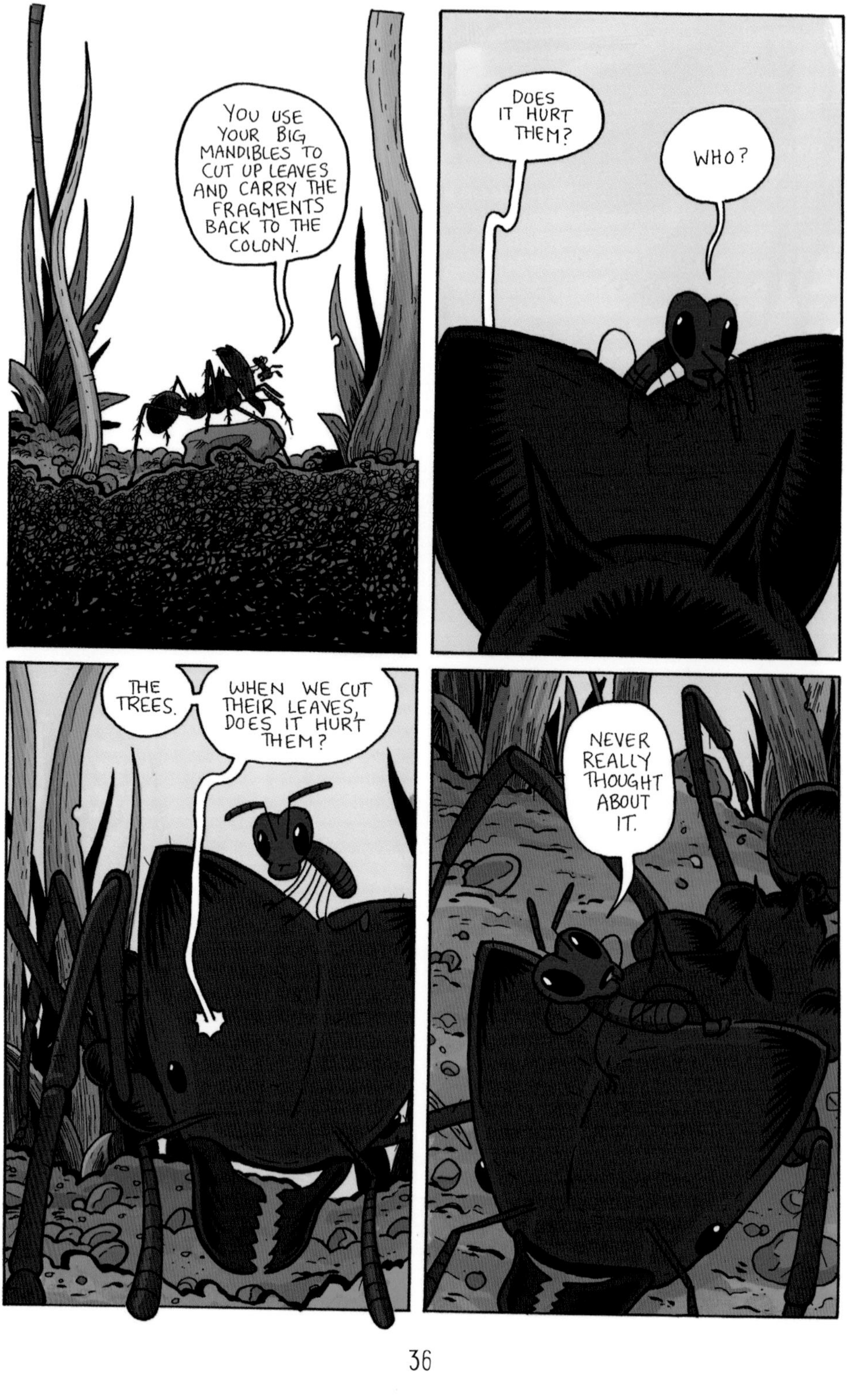
YOU USE YOUR BIG MANDIBLES TO CUT UP LEAVES AND CARRY THE FRAGMENTS BACK TO THE COLONY.
DOES IT HURT THEM?
WHO?
THE TREES.
WHEN WE CUT THEIR LEAVES, DOES IT HURT THEM?
NEVER REALLY THOUGHT ABOUT IT.

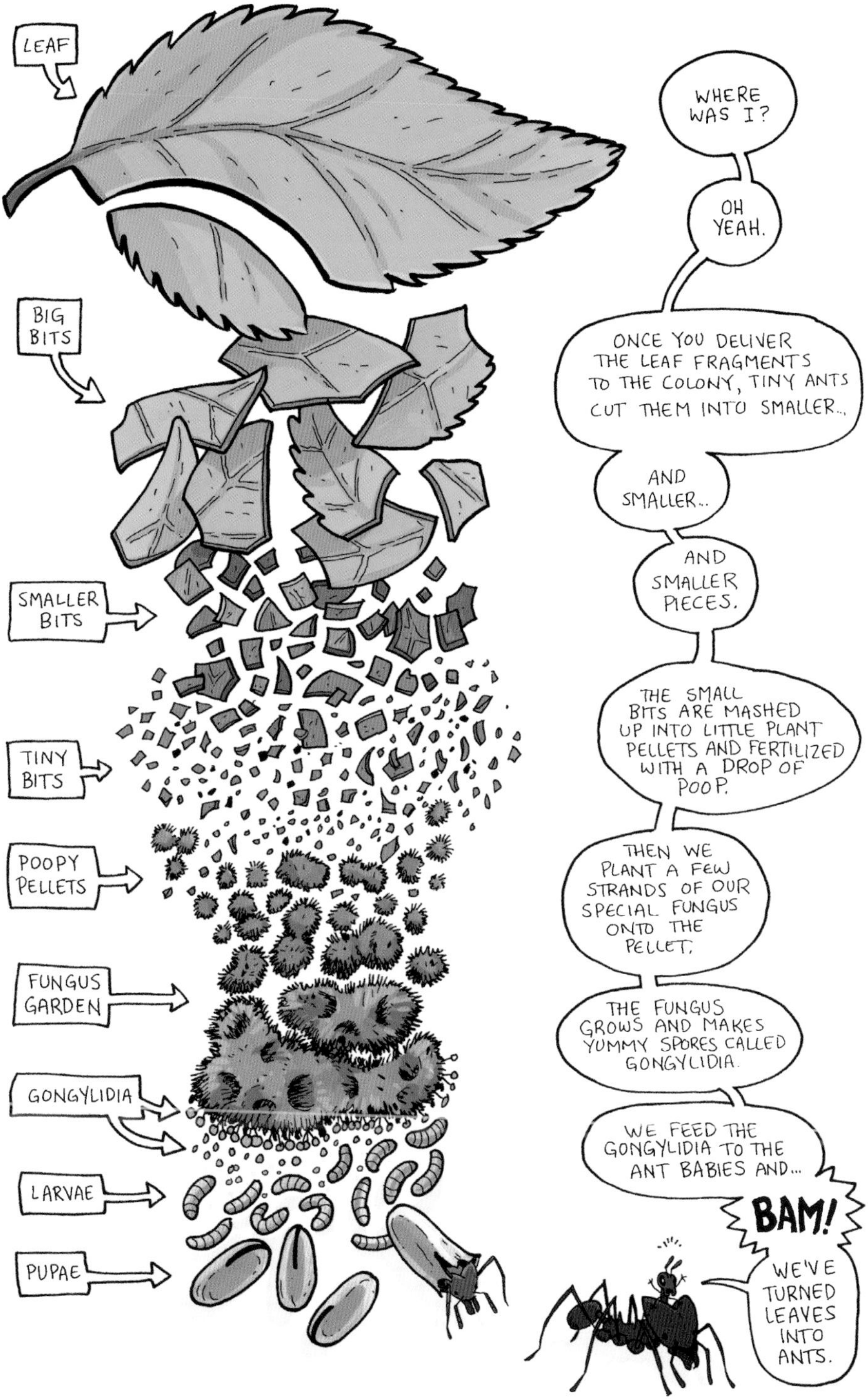
LEAF
BIG BITS
SMALLER BITS
TINY BITS
POOPY PELLETS
FUNGUS GARDEN
GONGYLIDIA
LARVAE
PUPAE
WHERE WAS I?
OH YEAH.
ONCE YOU DELIVER THE LEAF FRAGMENTS TO THE COLONY, TINY ANTS CUT THEM INTO SMALLER...
AND SMALLER...
AND SMALLER PIECES.
THE SMALL BITS ARE MASHED UP INTO LITTLE PLANT PELLETS AND FERTILIZED WITH A DROP OF POOP.
THEN WE PLANT A FEW STRANDS OF OUR SPECIAL FUNGUS ONTO THE PELLET.
THE FUNGUS GROWS AND MAKES YUMMY SPORES CALLED GONGYLIDIA.
WE FEED THE GONGYLIDIA TO THE ANT BABIES AND...
BAM!
WE'VE TURNED LEAVES INTO ANTS.

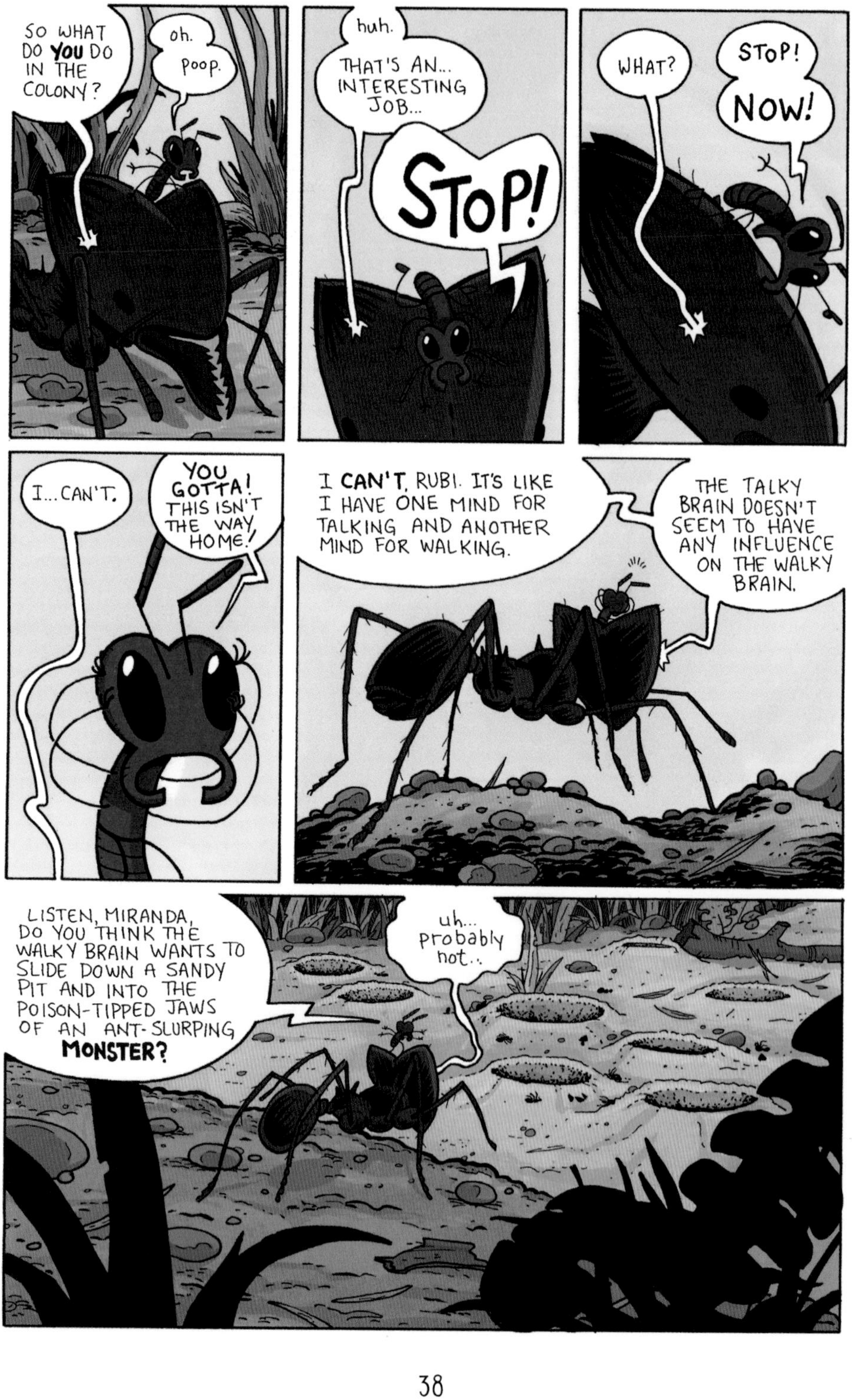
SO WHAT DO **YOU** DO IN THE COLONY?
oh.
poop.
huh.
THAT'S AN... INTERESTING JOB...
STOP!
WHAT?
STOP!
NOW!
I...CAN'T.
YOU GOTTA! THIS ISN'T THE WAY HOME!
I **CAN'T**, RUBI. IT'S LIKE I HAVE ONE MIND FOR TALKING AND ANOTHER MIND FOR WALKING.
THE TALKY BRAIN DOESN'T SEEM TO HAVE ANY INFLUENCE ON THE WALKY BRAIN.
LISTEN, MIRANDA, DO YOU THINK THE WALKY BRAIN WANTS TO SLIDE DOWN A SANDY PIT AND INTO THE POISON-TIPPED JAWS OF AN ANT-SLURPING **MONSTER?**
uh... probably not..

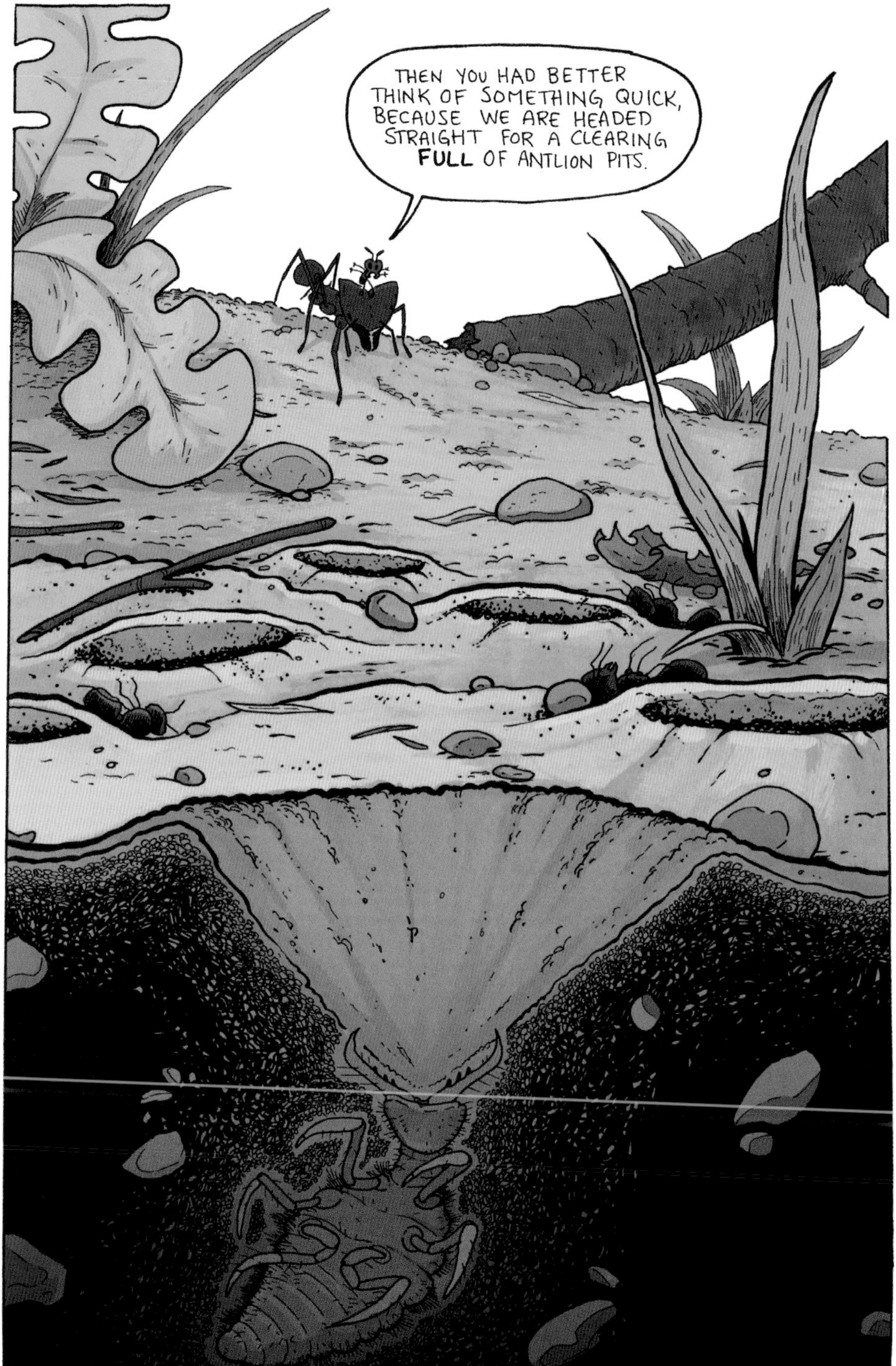
THEN YOU HAD BETTER THINK OF SOMETHING QUICK, BECAUSE WE ARE HEADED STRAIGHT FOR A CLEARING **FULL** OF ANTLION PITS.

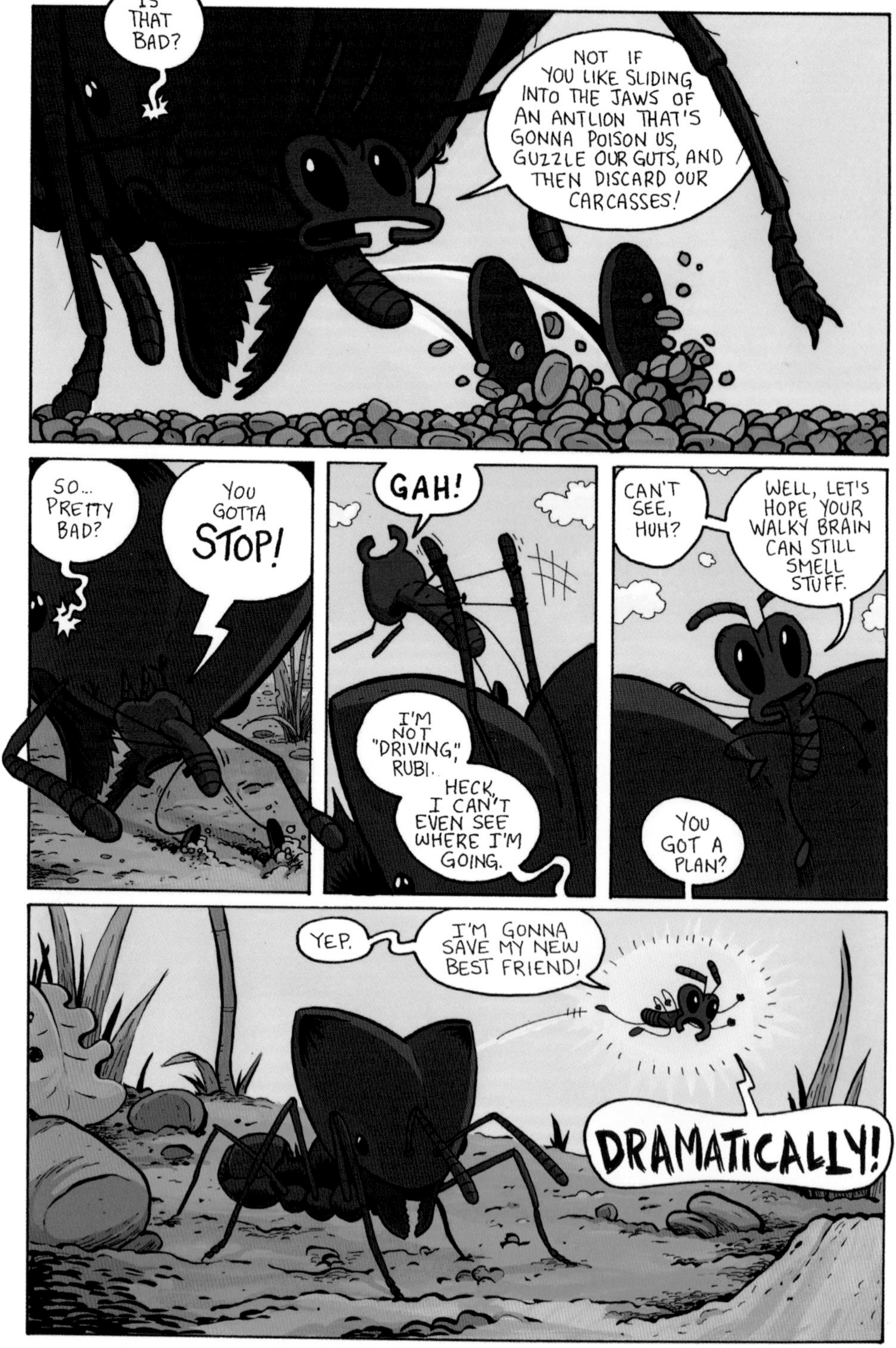
IS THAT BAD?
NOT IF YOU LIKE SLIDING INTO THE JAWS OF AN ANTLION THAT'S GONNA POISON US, GUZZLE OUR GUTS, AND THEN DISCARD OUR CARCASSES!
SO... PRETTY BAD?
YOU GOTTA STOP!
GAH!
I'M NOT "DRIVING," RUBI.
HECK, I CAN'T EVEN SEE WHERE I'M GOING.
CAN'T SEE, HUH?
WELL, LET'S HOPE YOUR WALKY BRAIN CAN STILL SMELL STUFF.
YOU GOT A PLAN?
YEP.
I'M GONNA SAVE MY NEW BEST FRIEND!
DRAMATICALLY!

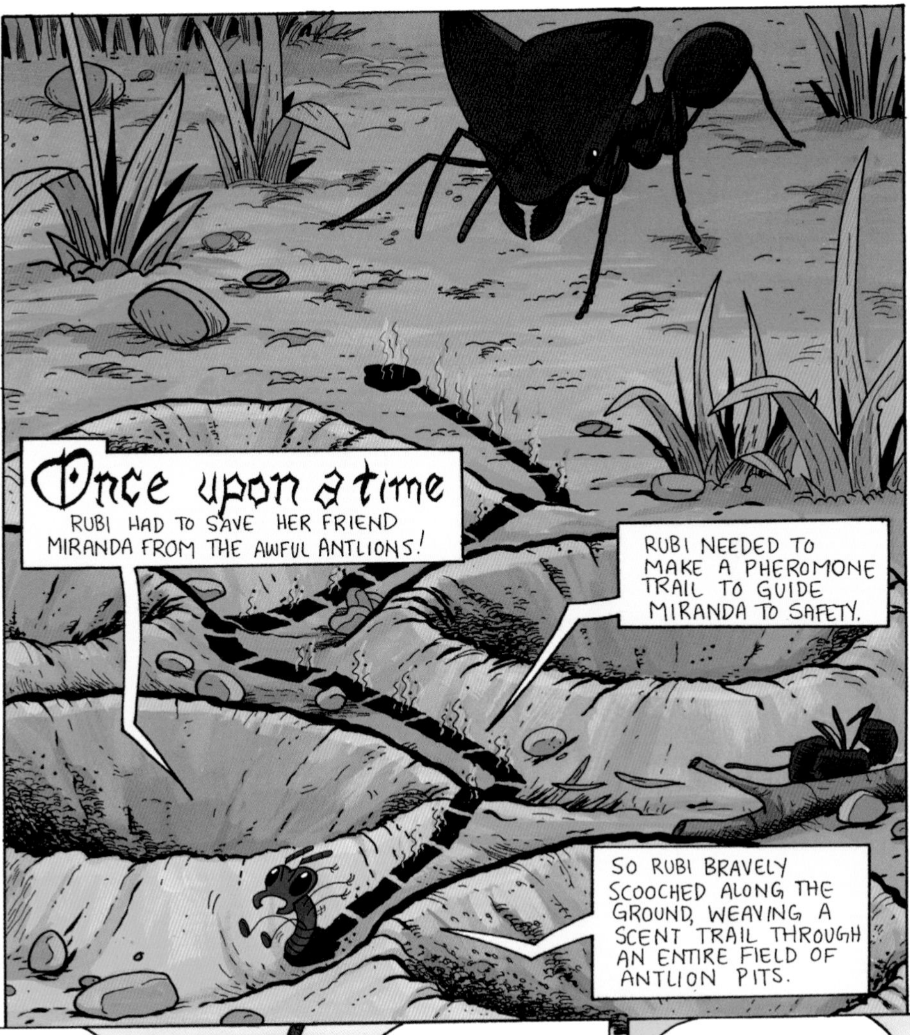
Once upon a time
RUBI HAD TO SAVE HER FRIEND MIRANDA FROM THE AWFUL ANTLIONS!
RUBI NEEDED TO MAKE A PHEROMONE TRAIL TO GUIDE MIRANDA TO SAFETY.
SO RUBI BRAVELY SCOOCHED ALONG THE GROUND, WEAVING A SCENT TRAIL THROUGH AN ENTIRE FIELD OF ANTLION PITS.

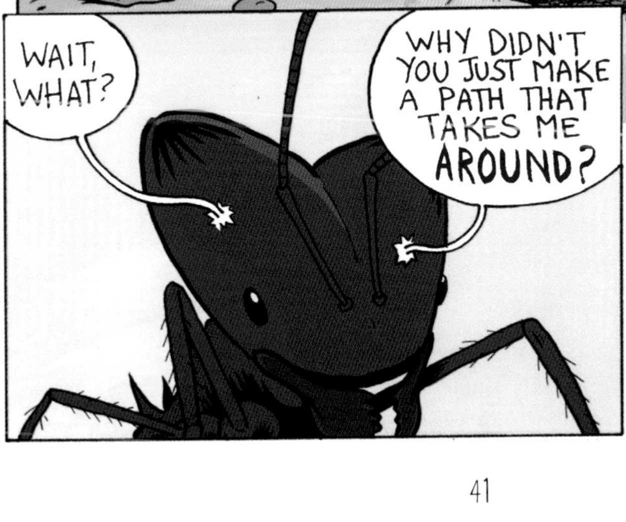
WAIT, WHAT?
WHY DIDN'T YOU JUST MAKE A PATH THAT TAKES ME AROUND?

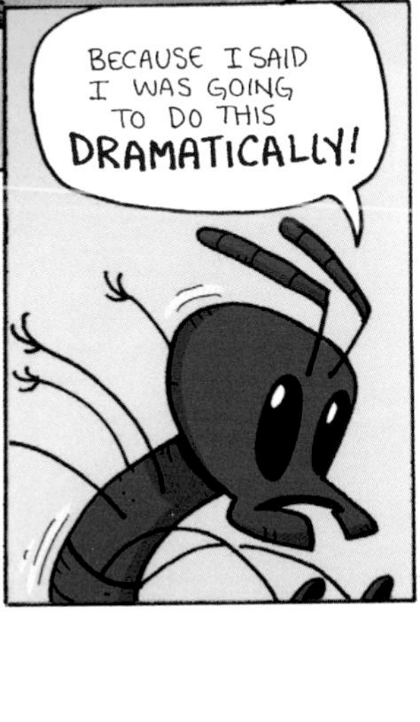
BECAUSE I SAID I WAS GOING TO DO THIS DRAMATICALLY!

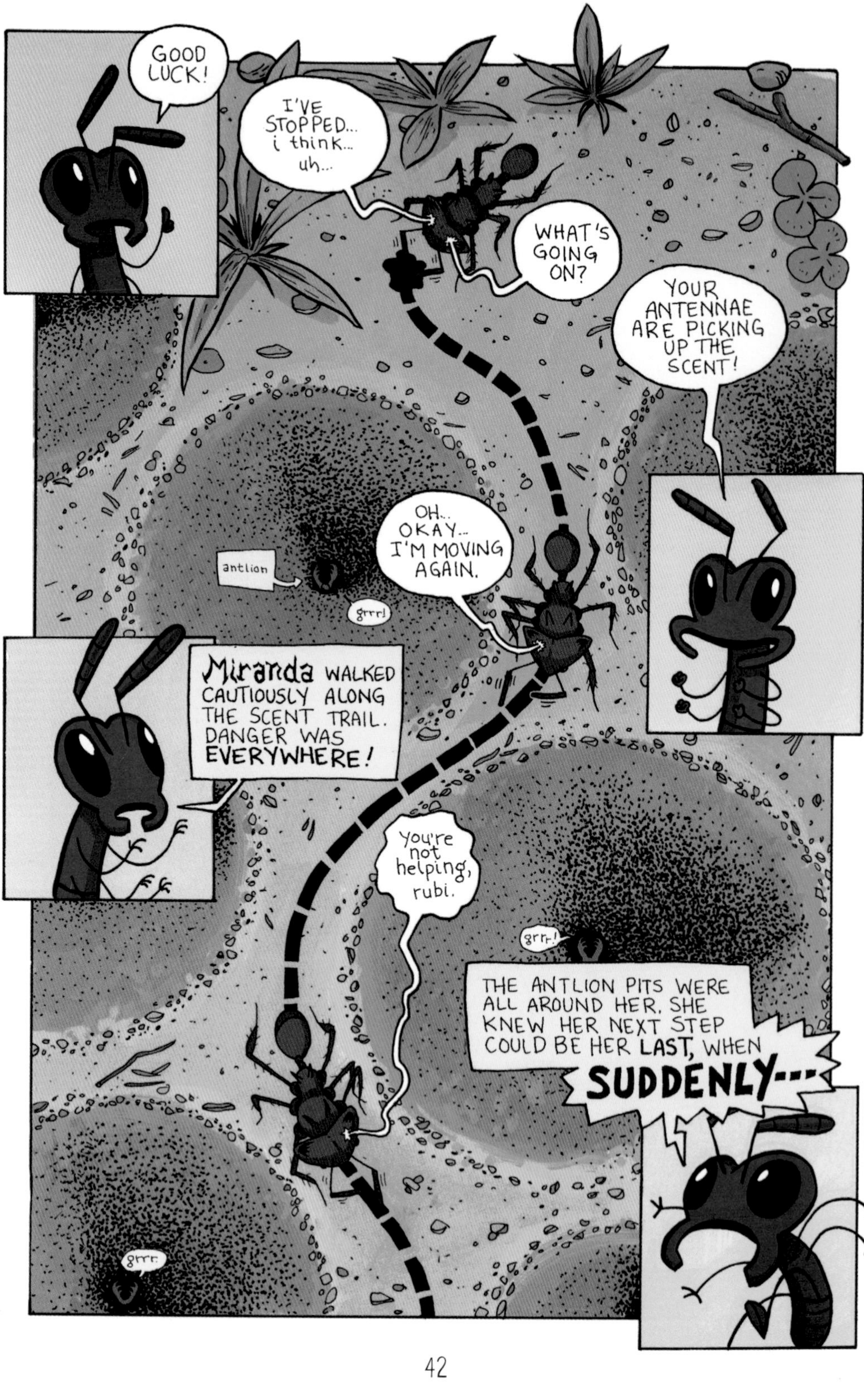
GOOD LUCK!
I'VE STOPPED... i think... uh...
WHAT'S GOING ON?
YOUR ANTENNAE ARE PICKING UP THE SCENT!
antlion
grrr!
OH... OKAY... I'M MOVING AGAIN.
Miranda WALKED CAUTIOUSLY ALONG THE SCENT TRAIL. DANGER WAS EVERYWHERE!
You're not helping, rubi.
grrr!
THE ANTLION PITS WERE ALL AROUND HER. SHE KNEW HER NEXT STEP COULD BE HER LAST, WHEN
SUDDENLY---
grrr.

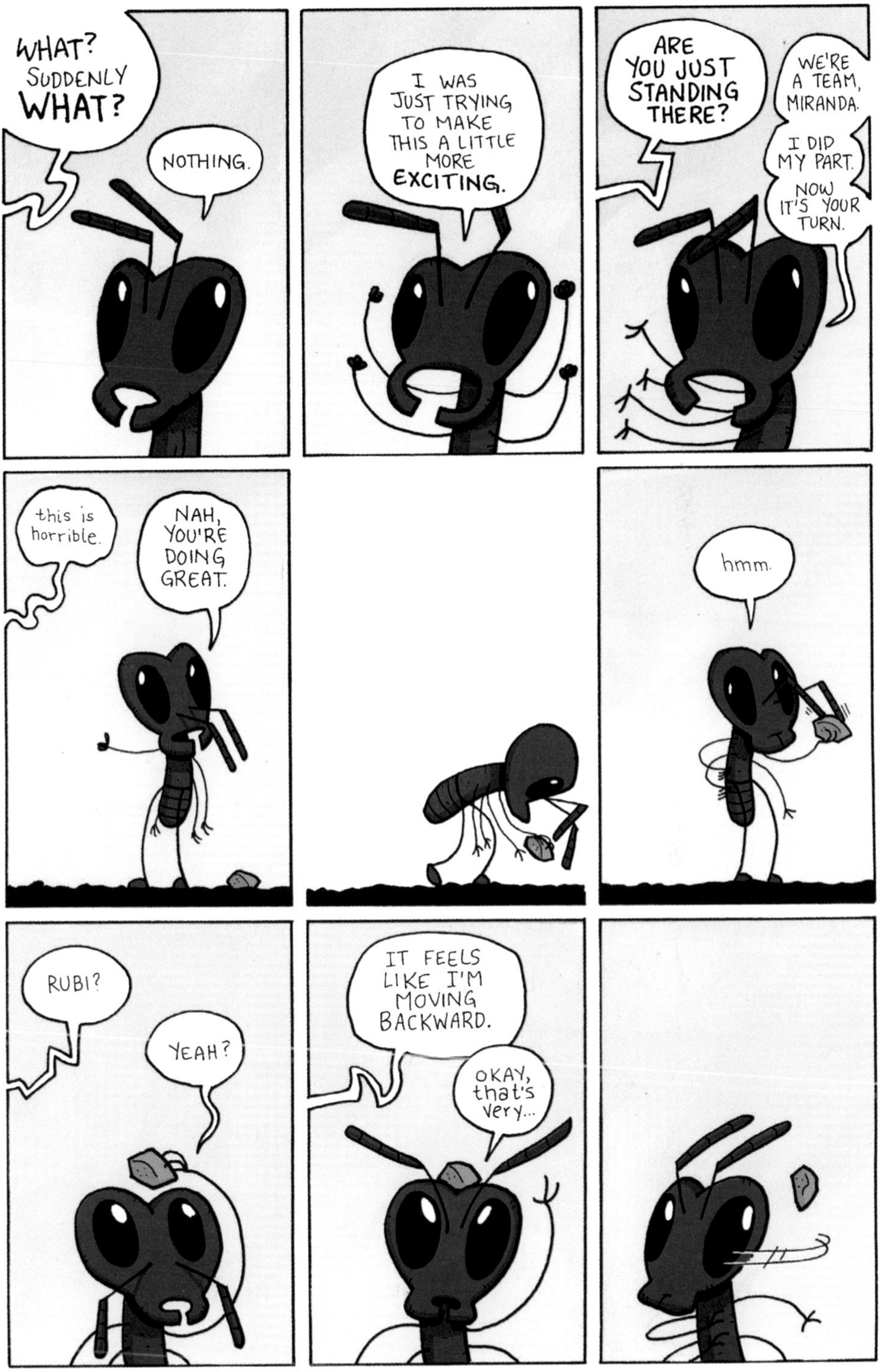
WHAT? SUDDENLY WHAT?
NOTHING.
I WAS JUST TRYING TO MAKE THIS A LITTLE MORE EXCITING.
ARE YOU JUST STANDING THERE?
WE'RE A TEAM, MIRANDA.
I DID MY PART.
NOW IT'S YOUR TURN.
this is horrible.
NAH, YOU'RE DOING GREAT.
hmm.
RUBI?
YEAH?
IT FEELS LIKE I'M MOVING BACKWARD.
OKAY, that's very...

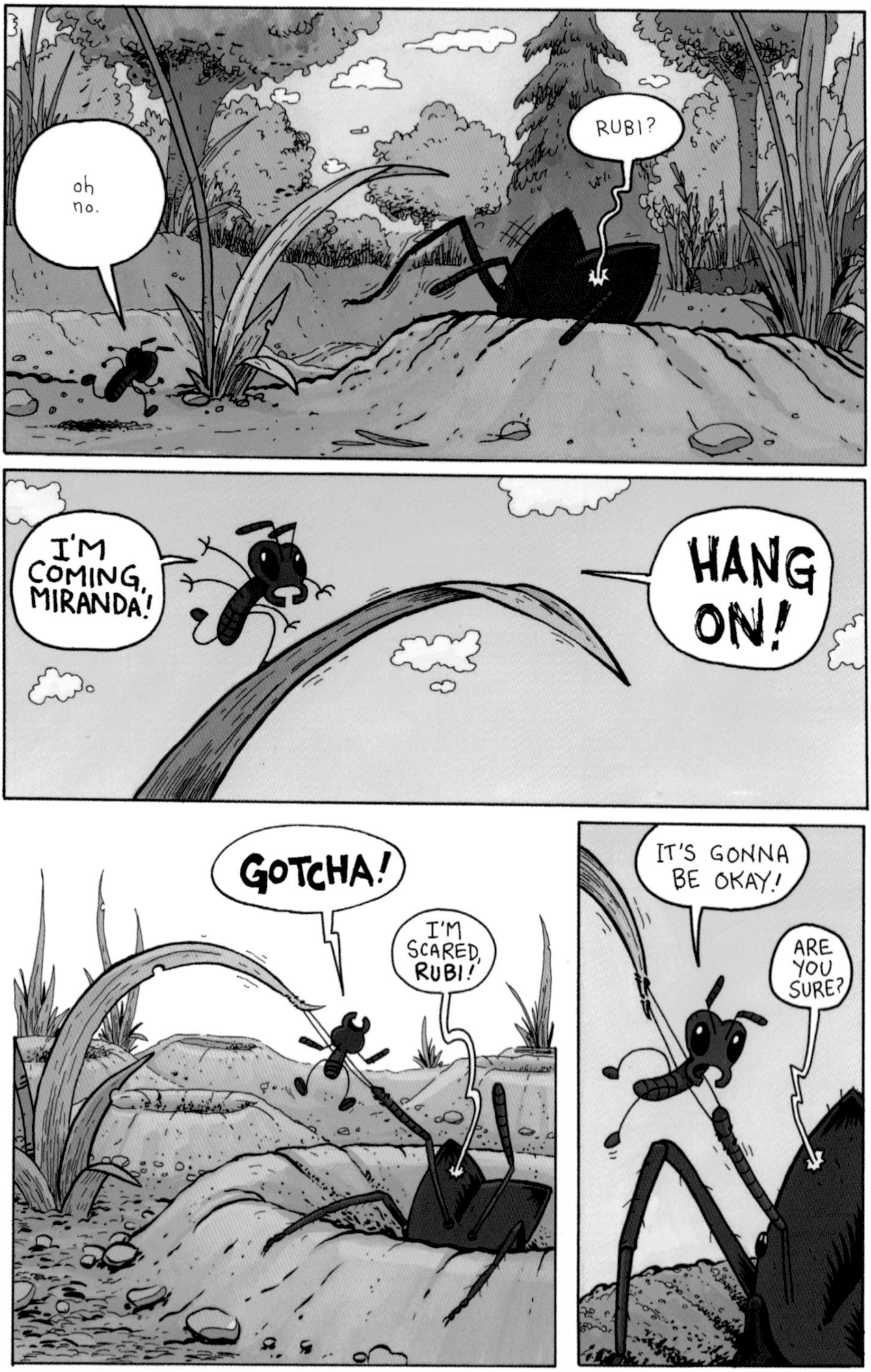
oh no.
RUBI?
I'M COMING, MIRANDA!
HANG ON!
GOTCHA!
I'M SCARED, RUBI!
IT'S GONNA BE OKAY!
ARE YOU SURE?

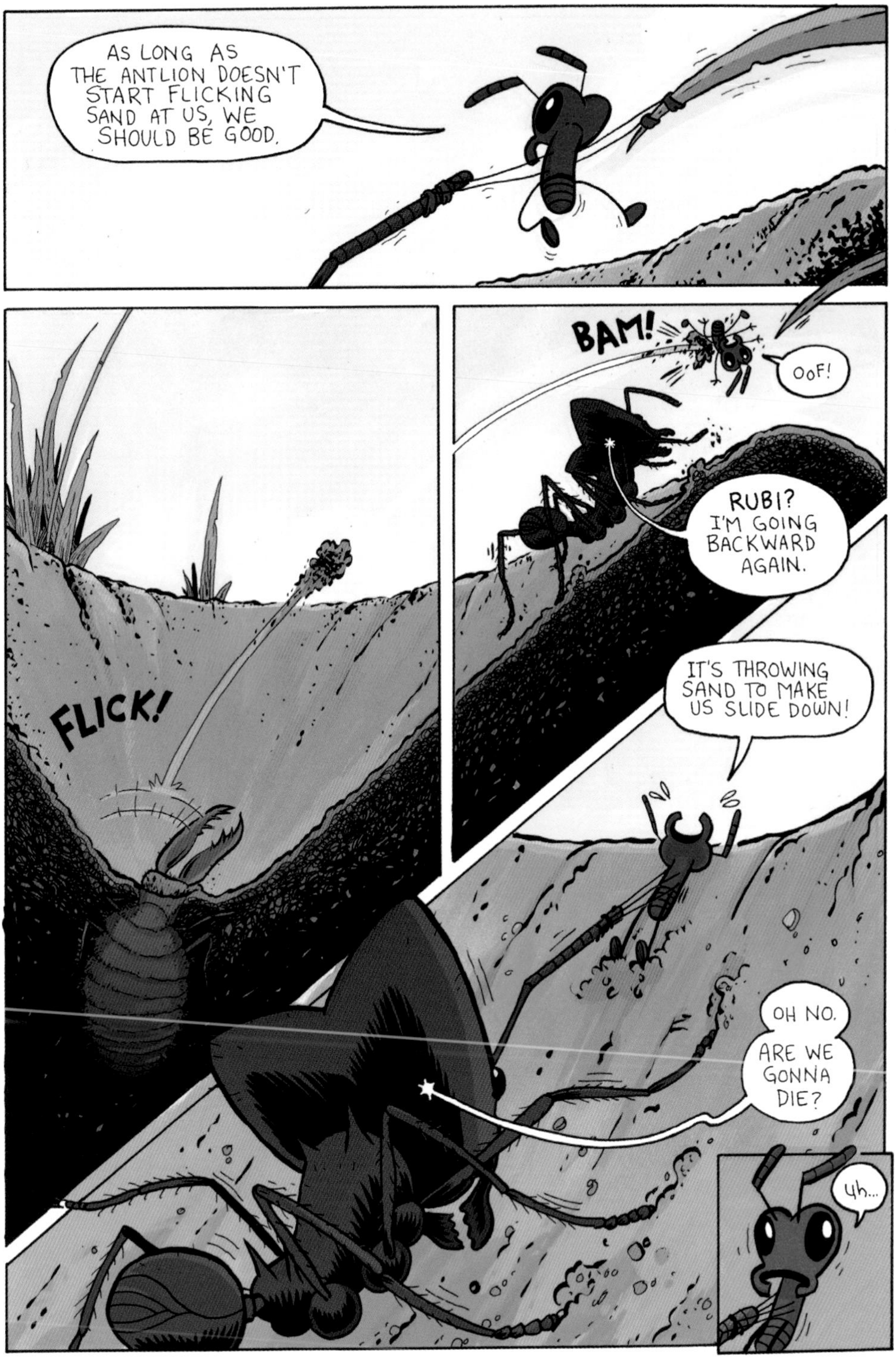
AS LONG AS THE ANTLION DOESN'T START FLICKING SAND AT US, WE SHOULD BE GOOD.
FLICK!
BAM!
OOF!
RUBI? I'M GOING BACKWARD AGAIN.
IT'S THROWING SAND TO MAKE US SLIDE DOWN!
OH NO.
ARE WE GONNA DIE?
Uh...

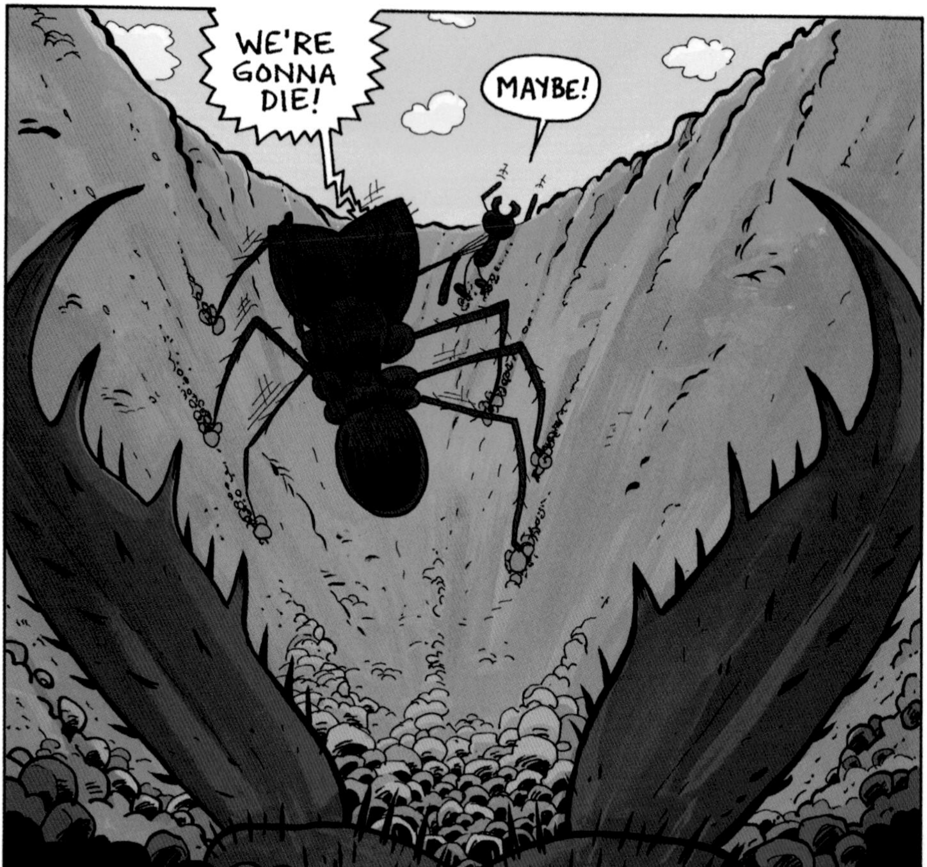
WE'RE GONNA DIE!
MAYBE!

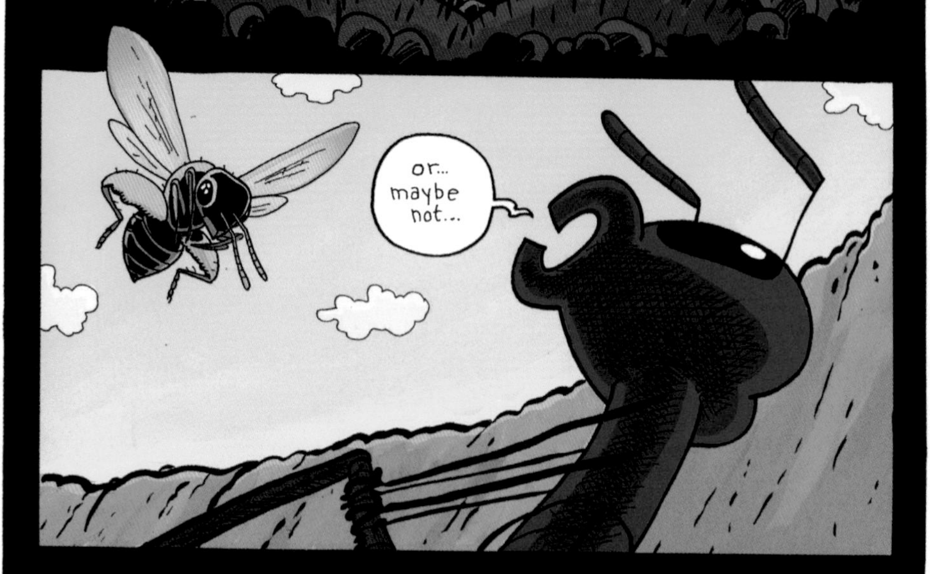
or... maybe not...

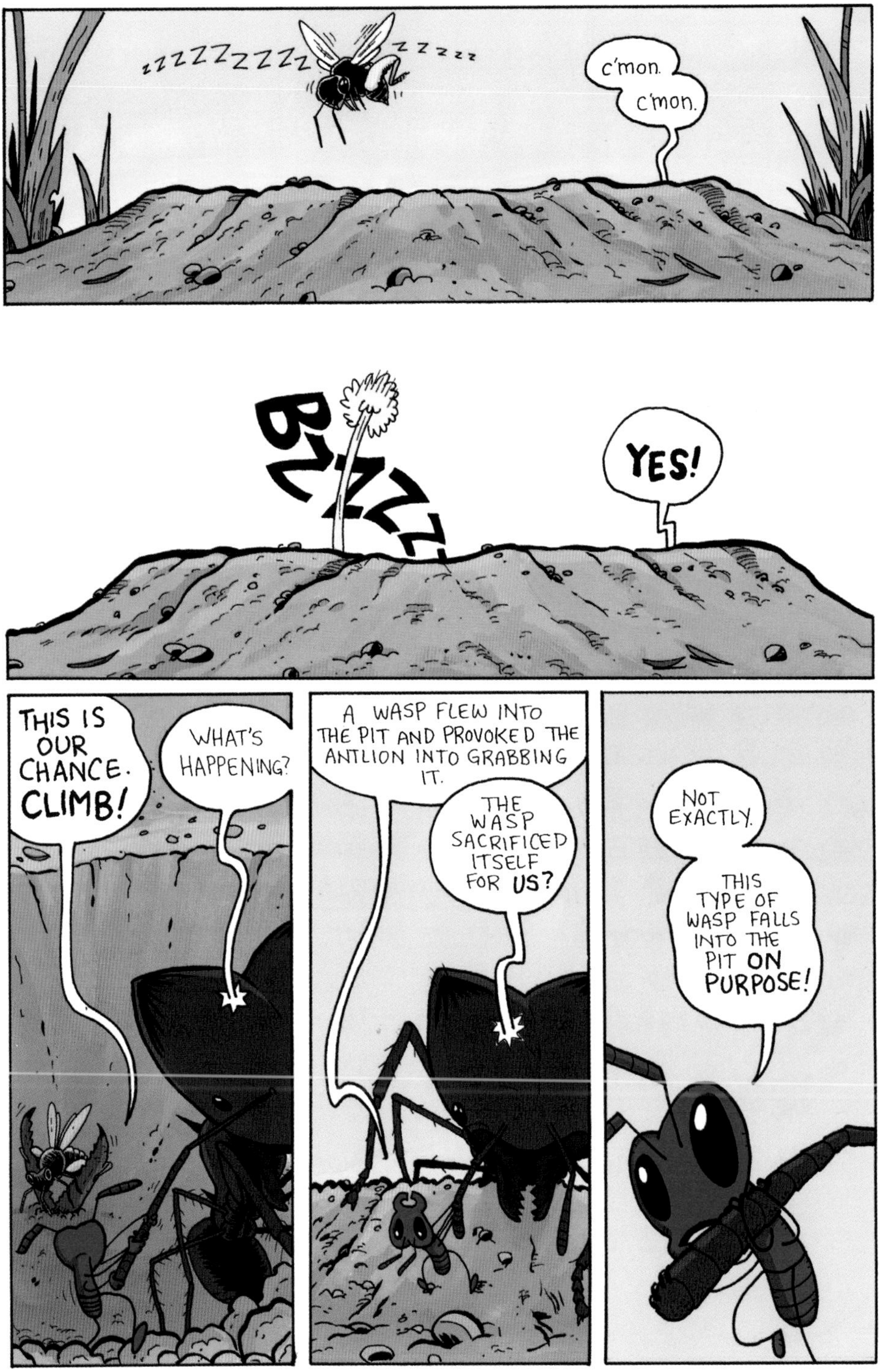
zzzzzzzzz zzzzz
c'mon.
c'mon.
BZZZZZ
YES!
THIS IS OUR CHANCE. CLIMB!
WHAT'S HAPPENING?
A WASP FLEW INTO THE PIT AND PROVOKED THE ANTLION INTO GRABBING IT.
THE WASP SACRIFICED ITSELF FOR US?
NOT EXACTLY.
THIS TYPE OF WASP FALLS INTO THE PIT ON PURPOSE!

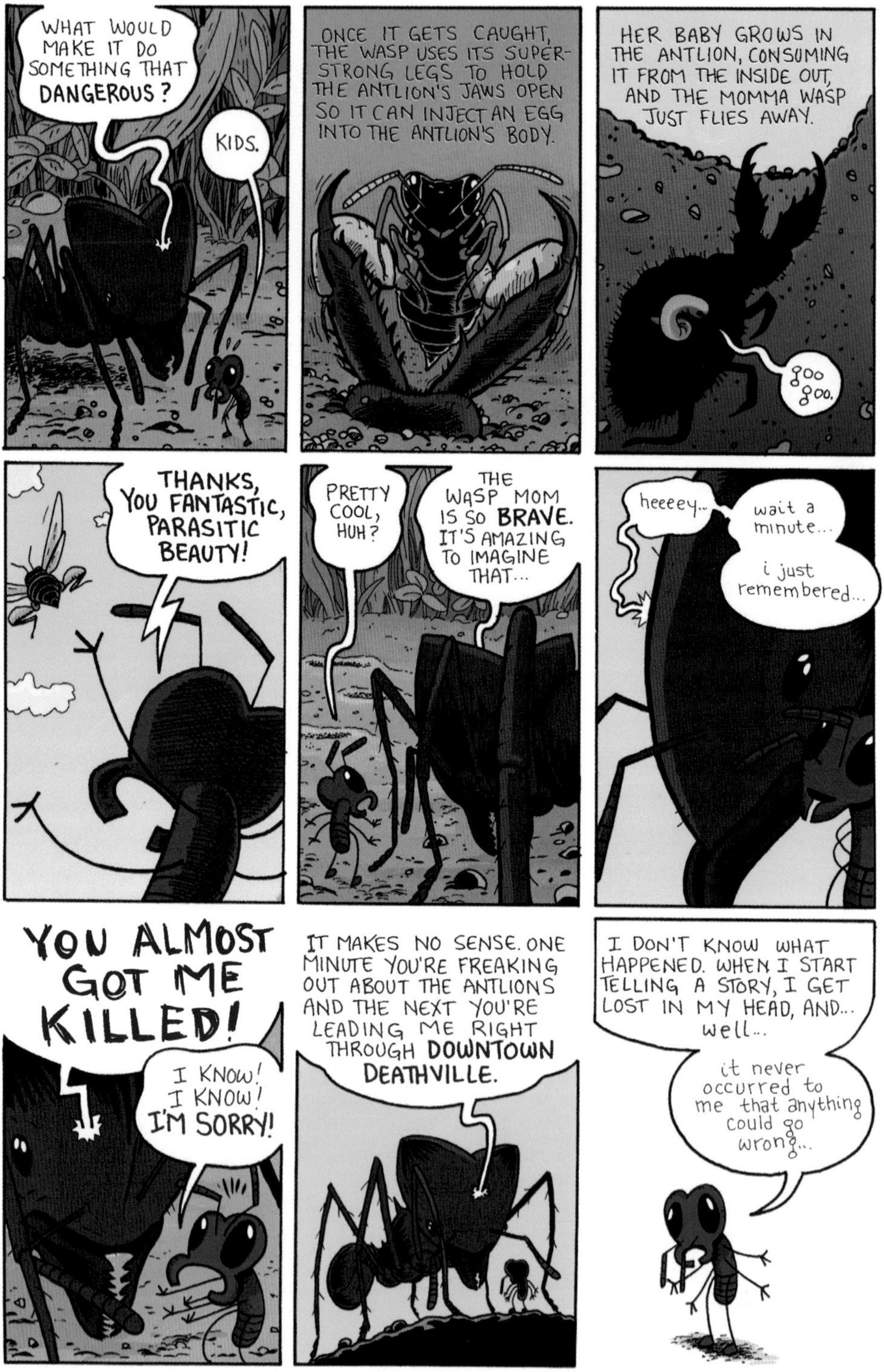
WHAT WOULD MAKE IT DO SOMETHING THAT DANGEROUS?
KIDS.
ONCE IT GETS CAUGHT, THE WASP USES ITS SUPER-STRONG LEGS TO HOLD THE ANTLION'S JAWS OPEN SO IT CAN INJECT AN EGG INTO THE ANTLION'S BODY.
HER BABY GROWS IN THE ANTLION, CONSUMING IT FROM THE INSIDE OUT, AND THE MOMMA WASP JUST FLIES AWAY.
goo goo.
THANKS, YOU FANTASTIC, PARASITIC BEAUTY!
PRETTY COOL, HUH?
THE WASP MOM IS SO BRAVE. IT'S AMAZING TO IMAGINE THAT...
heeeey...
wait a minute...
i just remembered...
YOU ALMOST GOT ME KILLED!
I KNOW! I KNOW! I'M SORRY!
IT MAKES NO SENSE. ONE MINUTE YOU'RE FREAKING OUT ABOUT THE ANTLIONS AND THE NEXT YOU'RE LEADING ME RIGHT THROUGH DOWNTOWN DEATHVILLE.
I DON'T KNOW WHAT HAPPENED. WHEN I START TELLING A STORY, I GET LOST IN MY HEAD, AND... well...
it never occurred to me that anything could go wrong...

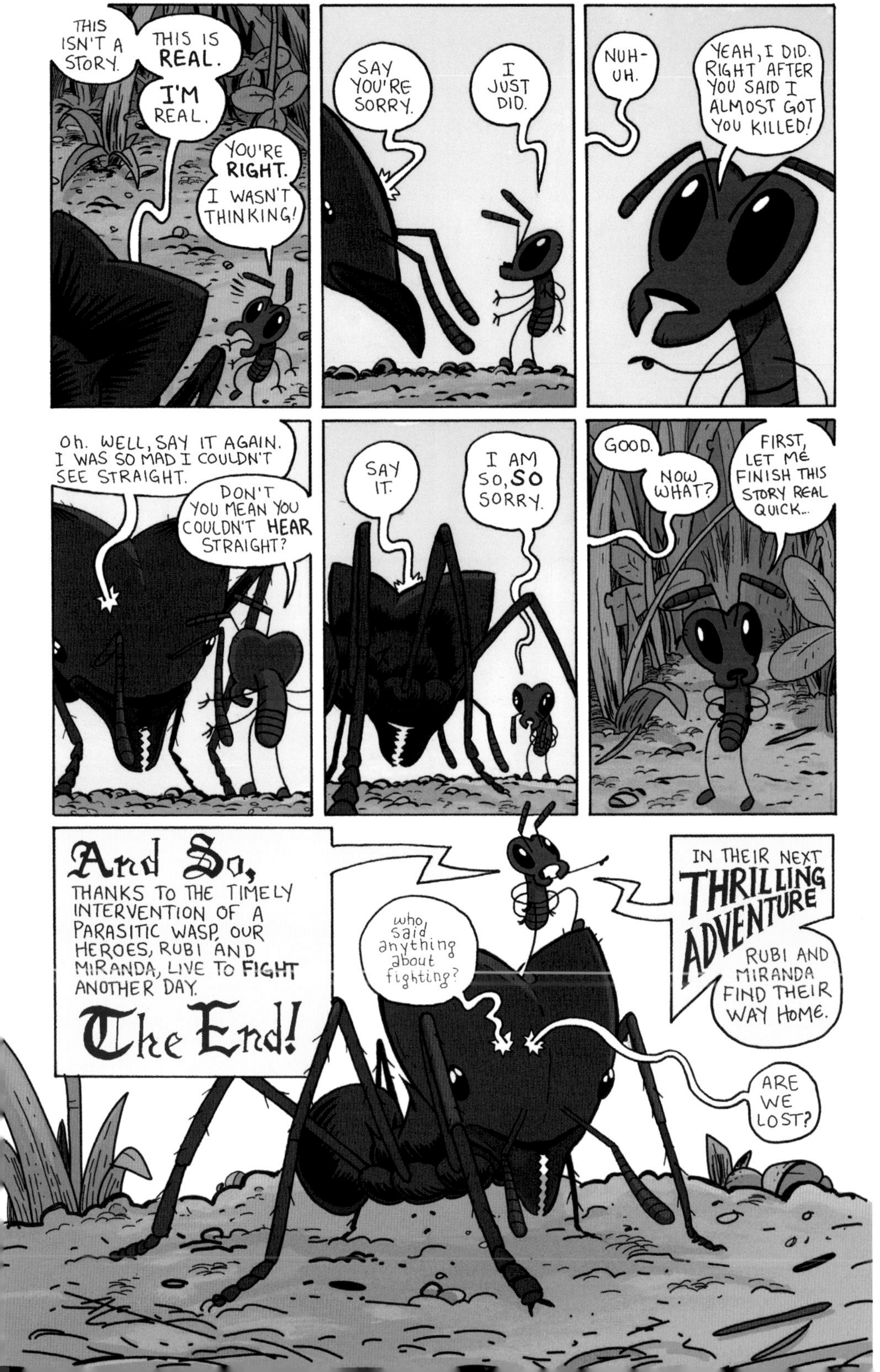

THIS ISN'T A STORY.
THIS IS REAL.
I'M REAL.
YOU'RE RIGHT. I WASN'T THINKING!
SAY YOU'RE SORRY.
I JUST DID.
NUH-UH.
YEAH, I DID. RIGHT AFTER YOU SAID I ALMOST GOT YOU KILLED!
Oh. WELL, SAY IT AGAIN. I WAS SO MAD I COULDN'T SEE STRAIGHT.
DON'T YOU MEAN YOU COULDN'T HEAR STRAIGHT?
SAY IT.
I AM SO, SO SORRY.
GOOD.
NOW WHAT?
FIRST, LET ME FINISH THIS STORY REAL QUICK...
And So,
THANKS TO THE TIMELY INTERVENTION OF A PARASITIC WASP, OUR HEROES, RUBI AND MIRANDA, LIVE TO FIGHT ANOTHER DAY.
The End!
who said anything about fighting?
IN THEIR NEXT THRILLING ADVENTURE RUBI AND MIRANDA FIND THEIR WAY HOME.
ARE WE LOST?

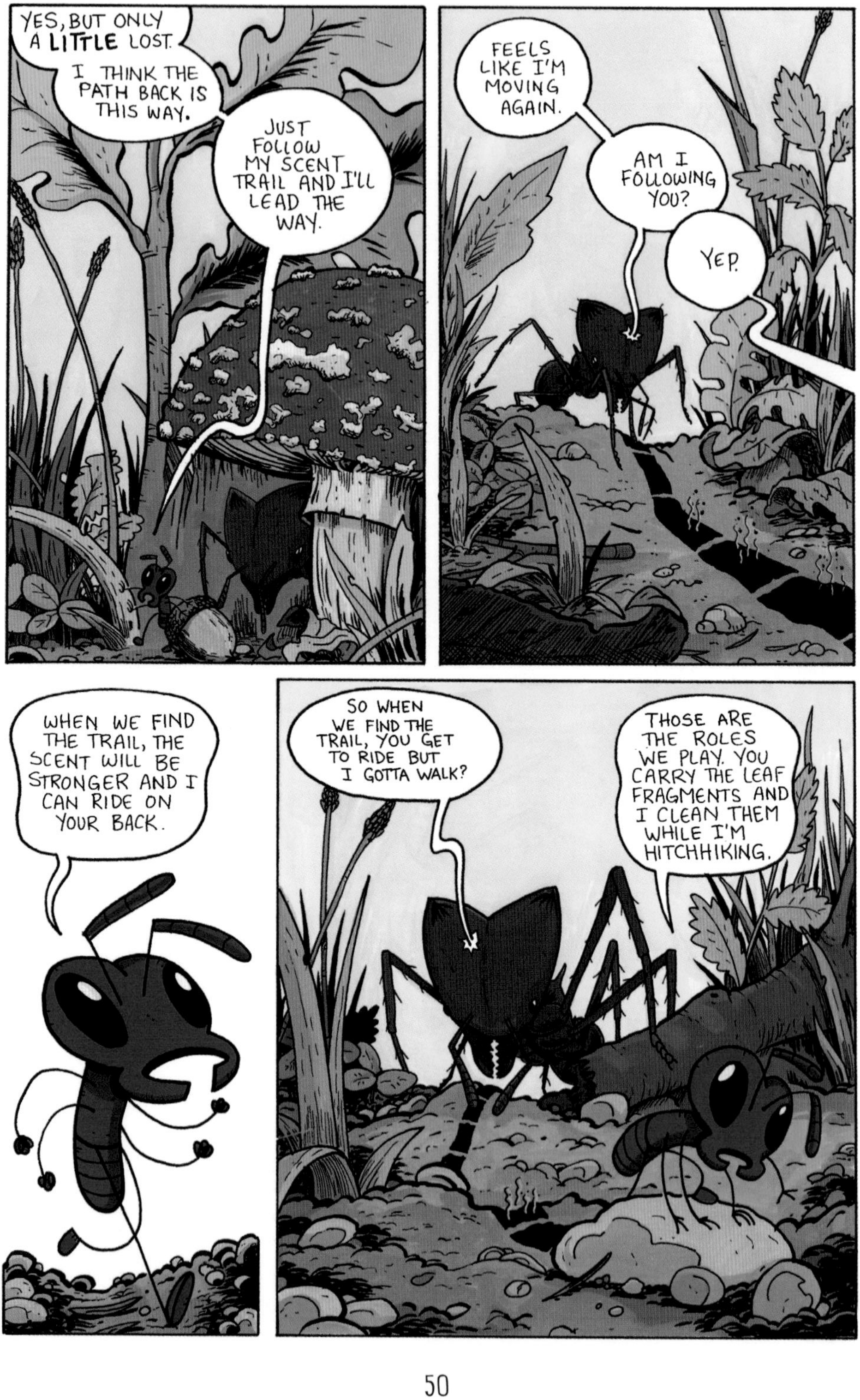
YES, BUT ONLY A LITTLE LOST.
I THINK THE PATH BACK IS THIS WAY.
JUST FOLLOW MY SCENT TRAIL AND I'LL LEAD THE WAY.
FEELS LIKE I'M MOVING AGAIN.
AM I FOLLOWING YOU?
YEP.
WHEN WE FIND THE TRAIL, THE SCENT WILL BE STRONGER AND I CAN RIDE ON YOUR BACK.
SO WHEN WE FIND THE TRAIL, YOU GET TO RIDE BUT I GOTTA WALK?
THOSE ARE THE ROLES WE PLAY. YOU CARRY THE LEAF FRAGMENTS AND I CLEAN THEM WHILE I'M HITCHHIKING.

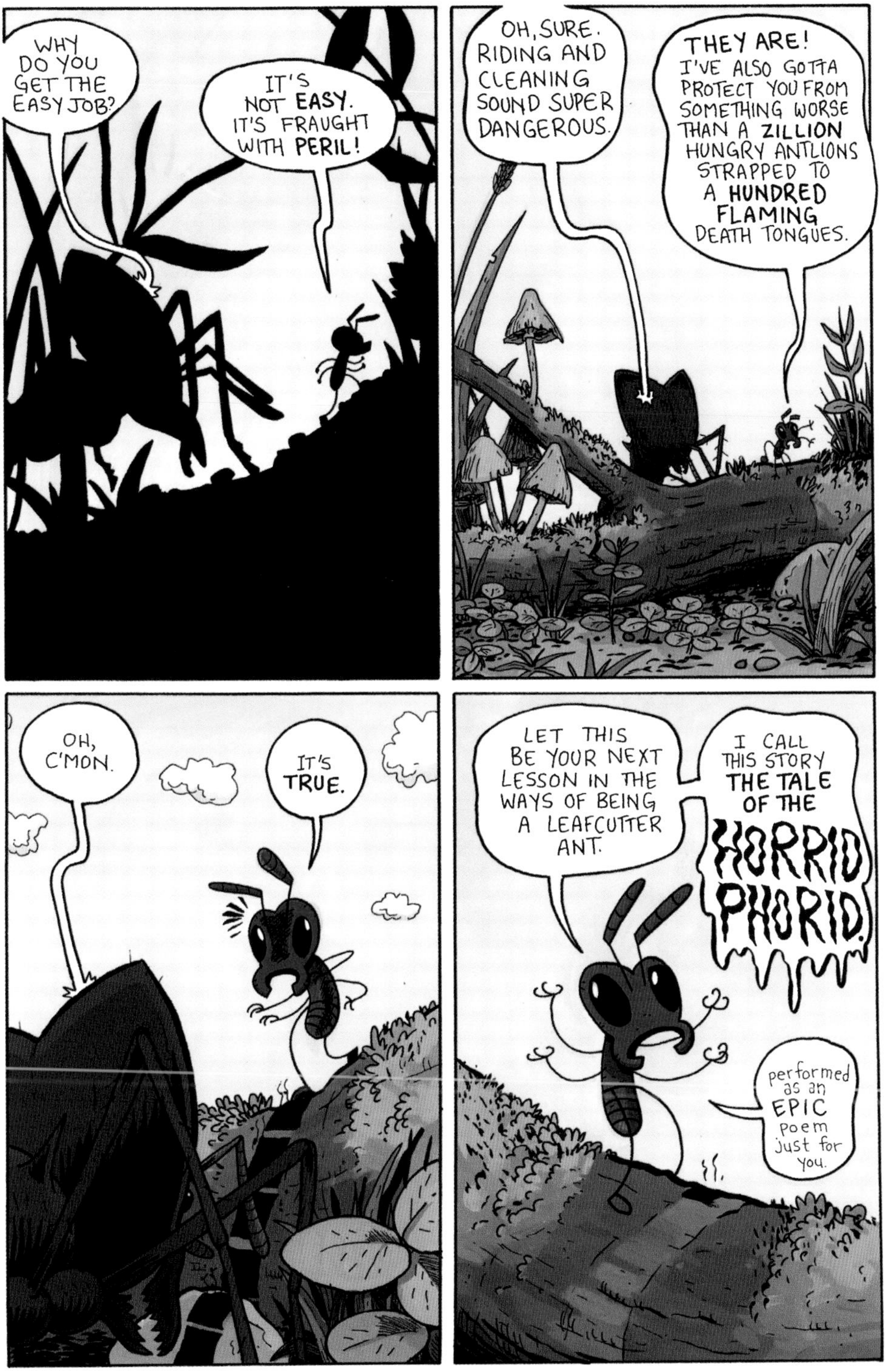
WHY DO YOU GET THE EASY JOB?
IT'S NOT **EASY**. IT'S FRAUGHT WITH **PERIL**!
OH, SURE. RIDING AND CLEANING SOUND SUPER DANGEROUS.
THEY ARE! I'VE ALSO GOTTA PROTECT YOU FROM SOMETHING WORSE THAN A **ZILLION** HUNGRY ANTLIONS STRAPPED TO A **HUNDRED FLAMING** DEATH TONGUES.
OH, C'MON.
IT'S **TRUE**.
LET THIS BE YOUR NEXT LESSON IN THE WAYS OF BEING A LEAFCUTTER ANT.
I CALL THIS STORY **THE TALE OF THE**
HORRID PHORID.
performed as an EPIC poem just for you.

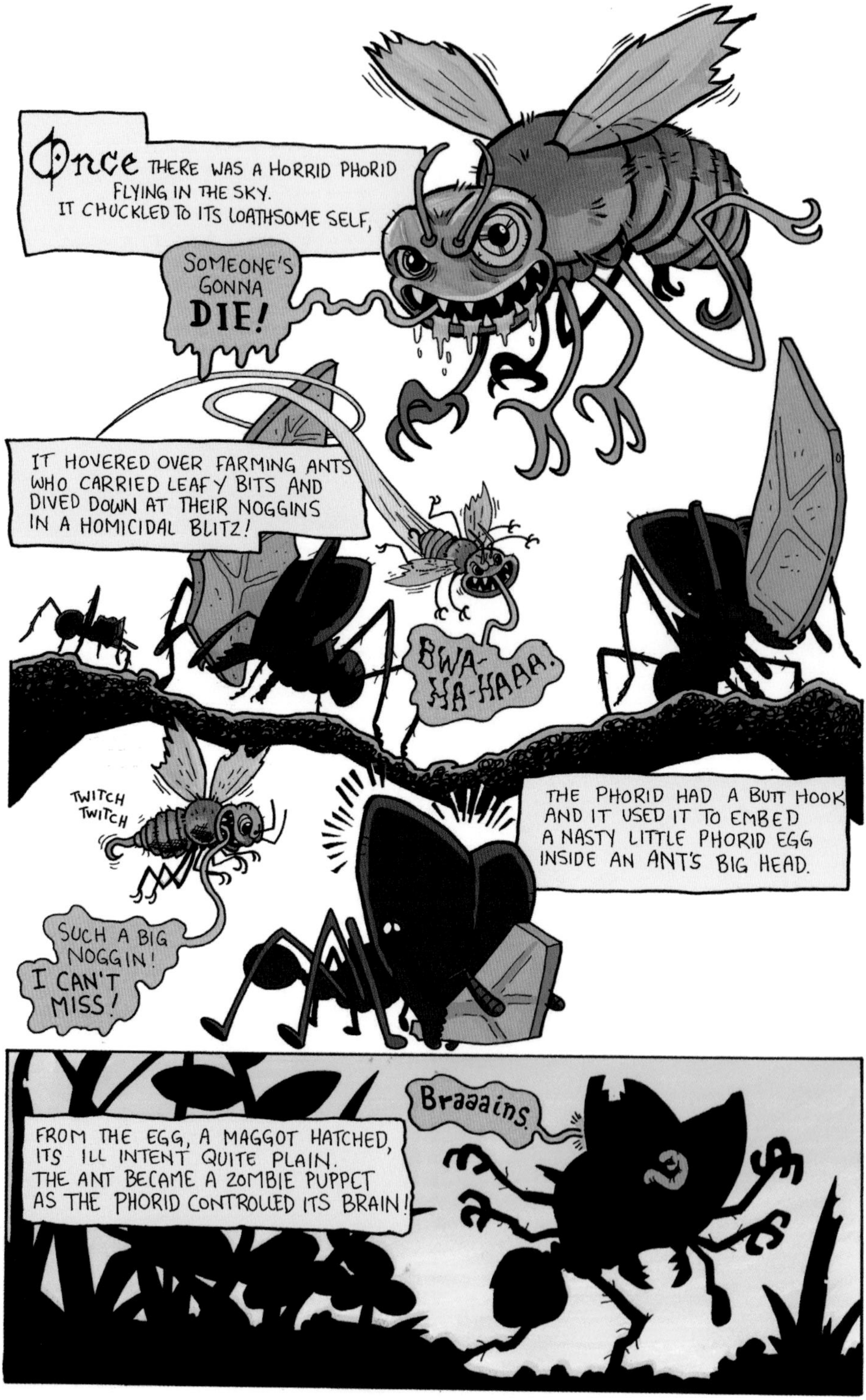

Once there was a horrid phorid flying in the sky. It chuckled to its loathsome self,
SOMEONE'S GONNA DIE!
IT HOVERED OVER FARMING ANTS WHO CARRIED LEAFY BITS AND DIVED DOWN AT THEIR NOGGINS IN A HOMICIDAL BLITZ!
BWA-HA-HAAA.
TWITCH TWITCH
THE PHORID HAD A BUTT HOOK AND IT USED IT TO EMBED A NASTY LITTLE PHORID EGG INSIDE AN ANT'S BIG HEAD.
SUCH A BIG NOGGIN! I CAN'T MISS!
FROM THE EGG, A MAGGOT HATCHED, ITS ILL INTENT QUITE PLAIN. THE ANT BECAME A ZOMBIE PUPPET AS THE PHORID CONTROLLED ITS BRAIN!
Braaains.

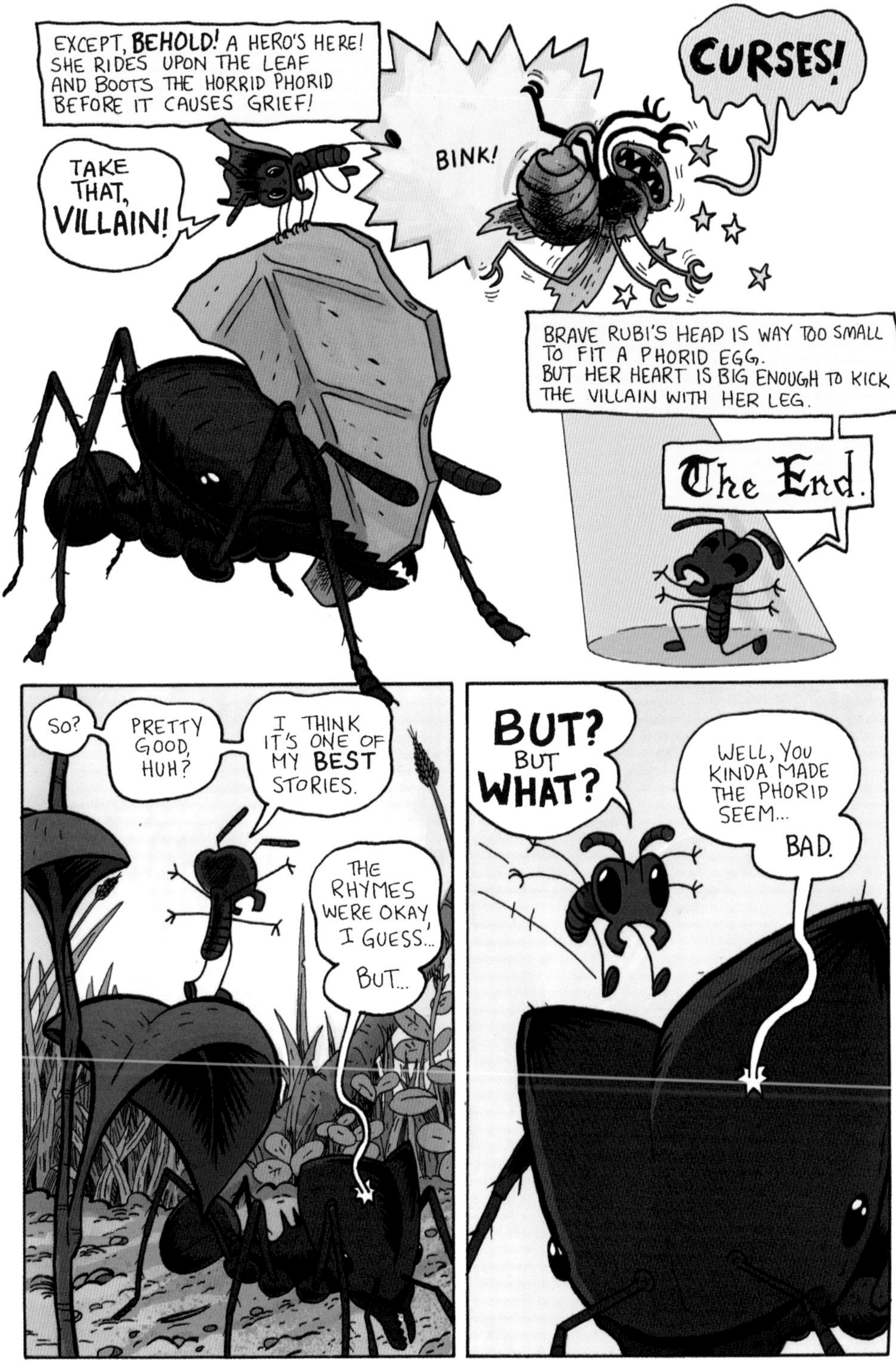
EXCEPT, BEHOLD! A HERO'S HERE! SHE RIDES UPON THE LEAF AND BOOTS THE HORRID PHORID BEFORE IT CAUSES GRIEF!
TAKE THAT, VILLAIN!
BINK!
CURSES!
BRAVE RUBI'S HEAD IS WAY TOO SMALL TO FIT A PHORID EGG. BUT HER HEART IS BIG ENOUGH TO KICK THE VILLAIN WITH HER LEG.
The End.
SO?
PRETTY GOOD, HUH?
I THINK IT'S ONE OF MY BEST STORIES.
THE RHYMES WERE OKAY, I GUESS...
BUT...
BUT? BUT WHAT?
WELL, YOU KINDA MADE THE PHORID SEEM...
BAD.

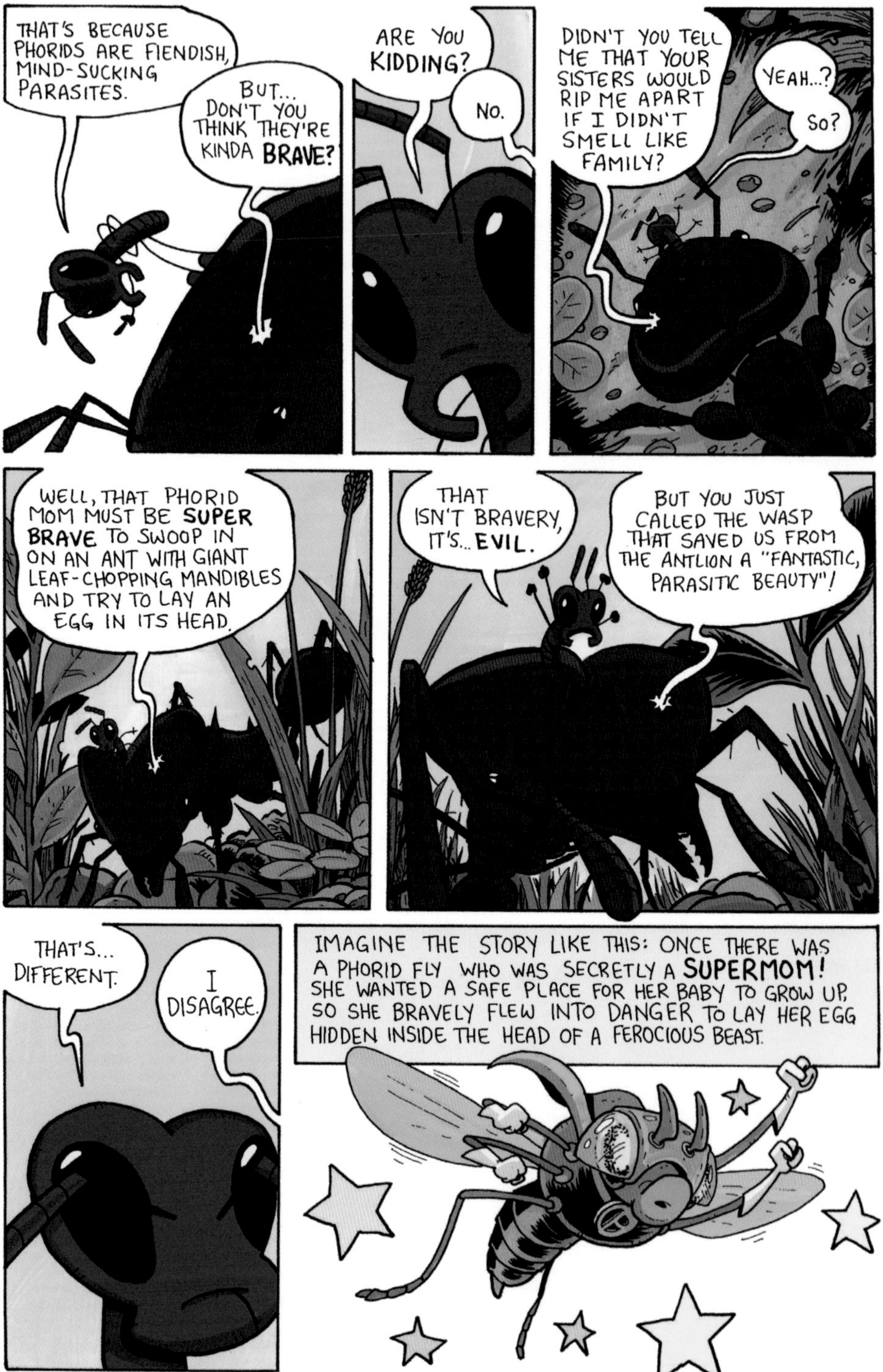
THAT'S BECAUSE PHORIDS ARE FIENDISH, MIND-SUCKING PARASITES.
BUT... DON'T YOU THINK THEY'RE KINDA BRAVE?
ARE YOU KIDDING?
NO.
DIDN'T YOU TELL ME THAT YOUR SISTERS WOULD RIP ME APART IF I DIDN'T SMELL LIKE FAMILY?
YEAH...?
SO?
WELL, THAT PHORID MOM MUST BE SUPER BRAVE TO SWOOP IN ON AN ANT WITH GIANT LEAF-CHOPPING MANDIBLES AND TRY TO LAY AN EGG IN ITS HEAD.
THAT ISN'T BRAVERY, IT'S... EVIL.
BUT YOU JUST CALLED THE WASP THAT SAVED US FROM THE ANTLION A "FANTASTIC, PARASITIC BEAUTY"!
THAT'S... DIFFERENT.
I DISAGREE.
IMAGINE THE STORY LIKE THIS: ONCE THERE WAS A PHORID FLY WHO WAS SECRETLY A SUPERMOM! SHE WANTED A SAFE PLACE FOR HER BABY TO GROW UP, SO SHE BRAVELY FLEW INTO DANGER TO LAY HER EGG HIDDEN INSIDE THE HEAD OF A FEROCIOUS BEAST.

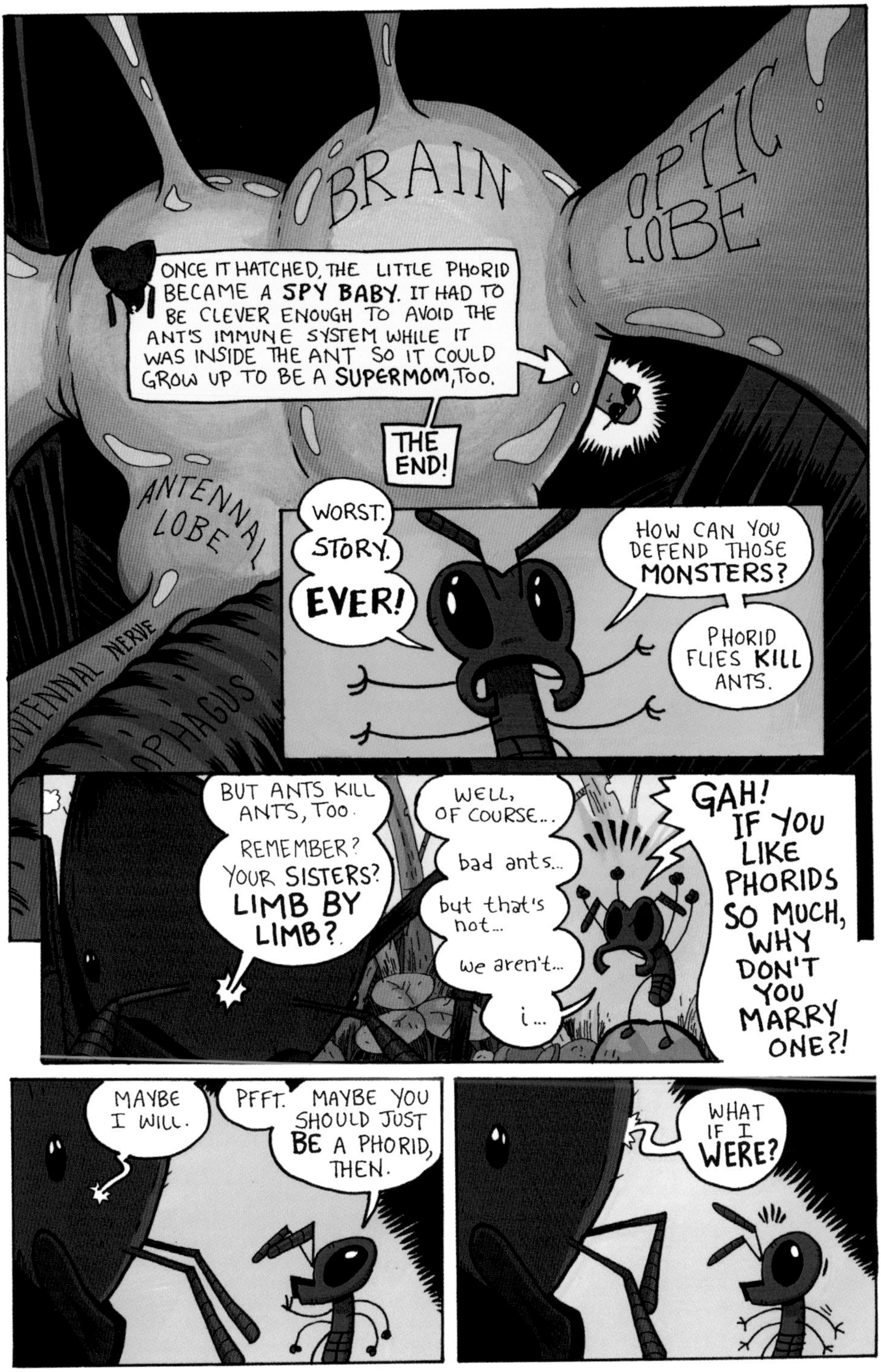
BRAIN
OPTIC LOBE
ONCE IT HATCHED, THE LITTLE PHORID BECAME A SPY BABY. IT HAD TO BE CLEVER ENOUGH TO AVOID THE ANT'S IMMUNE SYSTEM WHILE IT WAS INSIDE THE ANT SO IT COULD GROW UP TO BE A SUPERMOM, TOO.
THE END!
ANTENNAL LOBE
ANTENNAL NERVE
OPHAGUS
WORST. STORY. EVER!
HOW CAN YOU DEFEND THOSE MONSTERS?
PHORID FLIES KILL ANTS.
BUT ANTS KILL ANTS, TOO.
REMEMBER? YOUR SISTERS? LIMB BY LIMB?
WELL, OF COURSE...
bad ants...
but that's not...
we aren't...
i...
GAH! IF YOU LIKE PHORIDS SO MUCH, WHY DON'T YOU MARRY ONE?!
MAYBE I WILL.
PFFT. MAYBE YOU SHOULD JUST BE A PHORID, THEN.
WHAT IF I WERE?

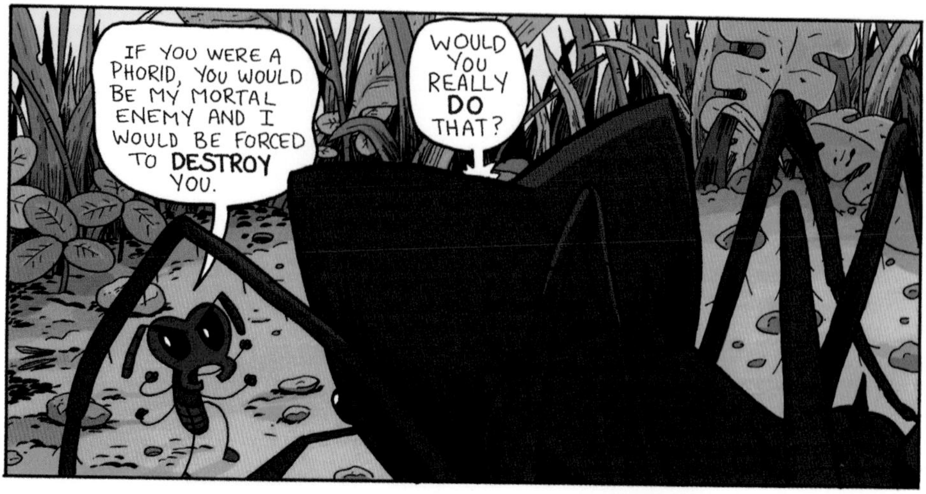
IF YOU WERE A PHORID, YOU WOULD BE MY MORTAL ENEMY AND I WOULD BE FORCED TO **DESTROY** YOU.
WOULD YOU REALLY **DO** THAT?

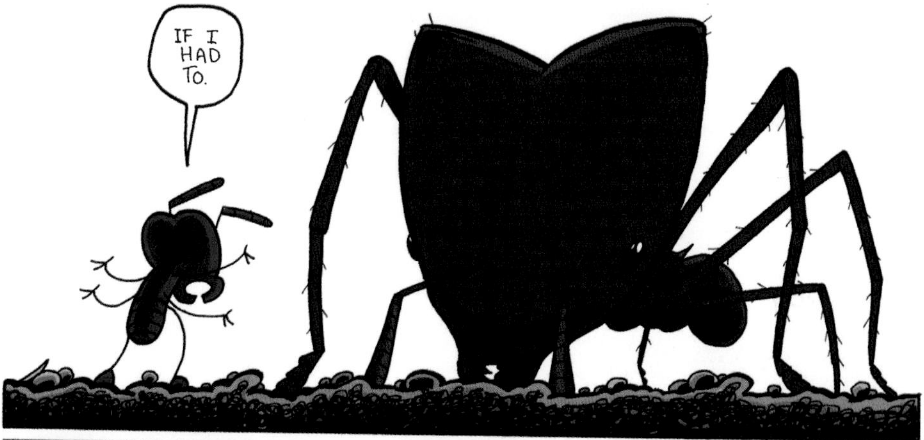
IF I HAD TO.

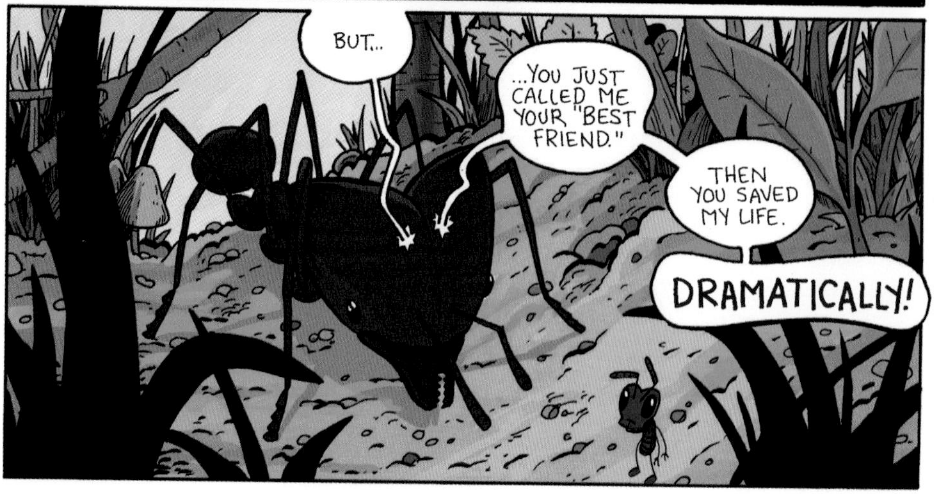
BUT...
...YOU JUST CALLED ME YOUR "BEST FRIEND."
THEN YOU SAVED MY LIFE.
DRAMATICALLY!

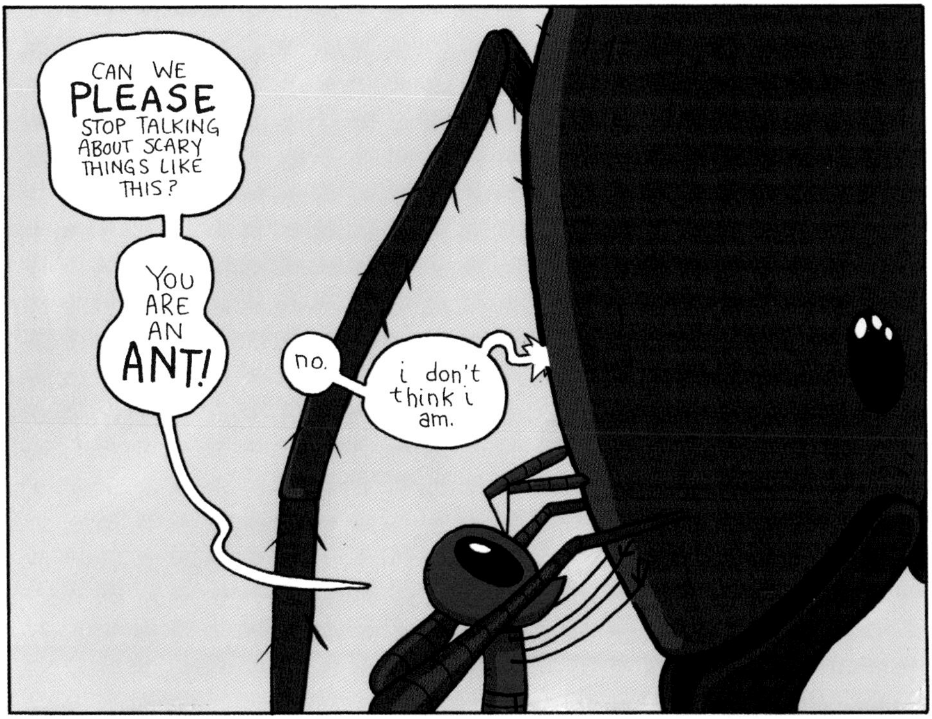
CAN WE PLEASE STOP TALKING ABOUT SCARY THINGS LIKE THIS?
YOU ARE AN ANT!
no.
i don't think i am.

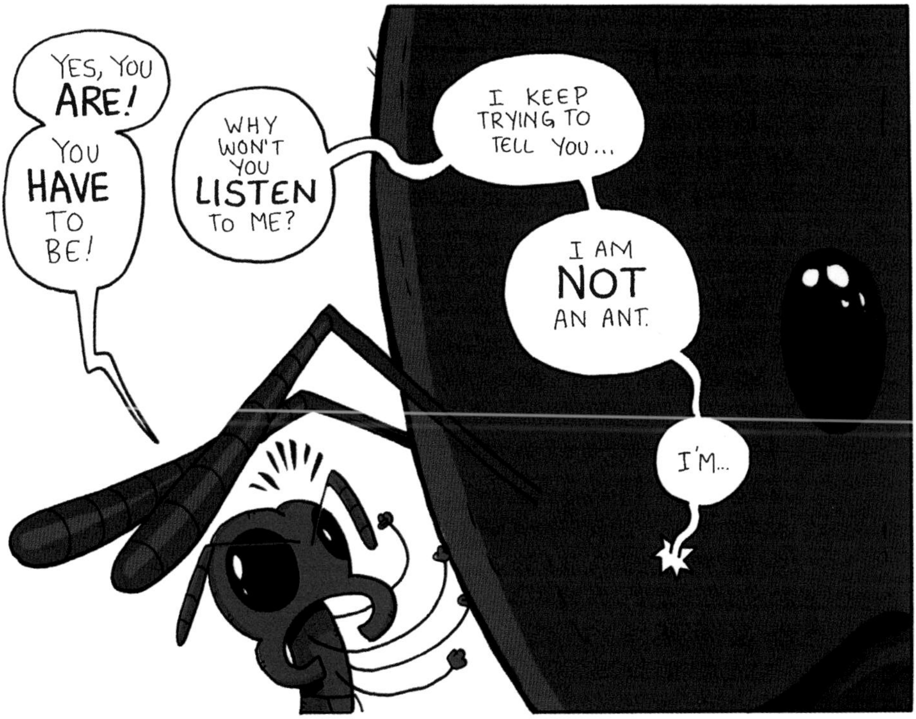
YES, YOU ARE!
YOU HAVE TO BE!
WHY WON'T YOU LISTEN TO ME?
I KEEP TRYING TO TELL YOU...
I AM NOT AN ANT.
I'M...

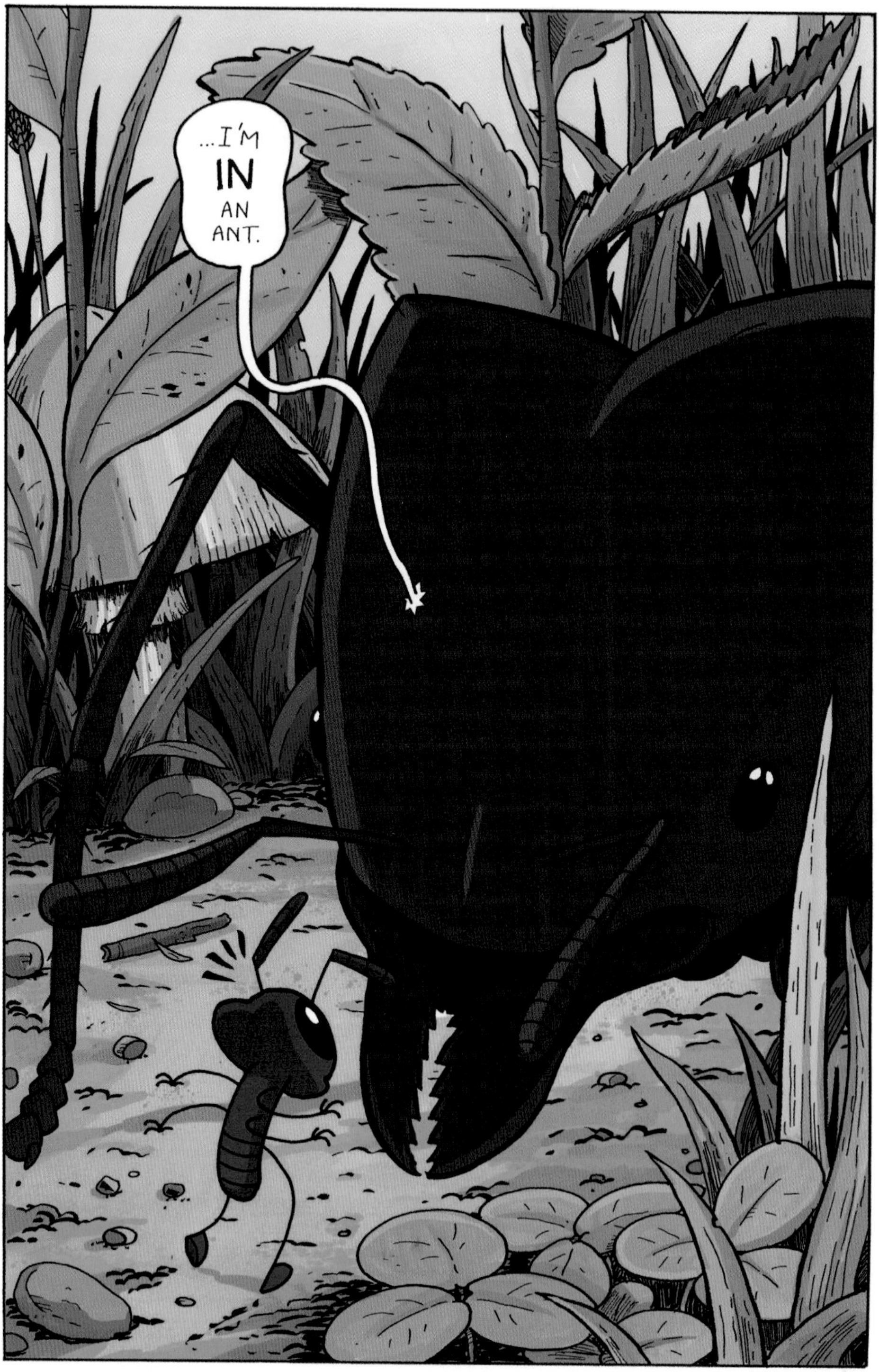
...I'M IN AN ANT.

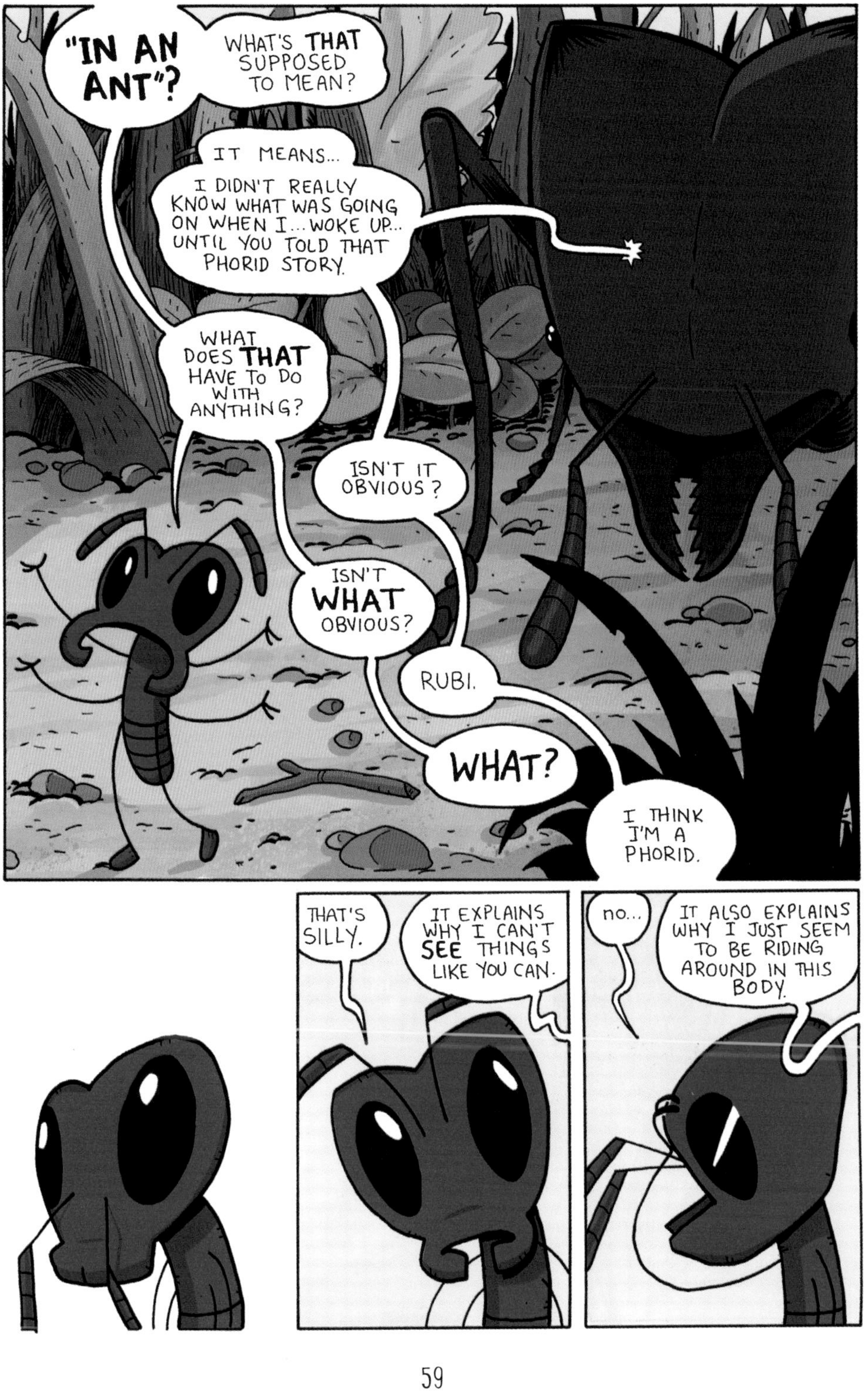
"IN AN ANT"?
WHAT'S THAT SUPPOSED TO MEAN?
IT MEANS...
I DIDN'T REALLY KNOW WHAT WAS GOING ON WHEN I... WOKE UP... UNTIL YOU TOLD THAT PHORID STORY.
WHAT DOES THAT HAVE TO DO WITH ANYTHING?
ISN'T IT OBVIOUS?
ISN'T WHAT OBVIOUS?
RUBI.
WHAT?
I THINK I'M A PHORID.
THAT'S SILLY.
IT EXPLAINS WHY I CAN'T SEE THINGS LIKE YOU CAN.
no...
IT ALSO EXPLAINS WHY I JUST SEEM TO BE RIDING AROUND IN THIS BODY.

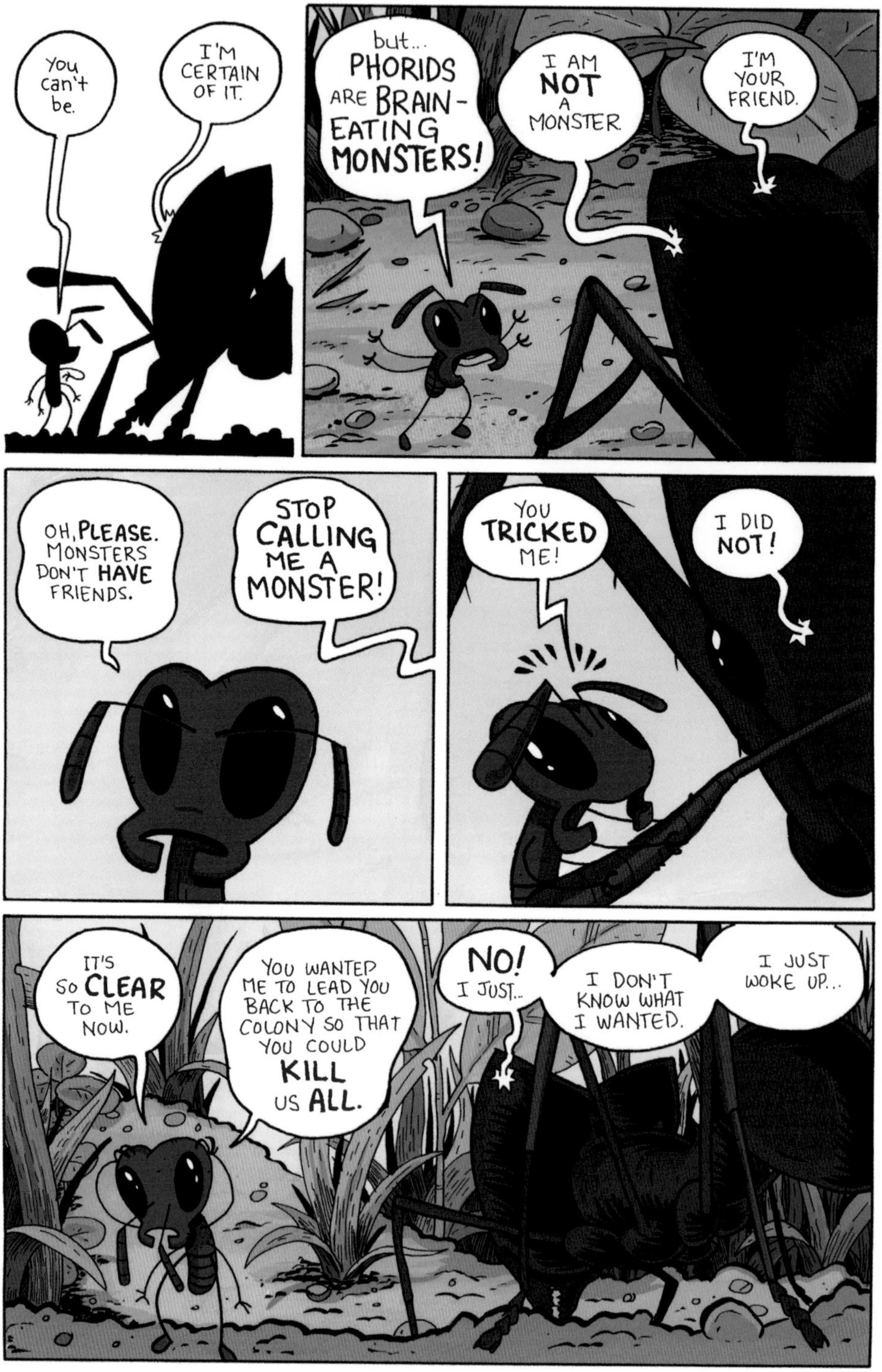
You can't be.
I'M CERTAIN OF IT.
but... PHORIDS ARE BRAIN-EATING MONSTERS!
I AM NOT A MONSTER.
I'M YOUR FRIEND.
OH, PLEASE. MONSTERS DON'T HAVE FRIENDS.
STOP CALLING ME A MONSTER!
YOU TRICKED ME!
I DID NOT!
IT'S SO CLEAR TO ME NOW.
YOU WANTED ME TO LEAD YOU BACK TO THE COLONY SO THAT YOU COULD KILL US ALL.
NO! I JUST...
I DON'T KNOW WHAT I WANTED.
I JUST WOKE UP...

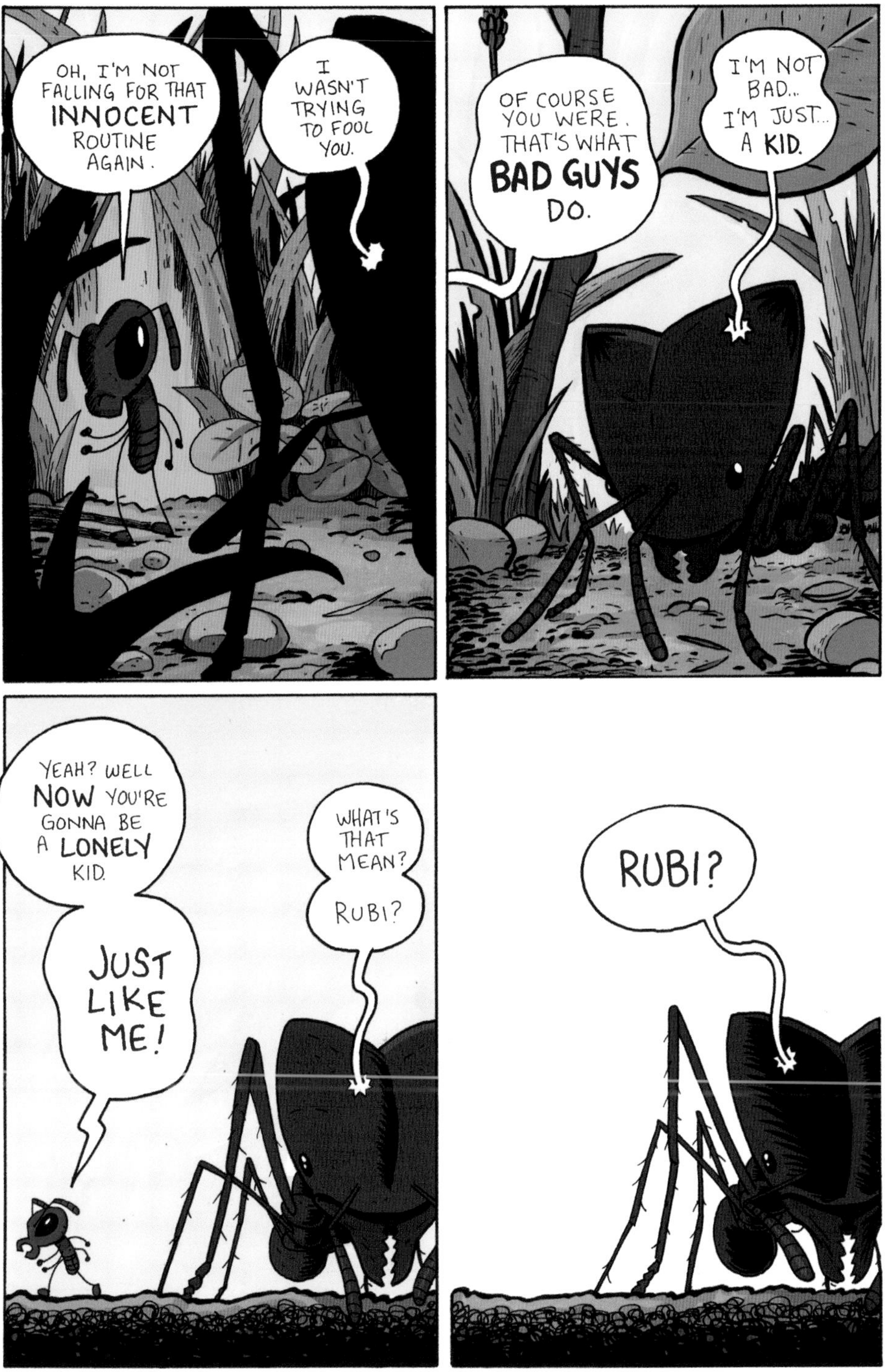
OH, I'M NOT FALLING FOR THAT INNOCENT ROUTINE AGAIN.
I WASN'T TRYING TO FOOL YOU.
OF COURSE YOU WERE. THAT'S WHAT BAD GUYS DO.
I'M NOT BAD... I'M JUST... A KID.
YEAH? WELL NOW YOU'RE GONNA BE A LONELY KID.
JUST LIKE ME!
WHAT'S THAT MEAN?
RUBI?
RUBI?

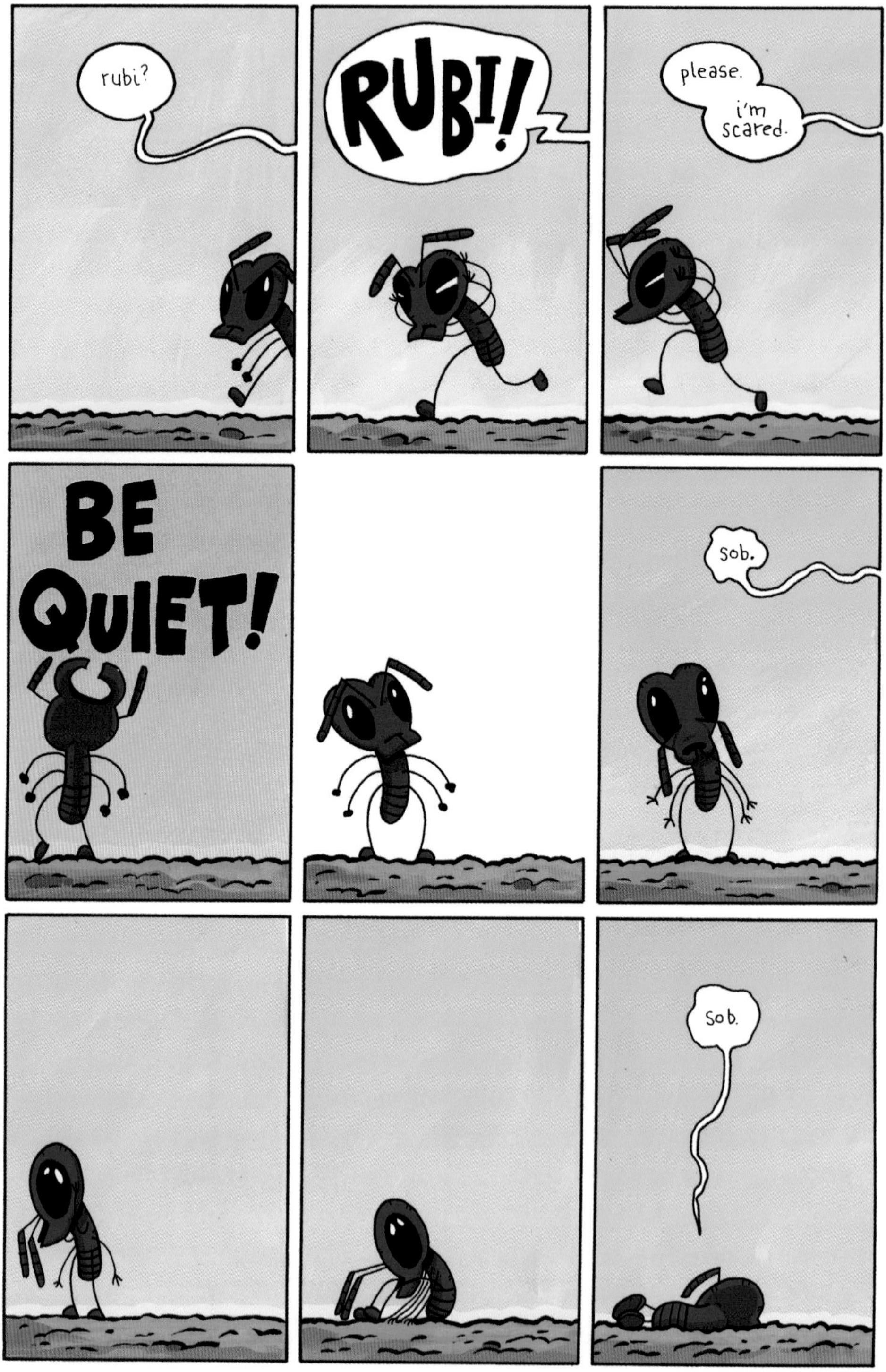
rubi?
RUBI!
please.
i'm scared.
BE QUIET!
sob.
sob.

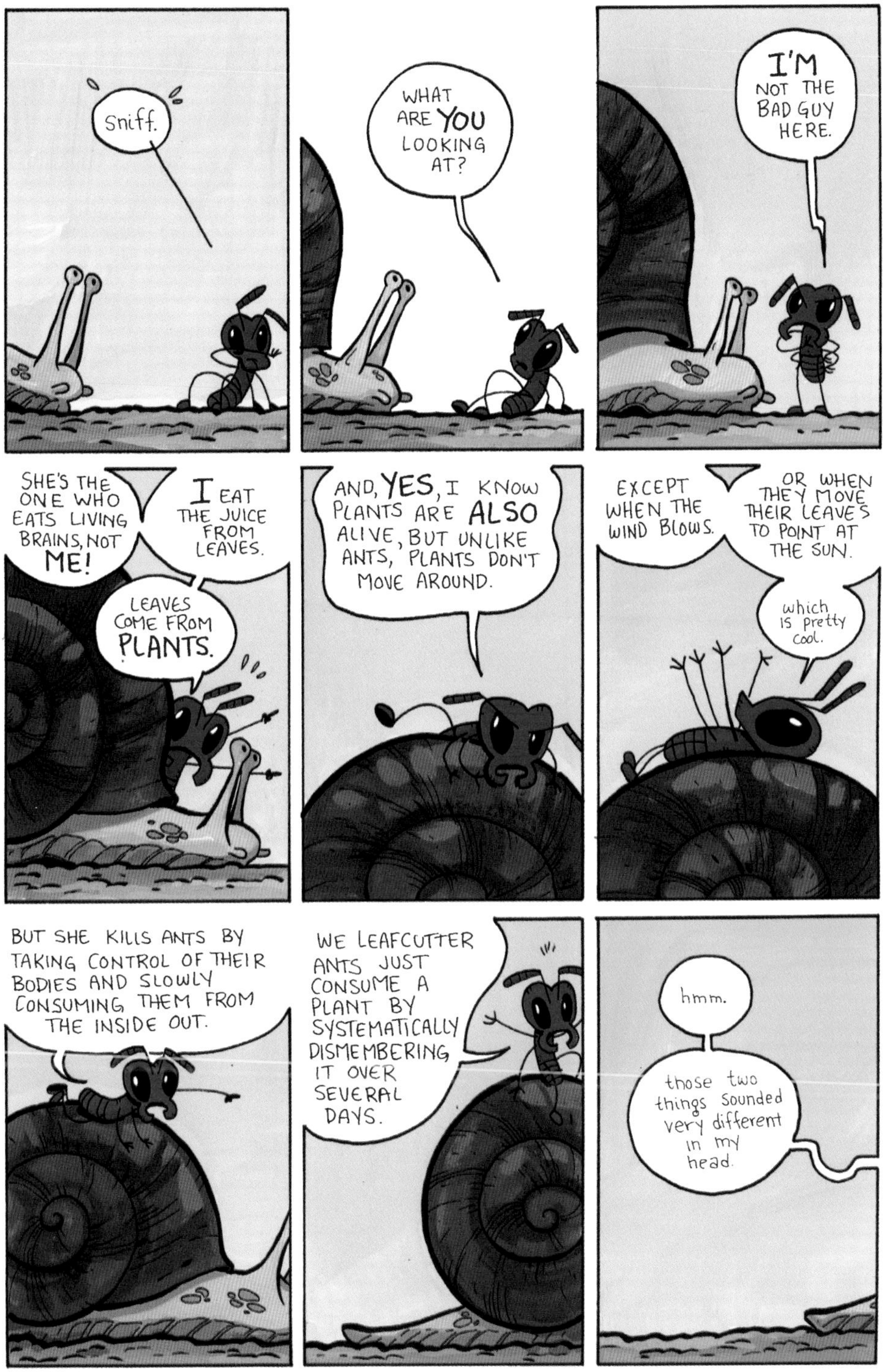
Sniff.
WHAT ARE YOU LOOKING AT?
I'M NOT THE BAD GUY HERE.
SHE'S THE ONE WHO EATS LIVING BRAINS, NOT ME!
I EAT THE JUICE FROM LEAVES.
LEAVES COME FROM PLANTS.
AND, YES, I KNOW PLANTS ARE ALSO ALIVE, BUT UNLIKE ANTS, PLANTS DON'T MOVE AROUND.
EXCEPT WHEN THE WIND BLOWS.
OR WHEN THEY MOVE THEIR LEAVES TO POINT AT THE SUN.
which is pretty cool.
BUT SHE KILLS ANTS BY TAKING CONTROL OF THEIR BODIES AND SLOWLY CONSUMING THEM FROM THE INSIDE OUT.
WE LEAFCUTTER ANTS JUST CONSUME A PLANT BY SYSTEMATICALLY DISMEMBERING IT OVER SEVERAL DAYS.
hmm.
those two things sounded very different in my head.

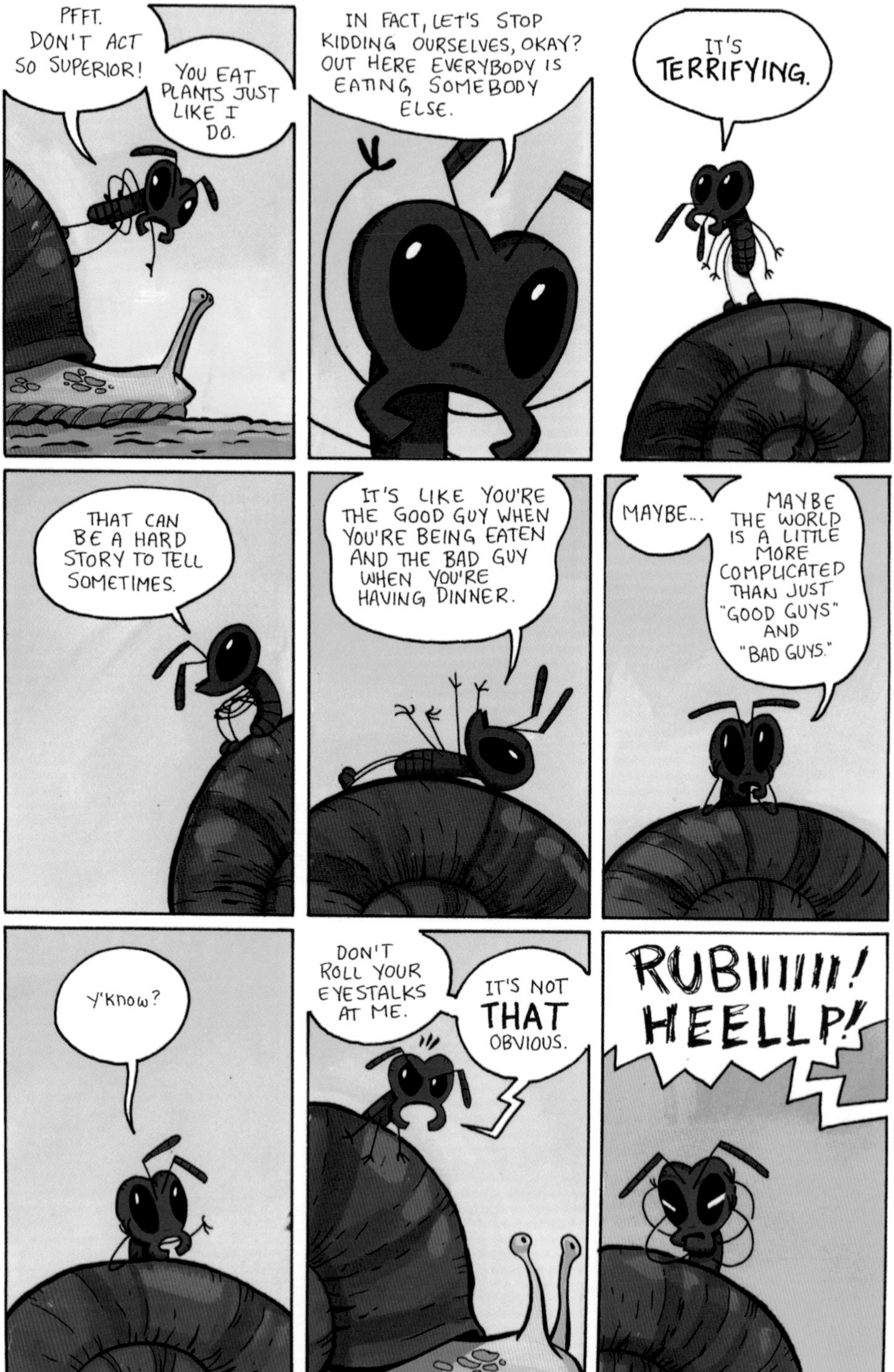
PFFT. DON'T ACT SO SUPERIOR!
YOU EAT PLANTS JUST LIKE I DO.
IN FACT, LET'S STOP KIDDING OURSELVES, OKAY? OUT HERE EVERYBODY IS EATING SOMEBODY ELSE.
IT'S TERRIFYING.
THAT CAN BE A HARD STORY TO TELL SOMETIMES.
IT'S LIKE YOU'RE THE GOOD GUY WHEN YOU'RE BEING EATEN AND THE BAD GUY WHEN YOU'RE HAVING DINNER.
MAYBE...
MAYBE THE WORLD IS A LITTLE MORE COMPLICATED THAN JUST "GOOD GUYS" AND "BAD GUYS."
Y'KNOW?
DON'T ROLL YOUR EYESTALKS AT ME.
IT'S NOT THAT OBVIOUS.
RUBIIIIII! HEELLP!

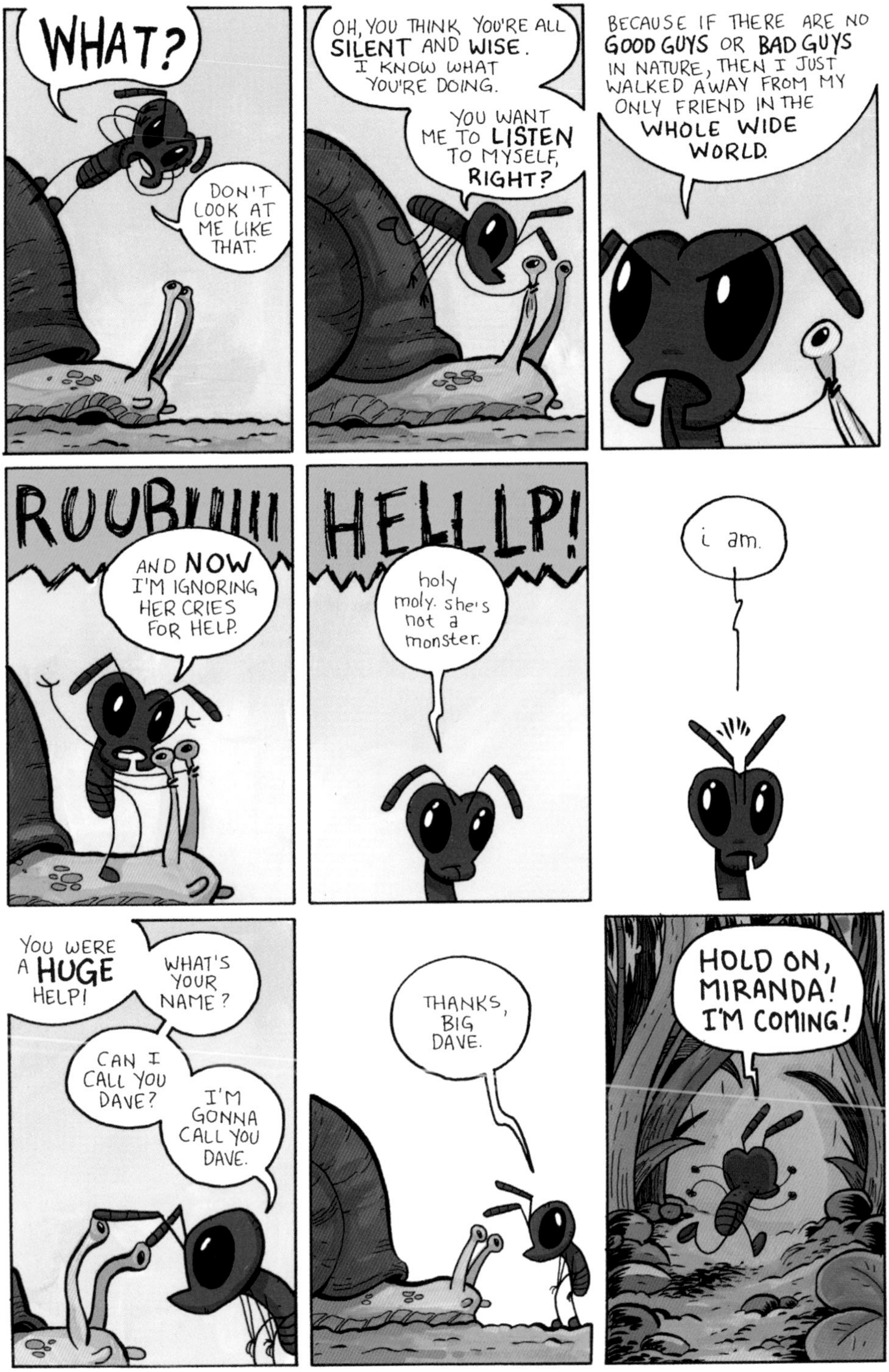
WHAT?
DON'T LOOK AT ME LIKE THAT.
OH, YOU THINK YOU'RE ALL SILENT AND WISE. I KNOW WHAT YOU'RE DOING.
YOU WANT ME TO LISTEN TO MYSELF, RIGHT?
BECAUSE IF THERE ARE NO GOOD GUYS OR BAD GUYS IN NATURE, THEN I JUST WALKED AWAY FROM MY ONLY FRIEND IN THE WHOLE WIDE WORLD.
RUUBIIIII
AND NOW I'M IGNORING HER CRIES FOR HELP.
HELLLP!
holy moly. she's not a monster.
i am.
YOU WERE A HUGE HELP!
WHAT'S YOUR NAME?
CAN I CALL YOU DAVE?
I'M GONNA CALL YOU DAVE.
THANKS, BIG DAVE.
HOLD ON, MIRANDA! I'M COMING!

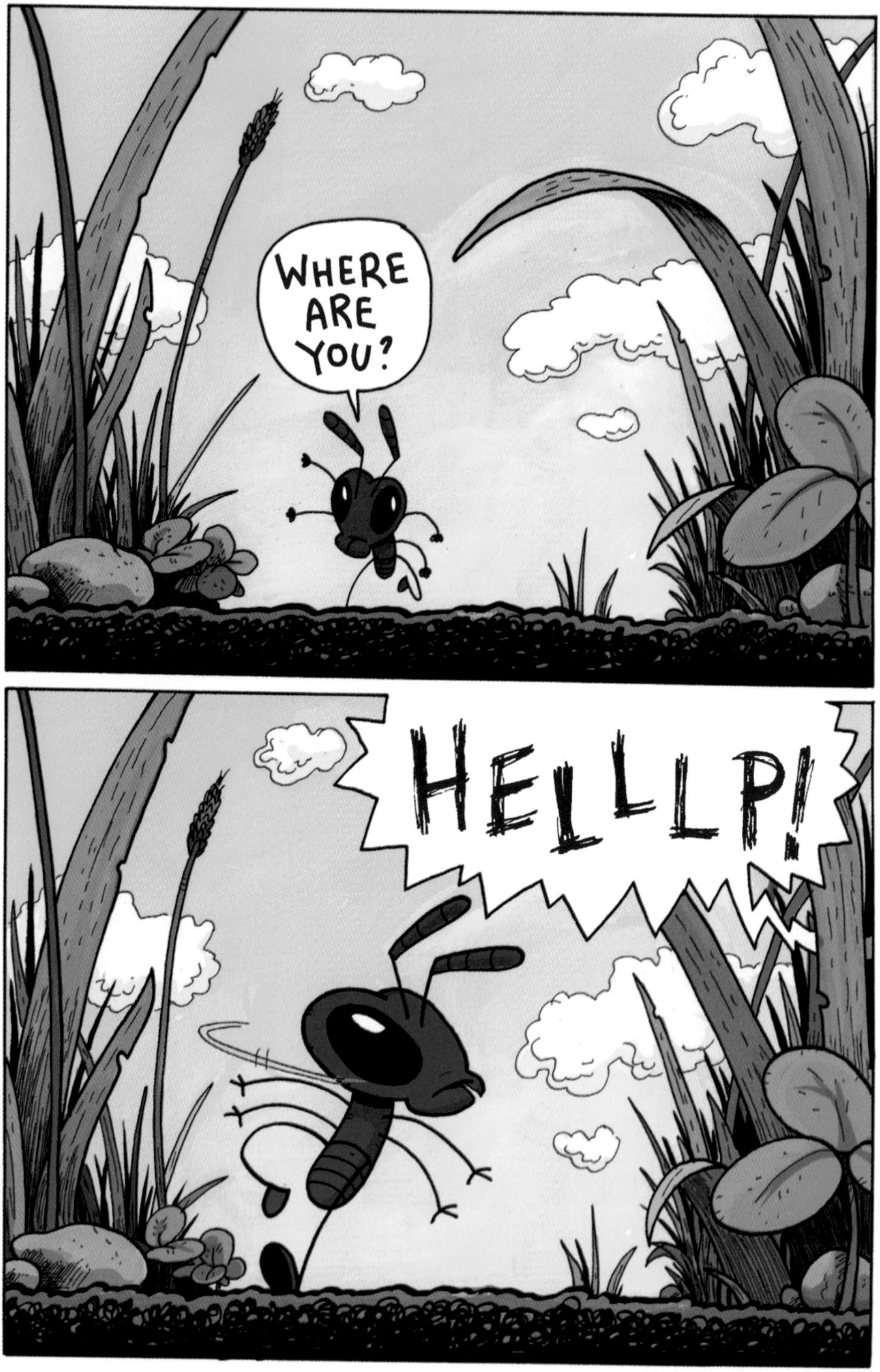
WHERE ARE YOU?
HELLLP!

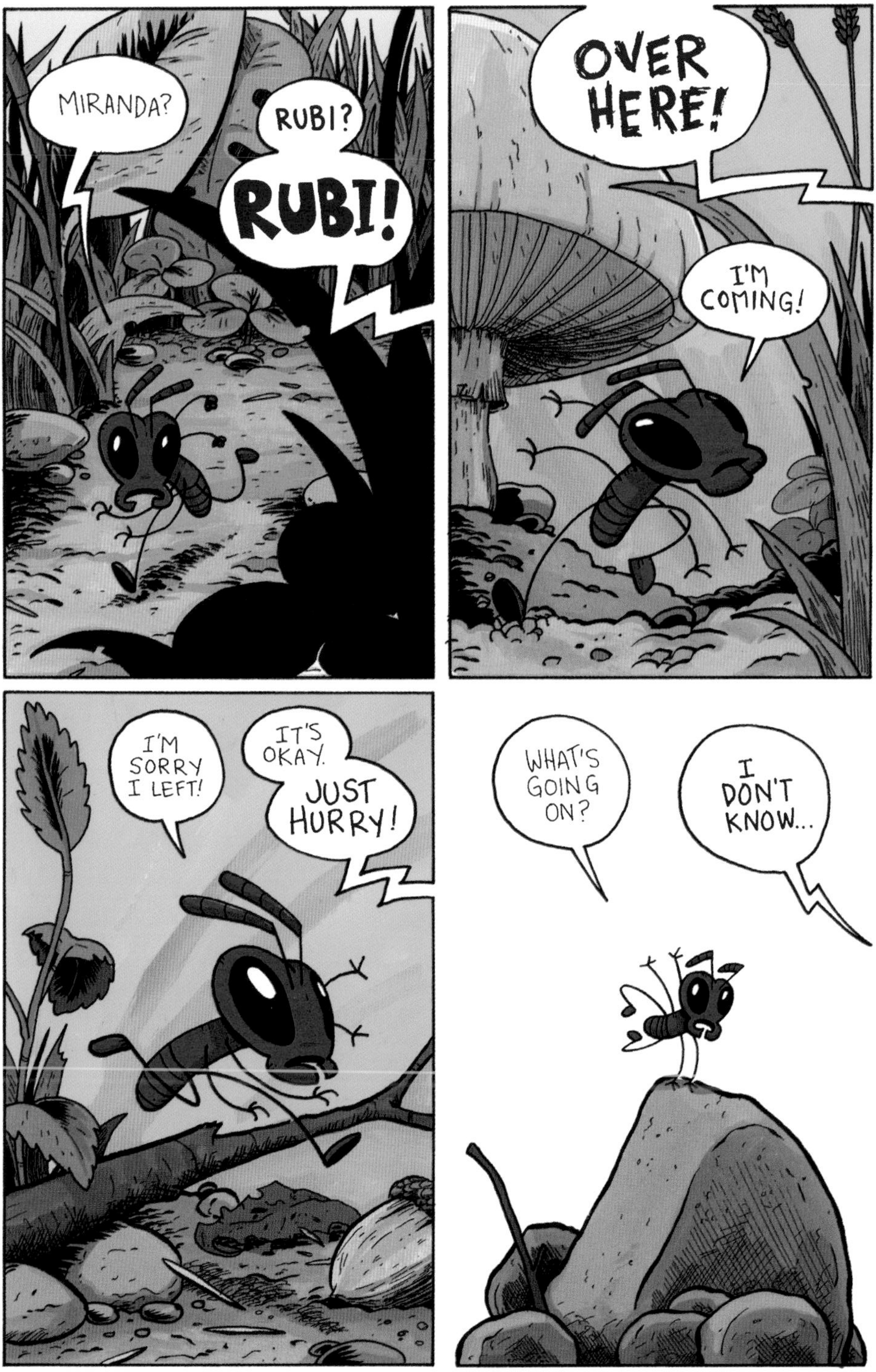
MIRANDA?
RUBI?
RUBI!
OVER HERE!
I'M COMING!
I'M SORRY I LEFT!
IT'S OKAY. JUST HURRY!
WHAT'S GOING ON?
I DON'T KNOW...

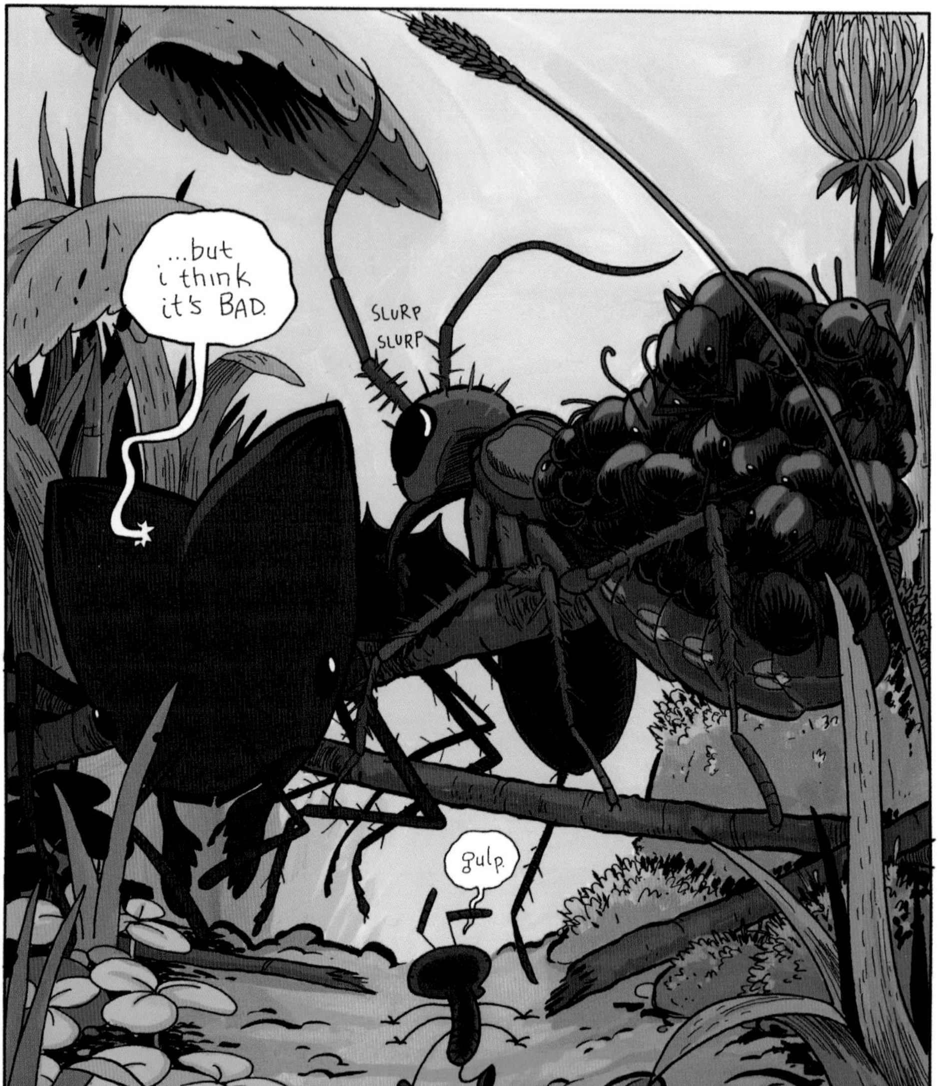
...but
i think
it's BAD.
SLURP
SLURP
gulp.

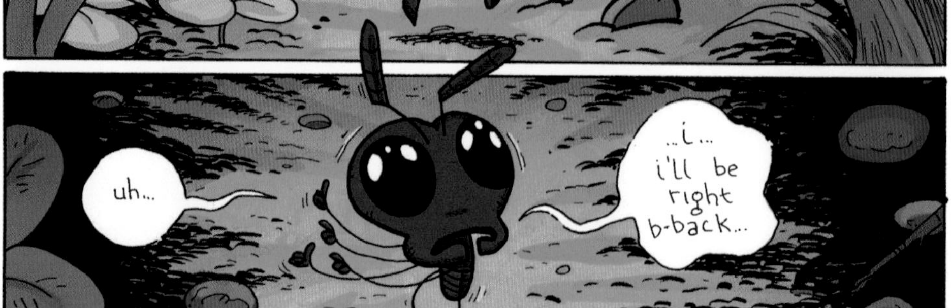
uh...
..i..
i'll be
right
b-back...

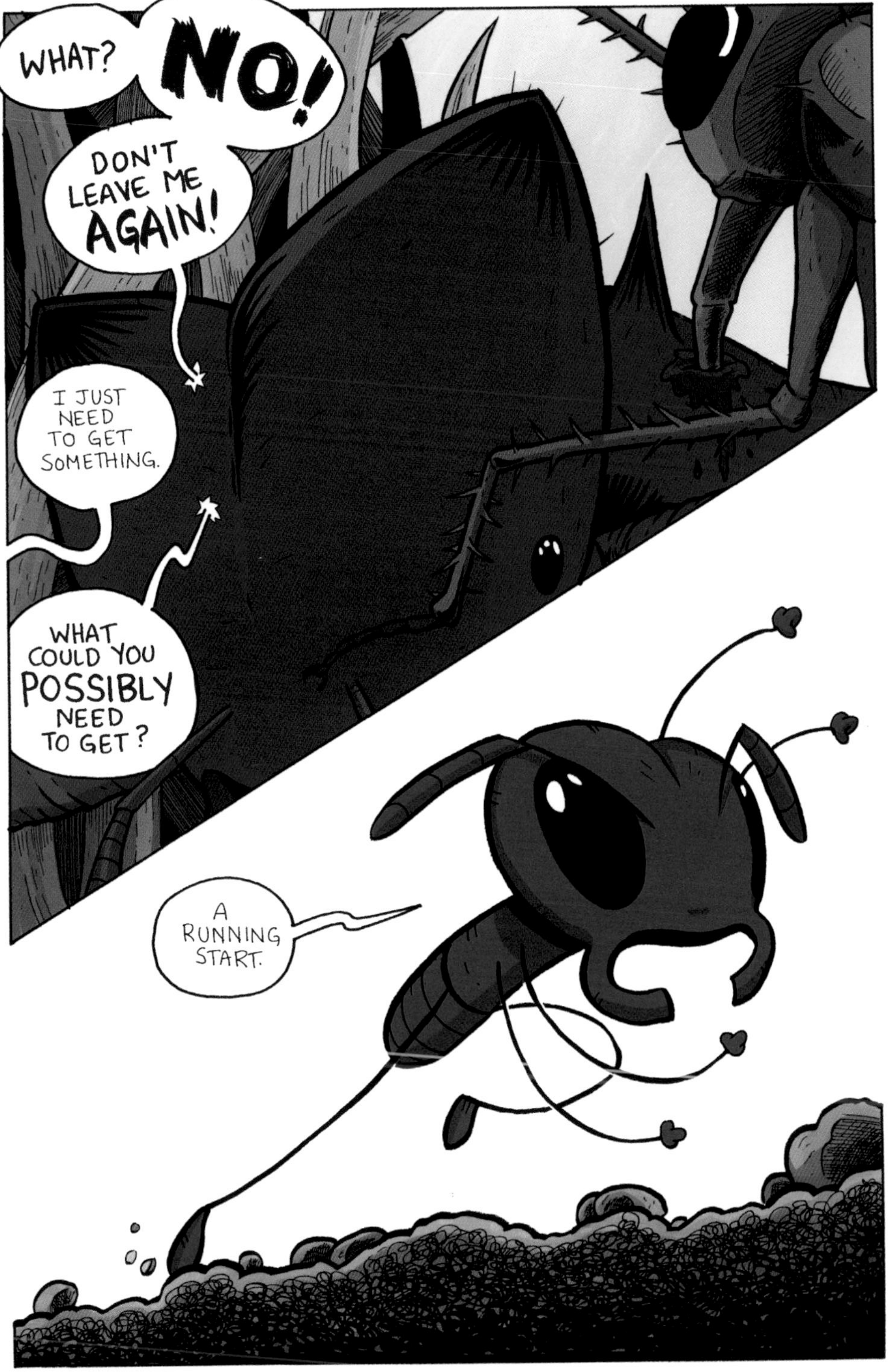
WHAT?
NO!
DON'T LEAVE ME AGAIN!
I JUST NEED TO GET SOMETHING.
WHAT COULD YOU POSSIBLY NEED TO GET?
A RUNNING START.

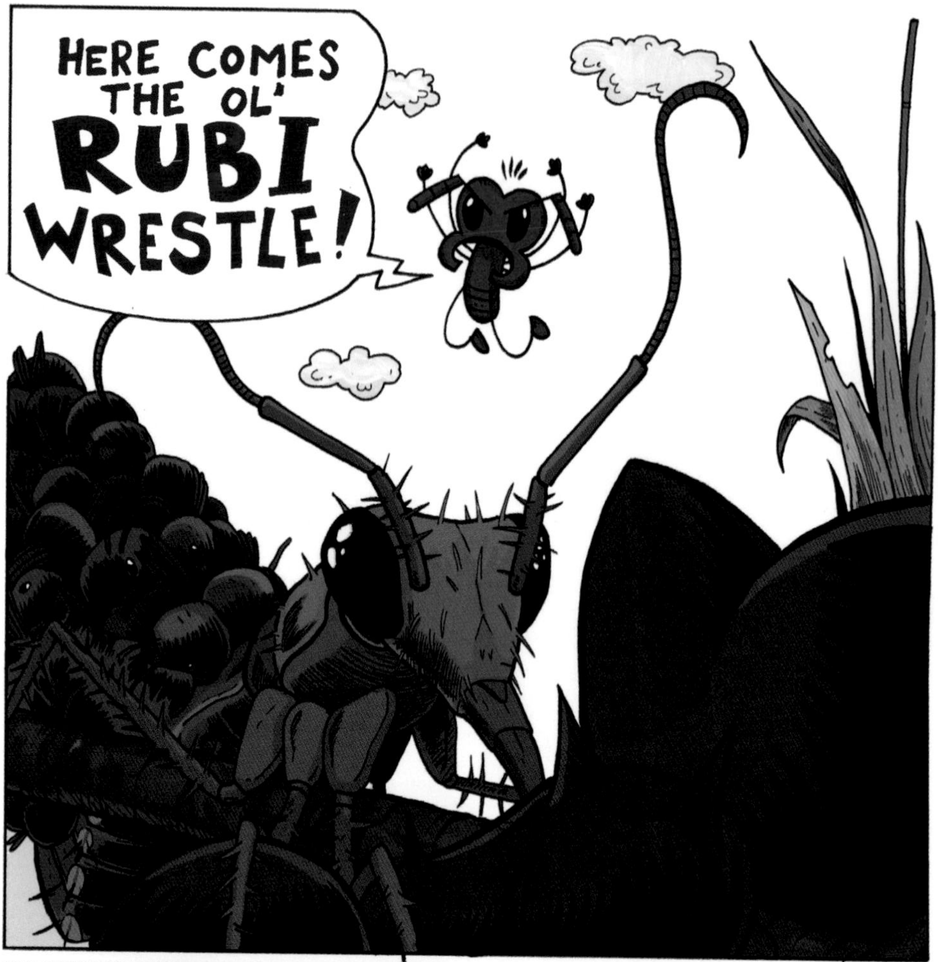
HERE COMES THE OL' RUBI WRESTLE!

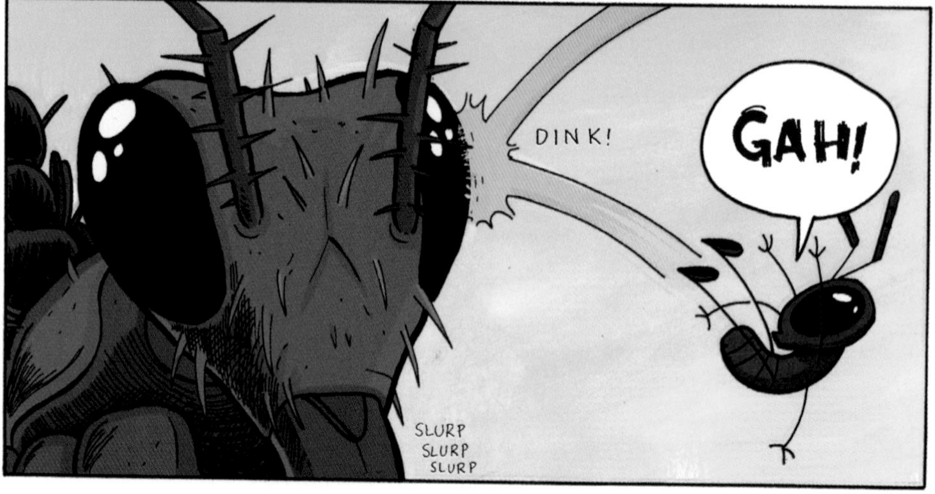
DINK!
GAH!
SLURP SLURP SLURP

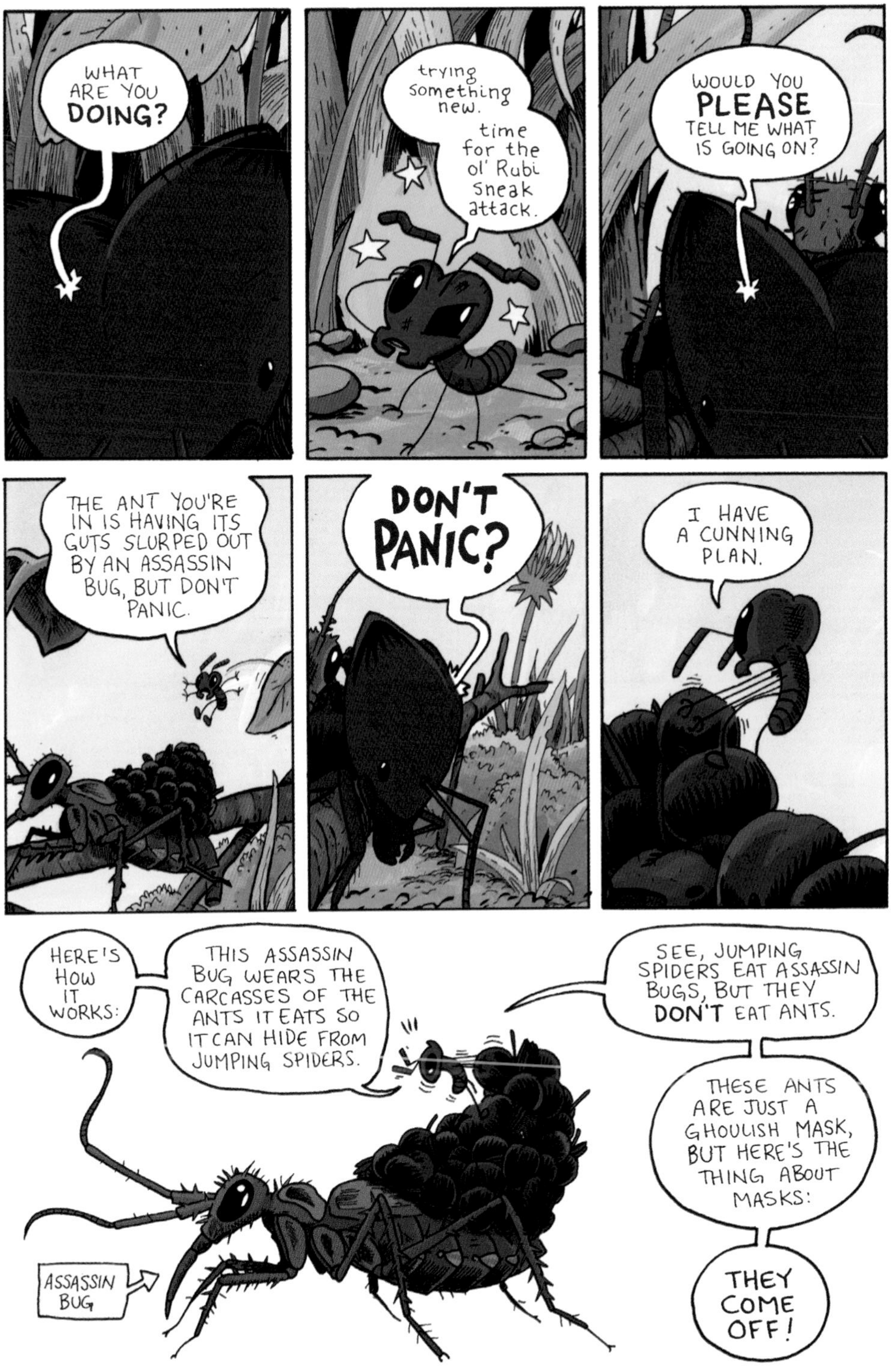
WHAT ARE YOU DOING?
trying something new.
time for the ol' Rubi Sneak attack.
WOULD YOU PLEASE TELL ME WHAT IS GOING ON?
THE ANT YOU'RE IN IS HAVING ITS GUTS SLURPED OUT BY AN ASSASSIN BUG, BUT DON'T PANIC.
DON'T PANIC?
I HAVE A CUNNING PLAN.
HERE'S HOW IT WORKS:
THIS ASSASSIN BUG WEARS THE CARCASSES OF THE ANTS IT EATS SO IT CAN HIDE FROM JUMPING SPIDERS.
SEE, JUMPING SPIDERS EAT ASSASSIN BUGS, BUT THEY DON'T EAT ANTS.
THESE ANTS ARE JUST A GHOULISH MASK, BUT HERE'S THE THING ABOUT MASKS:
THEY COME OFF!
ASSASSIN BUG

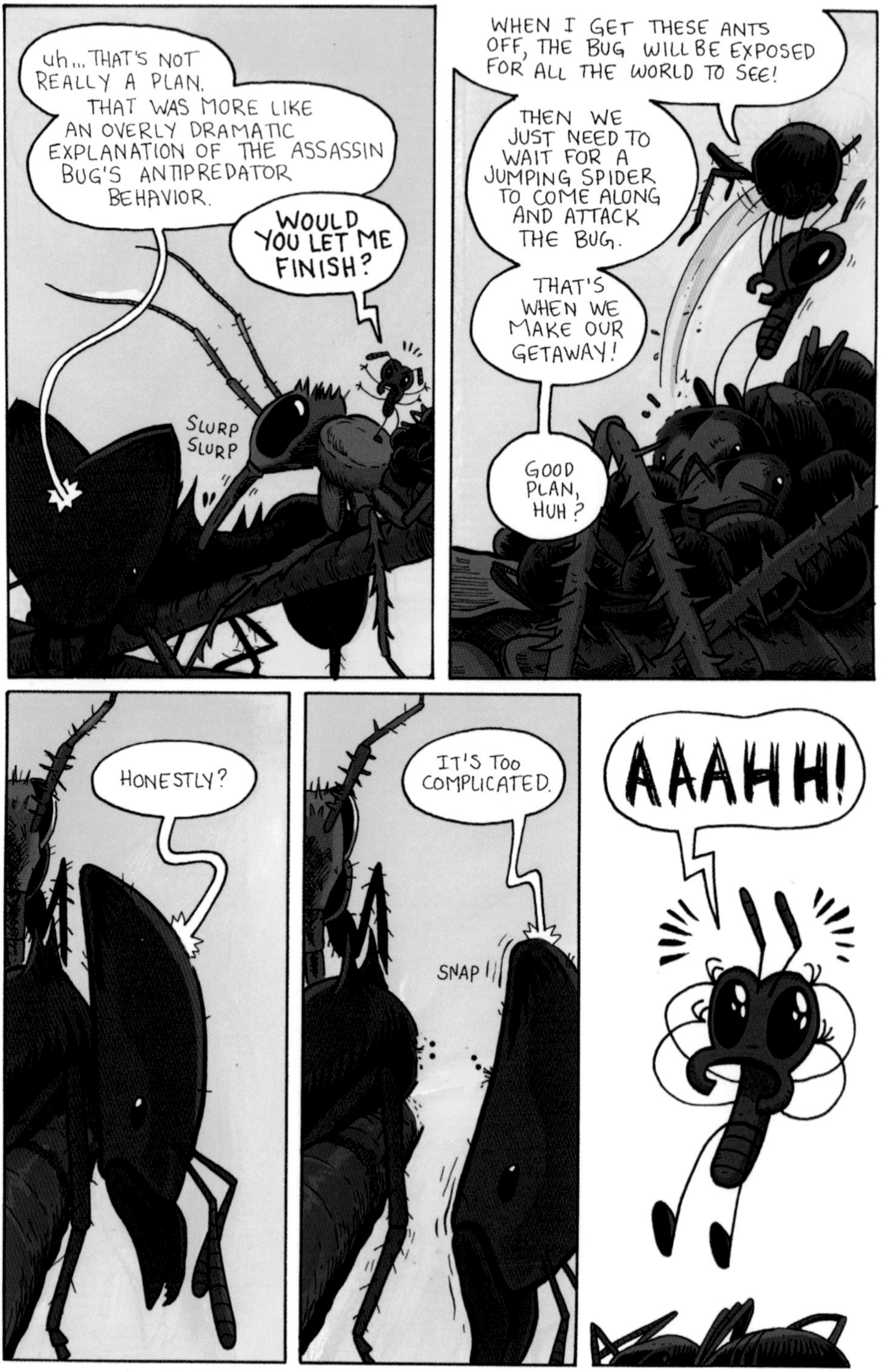
uh... THAT'S NOT REALLY A PLAN. THAT WAS MORE LIKE AN OVERLY DRAMATIC EXPLANATION OF THE ASSASSIN BUG'S ANTIPREDATOR BEHAVIOR.
WOULD YOU LET ME FINISH?
SLURP SLURP
WHEN I GET THESE ANTS OFF, THE BUG WILL BE EXPOSED FOR ALL THE WORLD TO SEE!
THEN WE JUST NEED TO WAIT FOR A JUMPING SPIDER TO COME ALONG AND ATTACK THE BUG.
THAT'S WHEN WE MAKE OUR GETAWAY!
GOOD PLAN, HUH?
HONESTLY?
IT'S TOO COMPLICATED.
SNAP
AAAHH!

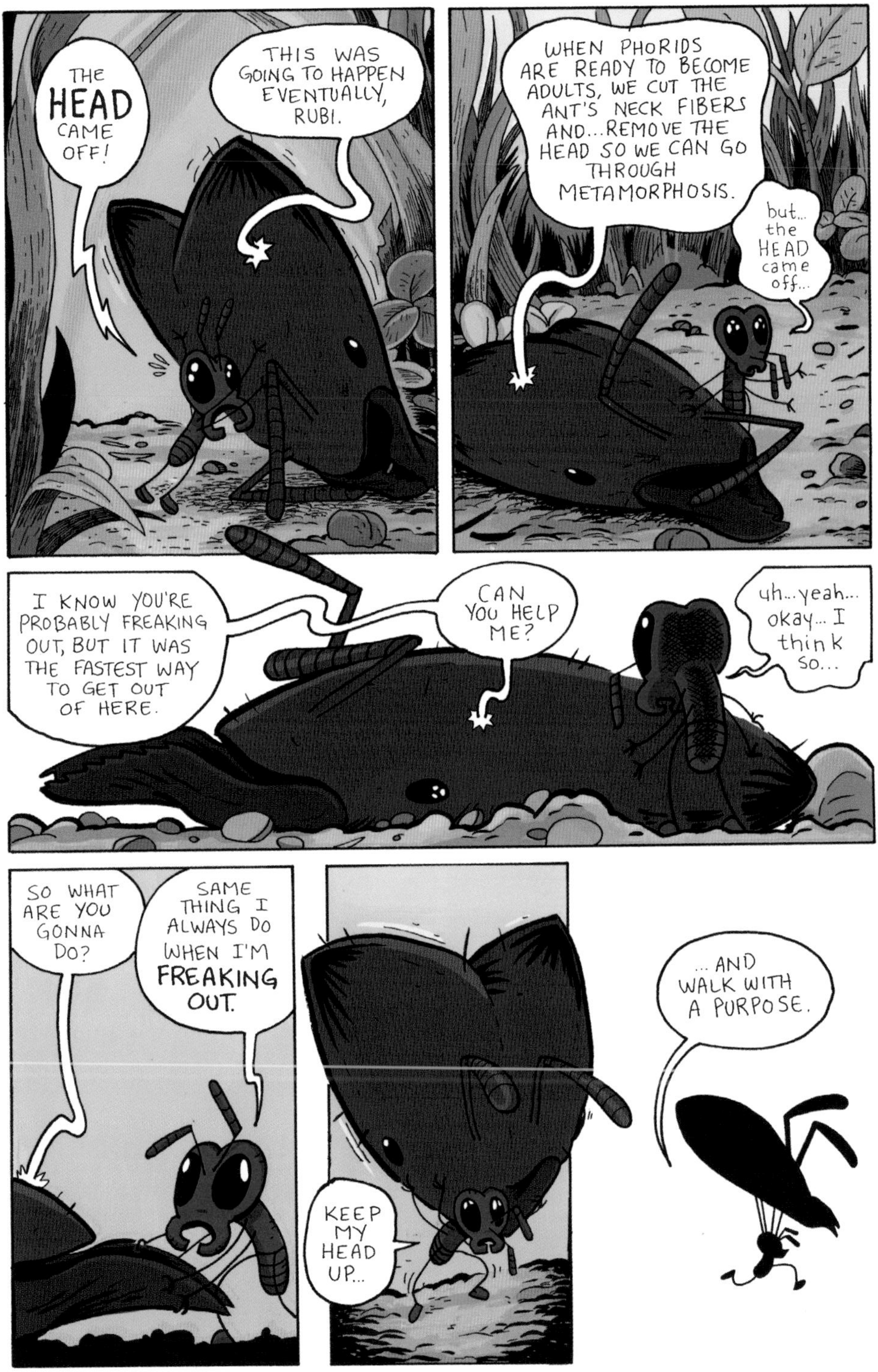
THE HEAD CAME OFF!
THIS WAS GOING TO HAPPEN EVENTUALLY, RUBI.
WHEN PHORIDS ARE READY TO BECOME ADULTS, WE CUT THE ANT'S NECK FIBERS AND...REMOVE THE HEAD SO WE CAN GO THROUGH METAMORPHOSIS.
but... the HEAD came off...
I KNOW YOU'RE PROBABLY FREAKING OUT, BUT IT WAS THE FASTEST WAY TO GET OUT OF HERE.
CAN YOU HELP ME?
uh...yeah... okay... I think so...
SO WHAT ARE YOU GONNA DO?
SAME THING I ALWAYS DO WHEN I'M FREAKING OUT.
KEEP MY HEAD UP...
...AND WALK WITH A PURPOSE.

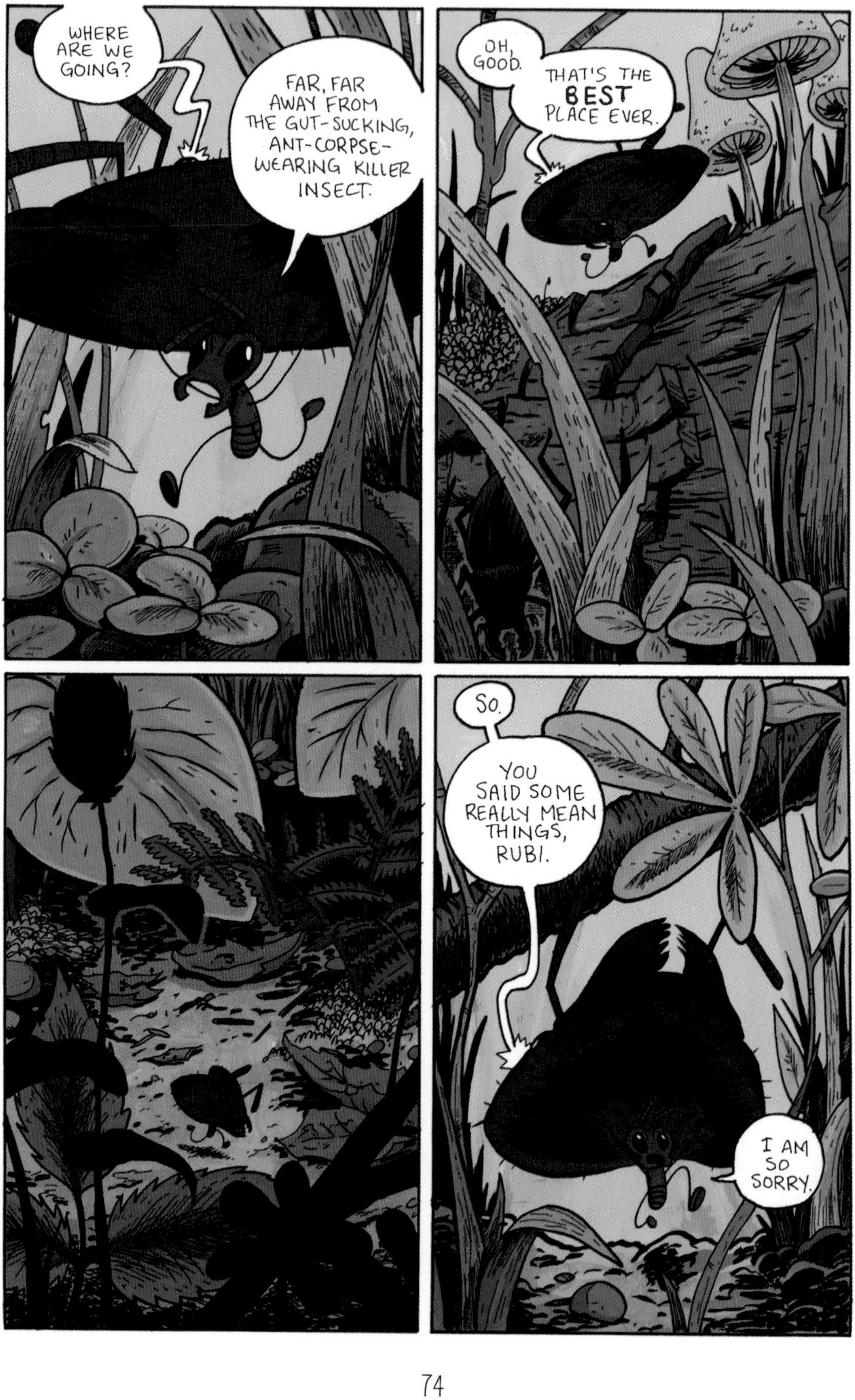
WHERE ARE WE GOING?
FAR, FAR AWAY FROM THE GUT-SUCKING, ANT-CORPSE-WEARING KILLER INSECT.
OH, GOOD.
THAT'S THE BEST PLACE EVER.
SO.
YOU SAID SOME REALLY MEAN THINGS, RUBI.
I AM SO SORRY.

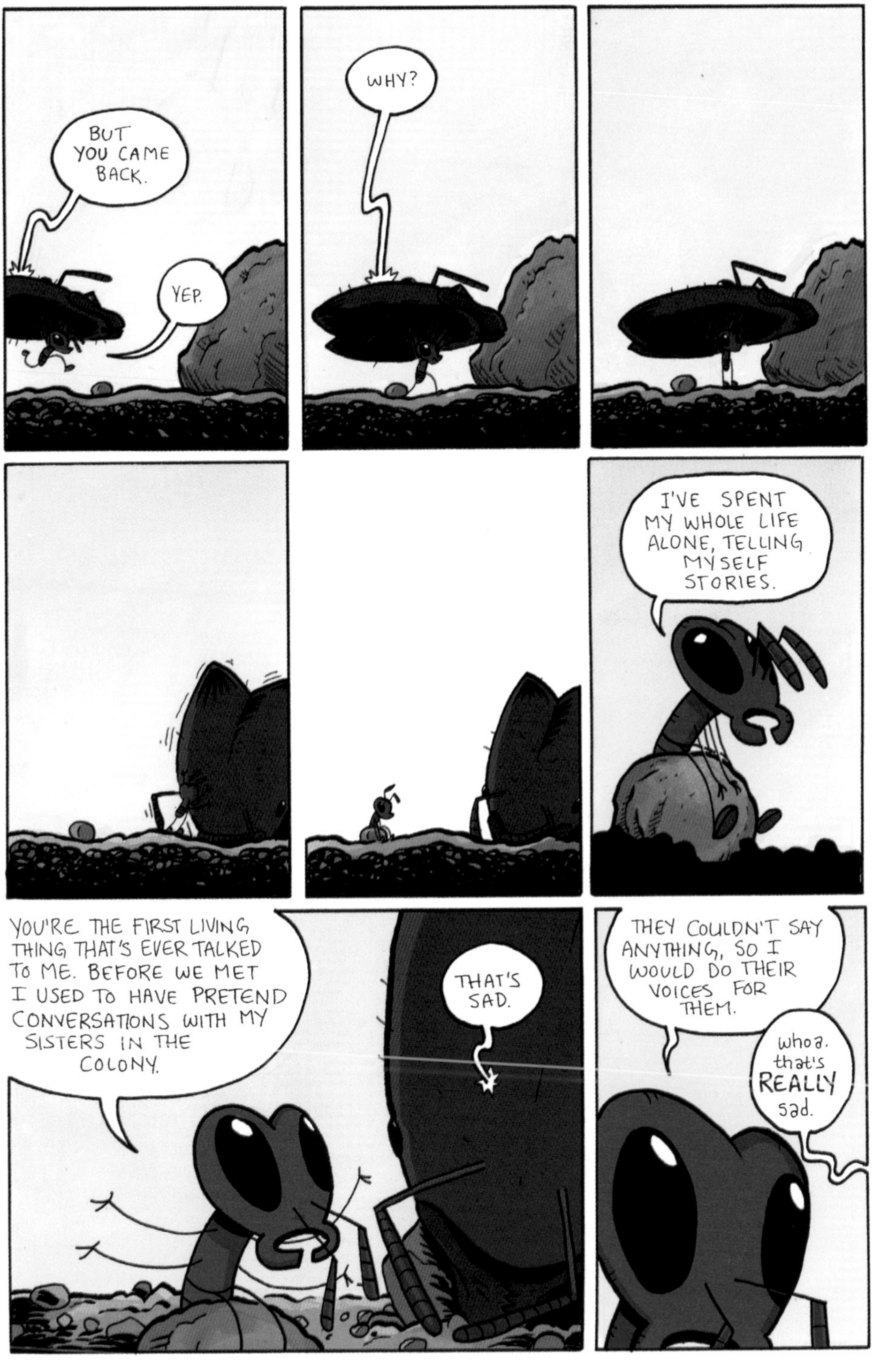
BUT YOU CAME BACK.
YEP.
WHY?
I'VE SPENT MY WHOLE LIFE ALONE, TELLING MYSELF STORIES.
YOU'RE THE FIRST LIVING THING THAT'S EVER TALKED TO ME. BEFORE WE MET I USED TO HAVE PRETEND CONVERSATIONS WITH MY SISTERS IN THE COLONY.
THAT'S SAD.
THEY COULDN'T SAY ANYTHING, SO I WOULD DO THEIR VOICES FOR THEM.
whoa. that's REALLY sad.

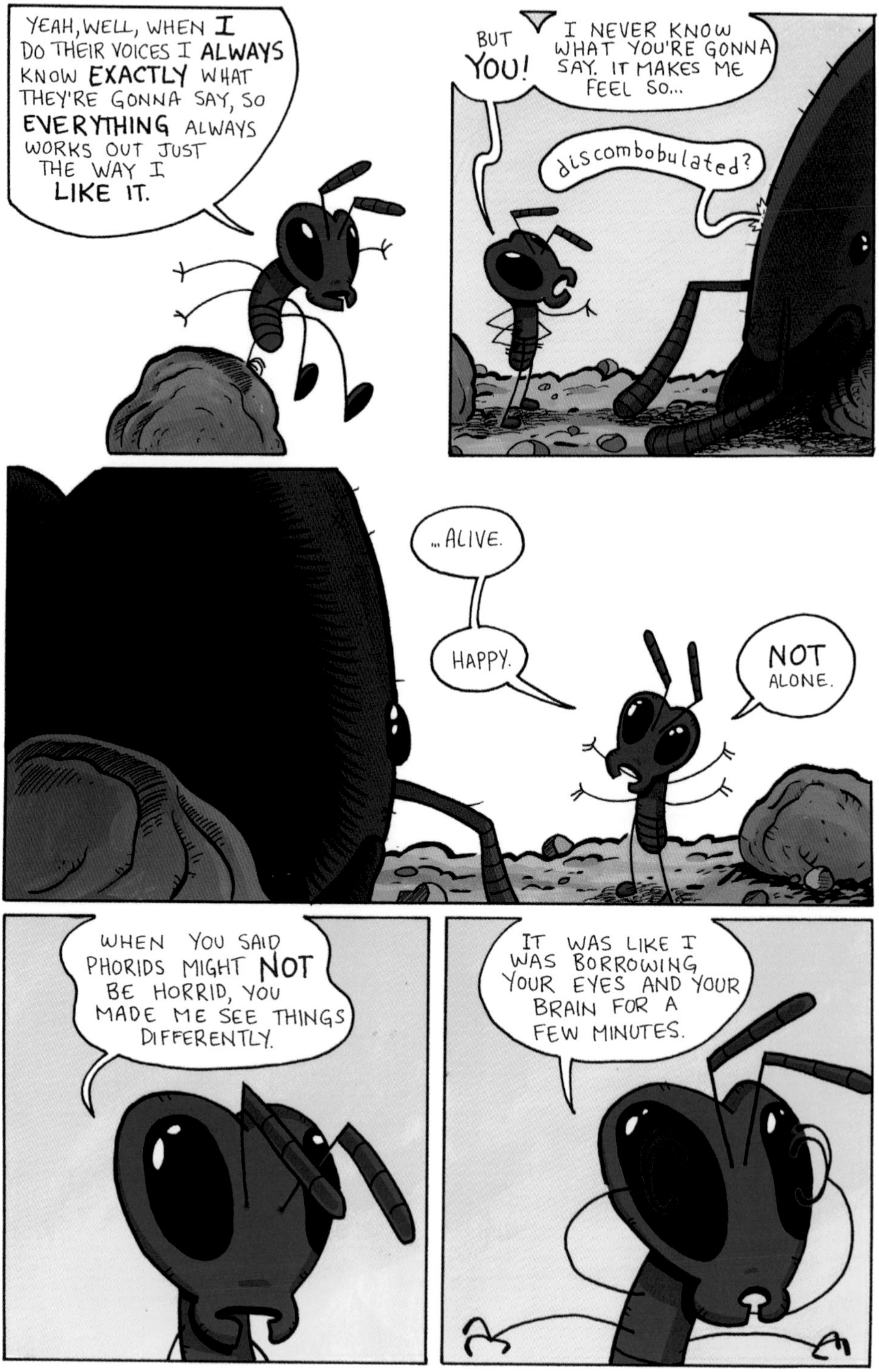
YEAH, WELL, WHEN I DO THEIR VOICES I ALWAYS KNOW EXACTLY WHAT THEY'RE GONNA SAY, SO EVERYTHING ALWAYS WORKS OUT JUST THE WAY I LIKE IT.
BUT YOU!
I NEVER KNOW WHAT YOU'RE GONNA SAY. IT MAKES ME FEEL SO...
discombobulated?
...ALIVE.
HAPPY.
NOT ALONE.
WHEN YOU SAID PHORIDS MIGHT NOT BE HORRID, YOU MADE ME SEE THINGS DIFFERENTLY.
IT WAS LIKE I WAS BORROWING YOUR EYES AND YOUR BRAIN FOR A FEW MINUTES.

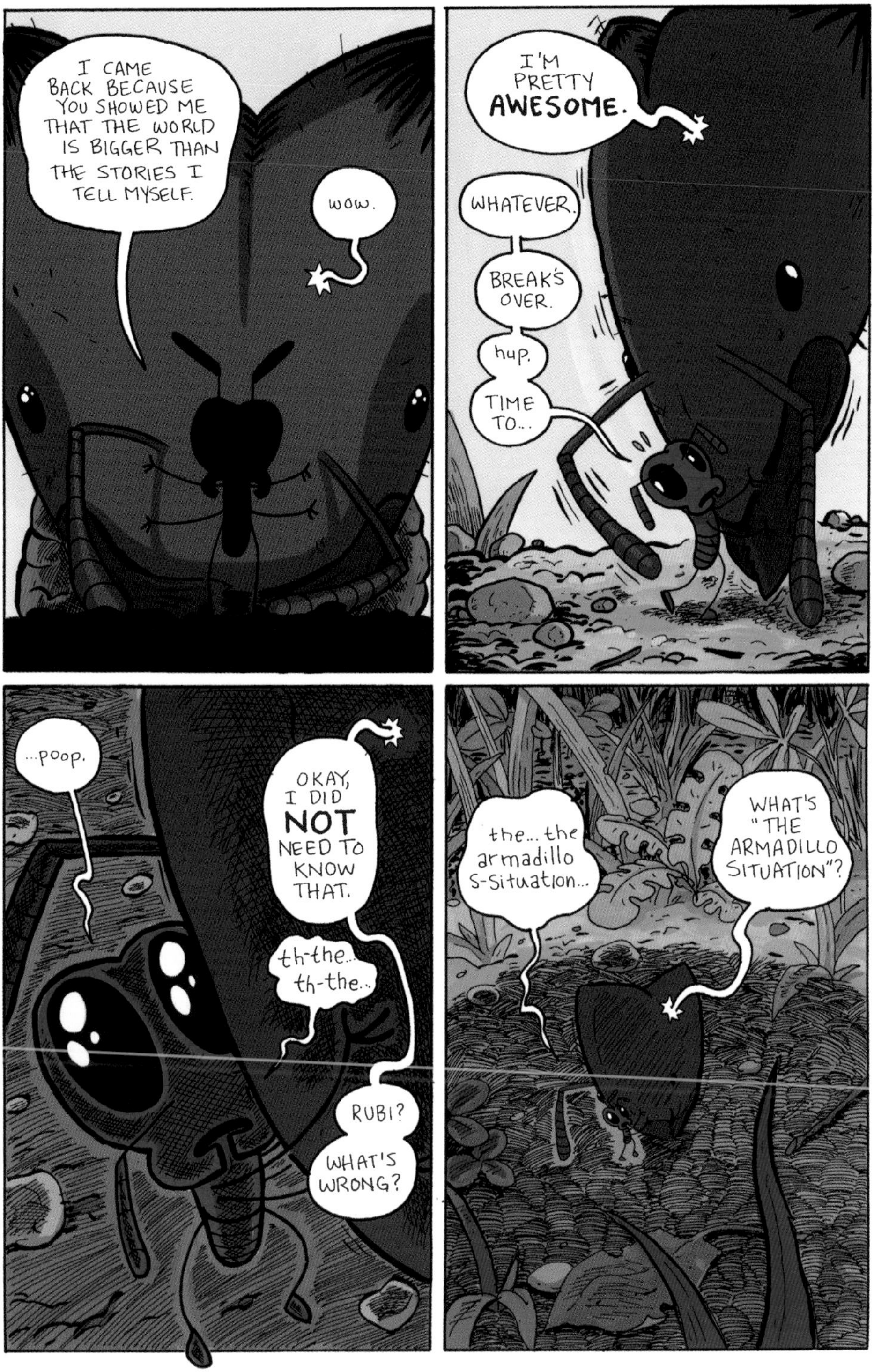
I CAME BACK BECAUSE YOU SHOWED ME THAT THE WORLD IS BIGGER THAN THE STORIES I TELL MYSELF.
wow.
I'M PRETTY **AWESOME.**
WHATEVER.
BREAK'S OVER.
hup.
TIME TO...
...poop.
OKAY, I DID **NOT** NEED TO KNOW THAT.
th-the... th-the...
RUBI?
WHAT'S WRONG?
the... the armadillo S-Situation...
WHAT'S "THE ARMADILLO SITUATION"?

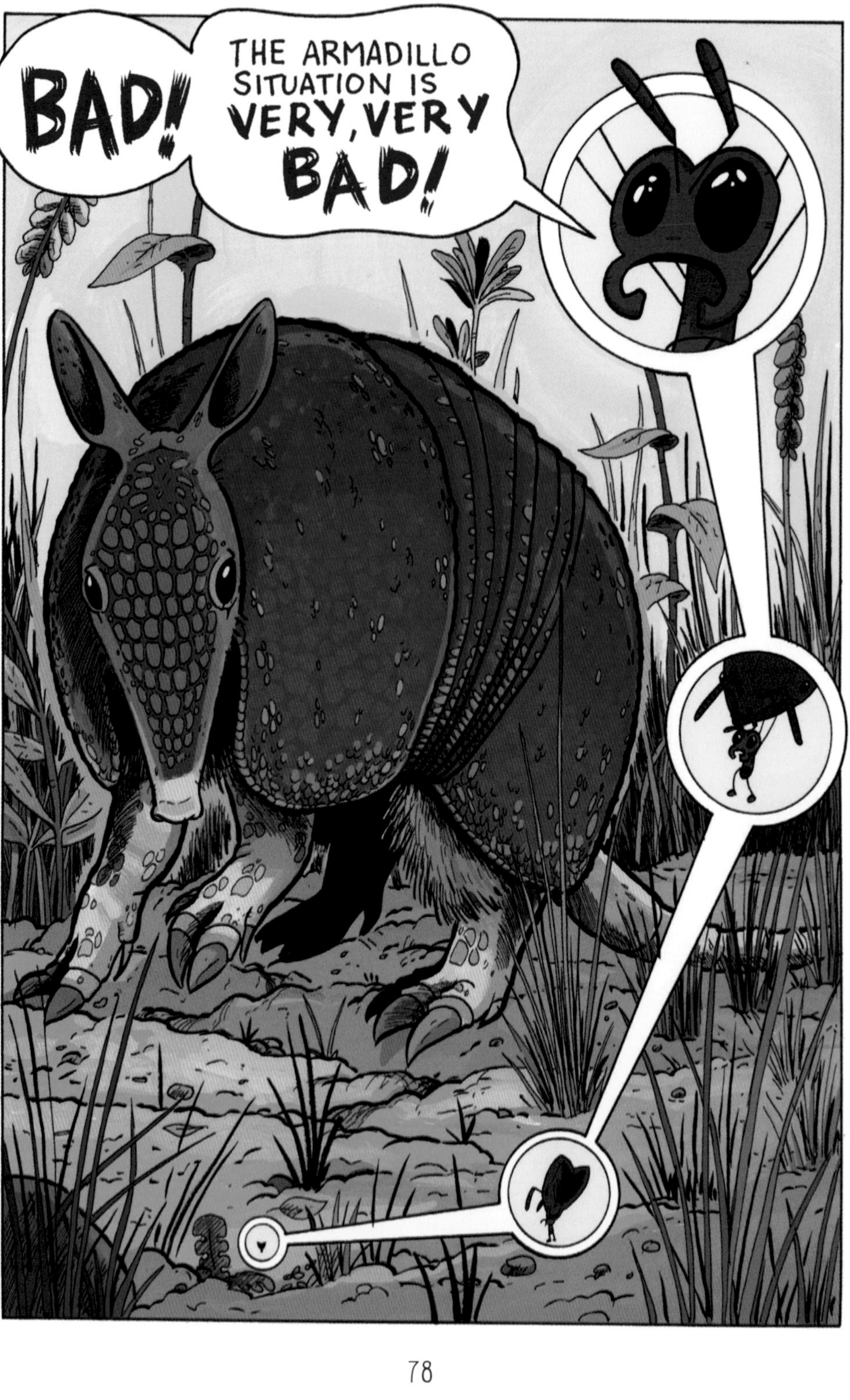
BAD!
THE ARMADILLO SITUATION IS VERY, VERY BAD!

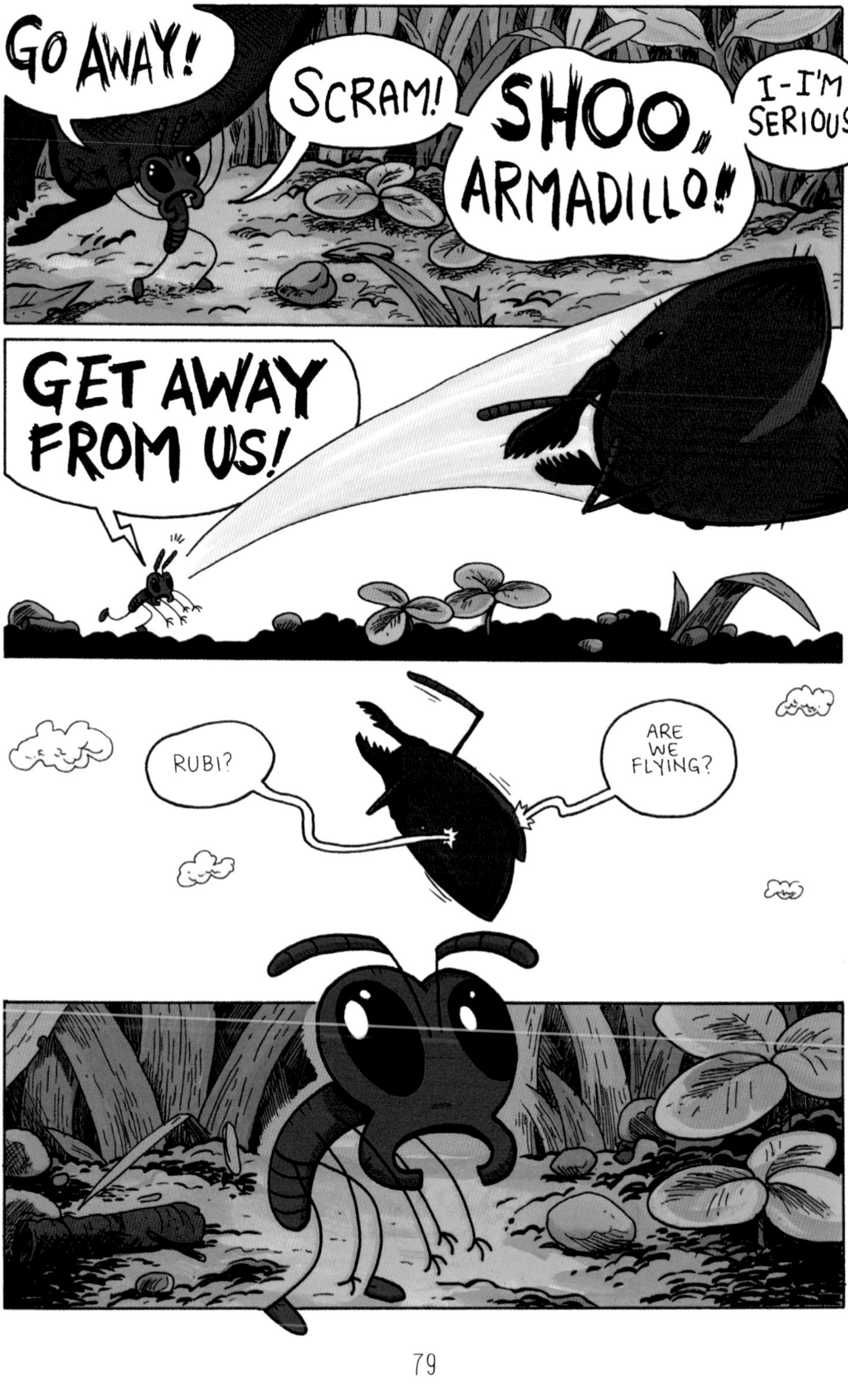
GO AWAY!
SCRAM!
SHOO, ARMADILLO!
I-I'M SERIOUS!
GET AWAY FROM US!
RUBI?
ARE WE FLYING?

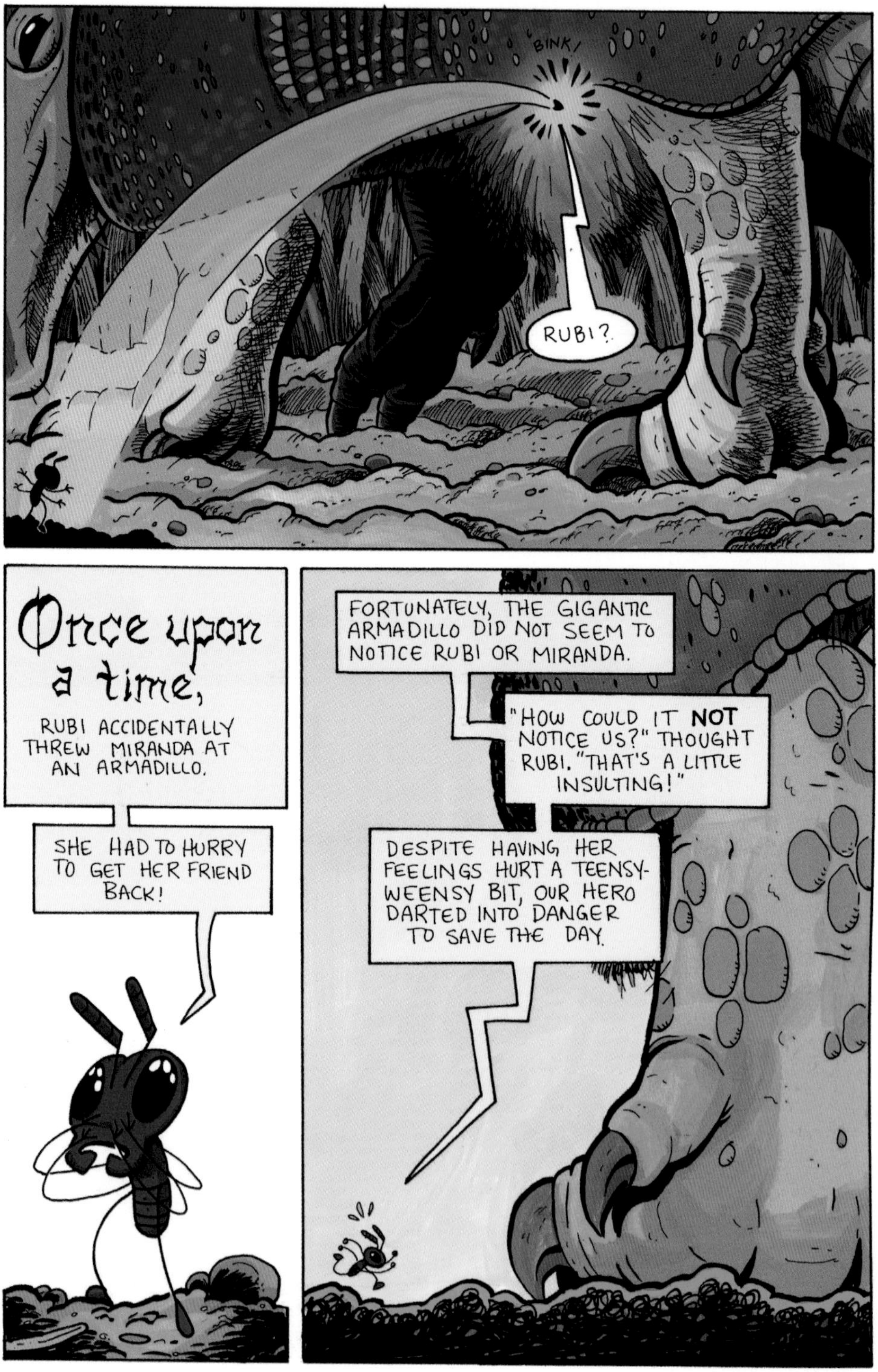
BINK!
RUBI?
Once upon a time,
RUBI ACCIDENTALLY THREW MIRANDA AT AN ARMADILLO.
SHE HAD TO HURRY TO GET HER FRIEND BACK!
FORTUNATELY, THE GIGANTIC ARMADILLO DID NOT SEEM TO NOTICE RUBI OR MIRANDA.
"HOW COULD IT **NOT** NOTICE US?" THOUGHT RUBI. "THAT'S A LITTLE INSULTING!"
DESPITE HAVING HER FEELINGS HURT A TEENSY-WEENSY BIT, OUR HERO DARTED INTO DANGER TO SAVE THE DAY.

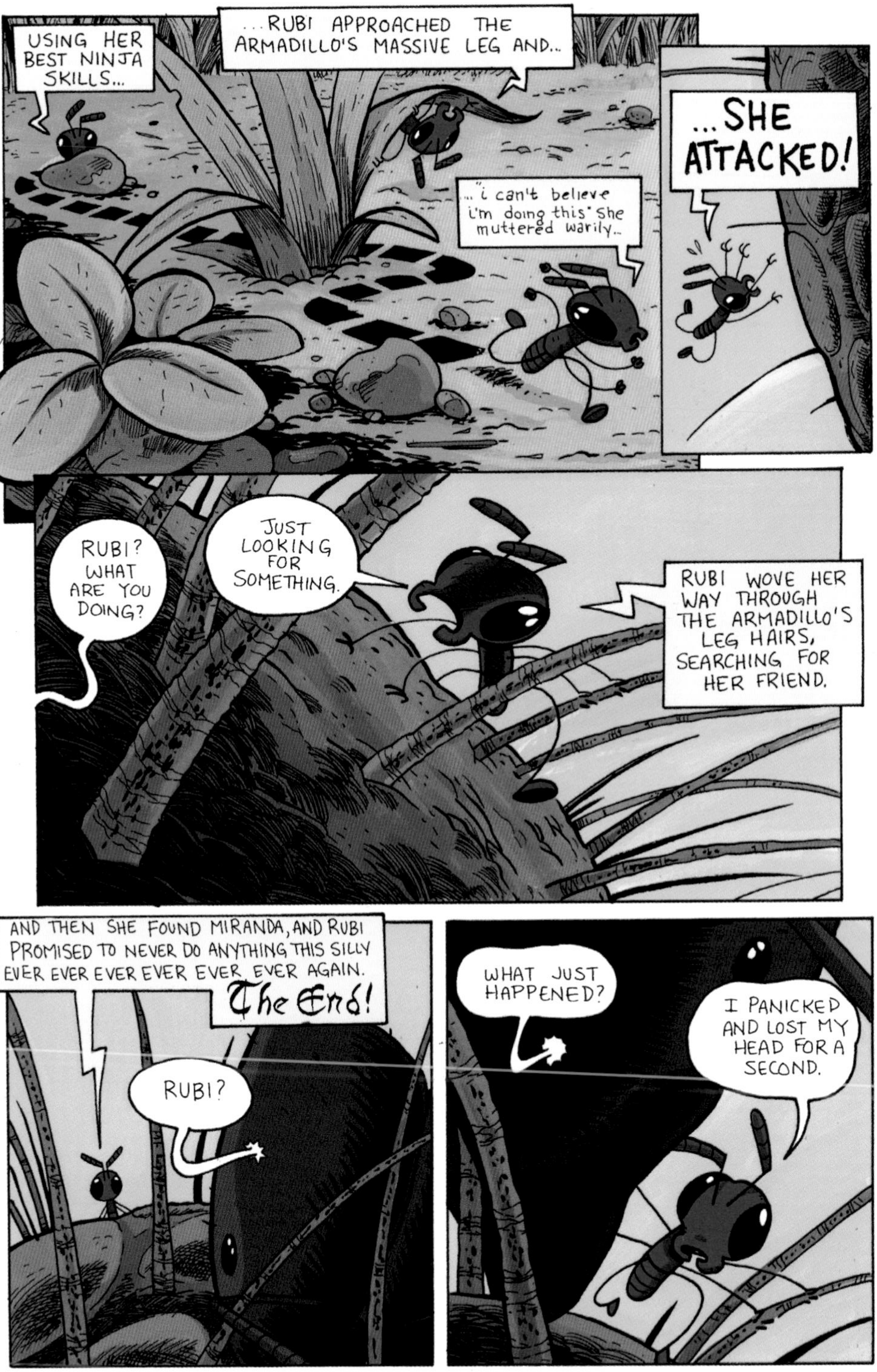
USING HER BEST NINJA SKILLS...
...RUBI APPROACHED THE ARMADILLO'S MASSIVE LEG AND...
..."i can't believe i'm doing this" she muttered warily...
...SHE ATTACKED!
RUBI? WHAT ARE YOU DOING?
JUST LOOKING FOR SOMETHING.
RUBI WOVE HER WAY THROUGH THE ARMADILLO'S LEG HAIRS, SEARCHING FOR HER FRIEND.
AND THEN SHE FOUND MIRANDA, AND RUBI PROMISED TO NEVER DO ANYTHING THIS SILLY EVER EVER EVER EVER EVER EVER AGAIN.
The End!
RUBI?
WHAT JUST HAPPENED?
I PANICKED AND LOST MY HEAD FOR A SECOND.

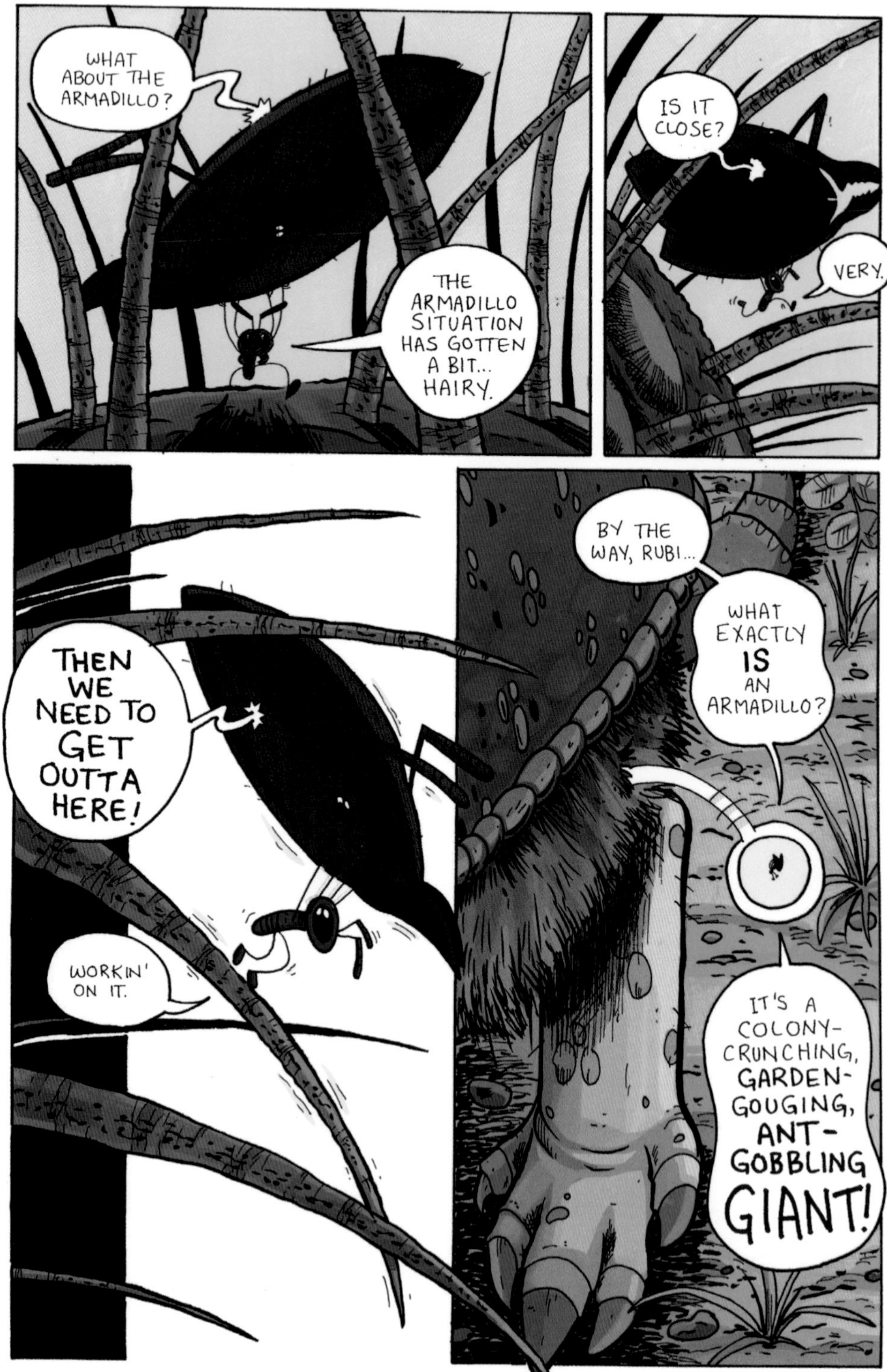
WHAT ABOUT THE ARMADILLO?
THE ARMADILLO SITUATION HAS GOTTEN A BIT... HAIRY.
IS IT CLOSE?
VERY.
THEN WE NEED TO GET OUTTA HERE!
WORKIN' ON IT.
BY THE WAY, RUBI...
WHAT EXACTLY IS AN ARMADILLO?
IT'S A COLONY-CRUNCHING, GARDEN-GOUGING, ANT-GOBBLING GIANT!

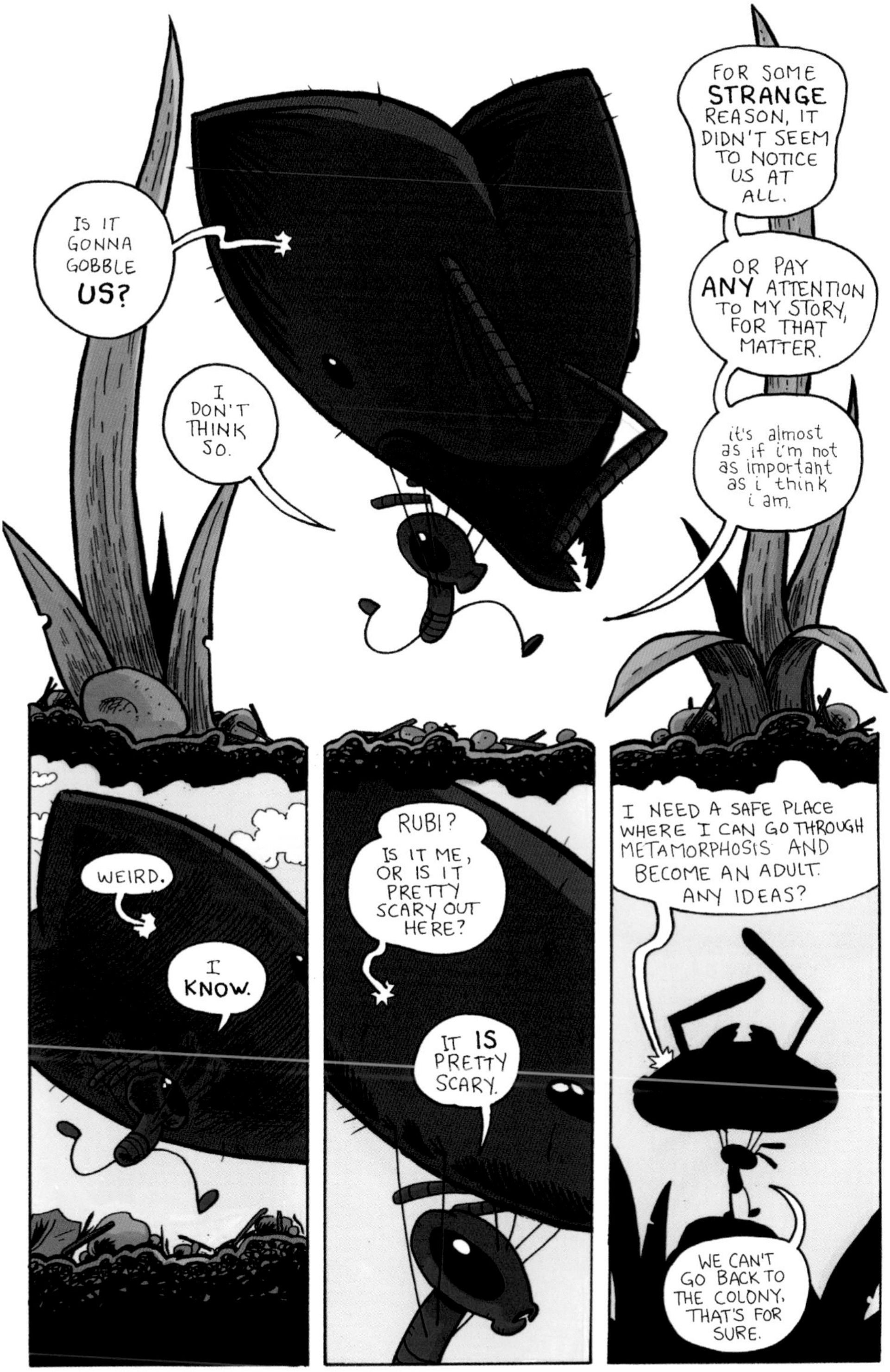
IS IT GONNA GOBBLE US?
I DON'T THINK SO.
FOR SOME STRANGE REASON, IT DIDN'T SEEM TO NOTICE US AT ALL.
OR PAY ANY ATTENTION TO MY STORY, FOR THAT MATTER.
it's almost as if i'm not as important as i think i am.
WEIRD.
I KNOW.
RUBI?
IS IT ME, OR IS IT PRETTY SCARY OUT HERE?
IT IS PRETTY SCARY.
I NEED A SAFE PLACE WHERE I CAN GO THROUGH METAMORPHOSIS AND BECOME AN ADULT. ANY IDEAS?
WE CAN'T GO BACK TO THE COLONY, THAT'S FOR SURE.

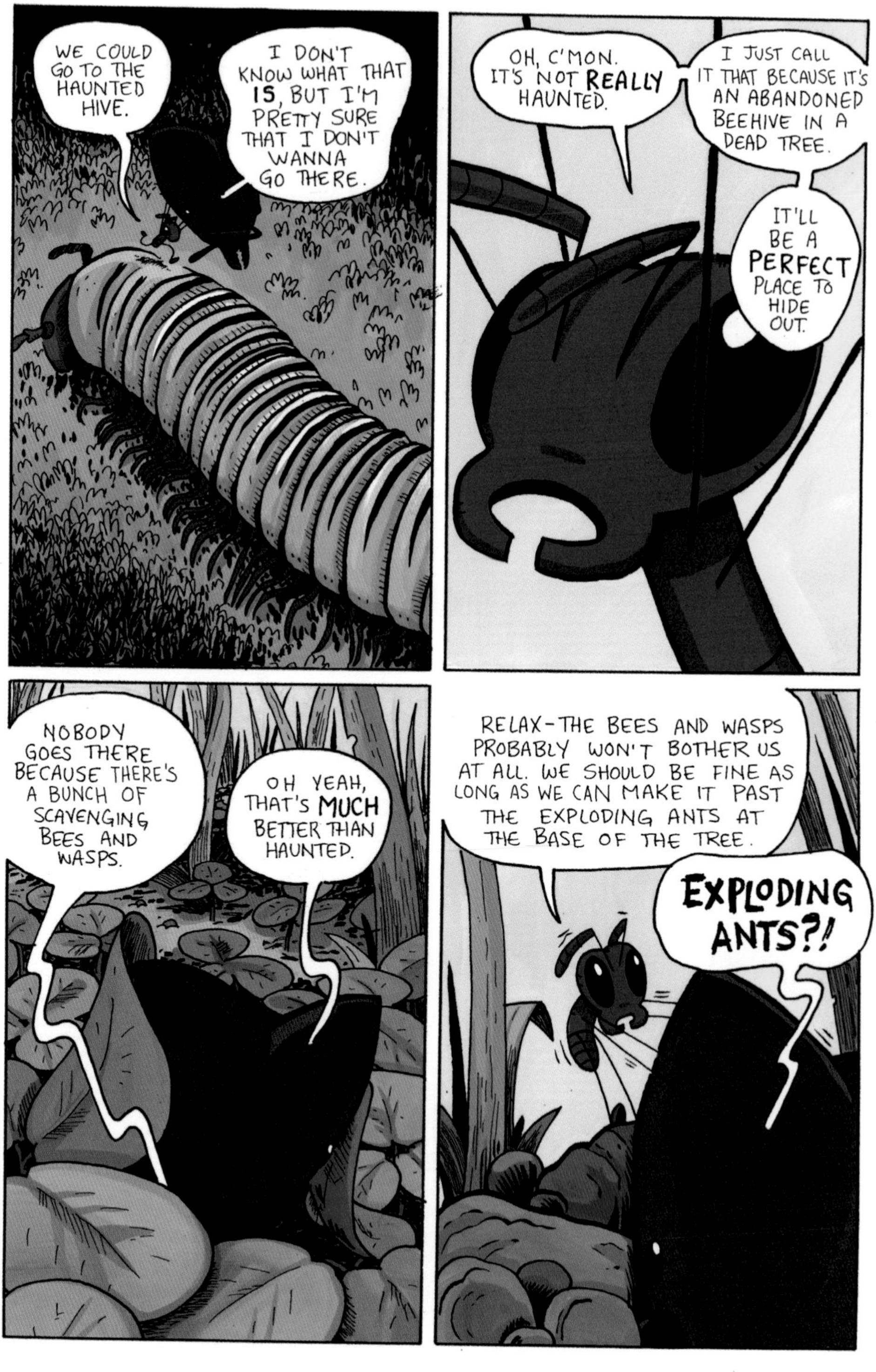
WE COULD GO TO THE HAUNTED HIVE.
I DON'T KNOW WHAT THAT IS, BUT I'M PRETTY SURE THAT I DON'T WANNA GO THERE.
OH, C'MON. IT'S NOT REALLY HAUNTED.
I JUST CALL IT THAT BECAUSE IT'S AN ABANDONED BEEHIVE IN A DEAD TREE.
IT'LL BE A PERFECT PLACE TO HIDE OUT.
NOBODY GOES THERE BECAUSE THERE'S A BUNCH OF SCAVENGING BEES AND WASPS.
OH YEAH, THAT'S MUCH BETTER THAN HAUNTED.
RELAX-THE BEES AND WASPS PROBABLY WON'T BOTHER US AT ALL. WE SHOULD BE FINE AS LONG AS WE CAN MAKE IT PAST THE EXPLODING ANTS AT THE BASE OF THE TREE.
EXPLODING ANTS?!

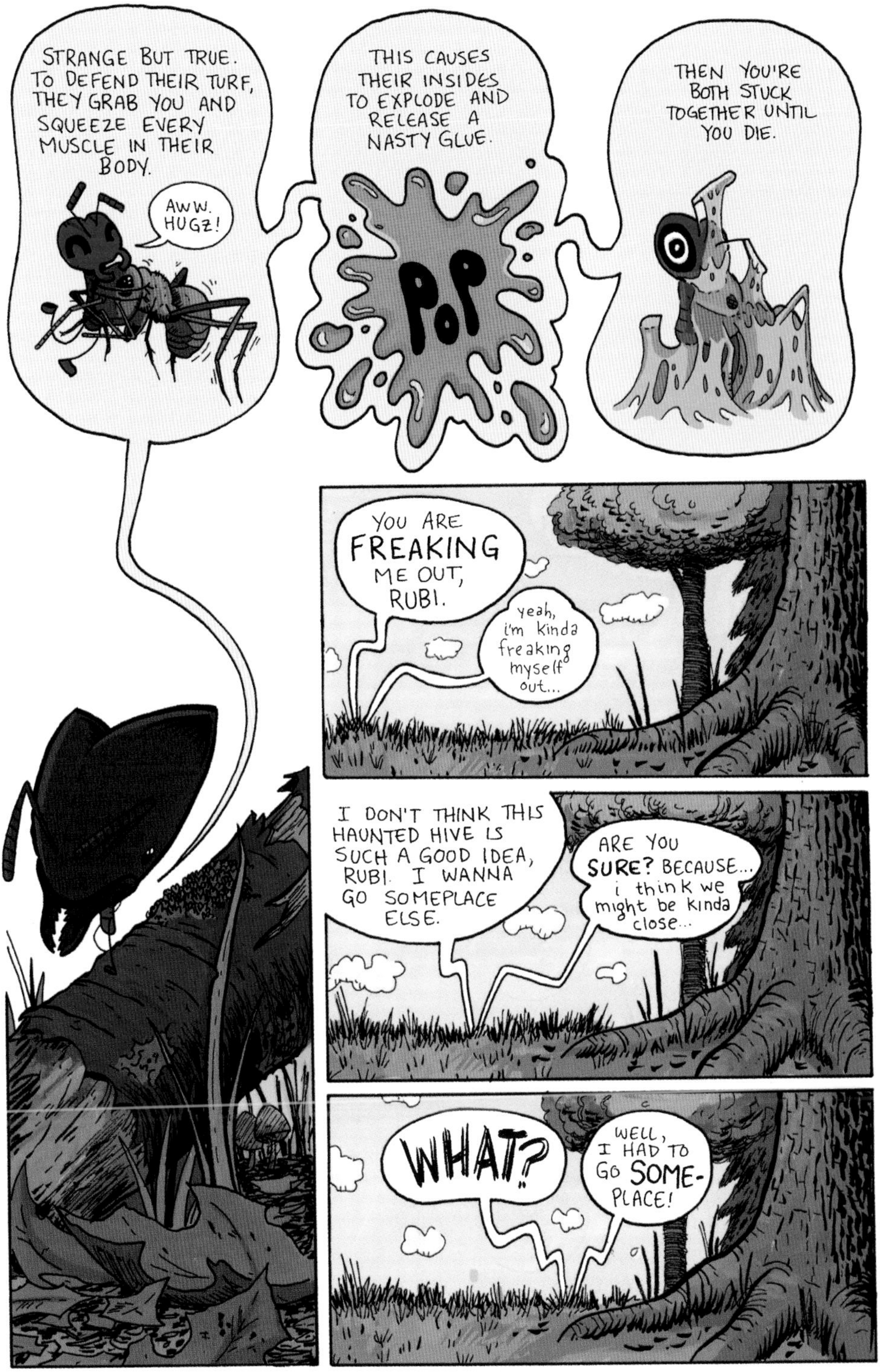
STRANGE BUT TRUE. TO DEFEND THEIR TURF, THEY GRAB YOU AND SQUEEZE EVERY MUSCLE IN THEIR BODY.
AWW. HUGZ!
THIS CAUSES THEIR INSIDES TO EXPLODE AND RELEASE A NASTY GLUE.
POP
THEN YOU'RE BOTH STUCK TOGETHER UNTIL YOU DIE.
YOU ARE FREAKING ME OUT, RUBI.
yeah, i'm kinda freaking myself out...
I DON'T THINK THIS HAUNTED HIVE IS SUCH A GOOD IDEA, RUBI. I WANNA GO SOMEPLACE ELSE.
ARE YOU SURE? BECAUSE... i think we might be kinda close...
WHAT?
WELL, I HAD TO GO SOME-PLACE!

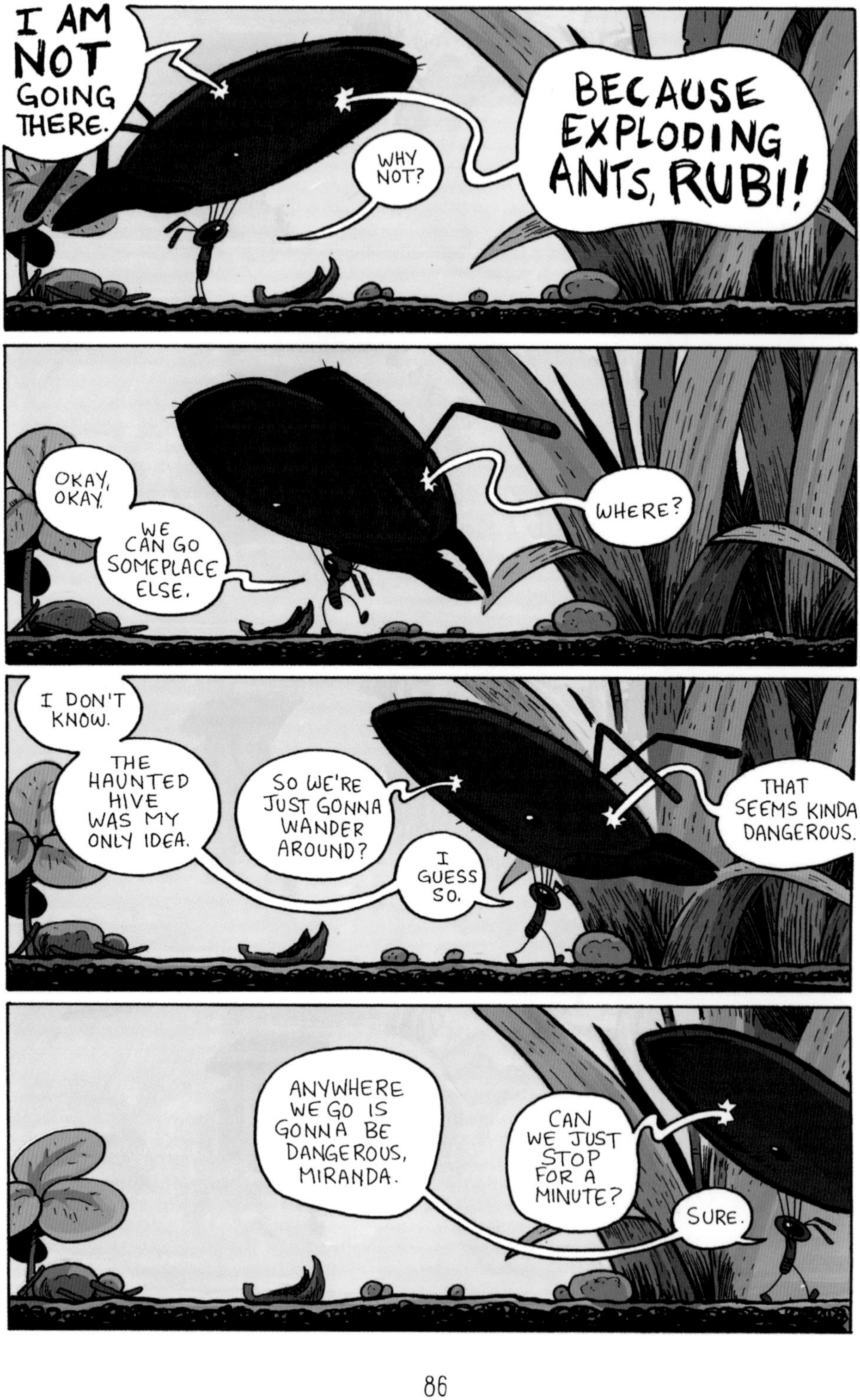
I AM NOT GOING THERE.
WHY NOT?
BECAUSE EXPLODING ANTS, RUBI!
OKAY, OKAY.
WE CAN GO SOMEPLACE ELSE.
WHERE?
I DON'T KNOW.
THE HAUNTED HIVE WAS MY ONLY IDEA.
SO WE'RE JUST GONNA WANDER AROUND?
I GUESS SO.
THAT SEEMS KINDA DANGEROUS.
ANYWHERE WE GO IS GONNA BE DANGEROUS, MIRANDA.
CAN WE JUST STOP FOR A MINUTE?
SURE.

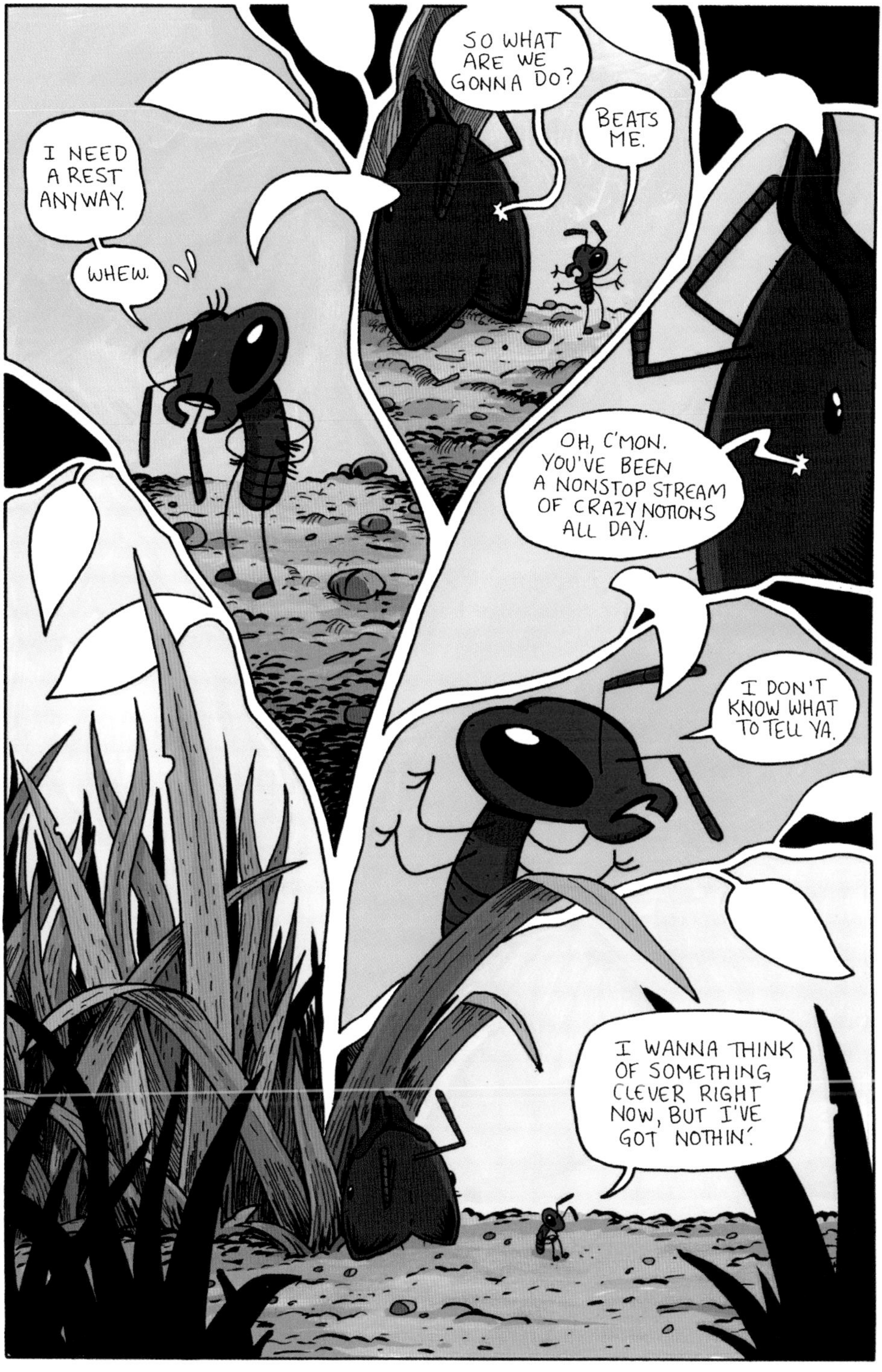
I NEED A REST ANYWAY.
WHEW.
SO WHAT ARE WE GONNA DO?
BEATS ME.
OH, C'MON. YOU'VE BEEN A NONSTOP STREAM OF CRAZY NOTIONS ALL DAY.
I DON'T KNOW WHAT TO TELL YA.
I WANNA THINK OF SOMETHING CLEVER RIGHT NOW, BUT I'VE GOT NOTHIN'.

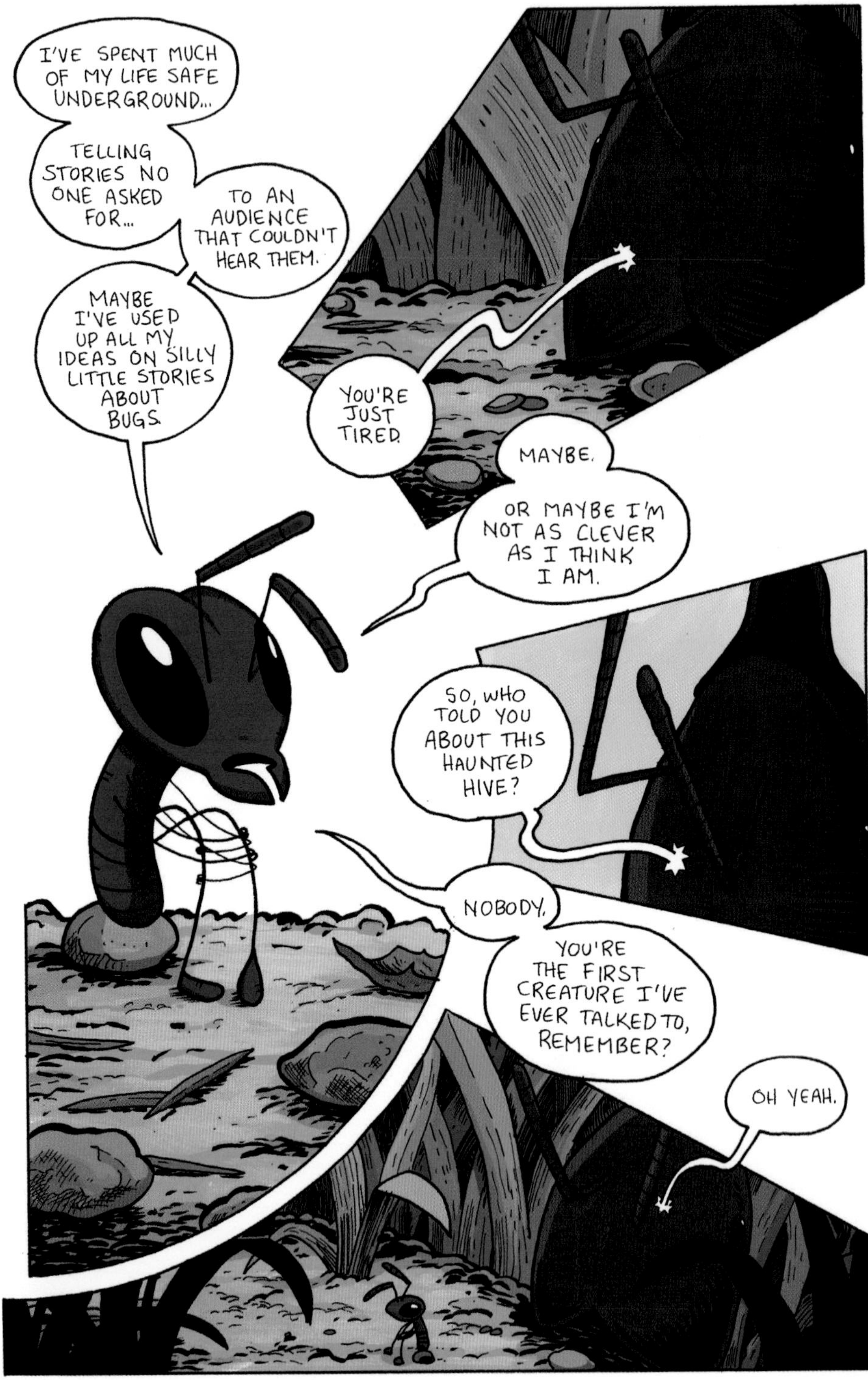
I'VE SPENT MUCH OF MY LIFE SAFE UNDERGROUND...
TELLING STORIES NO ONE ASKED FOR...
TO AN AUDIENCE THAT COULDN'T HEAR THEM.
MAYBE I'VE USED UP ALL MY IDEAS ON SILLY LITTLE STORIES ABOUT BUGS.
YOU'RE JUST TIRED.
MAYBE.
OR MAYBE I'M NOT AS CLEVER AS I THINK I AM.
SO, WHO TOLD YOU ABOUT THIS HAUNTED HIVE?
NOBODY.
YOU'RE THE FIRST CREATURE I'VE EVER TALKED TO, REMEMBER?
OH YEAH.

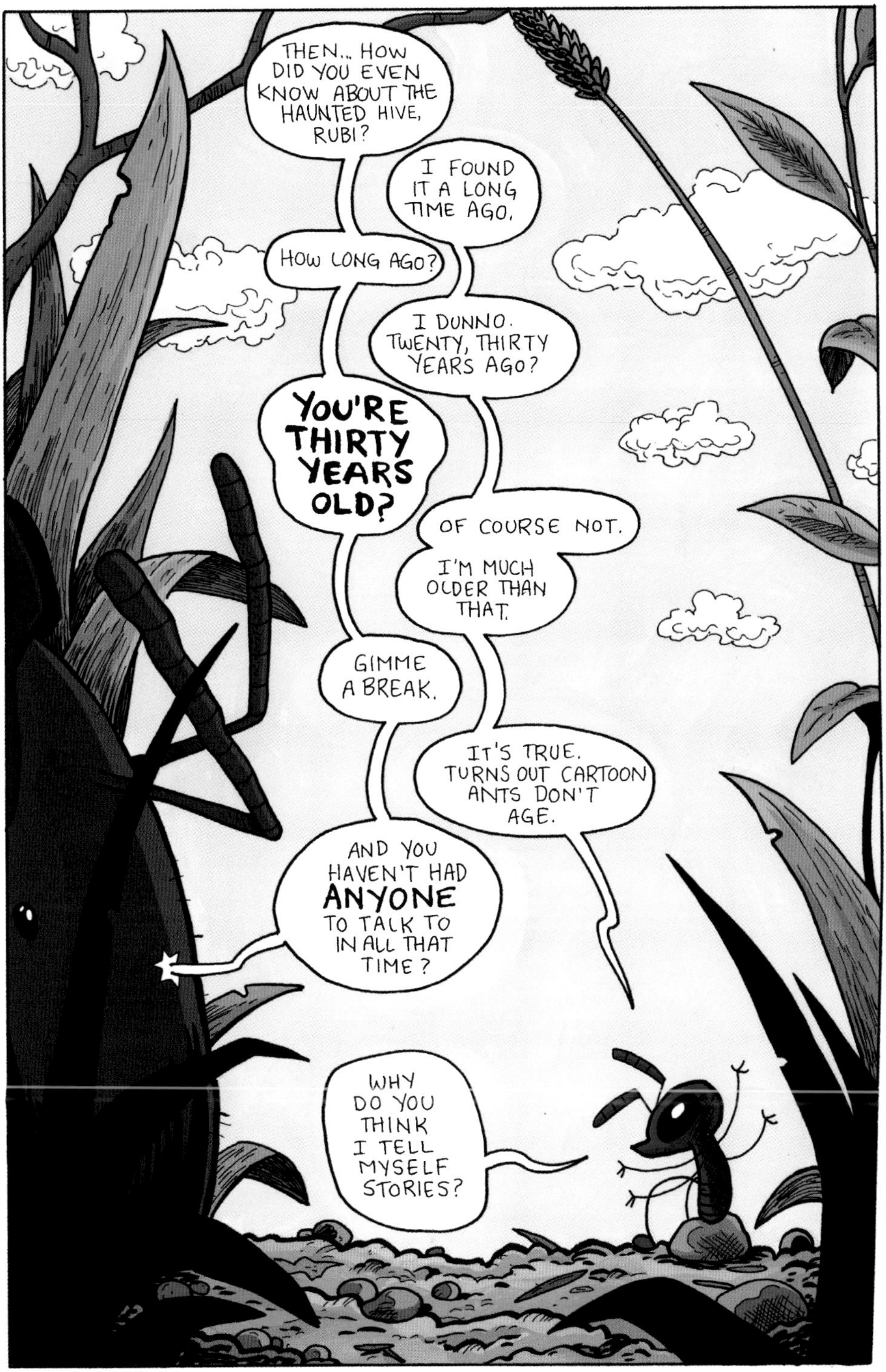
THEN... HOW DID YOU EVEN KNOW ABOUT THE HAUNTED HIVE, RUBI?
I FOUND IT A LONG TIME AGO.
HOW LONG AGO?
I DUNNO. TWENTY, THIRTY YEARS AGO?
YOU'RE THIRTY YEARS OLD?
OF COURSE NOT.
I'M MUCH OLDER THAN THAT.
GIMME A BREAK.
IT'S TRUE. TURNS OUT CARTOON ANTS DON'T AGE.
AND YOU HAVEN'T HAD ANYONE TO TALK TO IN ALL THAT TIME?
WHY DO YOU THINK I TELL MYSELF STORIES?

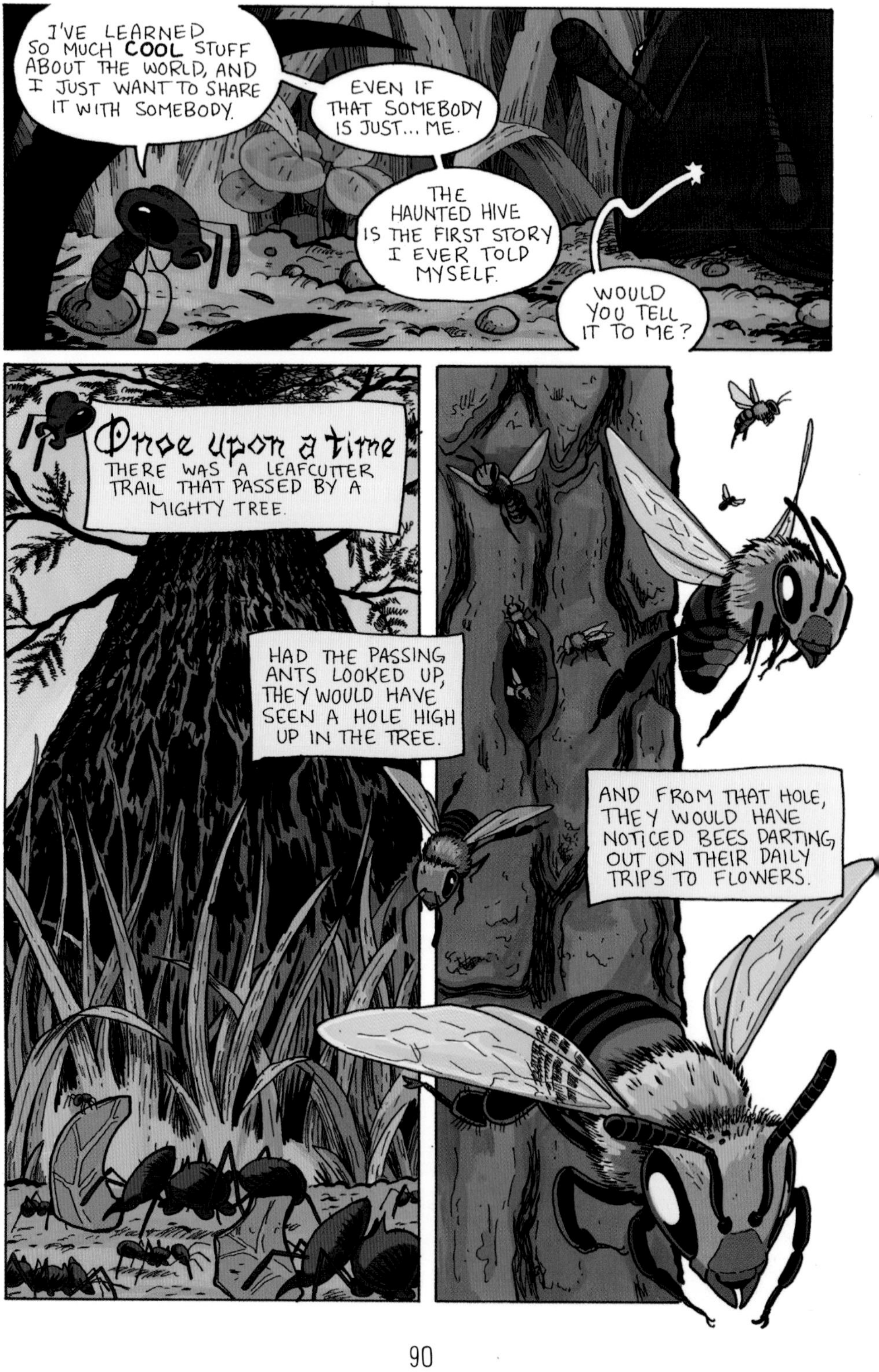
I'VE LEARNED SO MUCH **COOL** STUFF ABOUT THE WORLD, AND I JUST WANT TO SHARE IT WITH SOMEBODY.
EVEN IF THAT SOMEBODY IS JUST... ME.
THE HAUNTED HIVE IS THE FIRST STORY I EVER TOLD MYSELF.
WOULD YOU TELL IT TO ME?
Once upon a time THERE WAS A LEAFCUTTER TRAIL THAT PASSED BY A MIGHTY TREE.
HAD THE PASSING ANTS LOOKED UP, THEY WOULD HAVE SEEN A HOLE HIGH UP IN THE TREE.
AND FROM THAT HOLE, THEY WOULD HAVE NOTICED BEES DARTING OUT ON THEIR DAILY TRIPS TO FLOWERS.

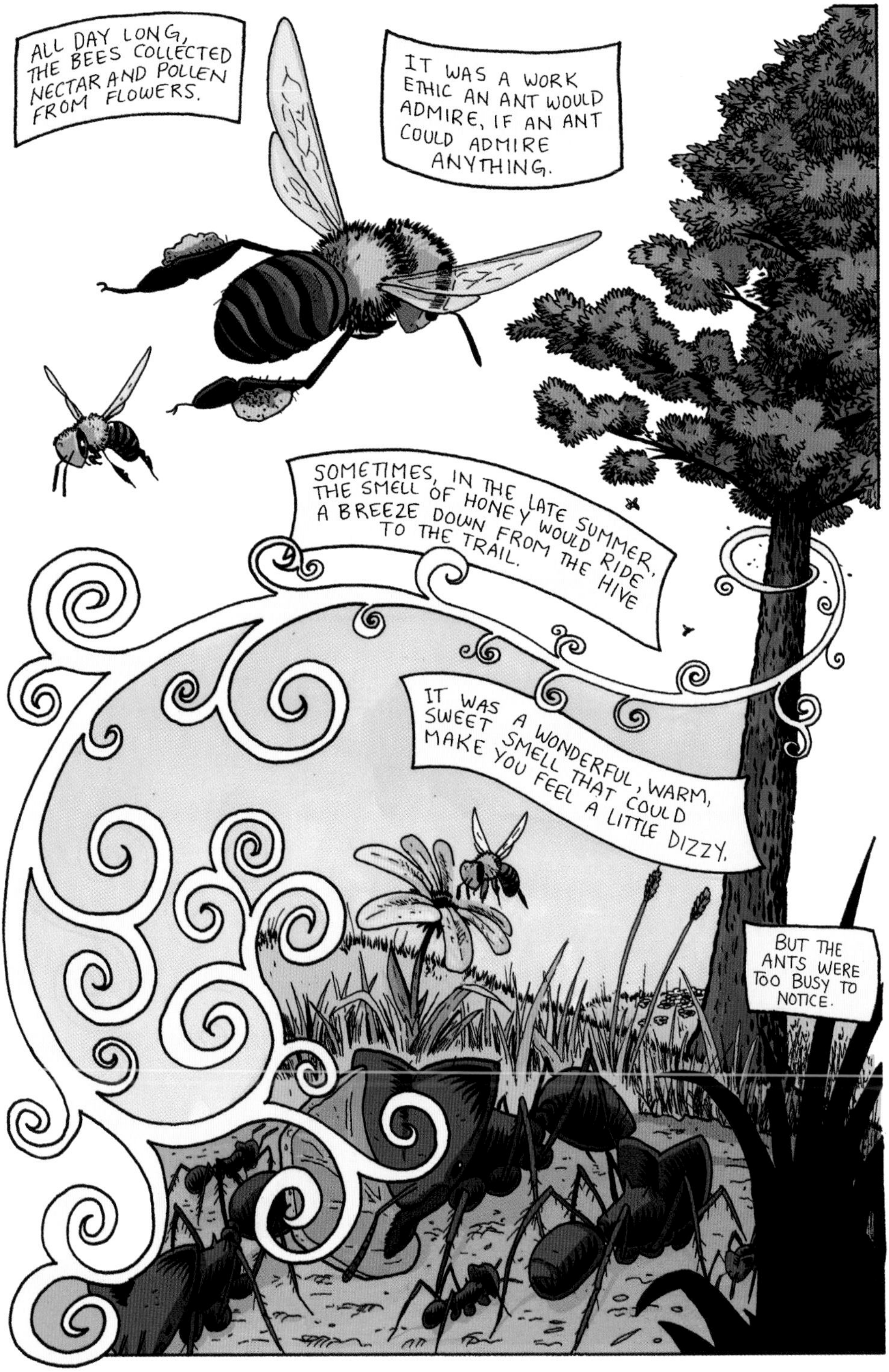
ALL DAY LONG, THE BEES COLLECTED NECTAR AND POLLEN FROM FLOWERS.
IT WAS A WORK ETHIC AN ANT WOULD ADMIRE, IF AN ANT COULD ADMIRE ANYTHING.
SOMETIMES, IN THE LATE SUMMER, THE SMELL OF HONEY WOULD RIDE A BREEZE DOWN FROM THE HIVE TO THE TRAIL.
IT WAS A WONDERFUL, WARM, SWEET SMELL THAT COULD MAKE YOU FEEL A LITTLE DIZZY.
BUT THE ANTS WERE TOO BUSY TO NOTICE.

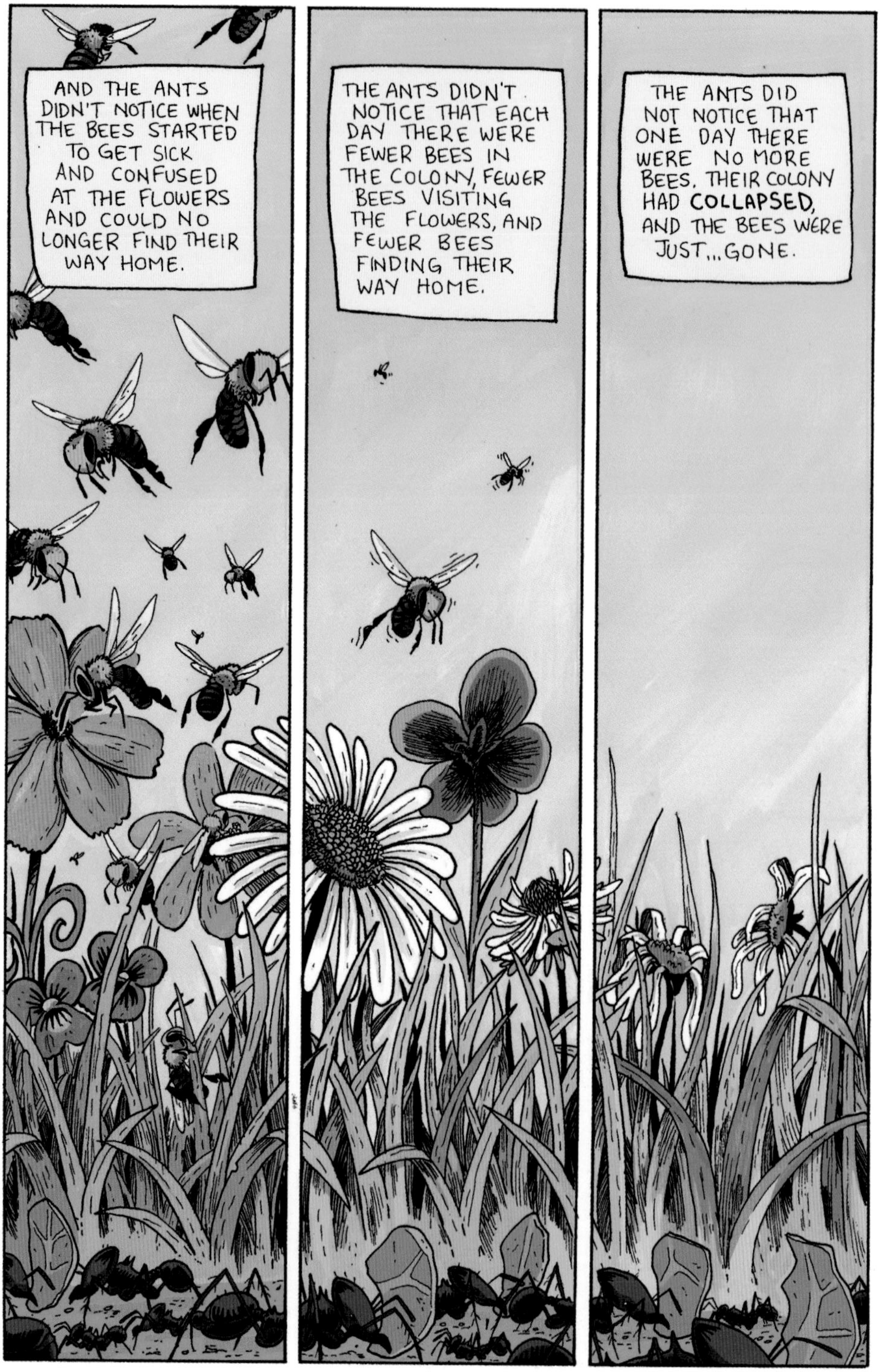
AND THE ANTS DIDN'T NOTICE WHEN THE BEES STARTED TO GET SICK AND CONFUSED AT THE FLOWERS AND COULD NO LONGER FIND THEIR WAY HOME.
THE ANTS DIDN'T NOTICE THAT EACH DAY THERE WERE FEWER BEES IN THE COLONY, FEWER BEES VISITING THE FLOWERS, AND FEWER BEES FINDING THEIR WAY HOME.
THE ANTS DID NOT NOTICE THAT ONE DAY THERE WERE NO MORE BEES. THEIR COLONY HAD **COLLAPSED**, AND THE BEES WERE JUST... GONE.

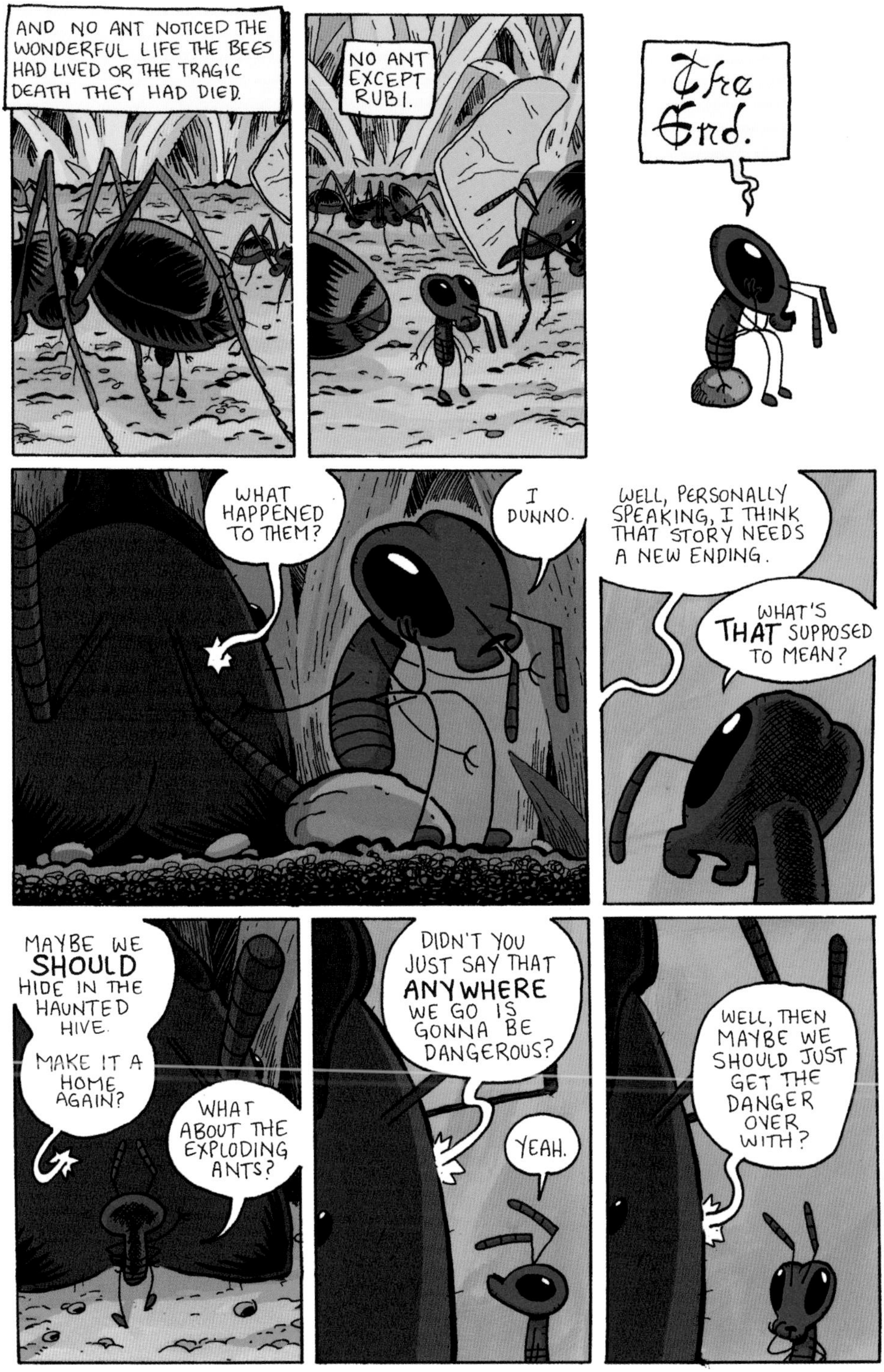
AND NO ANT NOTICED THE WONDERFUL LIFE THE BEES HAD LIVED OR THE TRAGIC DEATH THEY HAD DIED.
NO ANT EXCEPT RUBI.
The End.
WHAT HAPPENED TO THEM?
I DUNNO.
WELL, PERSONALLY SPEAKING, I THINK THAT STORY NEEDS A NEW ENDING.
WHAT'S THAT SUPPOSED TO MEAN?
MAYBE WE SHOULD HIDE IN THE HAUNTED HIVE.
MAKE IT A HOME AGAIN?
WHAT ABOUT THE EXPLODING ANTS?
DIDN'T YOU JUST SAY THAT ANYWHERE WE GO IS GONNA BE DANGEROUS?
YEAH.
WELL, THEN MAYBE WE SHOULD JUST GET THE DANGER OVER WITH?

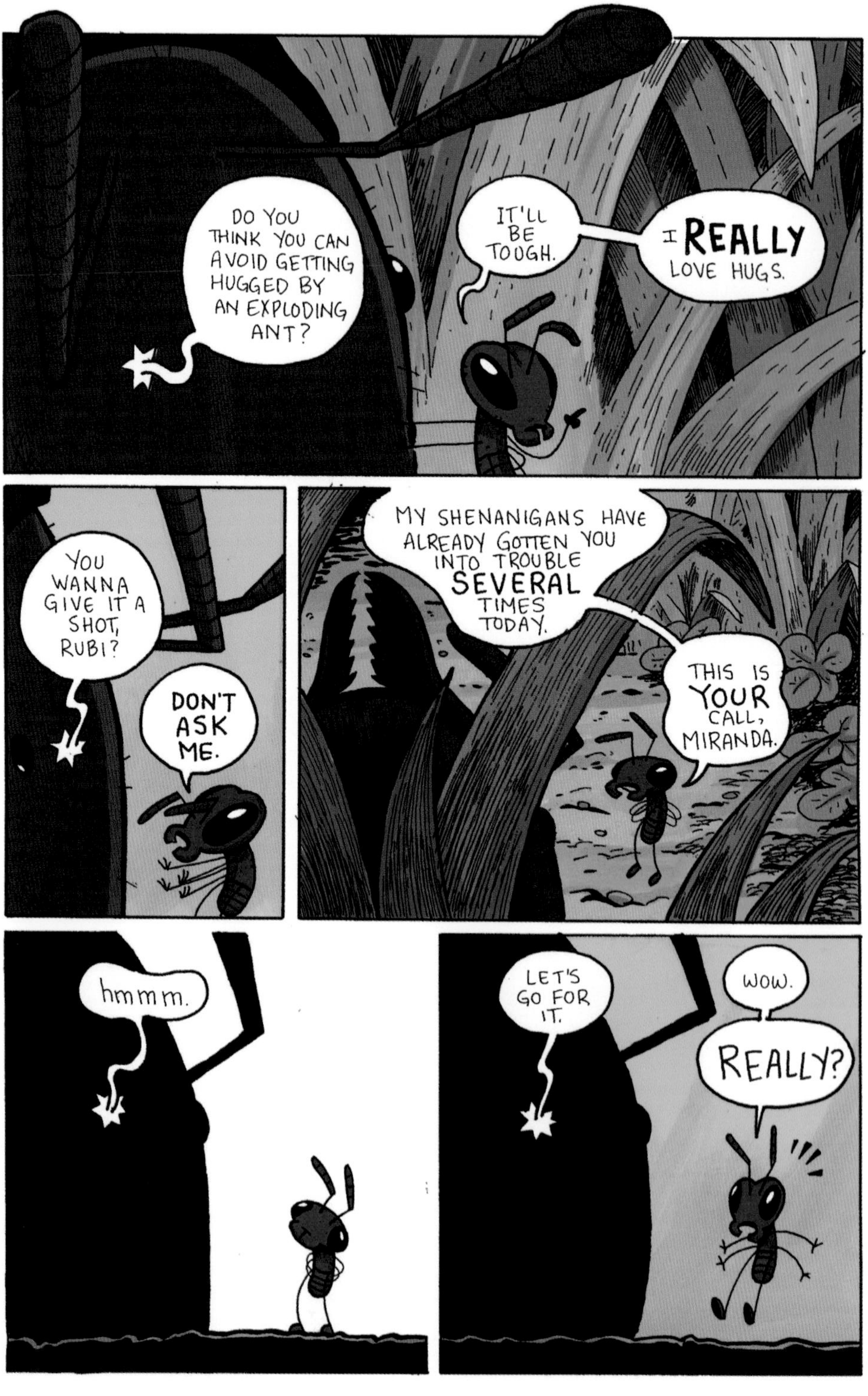
DO YOU THINK YOU CAN AVOID GETTING HUGGED BY AN EXPLODING ANT?
IT'LL BE TOUGH.
I REALLY LOVE HUGS.
YOU WANNA GIVE IT A SHOT, RUBI?
DON'T ASK ME.
MY SHENANIGANS HAVE ALREADY GOTTEN YOU INTO TROUBLE SEVERAL TIMES TODAY.
THIS IS YOUR CALL, MIRANDA.
hmmm.
LET'S GO FOR IT.
WOW.
REALLY?

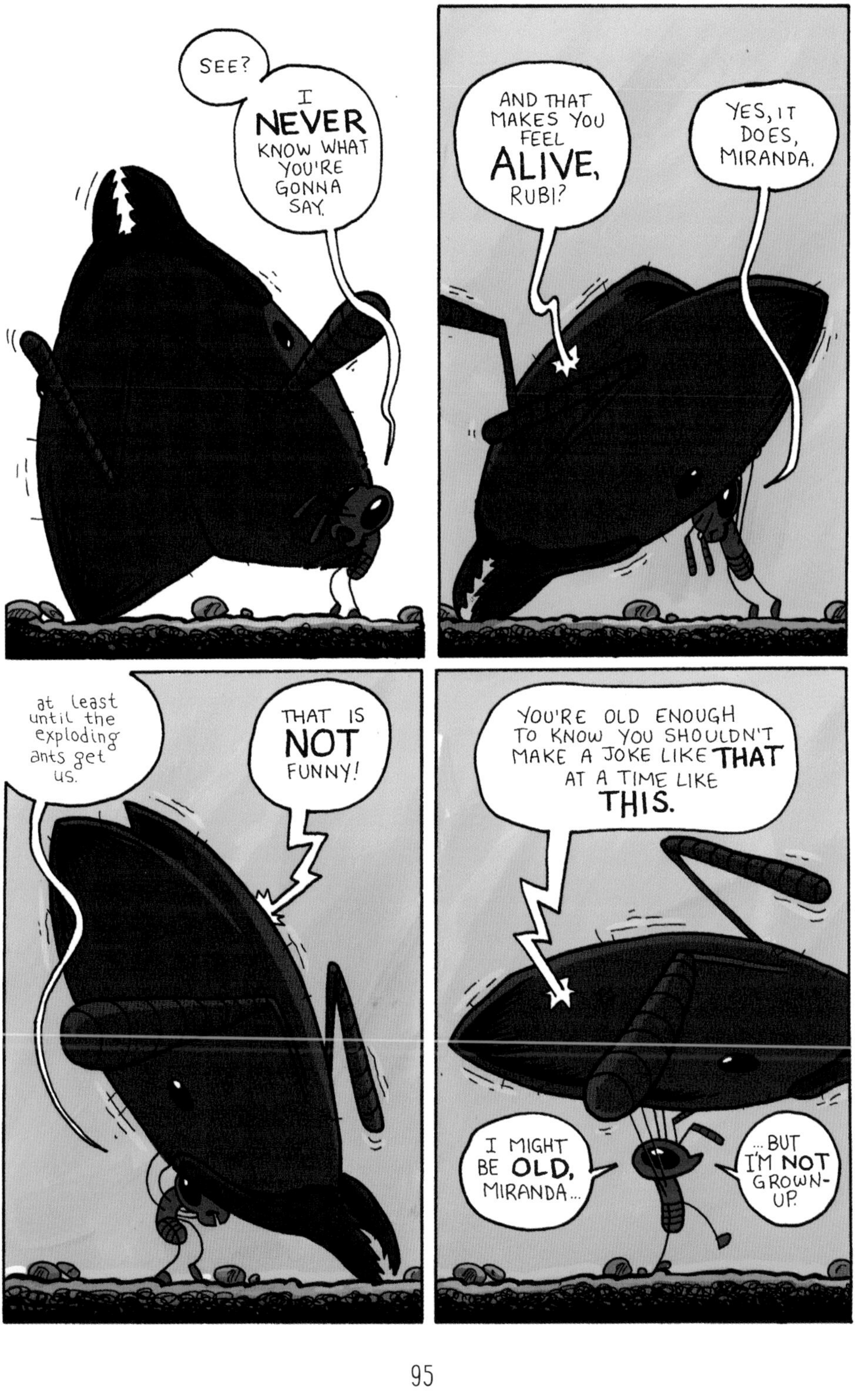
SEE?
I NEVER KNOW WHAT YOU'RE GONNA SAY.
AND THAT MAKES YOU FEEL ALIVE, RUBI?
YES, IT DOES, MIRANDA.
at least until the exploding ants get us.
THAT IS NOT FUNNY!
YOU'RE OLD ENOUGH TO KNOW YOU SHOULDN'T MAKE A JOKE LIKE THAT AT A TIME LIKE THIS.
I MIGHT BE OLD, MIRANDA...
...BUT I'M NOT GROWN-UP.

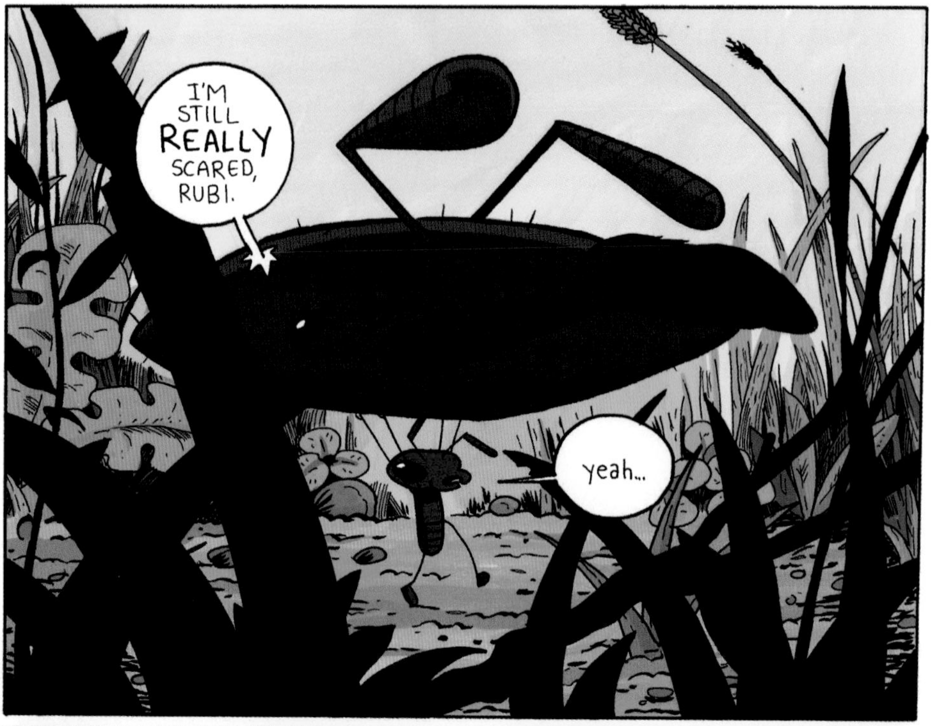
I'M STILL REALLY SCARED, RUBI.
yeah...

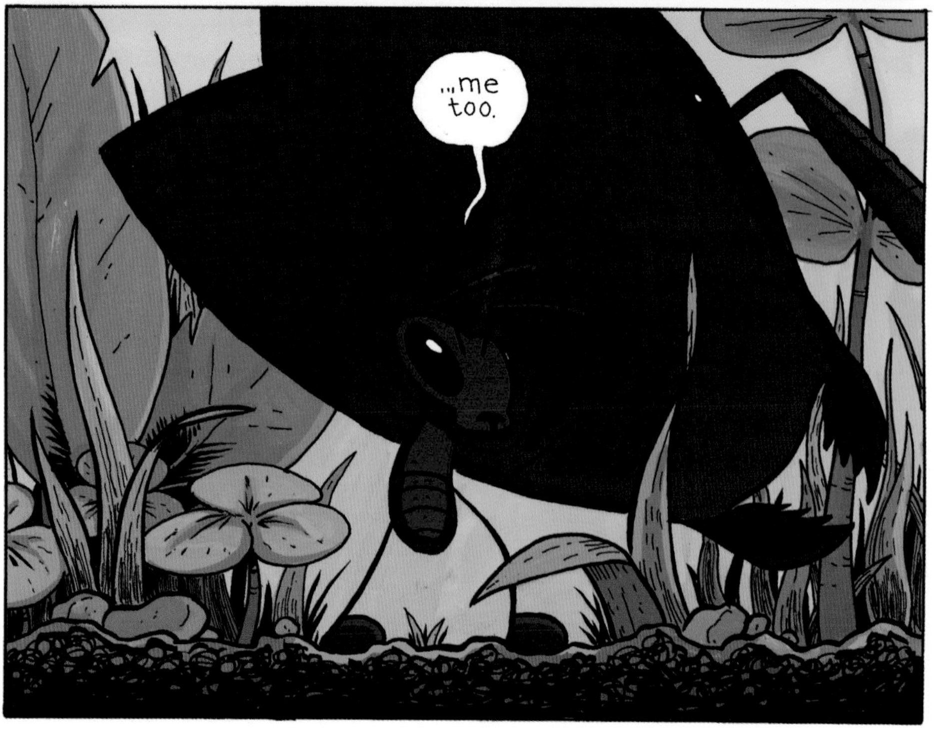
...me too.

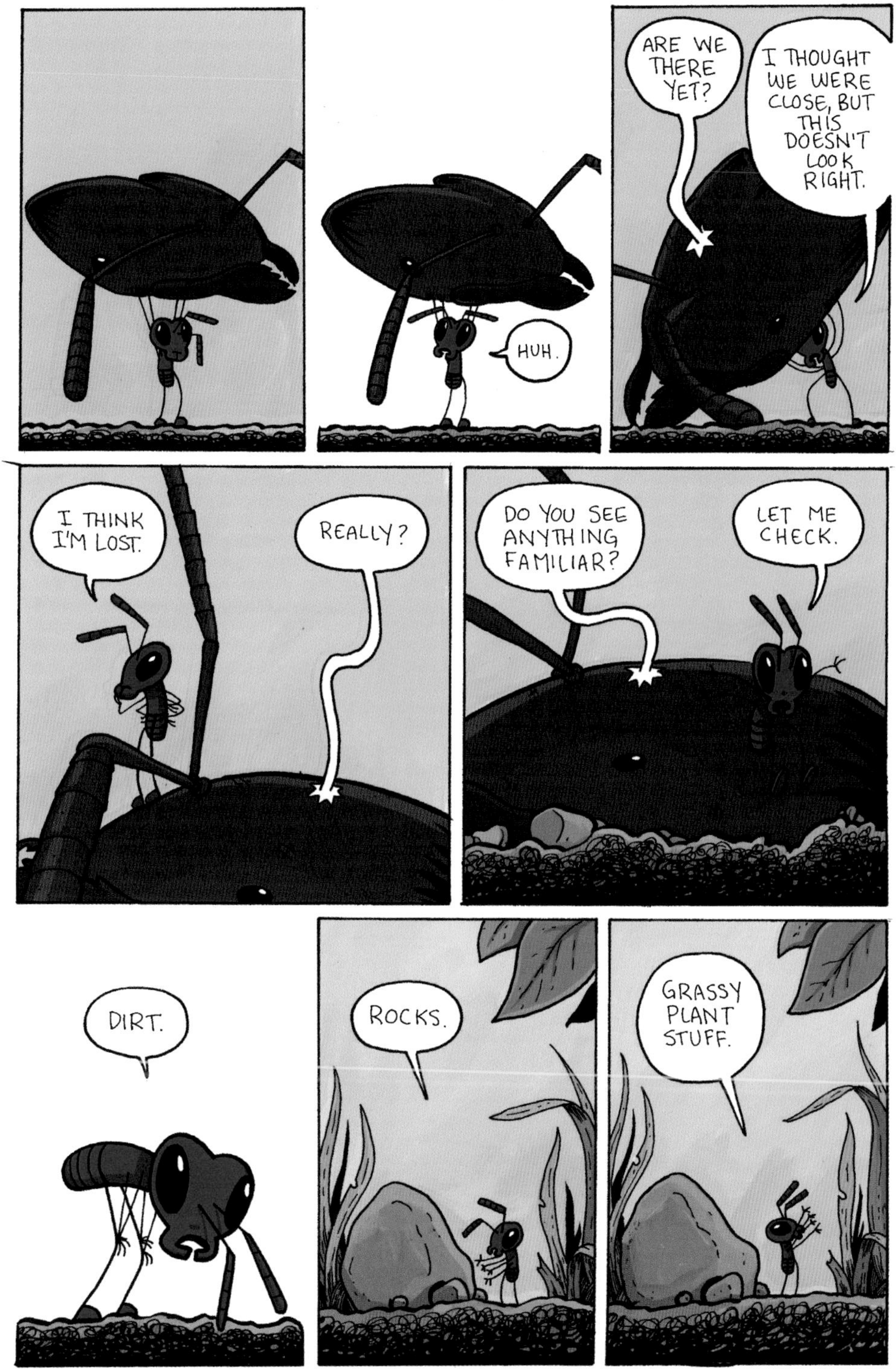
HUH.
ARE WE THERE YET?
I THOUGHT WE WERE CLOSE, BUT THIS DOESN'T LOOK RIGHT.
I THINK I'M LOST.
REALLY?
DO YOU SEE ANYTHING FAMILIAR?
LET ME CHECK.
DIRT.
ROCKS.
GRASSY PLANT STUFF.

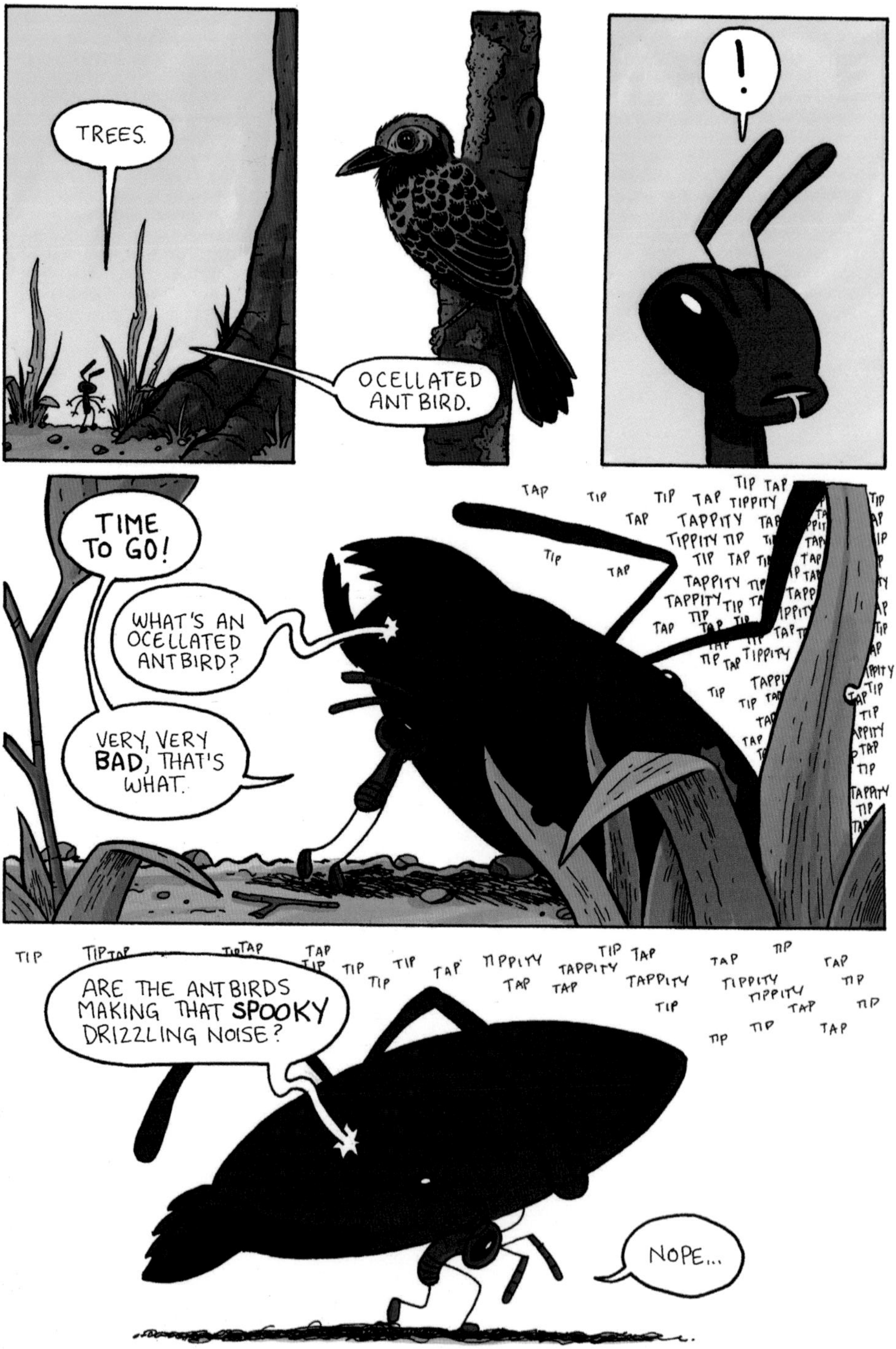

TREES.
OCELLATED ANT BIRD.
!
TIME TO GO!
WHAT'S AN OCELLATED ANTBIRD?
VERY, VERY BAD, THAT'S WHAT.
ARE THE ANTBIRDS MAKING THAT SPOOKY DRIZZLING NOISE?
NOPE...

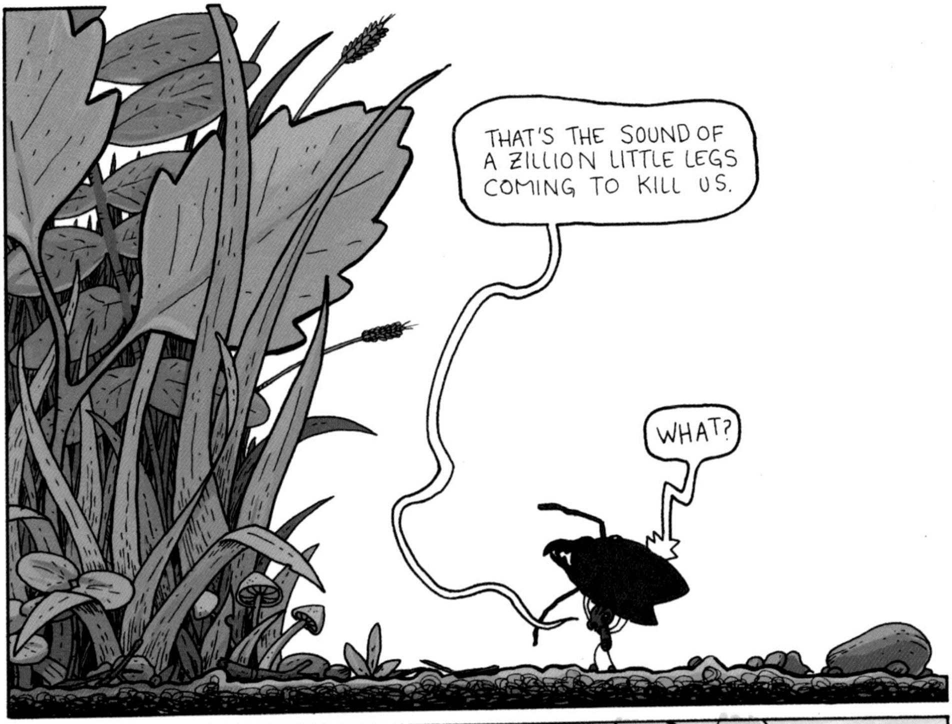
THAT'S THE SOUND OF A ZILLION LITTLE LEGS COMING TO KILL US.
WHAT?

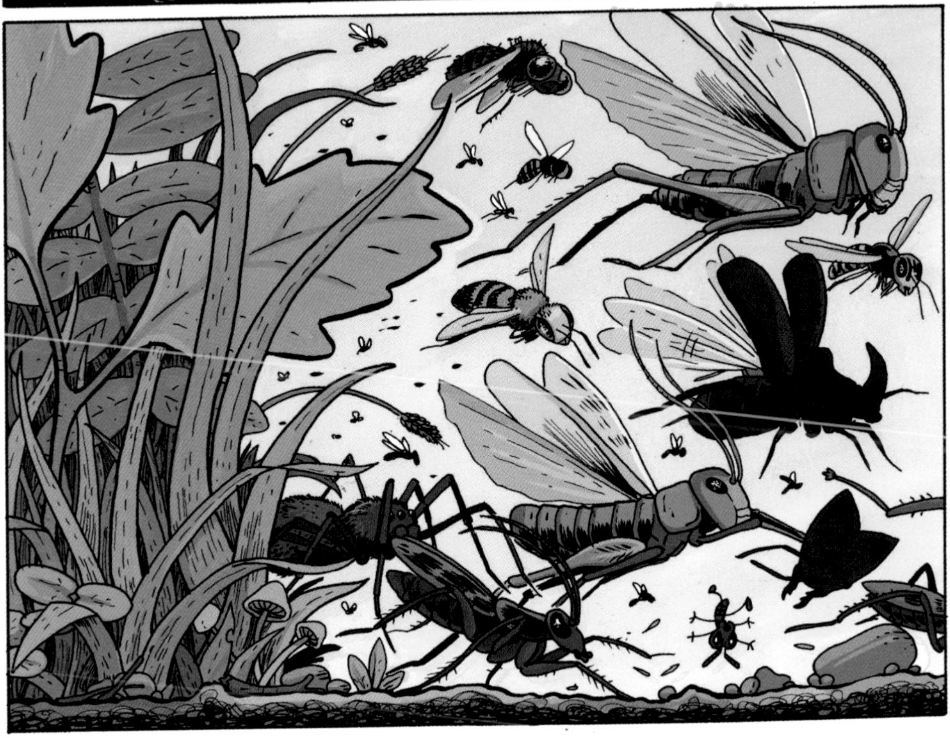

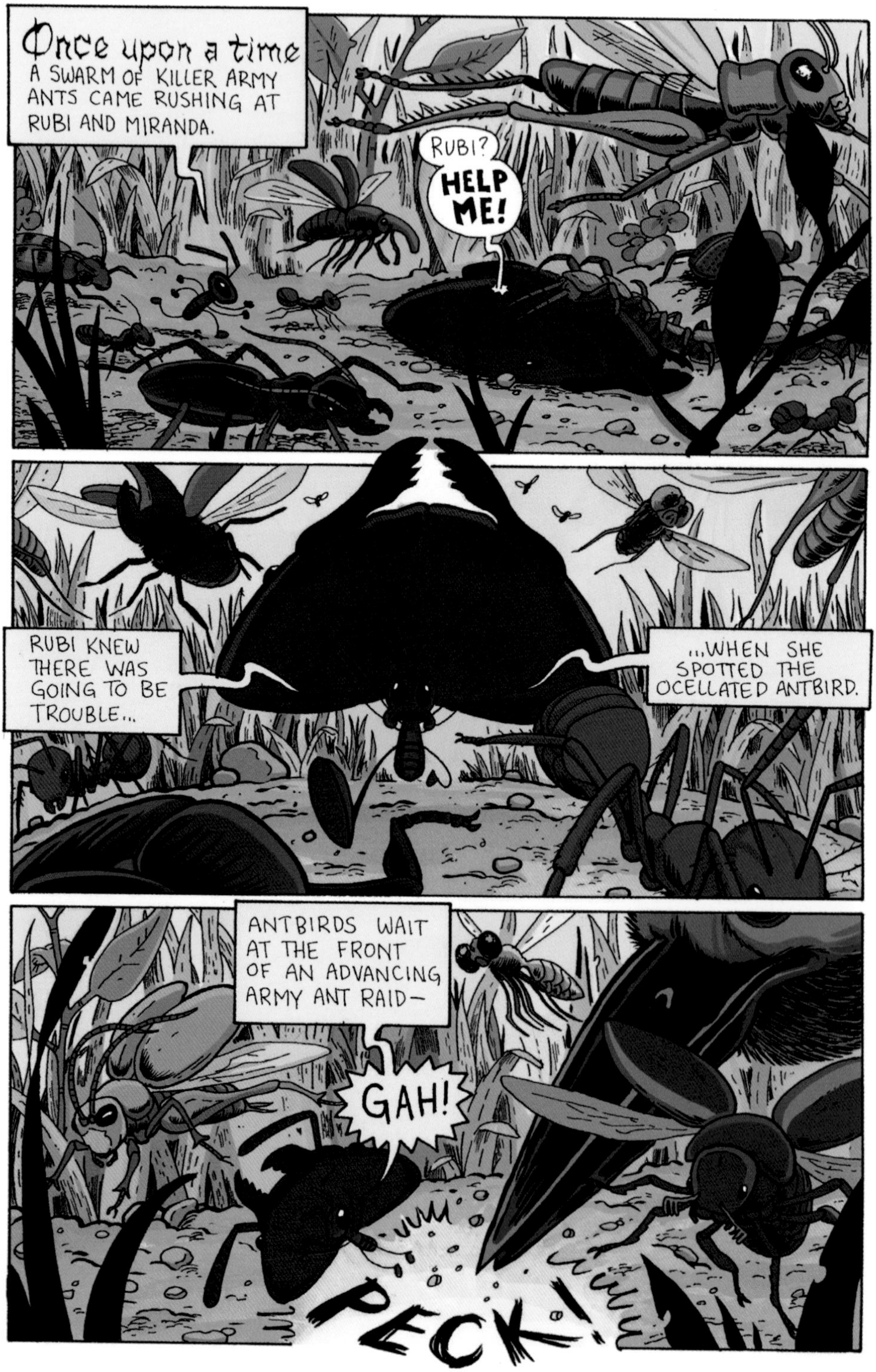
Once upon a time A SWARM OF KILLER ARMY ANTS CAME RUSHING AT RUBI AND MIRANDA.
RUBI?
HELP ME!
RUBI KNEW THERE WAS GOING TO BE TROUBLE...
...WHEN SHE SPOTTED THE OCELLATED ANTBIRD.
ANTBIRDS WAIT AT THE FRONT OF AN ADVANCING ARMY ANT RAID—
GAH!
PECK!

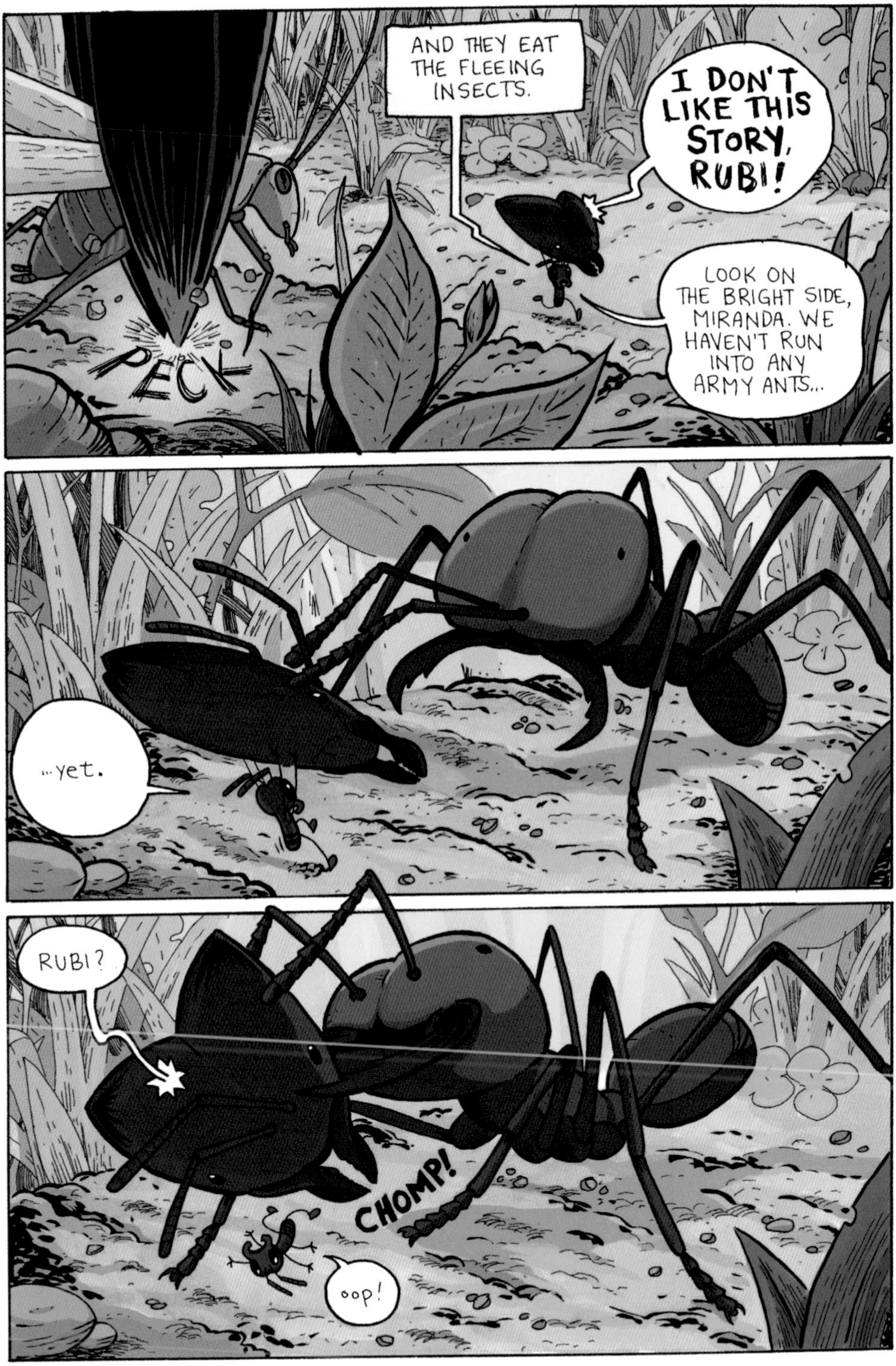
AND THEY EAT THE FLEEING INSECTS.
PECK
I DON'T LIKE THIS STORY, RUBI!
LOOK ON THE BRIGHT SIDE, MIRANDA. WE HAVEN'T RUN INTO ANY ARMY ANTS...
...yet.
RUBI?
CHOMP!
oop!

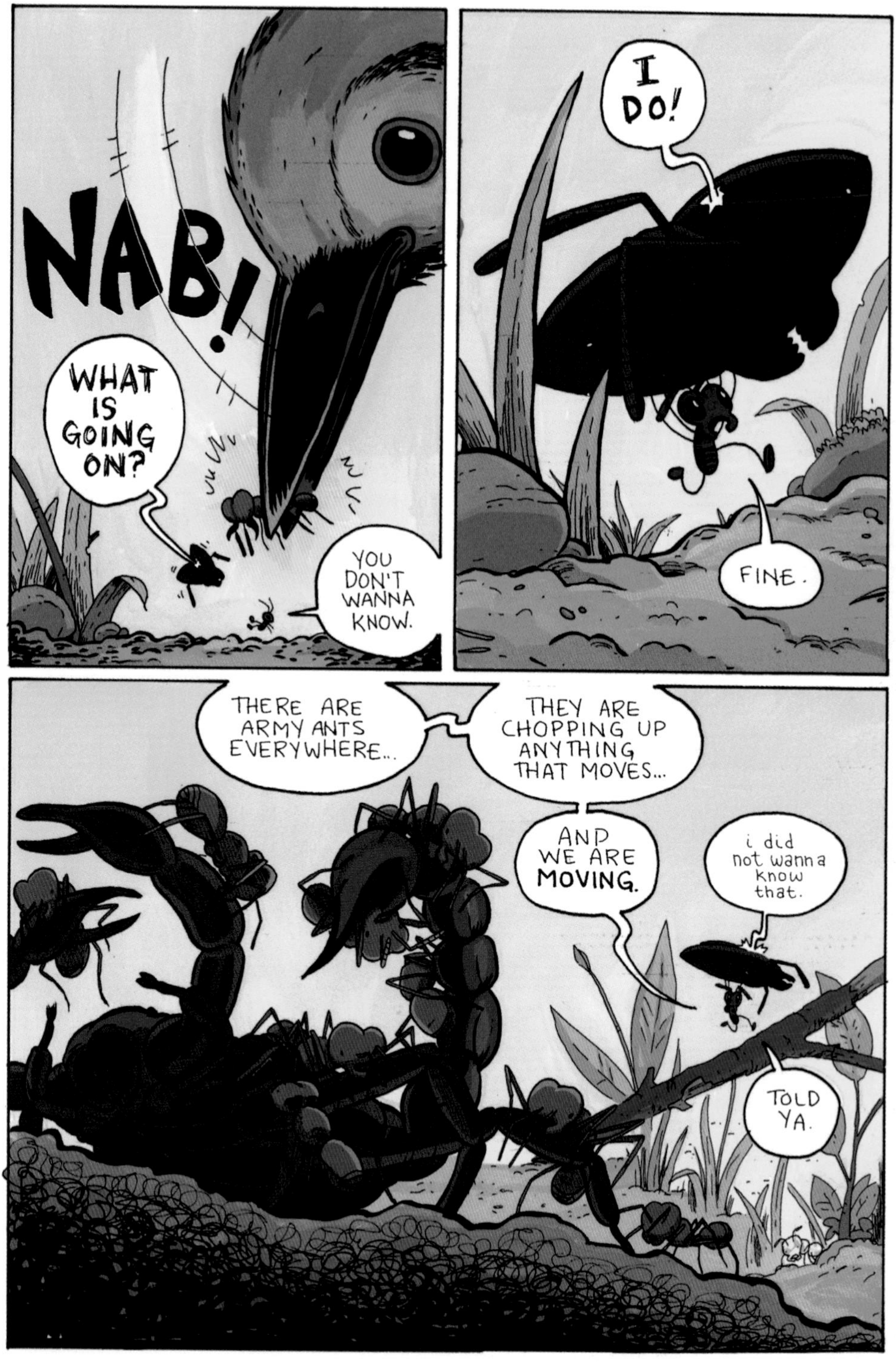
NAB!
WHAT IS GOING ON?
YOU DON'T WANNA KNOW.
I DO!
FINE.
THERE ARE ARMY ANTS EVERYWHERE...
THEY ARE CHOPPING UP ANYTHING THAT MOVES...
AND WE ARE MOVING.
i did not wanna know that.
TOLD YA.

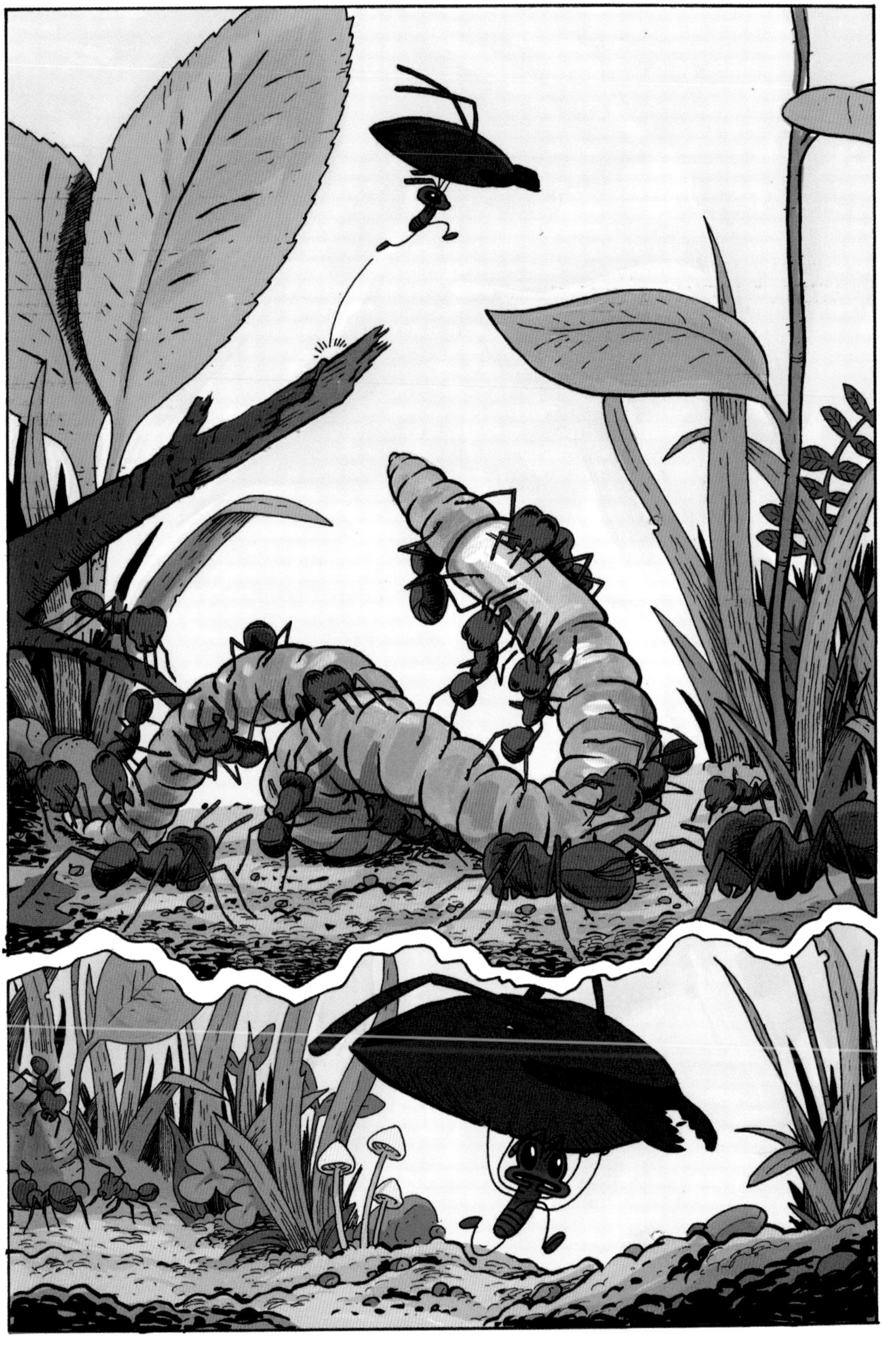

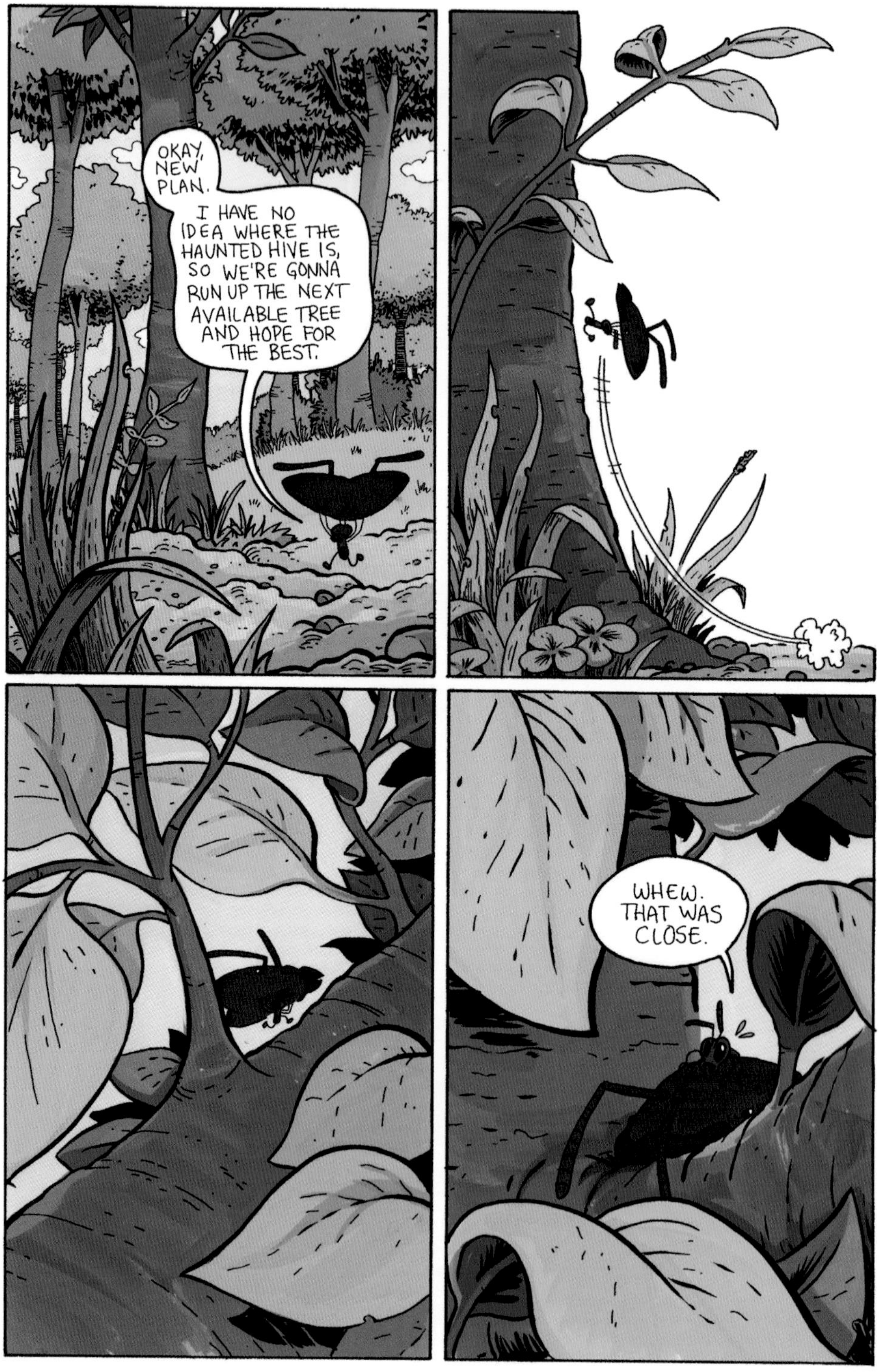
OKAY, NEW PLAN.
I HAVE NO IDEA WHERE THE HAUNTED HIVE IS, SO WE'RE GONNA RUN UP THE NEXT AVAILABLE TREE AND HOPE FOR THE BEST.
WHEW. THAT WAS CLOSE.

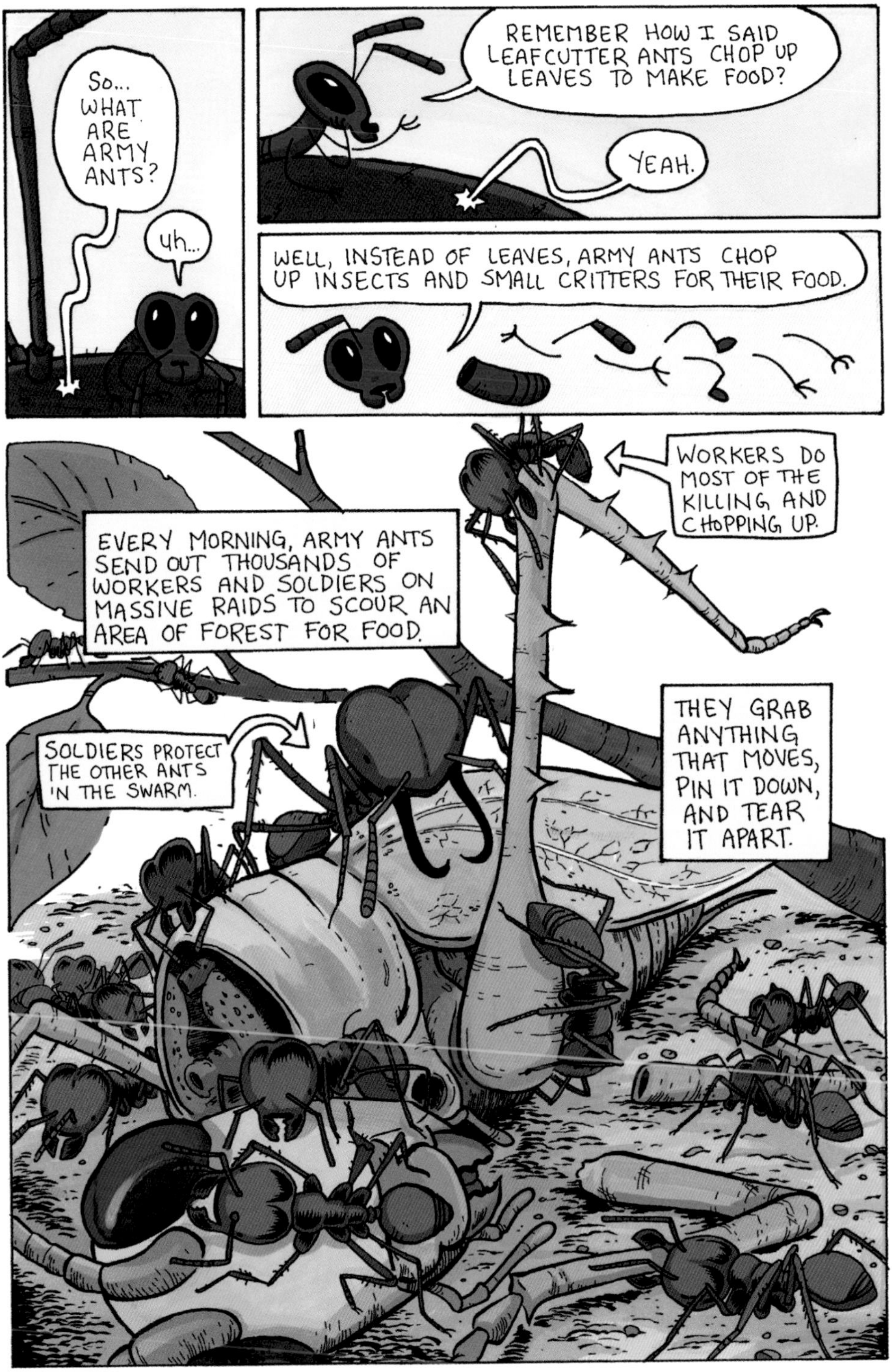
So... WHAT ARE ARMY ANTS?
uh...
REMEMBER HOW I SAID LEAFCUTTER ANTS CHOP UP LEAVES TO MAKE FOOD?
YEAH.
WELL, INSTEAD OF LEAVES, ARMY ANTS CHOP UP INSECTS AND SMALL CRITTERS FOR THEIR FOOD.
EVERY MORNING, ARMY ANTS SEND OUT THOUSANDS OF WORKERS AND SOLDIERS ON MASSIVE RAIDS TO SCOUR AN AREA OF FOREST FOR FOOD.
WORKERS DO MOST OF THE KILLING AND CHOPPING UP.
SOLDIERS PROTECT THE OTHER ANTS IN THE SWARM.
THEY GRAB ANYTHING THAT MOVES, PIN IT DOWN, AND TEAR IT APART.

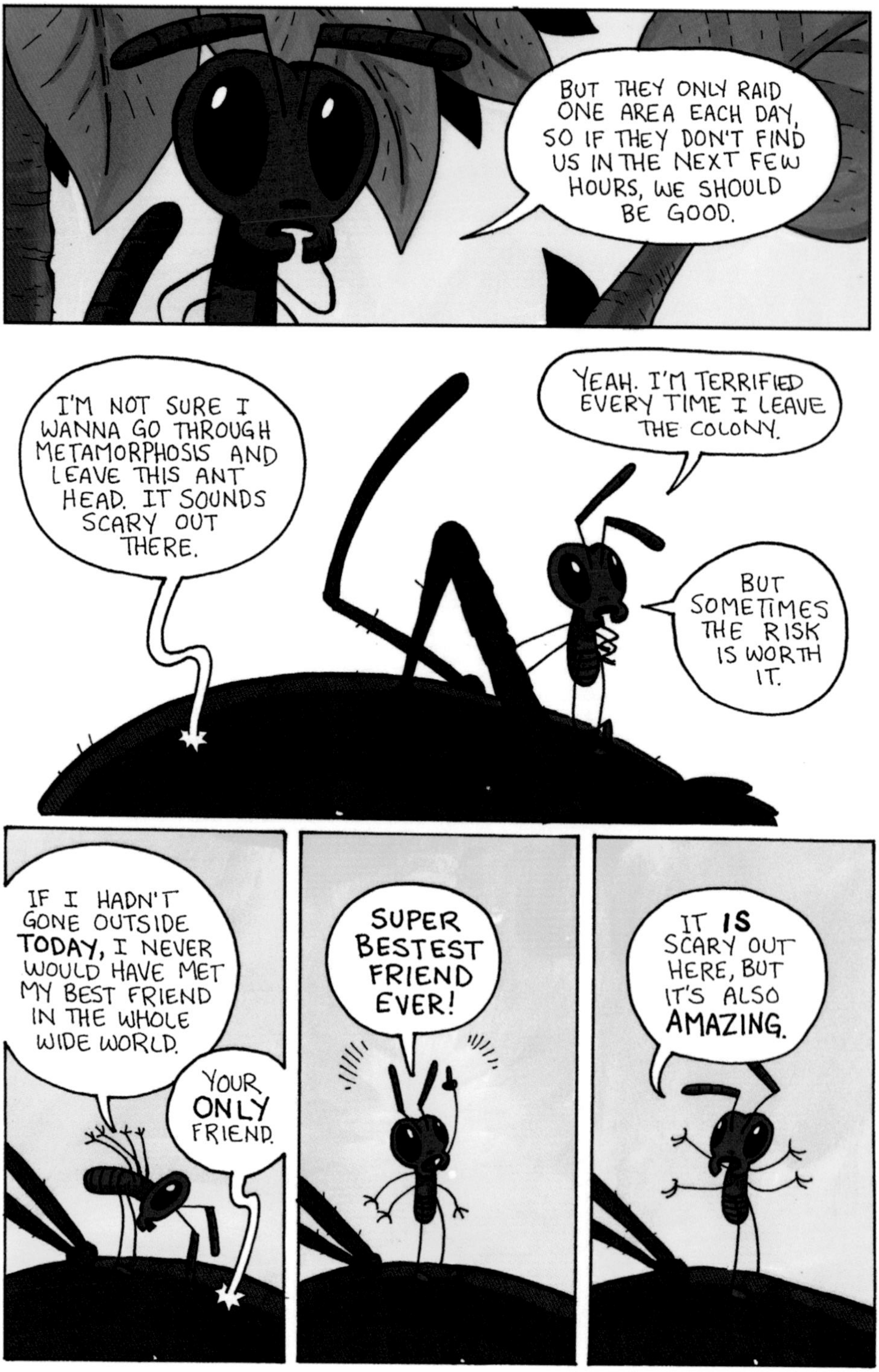
BUT THEY ONLY RAID ONE AREA EACH DAY, SO IF THEY DON'T FIND US IN THE NEXT FEW HOURS, WE SHOULD BE GOOD.
I'M NOT SURE I WANNA GO THROUGH METAMORPHOSIS AND LEAVE THIS ANT HEAD. IT SOUNDS SCARY OUT THERE.
YEAH. I'M TERRIFIED EVERY TIME I LEAVE THE COLONY.
BUT SOMETIMES THE RISK IS WORTH IT.
IF I HADN'T GONE OUTSIDE TODAY, I NEVER WOULD HAVE MET MY BEST FRIEND IN THE WHOLE WIDE WORLD.
YOUR ONLY FRIEND.
SUPER BESTEST FRIEND EVER!
IT IS SCARY OUT HERE, BUT IT'S ALSO AMAZING.

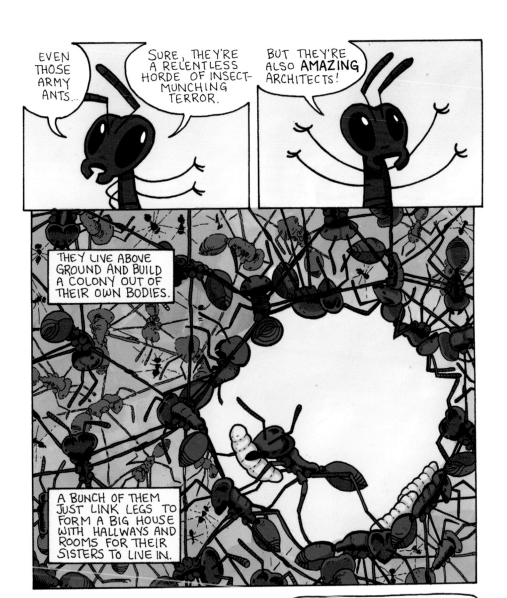

EVEN THOSE ARMY ANTS...

SURE, THEY'RE A RELENTLESS HORDE OF INSECT-MUNCHING TERROR.

BUT THEY'RE ALSO **AMAZING** ARCHITECTS!

THEY LIVE ABOVE GROUND AND BUILD A COLONY OUT OF THEIR OWN BODIES.

A BUNCH OF THEM JUST LINK LEGS TO FORM A BIG HOUSE WITH HALLWAYS AND ROOMS FOR THEIR SISTERS TO LIVE IN.

OH, C'MON.

IT'S TRUE. AND THEY DON'T STAY IN ONE PLACE VERY LONG EITHER. WHEN IT'S TIME TO MOVE, THE WHOLE STRUCTURE COMES APART AND THEY STROLL TO THEIR NEW HUNTING GROUNDS.

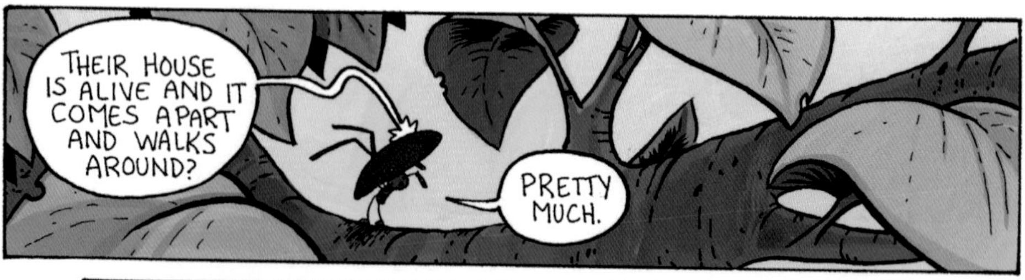
THEIR HOUSE IS ALIVE AND IT COMES APART AND WALKS AROUND?
PRETTY MUCH.

AND WHILE THEY'RE MOVING TO THEIR NEW HOME, SOME OF THEM BUILD BRIDGES WITH THEIR BODIES TO MAKE THE TRIP GO EASIER FOR THEIR SISTERS.

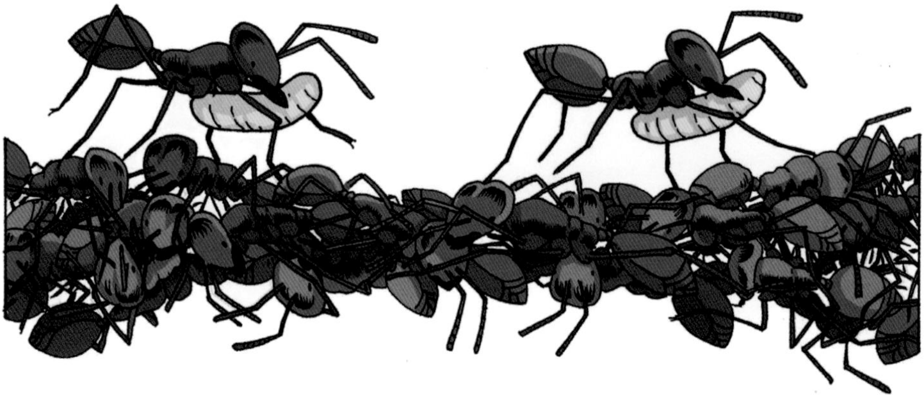

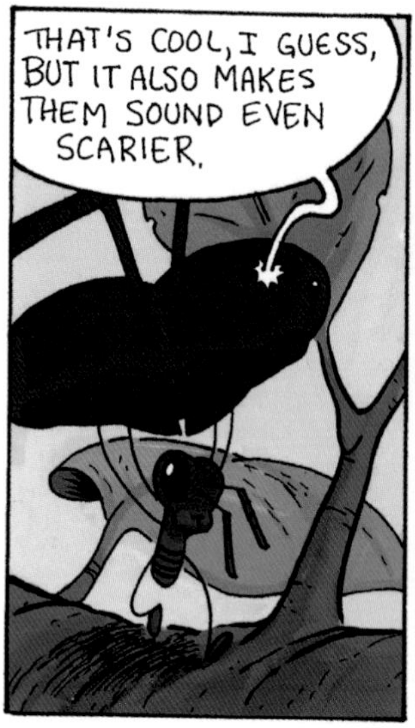
THAT'S COOL, I GUESS, BUT IT ALSO MAKES THEM SOUND EVEN SCARIER.

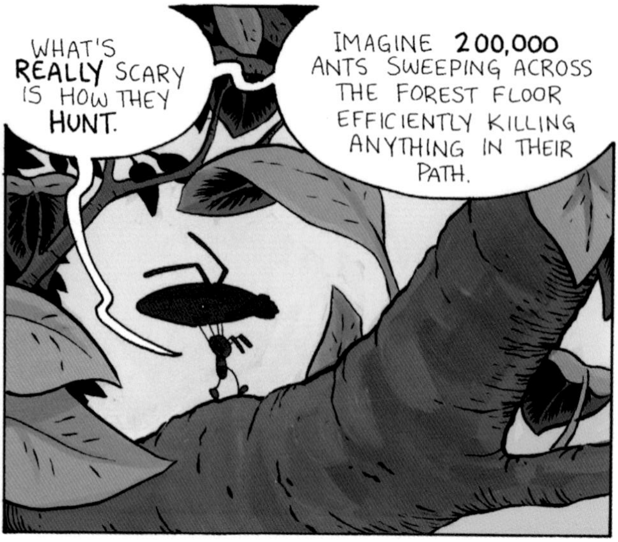
WHAT'S **REALLY** SCARY IS HOW THEY **HUNT**.
IMAGINE **200,000** ANTS SWEEPING ACROSS THE FOREST FLOOR EFFICIENTLY KILLING ANYTHING IN THEIR PATH.

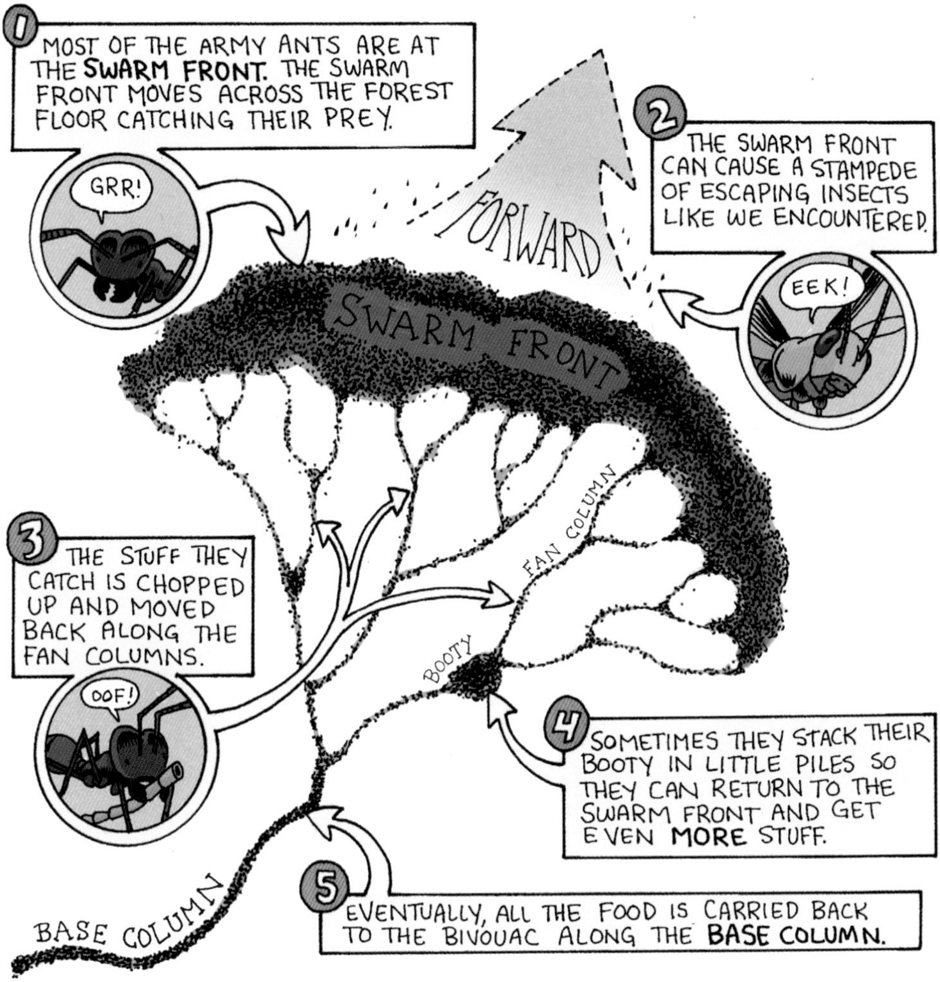
1
MOST OF THE ARMY ANTS ARE AT THE **SWARM FRONT.** THE SWARM FRONT MOVES ACROSS THE FOREST FLOOR CATCHING THEIR PREY.
GRR!
FORWARD
2
THE SWARM FRONT CAN CAUSE A STAMPEDE OF ESCAPING INSECTS LIKE WE ENCOUNTERED.
EEK!
SWARM FRONT
FAN COLUMN
3
THE STUFF THEY CATCH IS CHOPPED UP AND MOVED BACK ALONG THE FAN COLUMNS.
OOF!
BOOTY
4
SOMETIMES THEY STACK THEIR BOOTY IN LITTLE PILES SO THEY CAN RETURN TO THE SWARM FRONT AND GET EVEN **MORE** STUFF.
5
EVENTUALLY, ALL THE FOOD IS CARRIED BACK TO THE BIVOUAC ALONG THE **BASE COLUMN.**
BASE COLUMN

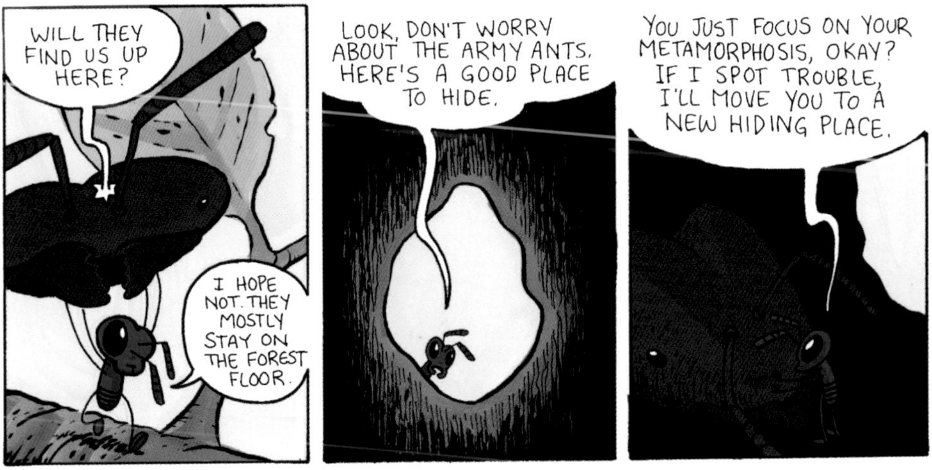
WILL THEY FIND US UP HERE?
I HOPE NOT. THEY MOSTLY STAY ON THE FOREST FLOOR.
LOOK, DON'T WORRY ABOUT THE ARMY ANTS. HERE'S A GOOD PLACE TO HIDE.
YOU JUST FOCUS ON YOUR METAMORPHOSIS, OKAY? IF I SPOT TROUBLE, I'LL MOVE YOU TO A NEW HIDING PLACE.

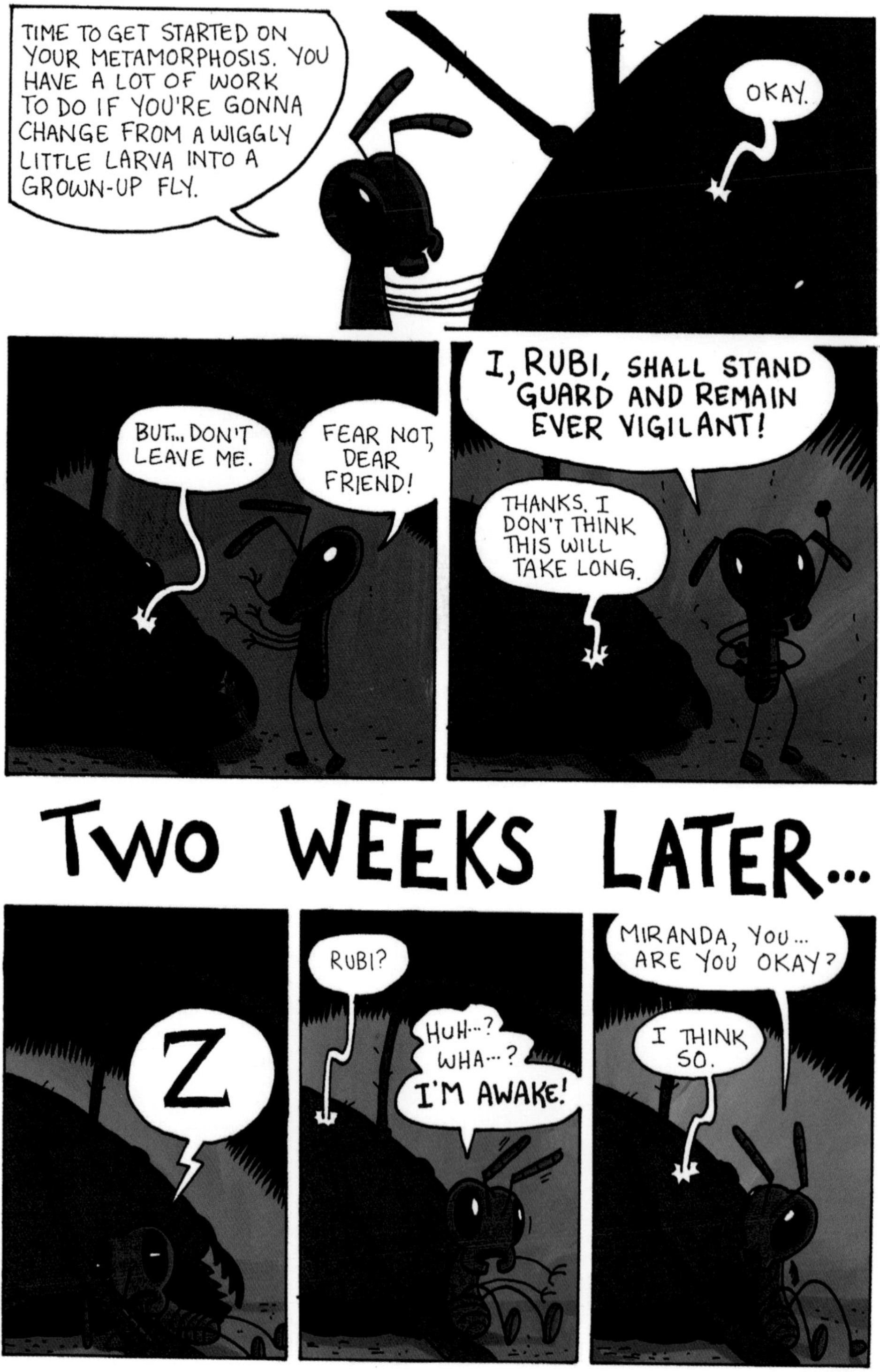
TIME TO GET STARTED ON YOUR METAMORPHOSIS. YOU HAVE A LOT OF WORK TO DO IF YOU'RE GONNA CHANGE FROM A WIGGLY LITTLE LARVA INTO A GROWN-UP FLY.
OKAY.
BUT... DON'T LEAVE ME.
FEAR NOT, DEAR FRIEND!
I, RUBI, SHALL STAND GUARD AND REMAIN EVER VIGILANT!
THANKS. I DON'T THINK THIS WILL TAKE LONG.
TWO WEEKS LATER...
Z
RUBI?
HUH...? WHA...? I'M AWAKE!
MIRANDA, YOU... ARE YOU OKAY?
I THINK SO.

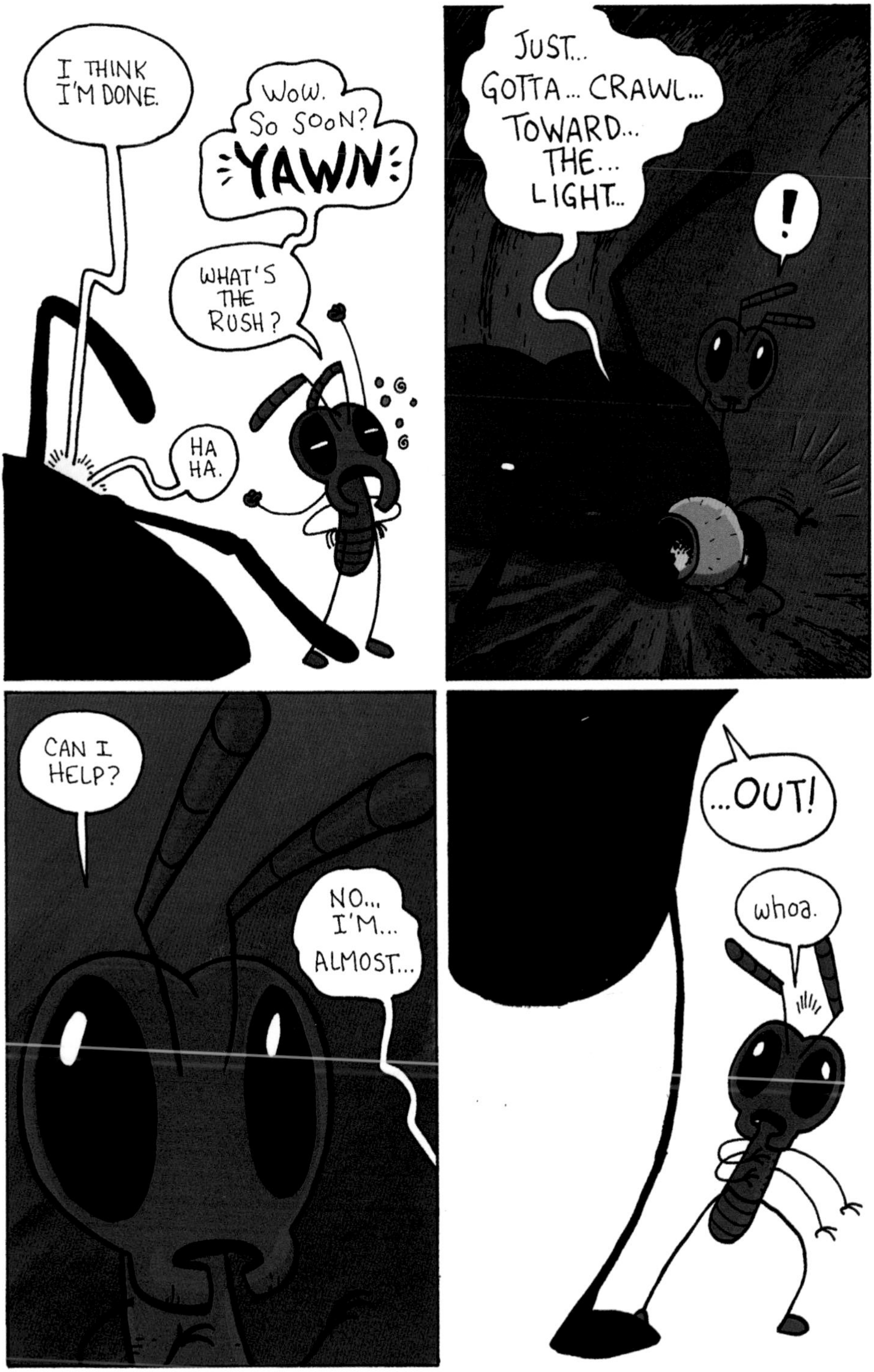
I THINK I'M DONE.
WoW. So SooN? YAWN
WHAT'S THE RUSH?
HA HA.
JUST... GOTTA... CRAWL... TOWARD... THE... LIGHT...
!
CAN I HELP?
NO... I'M... ALMOST...
...OUT!
whoa.

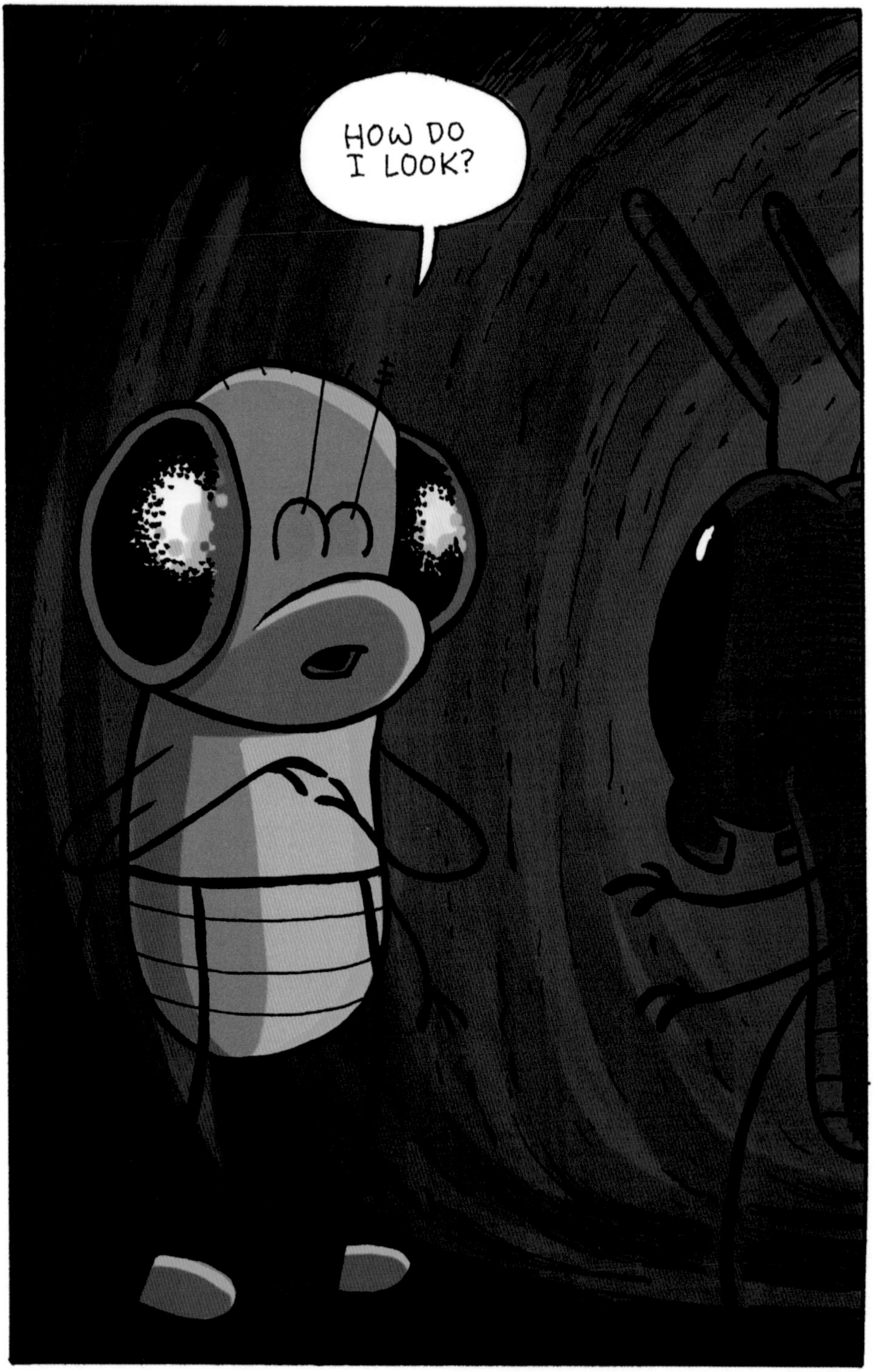
HOW DO I LOOK?

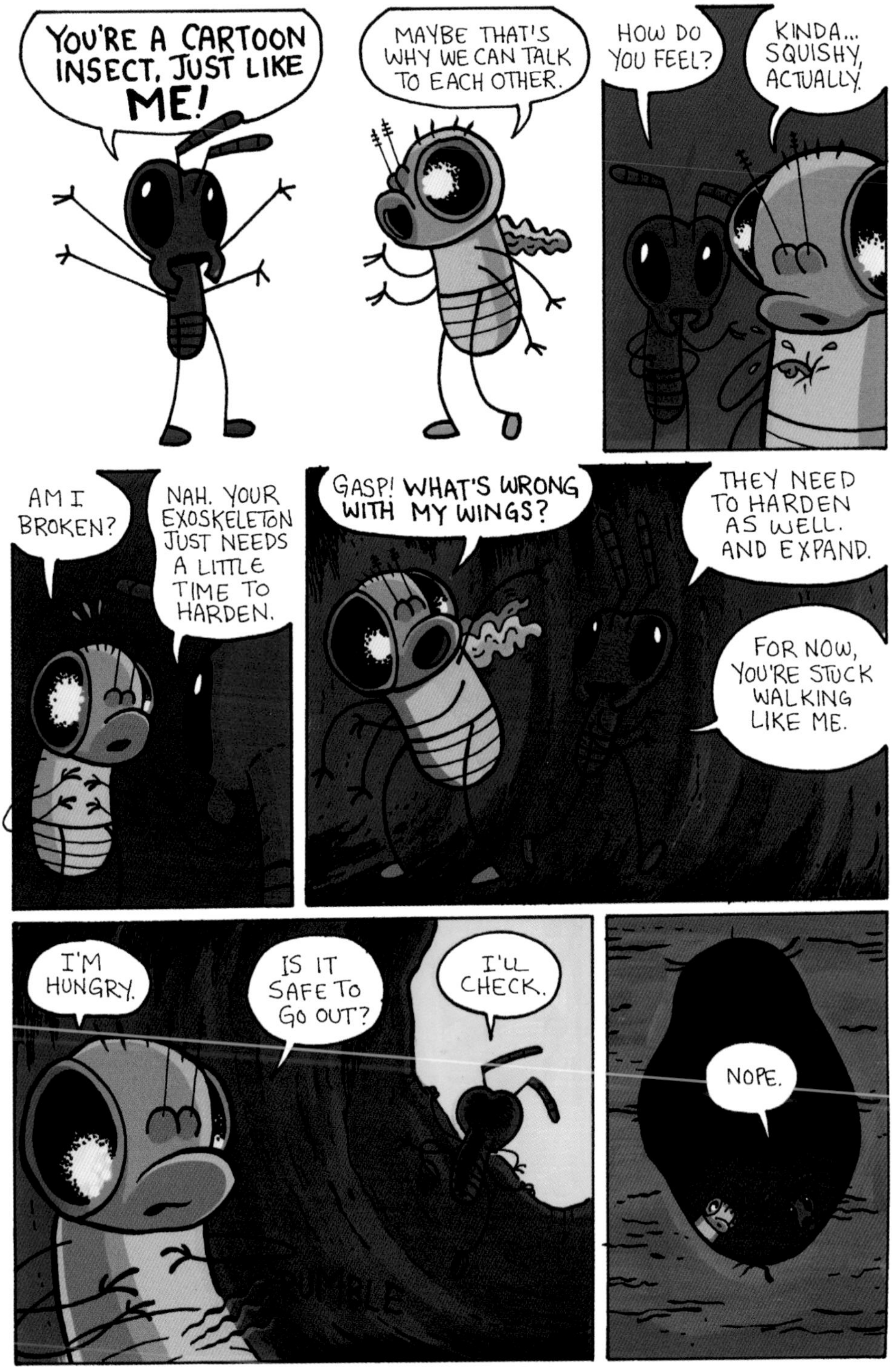
YOU'RE A CARTOON INSECT, JUST LIKE ME!
MAYBE THAT'S WHY WE CAN TALK TO EACH OTHER.
HOW DO YOU FEEL?
KINDA... SQUISHY, ACTUALLY.
AM I BROKEN?
NAH. YOUR EXOSKELETON JUST NEEDS A LITTLE TIME TO HARDEN.
GASP! WHAT'S WRONG WITH MY WINGS?
THEY NEED TO HARDEN AS WELL. AND EXPAND.
FOR NOW, YOU'RE STUCK WALKING LIKE ME.
I'M HUNGRY.
IS IT SAFE TO GO OUT?
I'LL CHECK.
NOPE.

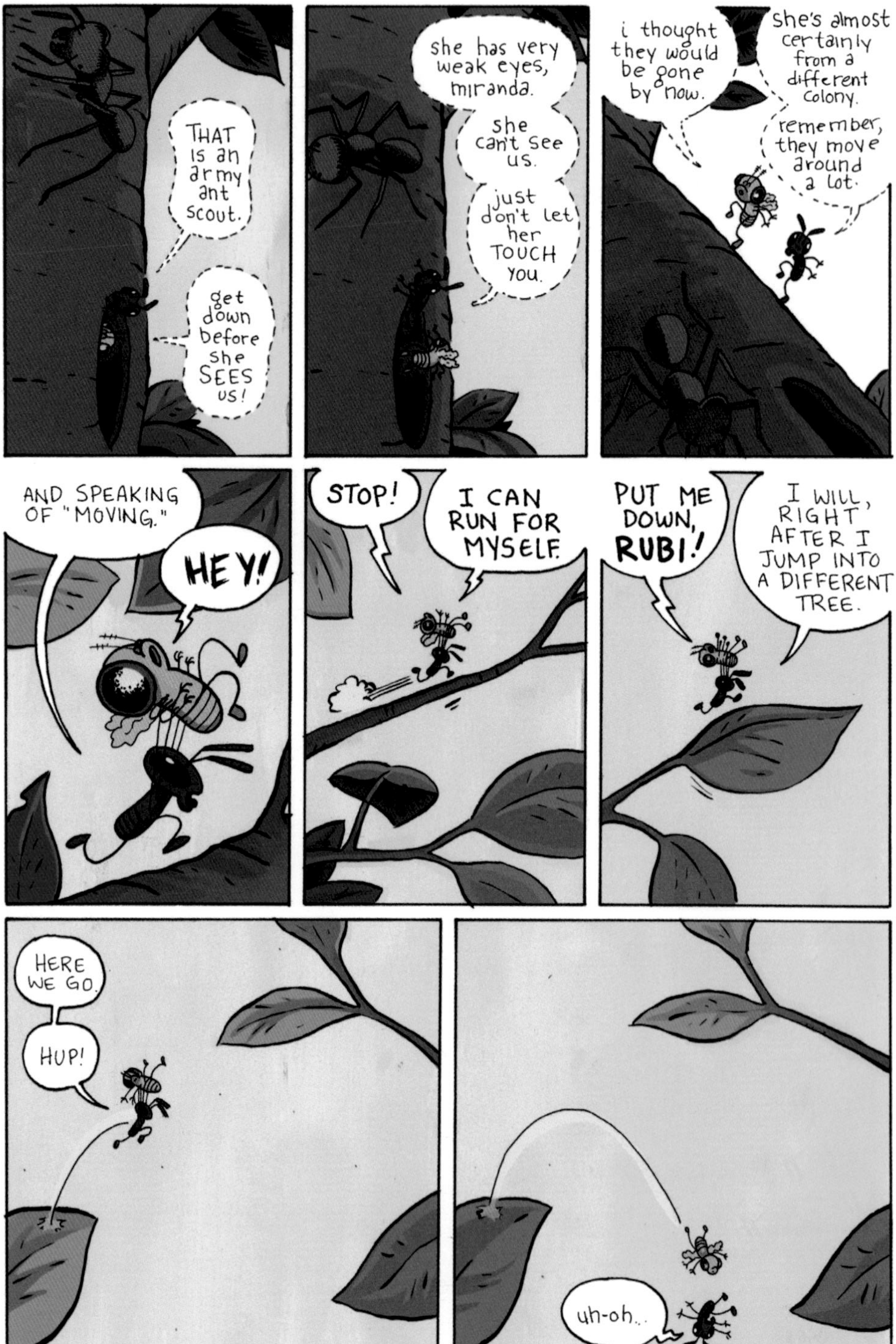
THAT is an army ant scout.
get down before she SEES us!
she has very weak eyes, miranda.
she can't see us.
just don't let her TOUCH you.
i thought they would be gone by now.
she's almost certainly from a different colony.
remember, they move around a lot.
AND SPEAKING OF "MOVING."
HEY!
STOP!
I CAN RUN FOR MYSELF.
PUT ME DOWN, RUBI!
I WILL, RIGHT AFTER I JUMP INTO A DIFFERENT TREE.
HERE WE GO.
HUP!
uh-oh..

DIINK!

HA! I LANDED ON A NICE SQUISHY CATERPILLAR.

YOU GOOD, MIRANDA?

NOT EXACTLY.

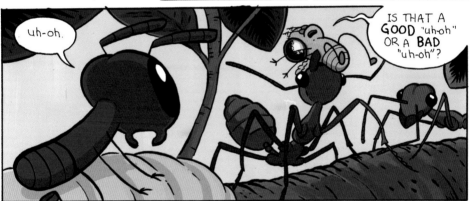

uh-oh.

IS THAT A **GOOD** "uh-oh" OR A **BAD** "uh-oh"?

WEAVER ANTS!

ARE THEY NICE?

NO. THEY SHOULD BE RIPPING US APART.

BUT THEY'RE **NOT.** THEY'RE TAKING US SOMEPLACE.

PROBABLY THAT BIG BUNDLE OF LEAVES SEWN TOGETHER WITH WHITE SILK.

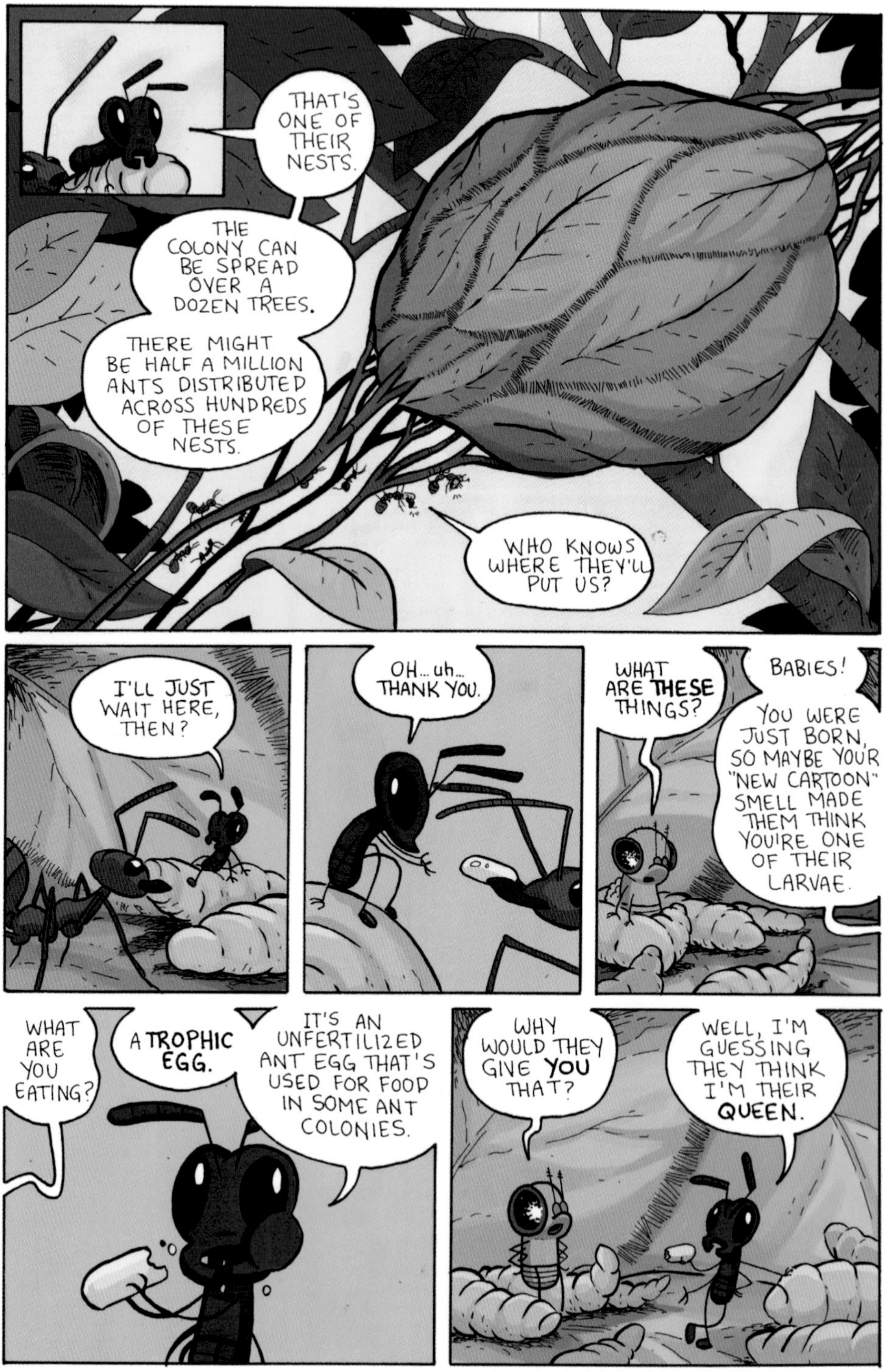
THAT'S ONE OF THEIR NESTS.
THE COLONY CAN BE SPREAD OVER A DOZEN TREES.
THERE MIGHT BE HALF A MILLION ANTS DISTRIBUTED ACROSS HUNDREDS OF THESE NESTS.
WHO KNOWS WHERE THEY'LL PUT US?
I'LL JUST WAIT HERE, THEN?
OH... uh... THANK YOU.
WHAT ARE **THESE** THINGS?
BABIES!
YOU WERE JUST BORN, SO MAYBE YOUR "NEW CARTOON" SMELL MADE THEM THINK YOU'RE ONE OF THEIR LARVAE.
WHAT ARE YOU EATING?
A **TROPHIC EGG.**
IT'S AN UNFERTILIZED ANT EGG THAT'S USED FOR FOOD IN SOME ANT COLONIES.
WHY WOULD THEY GIVE **YOU** THAT?
WELL, I'M GUESSING THEY THINK I'M THEIR **QUEEN.**

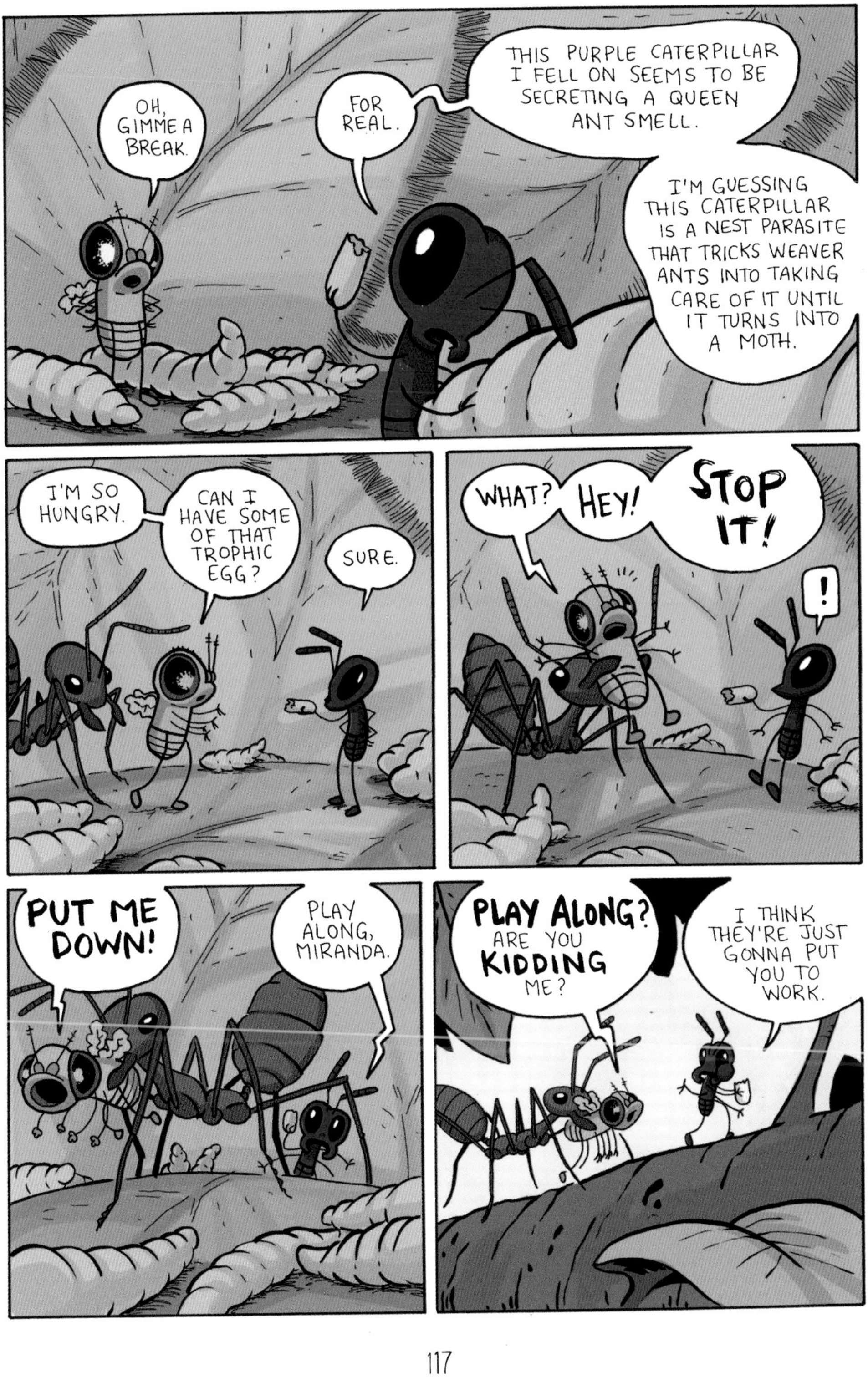
OH, GIMME A BREAK.
FOR REAL.
THIS PURPLE CATERPILLAR I FELL ON SEEMS TO BE SECRETING A QUEEN ANT SMELL.
I'M GUESSING THIS CATERPILLAR IS A NEST PARASITE THAT TRICKS WEAVER ANTS INTO TAKING CARE OF IT UNTIL IT TURNS INTO A MOTH.
I'M SO HUNGRY.
CAN I HAVE SOME OF THAT TROPHIC EGG?
SURE.
WHAT?
HEY!
STOP IT!
!
PUT ME DOWN!
PLAY ALONG, MIRANDA.
PLAY ALONG? ARE YOU KIDDING ME?
I THINK THEY'RE JUST GONNA PUT YOU TO WORK.

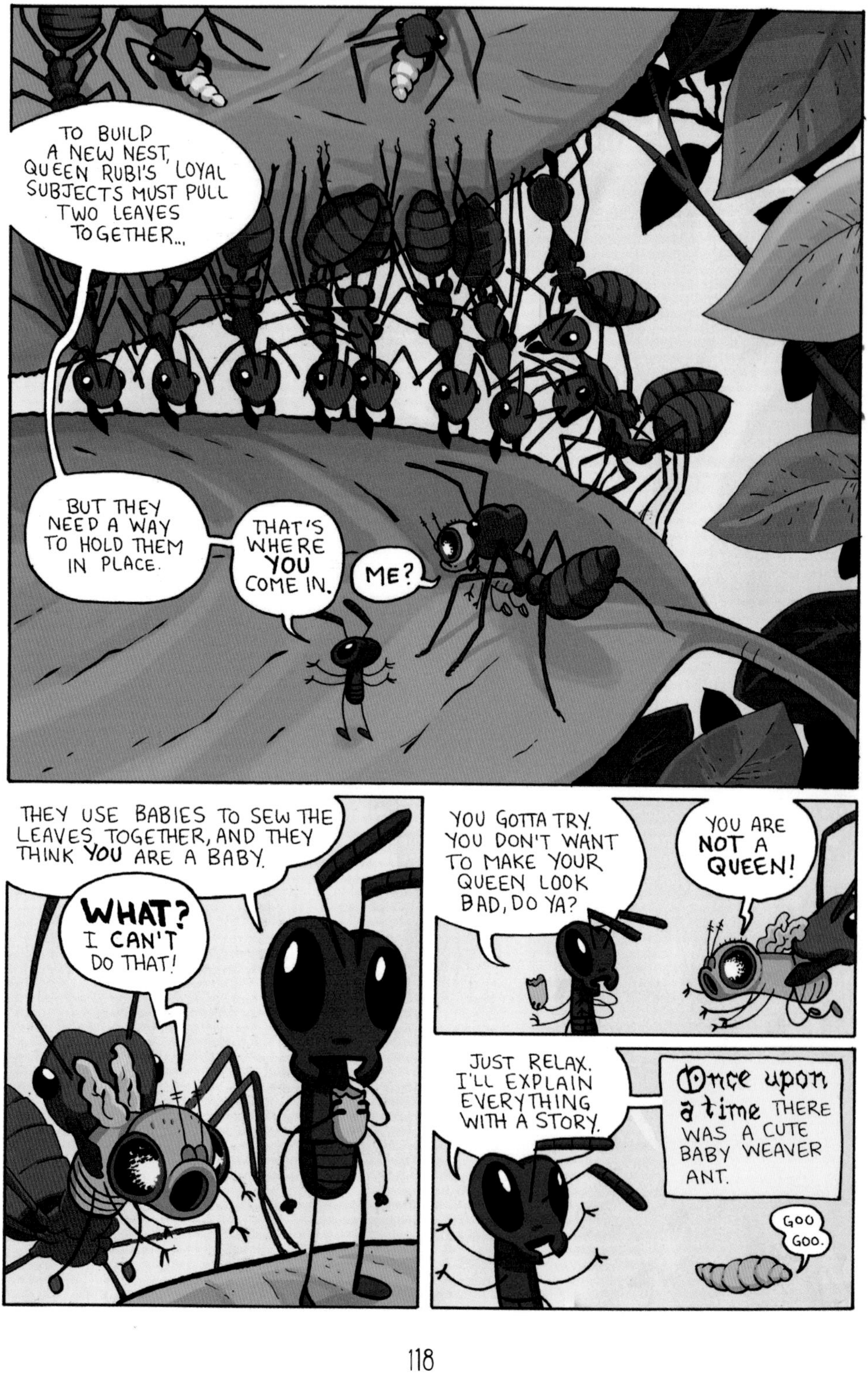
TO BUILD A NEW NEST, QUEEN RUBI'S LOYAL SUBJECTS MUST PULL TWO LEAVES TOGETHER...
BUT THEY NEED A WAY TO HOLD THEM IN PLACE.
THAT'S WHERE YOU COME IN.
ME?
THEY USE BABIES TO SEW THE LEAVES TOGETHER, AND THEY THINK YOU ARE A BABY.
WHAT? I CAN'T DO THAT!
YOU GOTTA TRY. YOU DON'T WANT TO MAKE YOUR QUEEN LOOK BAD, DO YA?
YOU ARE NOT A QUEEN!
JUST RELAX. I'LL EXPLAIN EVERYTHING WITH A STORY.
Once upon a time THERE WAS A CUTE BABY WEAVER ANT.
GOO GOO.

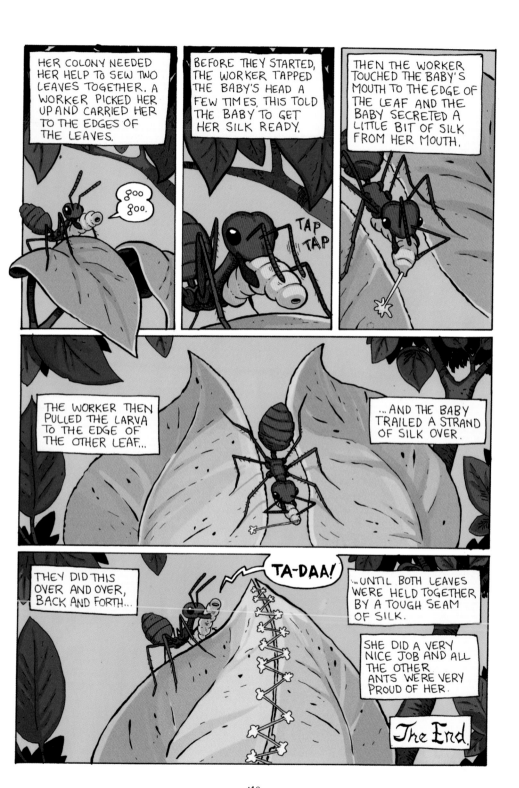

HER COLONY NEEDED HER HELP TO SEW TWO LEAVES TOGETHER. A WORKER PICKED HER UP AND CARRIED HER TO THE EDGES OF THE LEAVES.

goo goo.

BEFORE THEY STARTED, THE WORKER TAPPED THE BABY'S HEAD A FEW TIMES, THIS TOLD THE BABY TO GET HER SILK READY.

TAP TAP

THEN THE WORKER TOUCHED THE BABY'S MOUTH TO THE EDGE OF THE LEAF AND THE BABY SECRETED A LITTLE BIT OF SILK FROM HER MOUTH.

THE WORKER THEN PULLED THE LARVA TO THE EDGE OF THE OTHER LEAF...

...AND THE BABY TRAILED A STRAND OF SILK OVER.

THEY DID THIS OVER AND OVER, BACK AND FORTH...

TA-DAA!

...UNTIL BOTH LEAVES WERE HELD TOGETHER BY A TOUGH SEAM OF SILK.

SHE DID A VERY NICE JOB AND ALL THE OTHER ANTS WERE VERY PROUD OF HER.

The End.

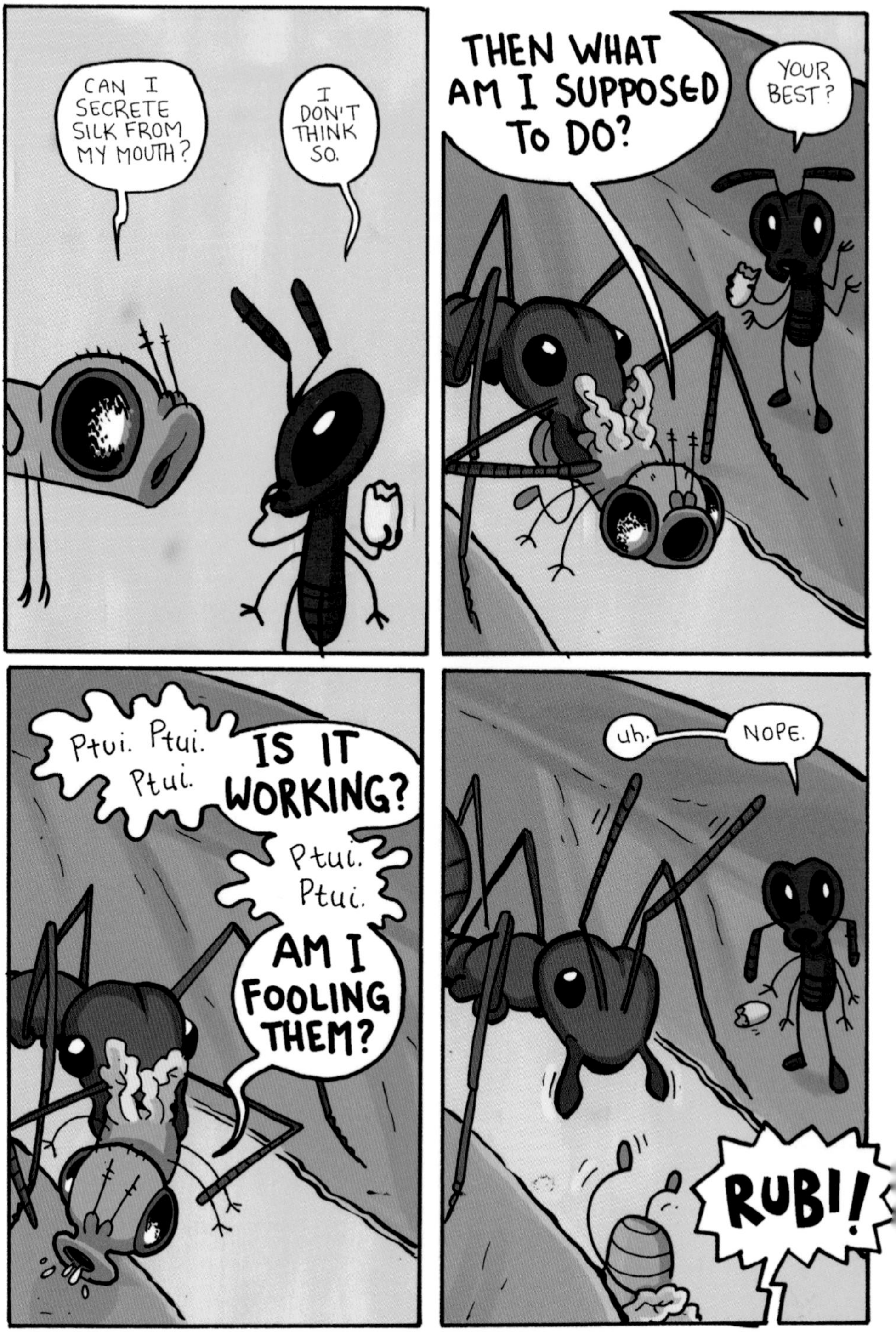
CAN I SECRETE SILK FROM MY MOUTH?
I DON'T THINK SO.
THEN WHAT AM I SUPPOSED TO DO?
YOUR BEST?
Ptui. Ptui. Ptui.
IS IT WORKING?
Ptui. Ptui.
AM I FOOLING THEM?
uh.
NOPE.
RUBI!

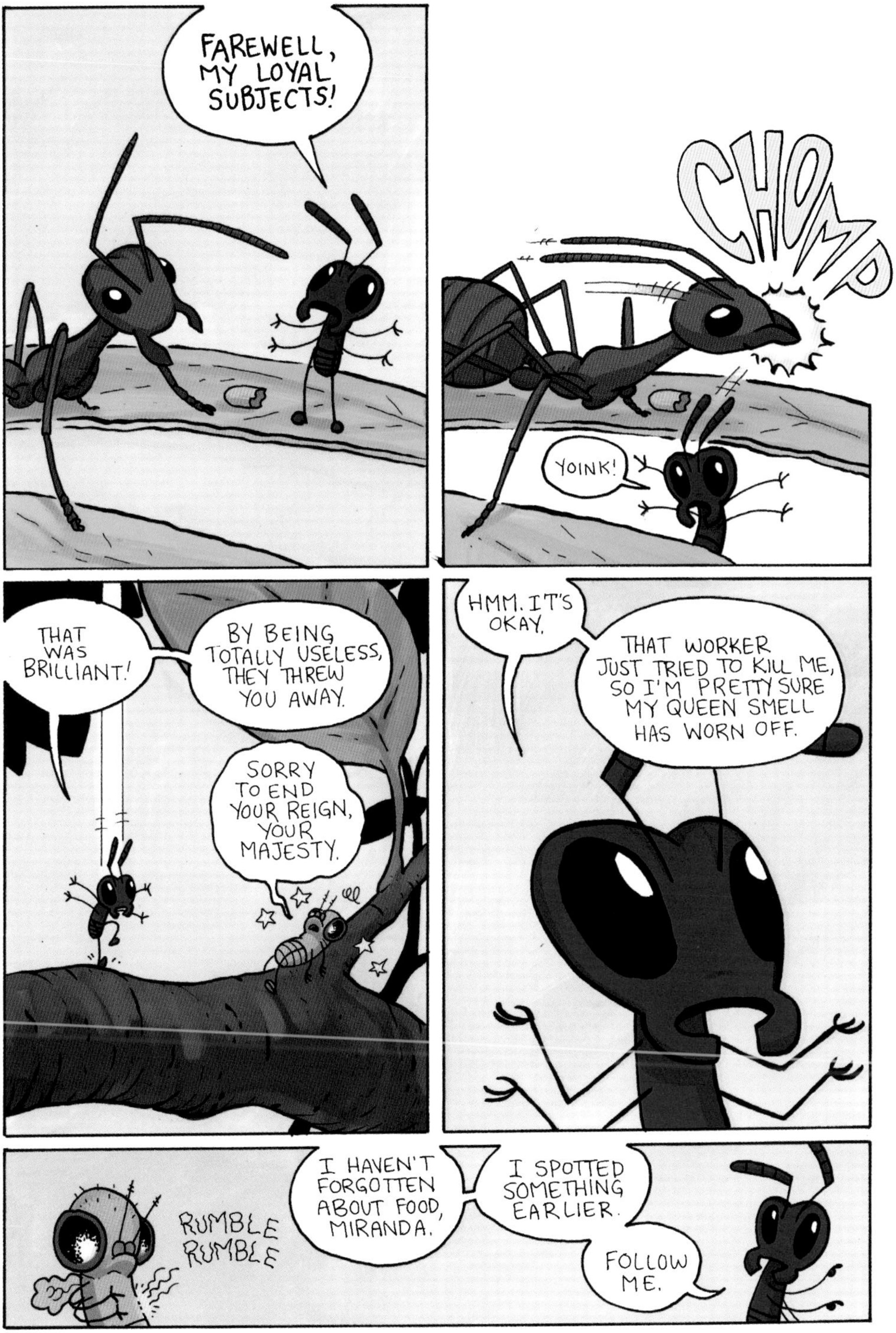
FAREWELL, MY LOYAL SUBJECTS!
CHOMP
YOINK!
THAT WAS BRILLIANT!
BY BEING TOTALLY USELESS, THEY THREW YOU AWAY.
SORRY TO END YOUR REIGN, YOUR MAJESTY.
HMM. IT'S OKAY.
THAT WORKER JUST TRIED TO KILL ME, SO I'M PRETTY SURE MY QUEEN SMELL HAS WORN OFF.
RUMBLE RUMBLE
I HAVEN'T FORGOTTEN ABOUT FOOD, MIRANDA.
I SPOTTED SOMETHING EARLIER.
FOLLOW ME.

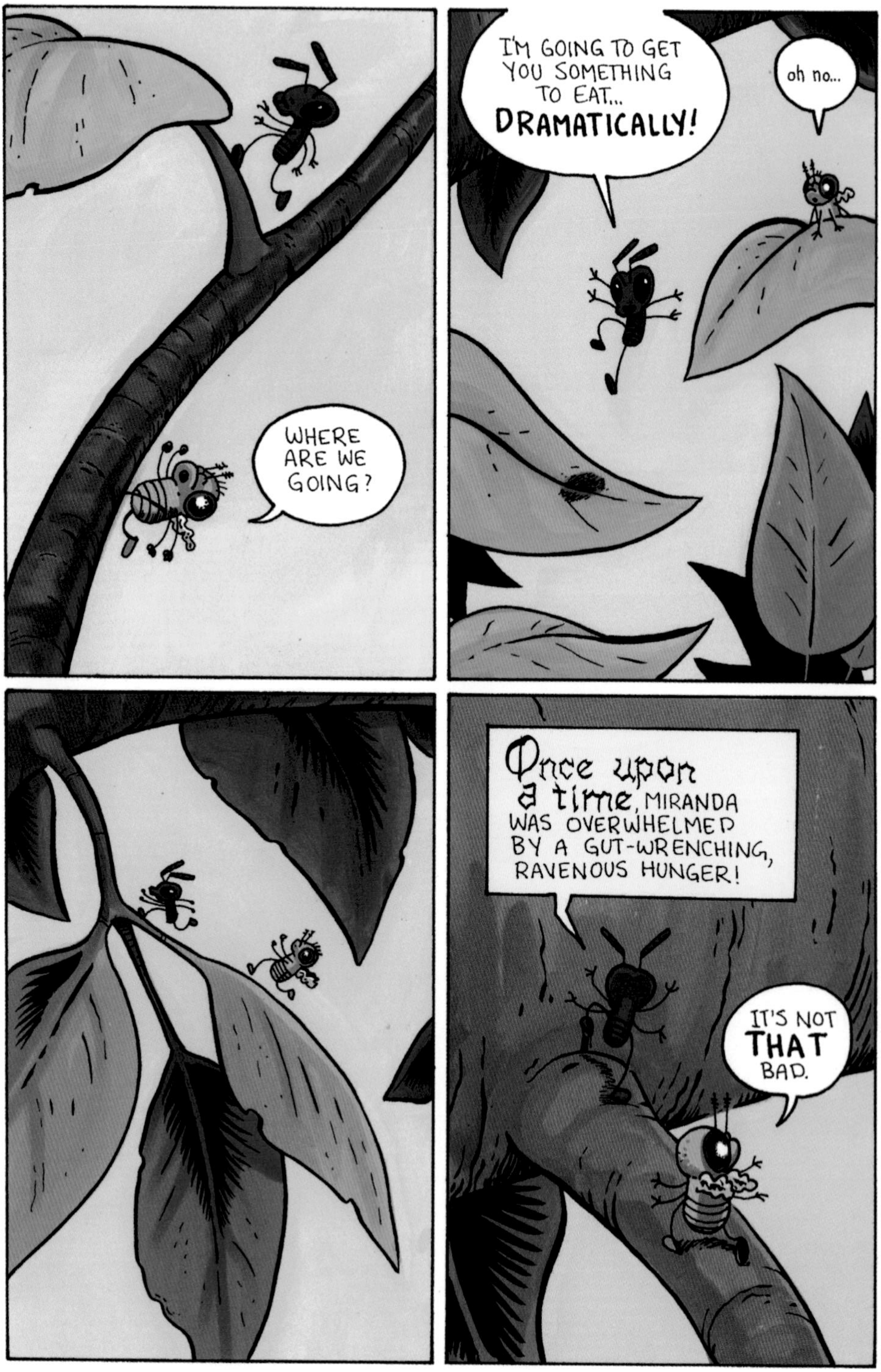
WHERE ARE WE GOING?
I'M GOING TO GET YOU SOMETHING TO EAT... DRAMATICALLY!
oh no...
Once upon a time, MIRANDA WAS OVERWHELMED BY A GUT-WRENCHING, RAVENOUS HUNGER!
IT'S NOT THAT BAD.

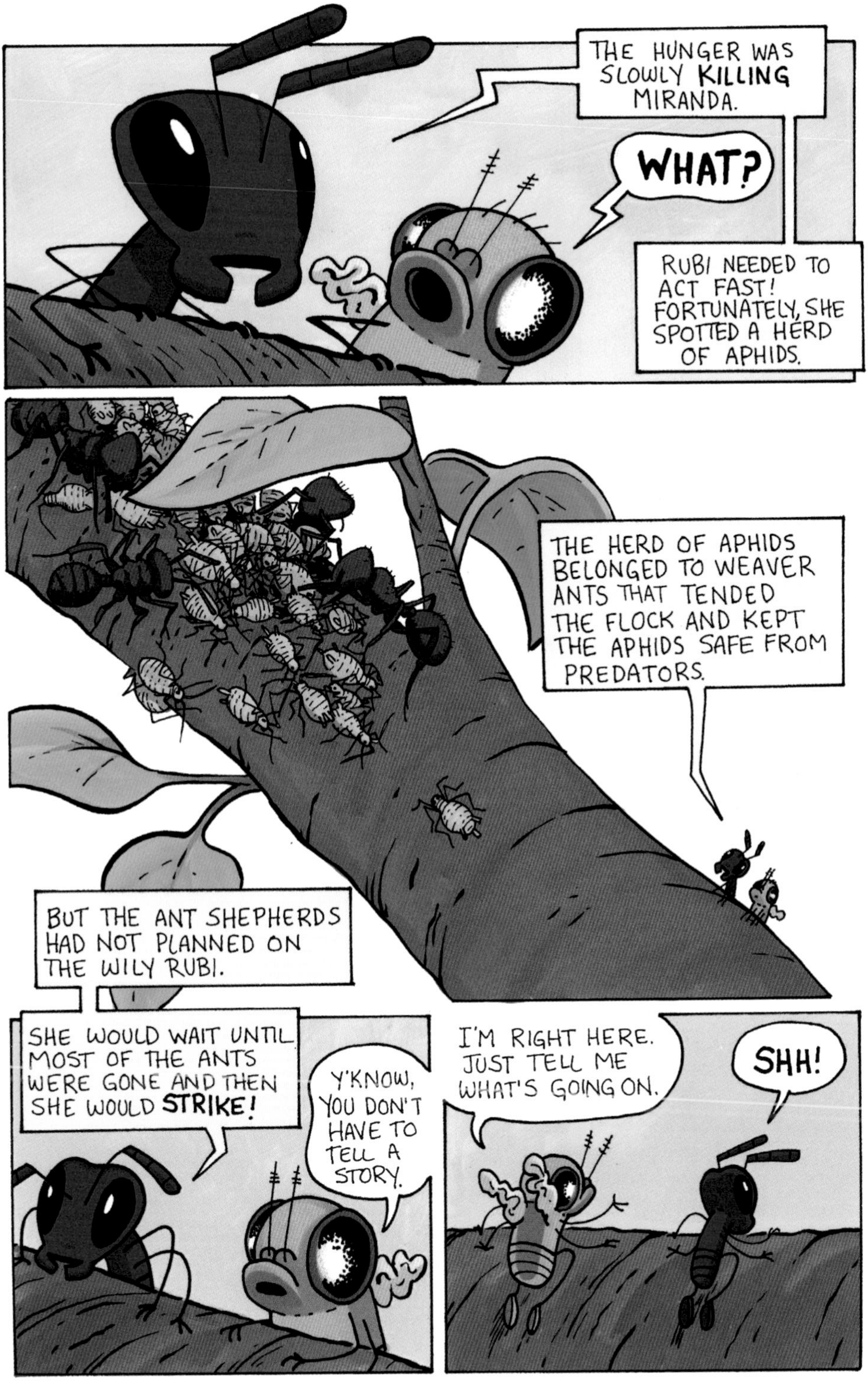

THE HUNGER WAS SLOWLY **KILLING** MIRANDA.
WHAT?
RUBI NEEDED TO ACT FAST! FORTUNATELY, SHE SPOTTED A HERD OF APHIDS.
THE HERD OF APHIDS BELONGED TO WEAVER ANTS THAT TENDED THE FLOCK AND KEPT THE APHIDS SAFE FROM PREDATORS.
BUT THE ANT SHEPHERDS HAD NOT PLANNED ON THE WILY RUBI.
SHE WOULD WAIT UNTIL MOST OF THE ANTS WERE GONE AND THEN SHE WOULD **STRIKE!**
Y'KNOW, YOU DON'T HAVE TO TELL A STORY.
I'M RIGHT HERE. JUST TELL ME WHAT'S GOING ON.
SHH!

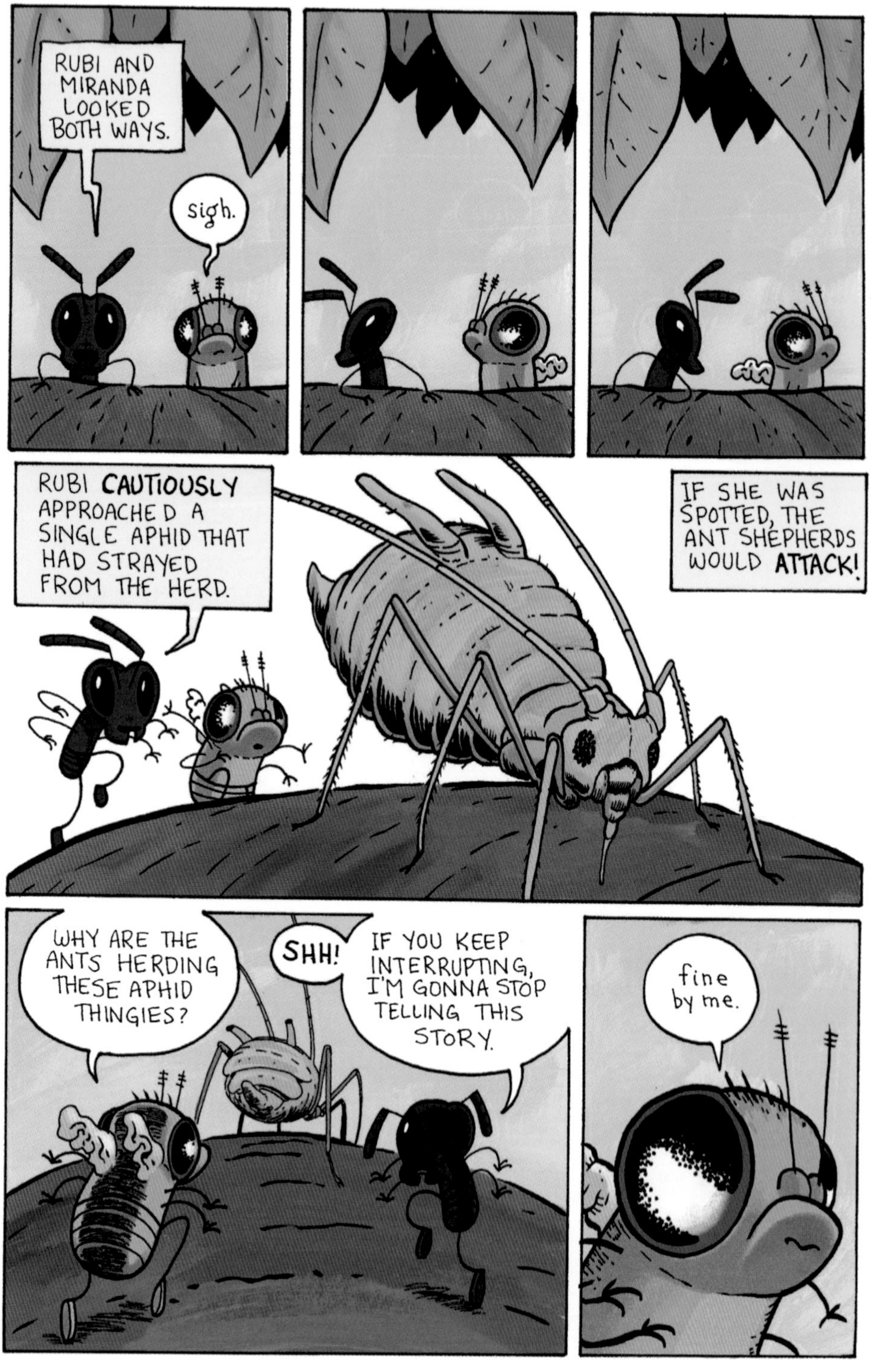
RUBI AND MIRANDA LOOKED BOTH WAYS.
sigh.
RUBI **CAUTIOUSLY** APPROACHED A SINGLE APHID THAT HAD STRAYED FROM THE HERD.
IF SHE WAS SPOTTED, THE ANT SHEPHERDS WOULD **ATTACK!**
WHY ARE THE ANTS HERDING THESE APHID THINGIES?
SHH!
IF YOU KEEP INTERRUPTING, I'M GONNA STOP TELLING THIS STORY.
fine by me.

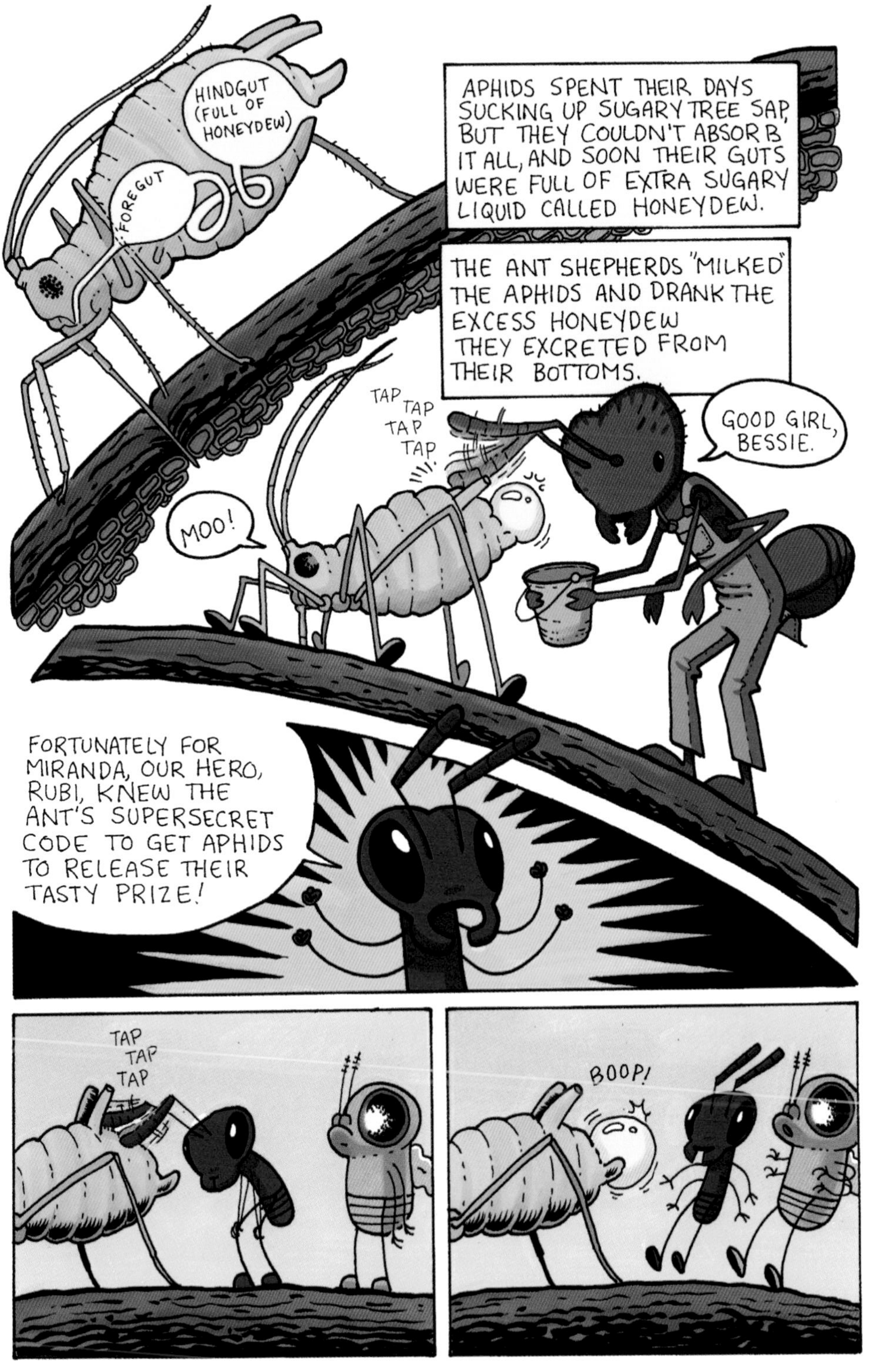
HINDGUT (FULL OF HONEYDEW)
FOREGUT
APHIDS SPENT THEIR DAYS SUCKING UP SUGARY TREE SAP, BUT THEY COULDN'T ABSORB IT ALL, AND SOON THEIR GUTS WERE FULL OF EXTRA SUGARY LIQUID CALLED HONEYDEW.
THE ANT SHEPHERDS "MILKED" THE APHIDS AND DRANK THE EXCESS HONEYDEW THEY EXCRETED FROM THEIR BOTTOMS.
TAP TAP TAP TAP
GOOD GIRL, BESSIE.
MOO!
FORTUNATELY FOR MIRANDA, OUR HERO, RUBI, KNEW THE ANT'S SUPERSECRET CODE TO GET APHIDS TO RELEASE THEIR TASTY PRIZE!
TAP TAP TAP
BOOP!

RUBI TURNED TO HER **STARVING** FRIEND. MIRANDA ONLY HAD **MOMENTS** TO LIVE.

You are ridiculous.

SHE HAD TO DRINK **NOW** OR THIS WOULD BE *The End!*

whatever.

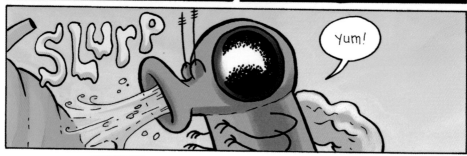

SLURP

Yum!

YOU GONNA HAVE SOME?

NO WAY. THAT STUFF CAME OUT OF ITS **BUTT. GROSS.**

WHA-? THEN WHY DID YOU HAVE **ME DRINK IT???**

I THOUGHT IT WOULD BE A HILARIOUS PRANK.

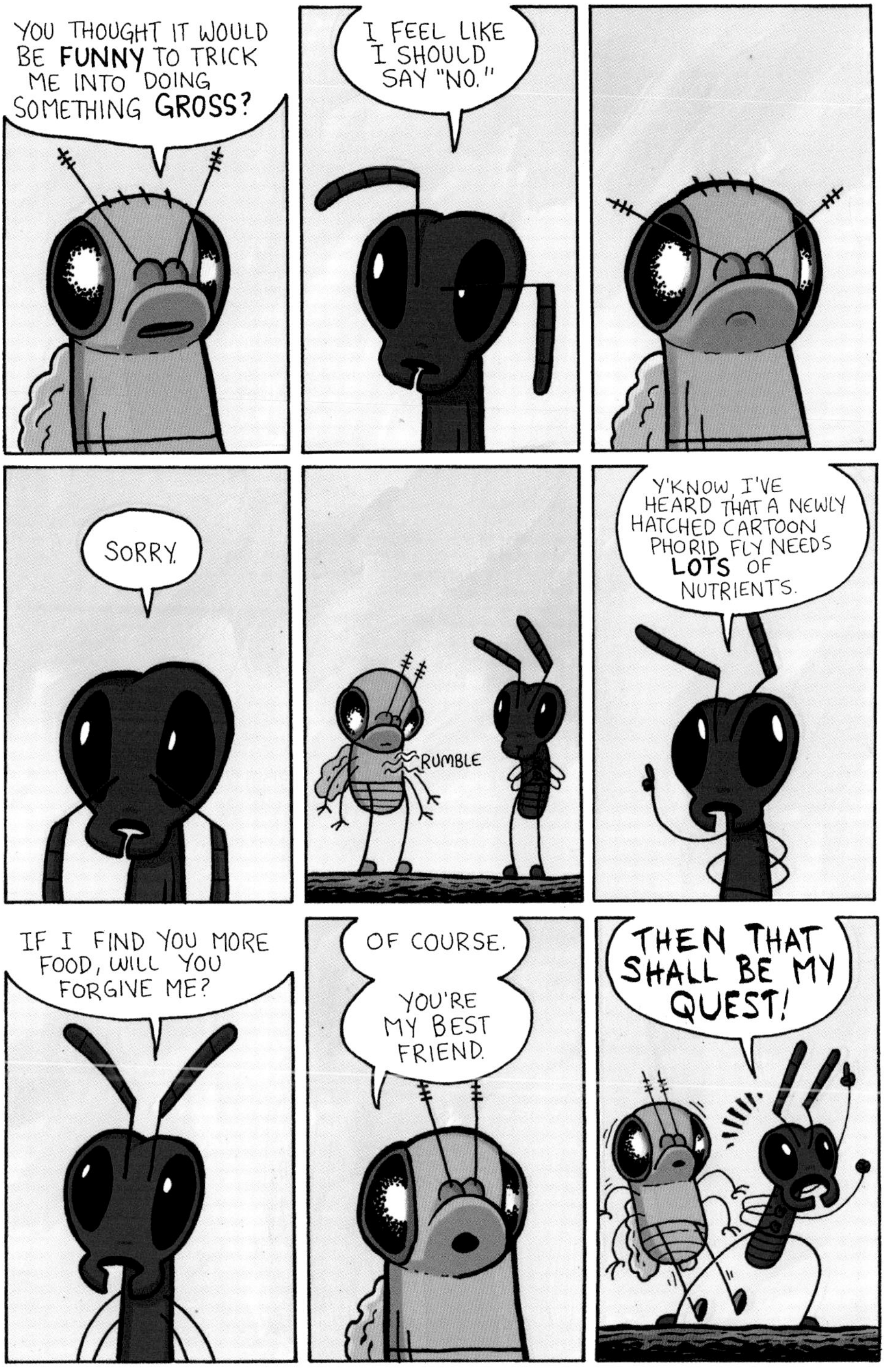
YOU THOUGHT IT WOULD BE FUNNY TO TRICK ME INTO DOING SOMETHING GROSS?
I FEEL LIKE I SHOULD SAY "NO."
SORRY.
RUMBLE
Y'KNOW, I'VE HEARD THAT A NEWLY HATCHED CARTOON PHORID FLY NEEDS LOTS OF NUTRIENTS.
IF I FIND YOU MORE FOOD, WILL YOU FORGIVE ME?
OF COURSE.
YOU'RE MY BEST FRIEND.
THEN THAT SHALL BE MY QUEST!

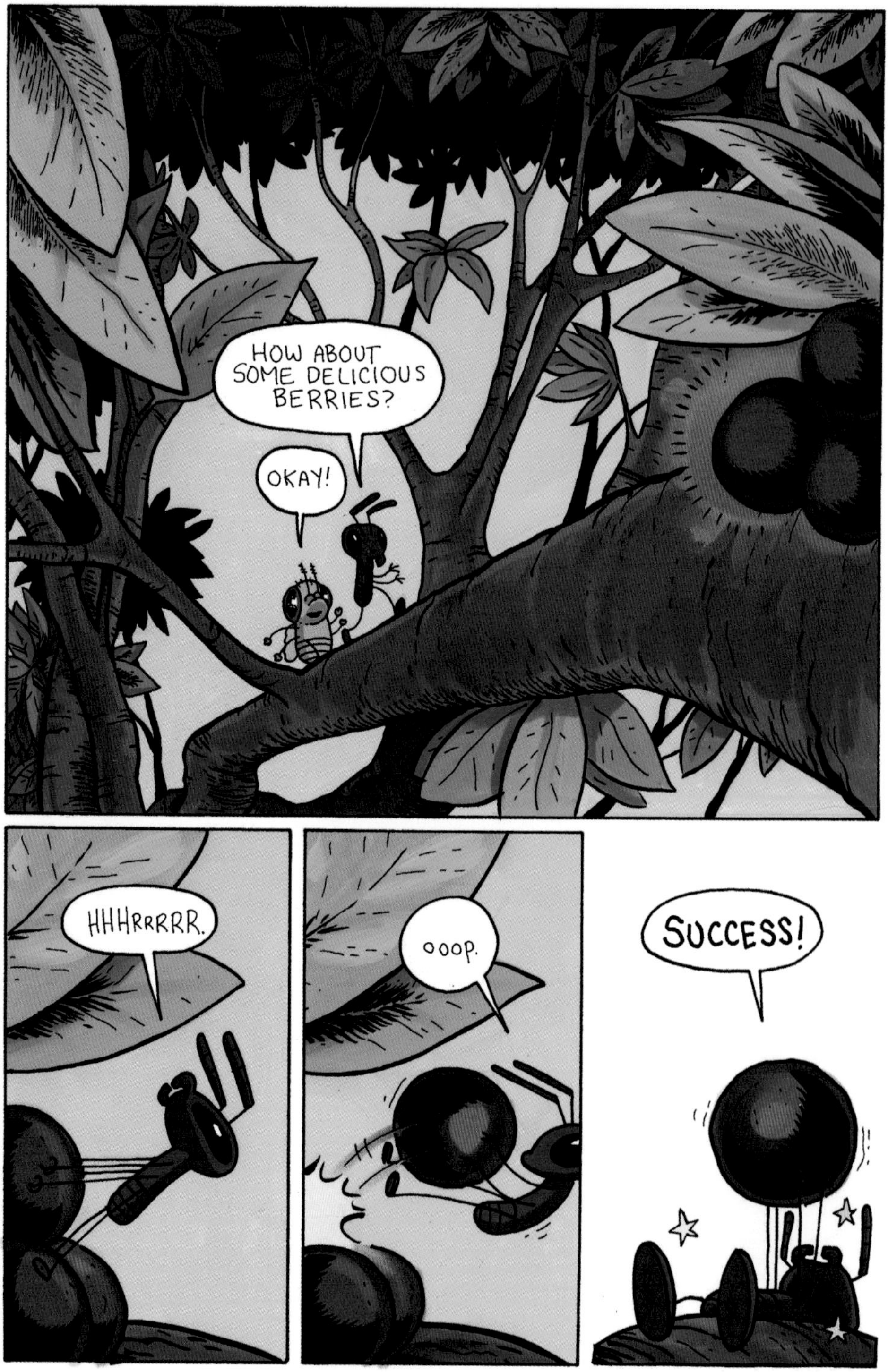
HOW ABOUT SOME DELICIOUS BERRIES?
OKAY!
HHHRRRRR.
ooop.
SUCCESS!

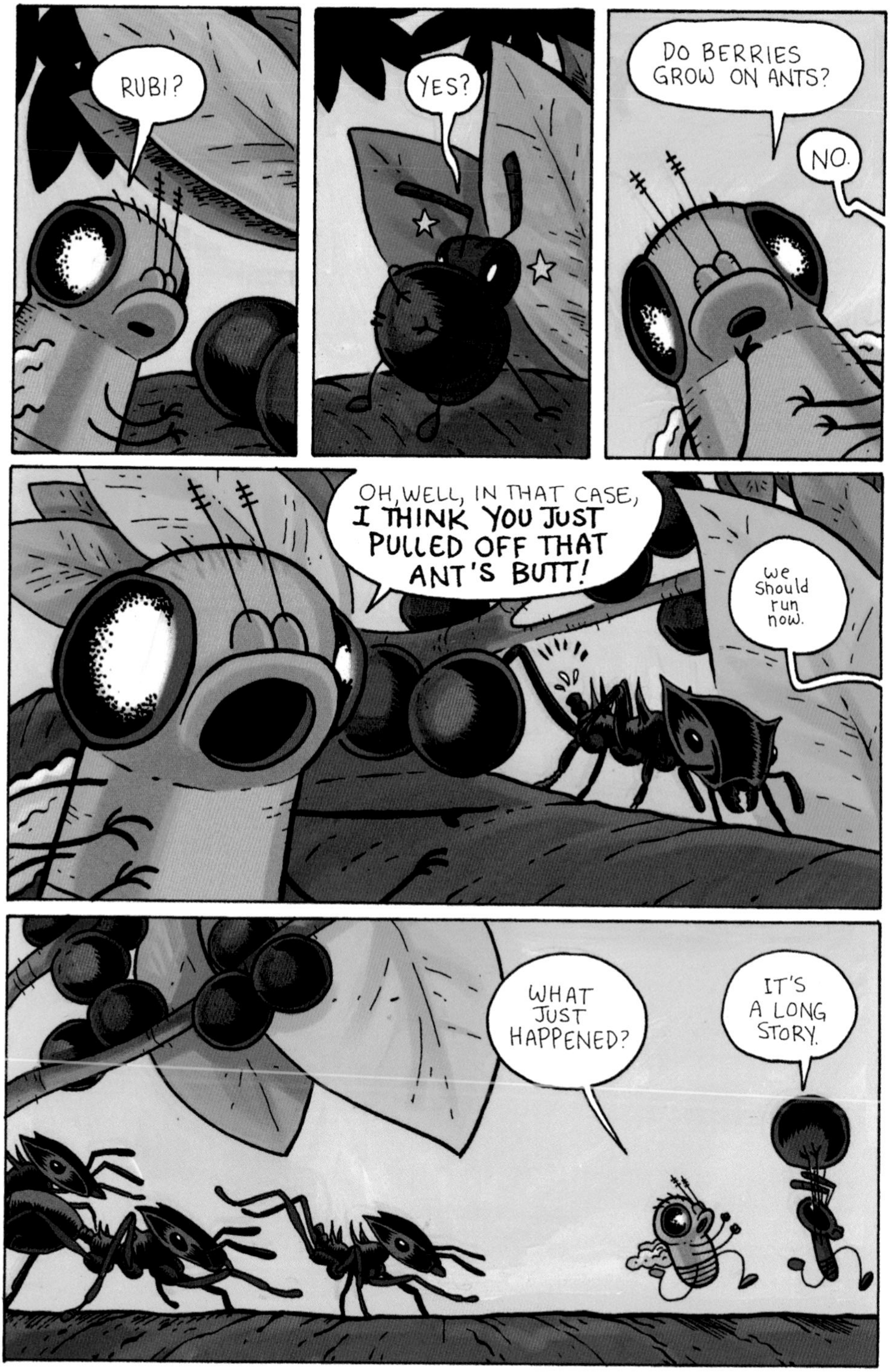
RUBI?
YES?
DO BERRIES GROW ON ANTS?
NO.
OH, WELL, IN THAT CASE, I THINK YOU JUST PULLED OFF THAT ANT'S BUTT!
we should run now.
WHAT JUST HAPPENED?
IT'S A LONG STORY.

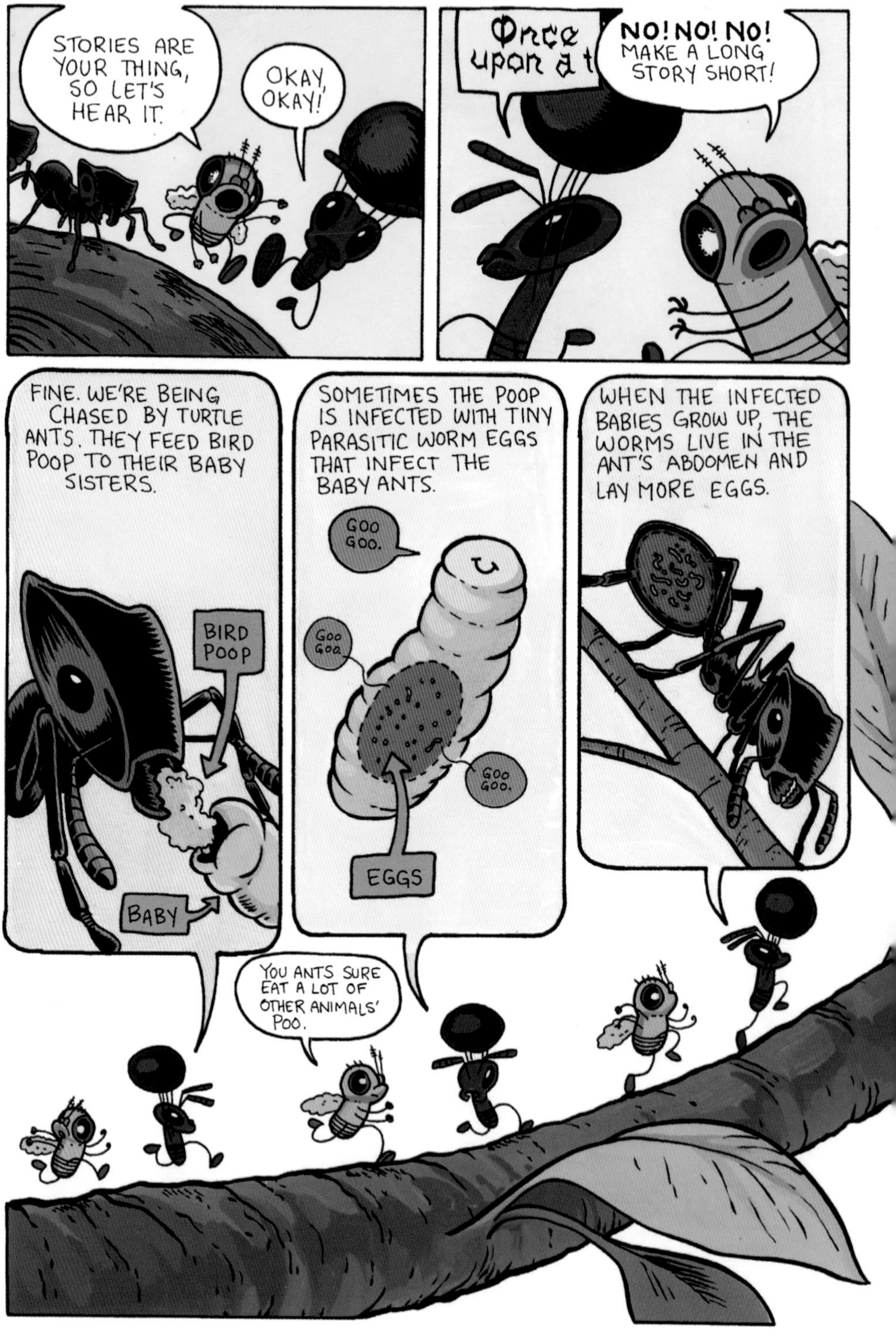
STORIES ARE YOUR THING, SO LET'S HEAR IT.
OKAY, OKAY!
Once upon a t
NO! NO! NO! MAKE A LONG STORY SHORT!
FINE. WE'RE BEING CHASED BY TURTLE ANTS. THEY FEED BIRD POOP TO THEIR BABY SISTERS.
BIRD POOP
BABY
SOMETIMES THE POOP IS INFECTED WITH TINY PARASITIC WORM EGGS THAT INFECT THE BABY ANTS.
GOO GOO.
GOO GOO.
GOO GOO.
EGGS
WHEN THE INFECTED BABIES GROW UP, THE WORMS LIVE IN THE ANT'S ABDOMEN AND LAY MORE EGGS.
YOU ANTS SURE EAT A LOT OF OTHER ANIMALS' POO.

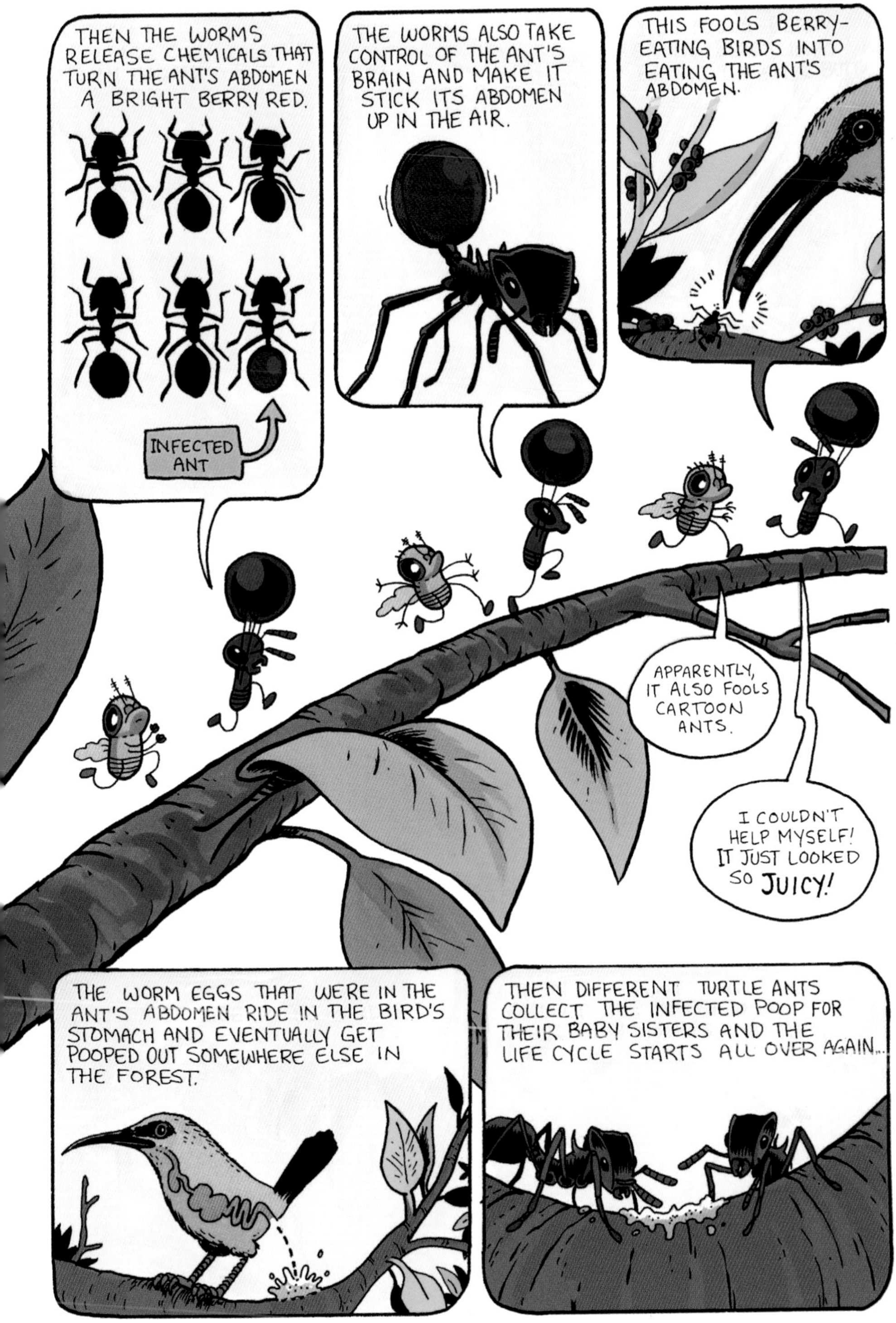
THEN THE WORMS RELEASE CHEMICALS THAT TURN THE ANT'S ABDOMEN A BRIGHT BERRY RED.
INFECTED ANT
THE WORMS ALSO TAKE CONTROL OF THE ANT'S BRAIN AND MAKE IT STICK ITS ABDOMEN UP IN THE AIR.
THIS FOOLS BERRY-EATING BIRDS INTO EATING THE ANT'S ABDOMEN.
APPARENTLY, IT ALSO FOOLS CARTOON ANTS.
I COULDN'T HELP MYSELF! IT JUST LOOKED SO JUICY!
THE WORM EGGS THAT WERE IN THE ANT'S ABDOMEN RIDE IN THE BIRD'S STOMACH AND EVENTUALLY GET POOPED OUT SOMEWHERE ELSE IN THE FOREST.
THEN DIFFERENT TURTLE ANTS COLLECT THE INFECTED POOP FOR THEIR BABY SISTERS AND THE LIFE CYCLE STARTS ALL OVER AGAIN...

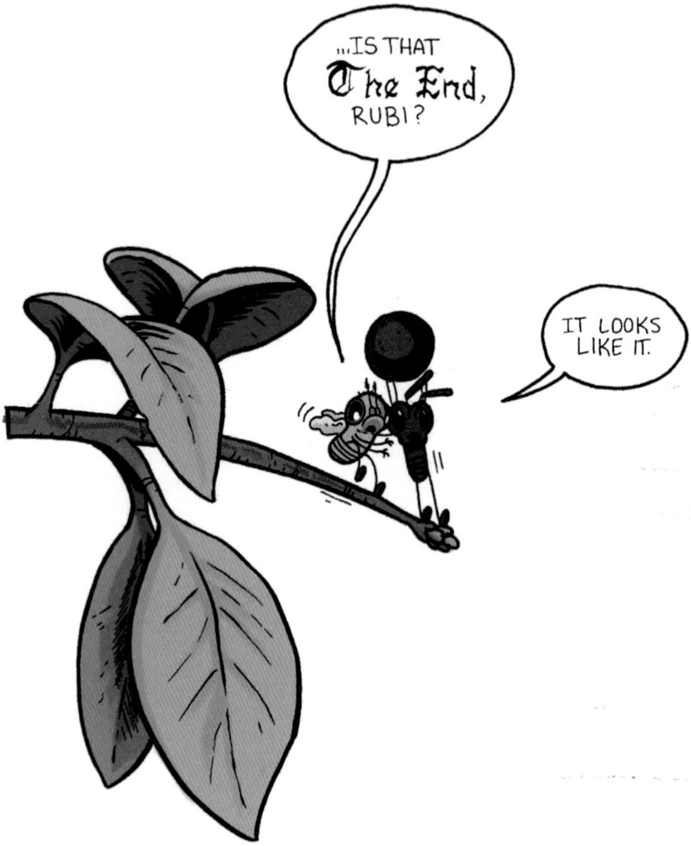
...IS THAT The End, RUBI?
IT LOOKS LIKE IT.

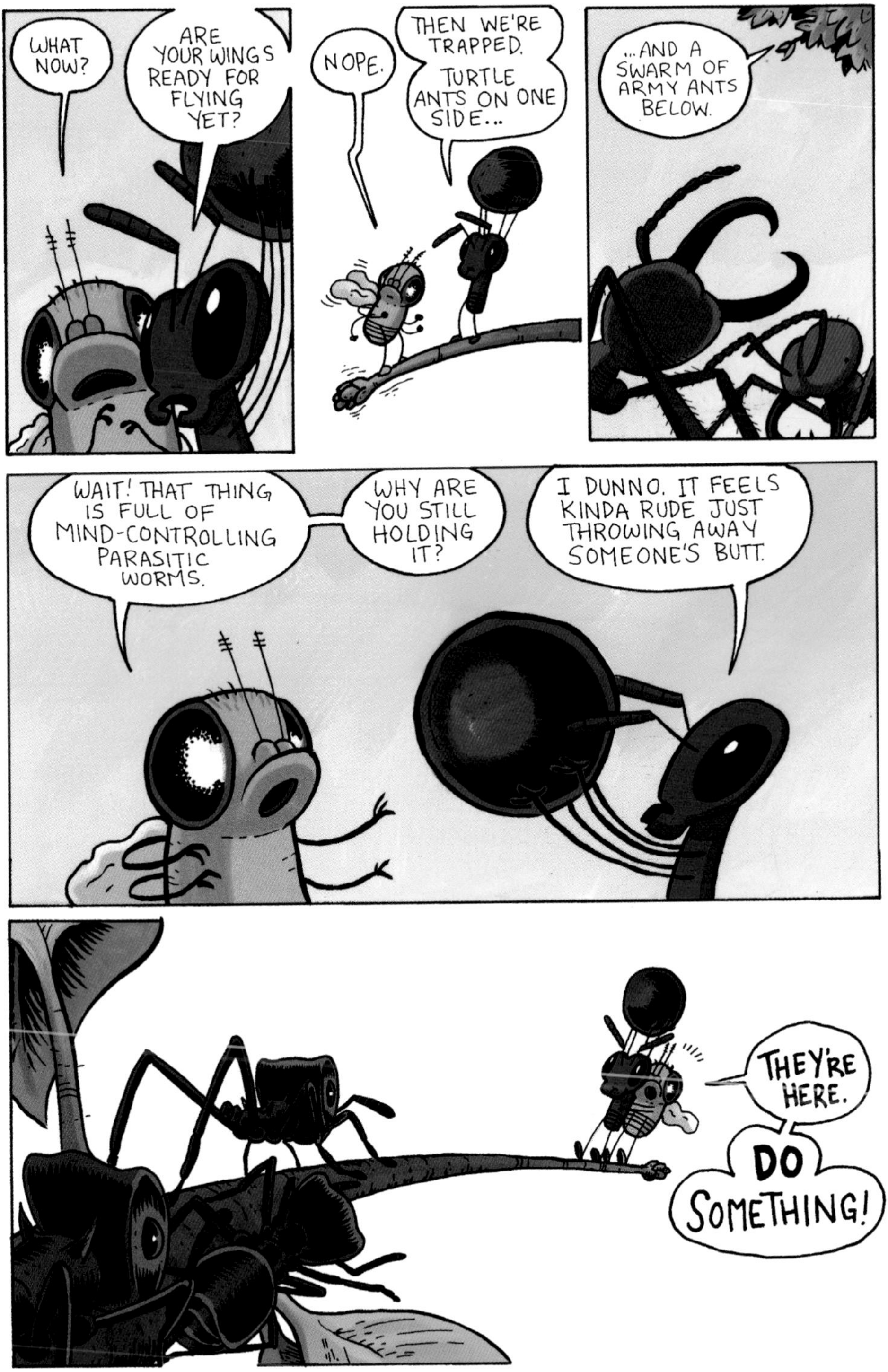
WHAT NOW?
ARE YOUR WINGS READY FOR FLYING YET?
NOPE.
THEN WE'RE TRAPPED.
TURTLE ANTS ON ONE SIDE...
...AND A SWARM OF ARMY ANTS BELOW.
WAIT! THAT THING IS FULL OF MIND-CONTROLLING PARASITIC WORMS.
WHY ARE YOU STILL HOLDING IT?
I DUNNO. IT FEELS KINDA RUDE JUST THROWING AWAY SOMEONE'S BUTT.
THEY'RE HERE.
DO SOMETHING!

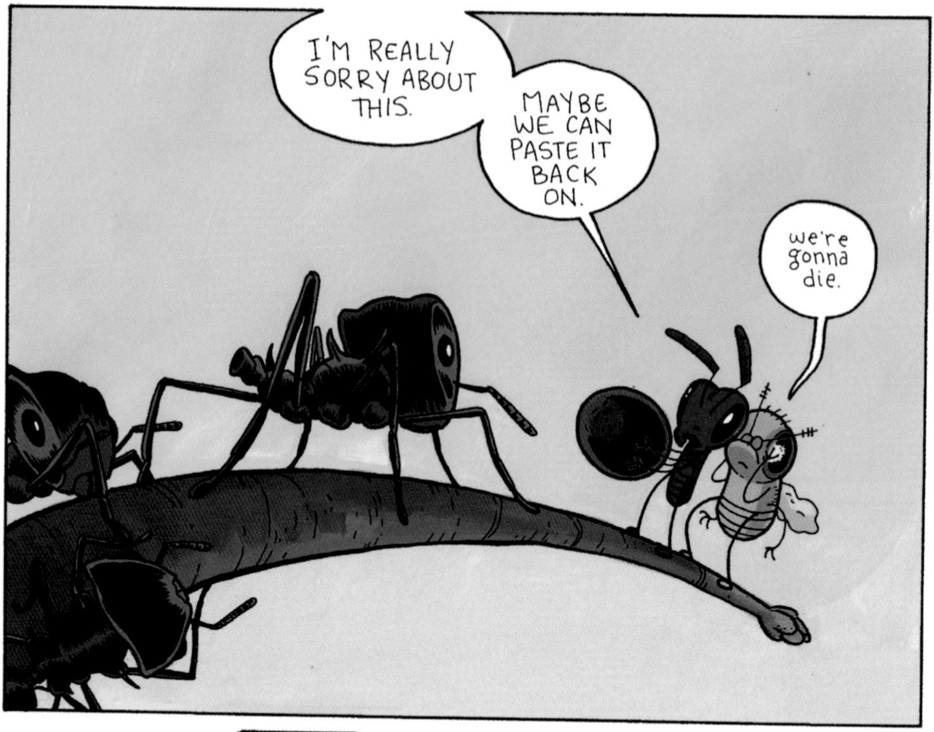
I'M REALLY SORRY ABOUT THIS.
MAYBE WE CAN PASTE IT BACK ON.
we're gonna die.

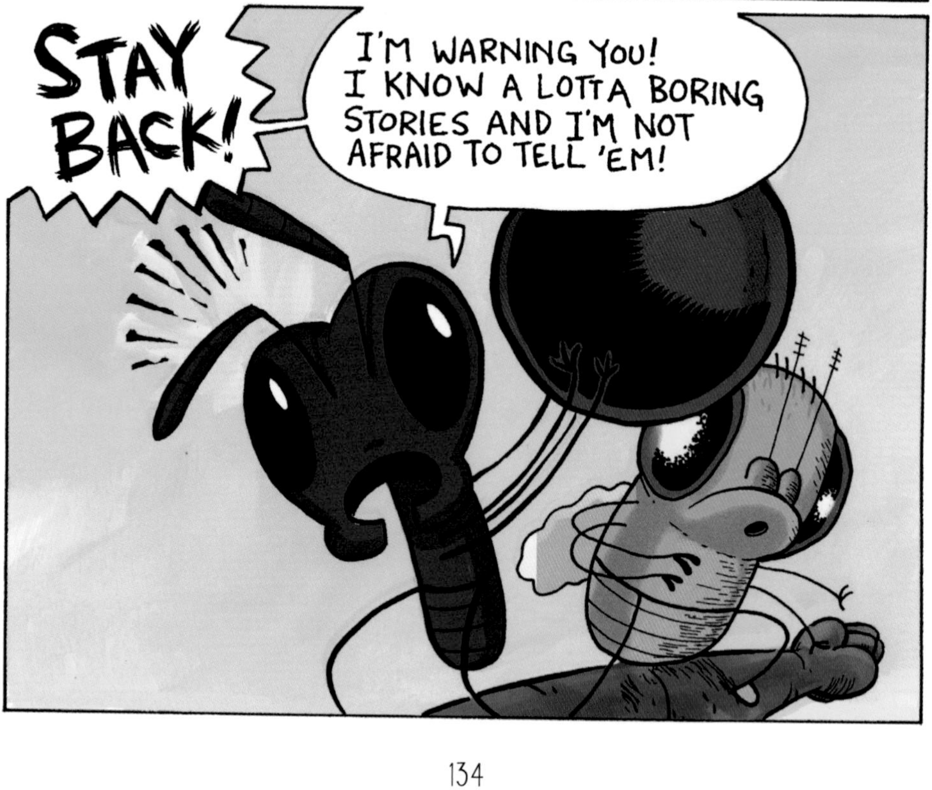
STAY BACK!
I'M WARNING YOU! I KNOW A LOTTA BORING STORIES AND I'M NOT AFRAID TO TELL 'EM!

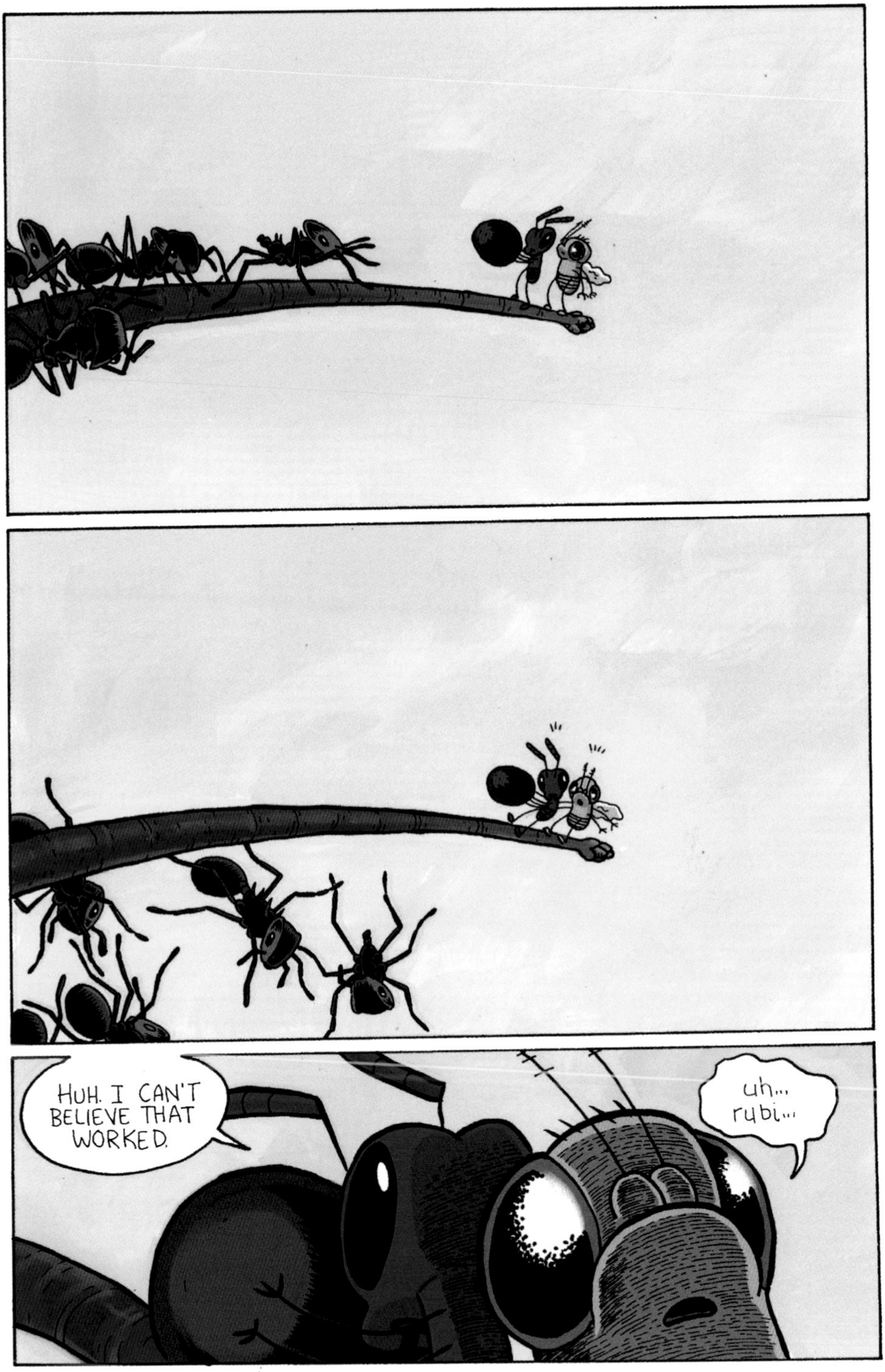
HUH. I CAN'T BELIEVE THAT WORKED.
uh... rubi...

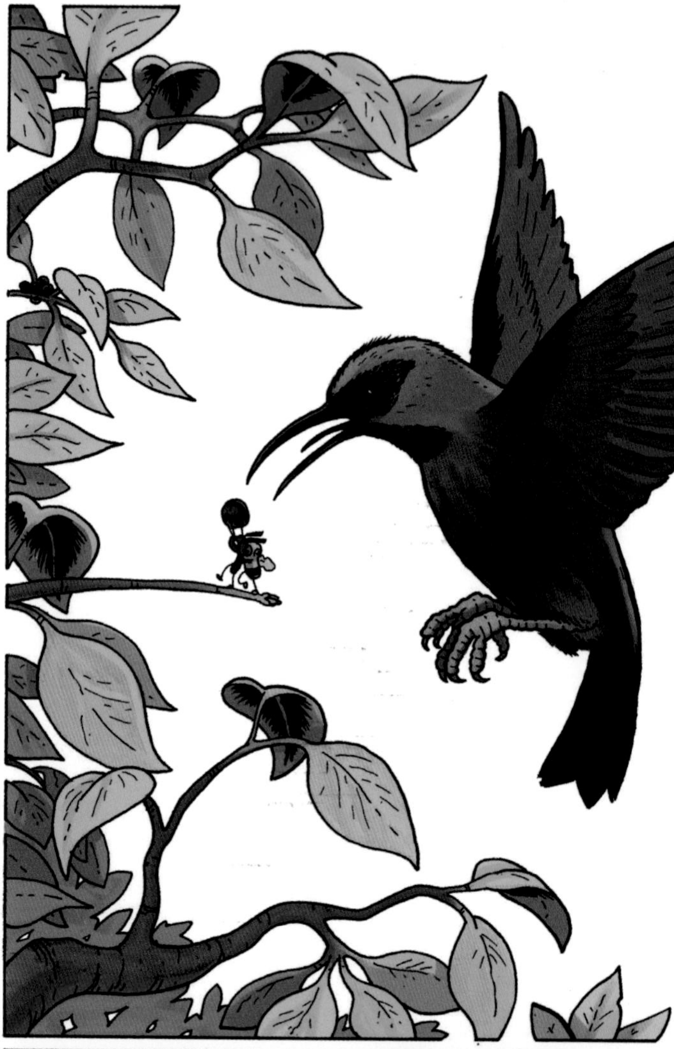

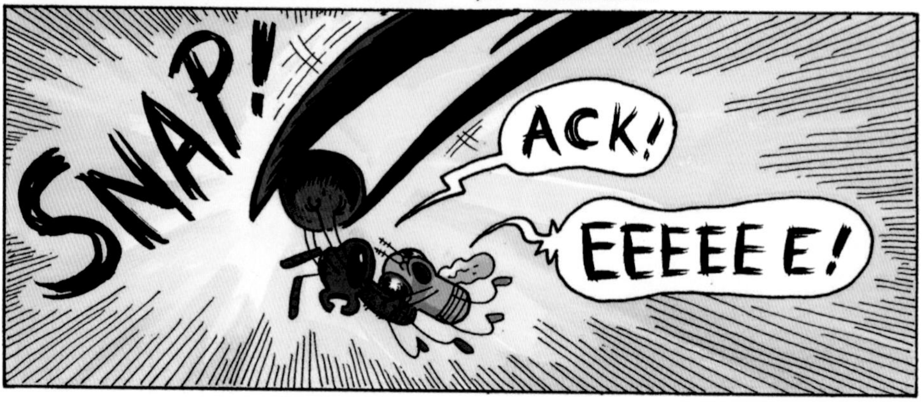

SNAP!
ACK!
EEEEE E!

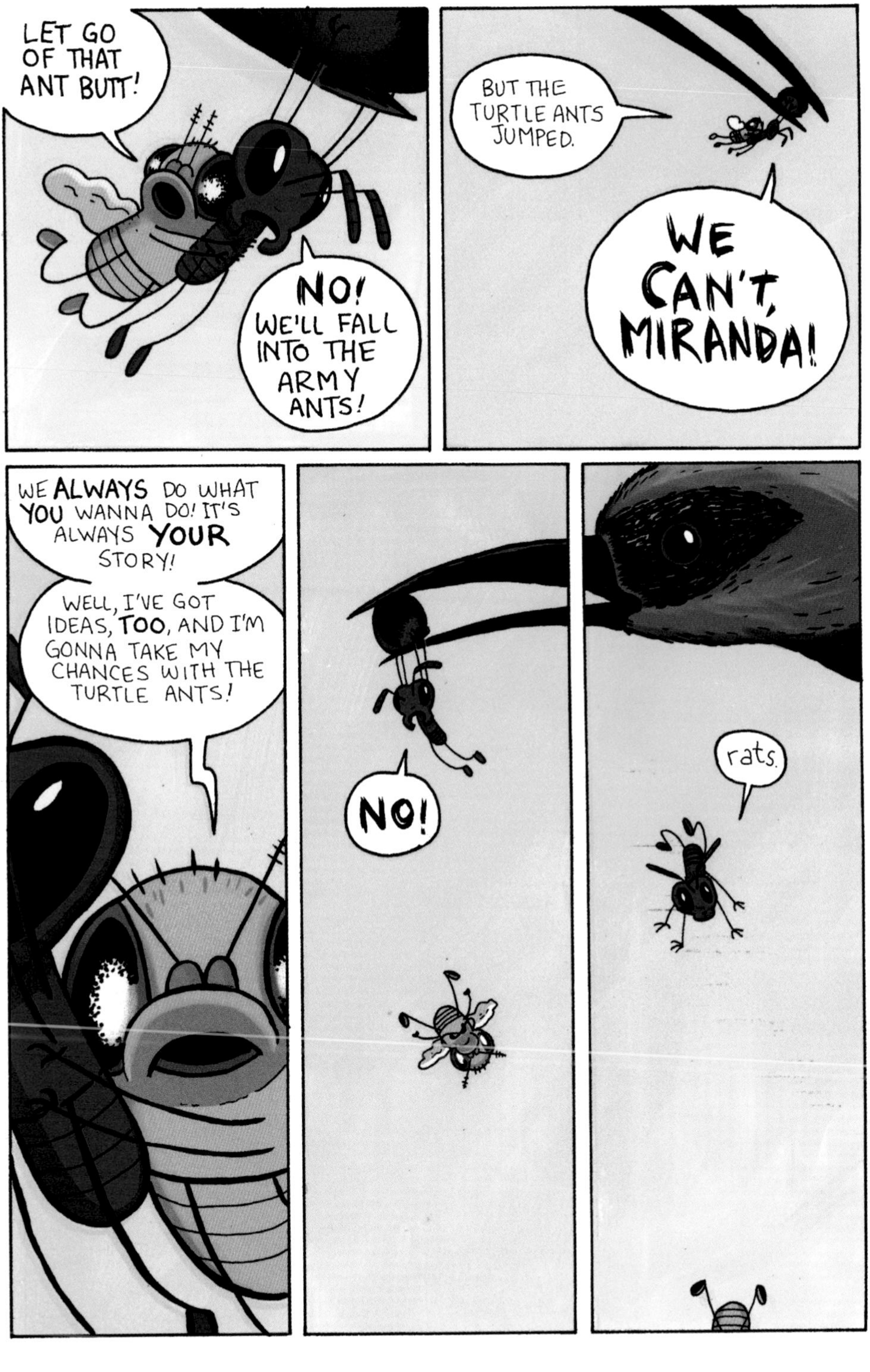
LET GO OF THAT ANT BUTT!
NO! WE'LL FALL INTO THE ARMY ANTS!
BUT THE TURTLE ANTS JUMPED.
WE CAN'T, MIRANDA!
WE ALWAYS DO WHAT YOU WANNA DO! IT'S ALWAYS YOUR STORY!
WELL, I'VE GOT IDEAS, TOO, AND I'M GONNA TAKE MY CHANCES WITH THE TURTLE ANTS!
NO!
rats.

SEE? WE'LL JUST FOLLOW THE TURTLE ANTS.

WAIT FOR IT...

WHAT THE-?

WHERE ARE THEY GOING?

TURTLE ANTS HAVE ANOTHER NAME, MIRANDA.

THEY'RE ALSO CALLED "GLIDING ANTS."

ZIP

ZIP

ZIP

WHEN THEY FALL (OR IN THIS CASE, JUMP) OFF A BRANCH, THEY CAN USE THEIR FLAT HEADS AND ABDOMENS TO CHANGE DIRECTION AND GLIDE BACK TO THE SAFETY OF THEIR HOME TREE TRUNK.

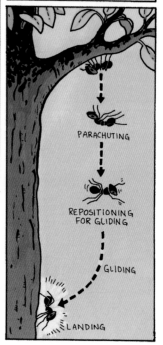

PARACHUTING

REPOSITIONING FOR GLIDING

GLIDING

LANDING

CAN YOU DO THAT?

NOPE.

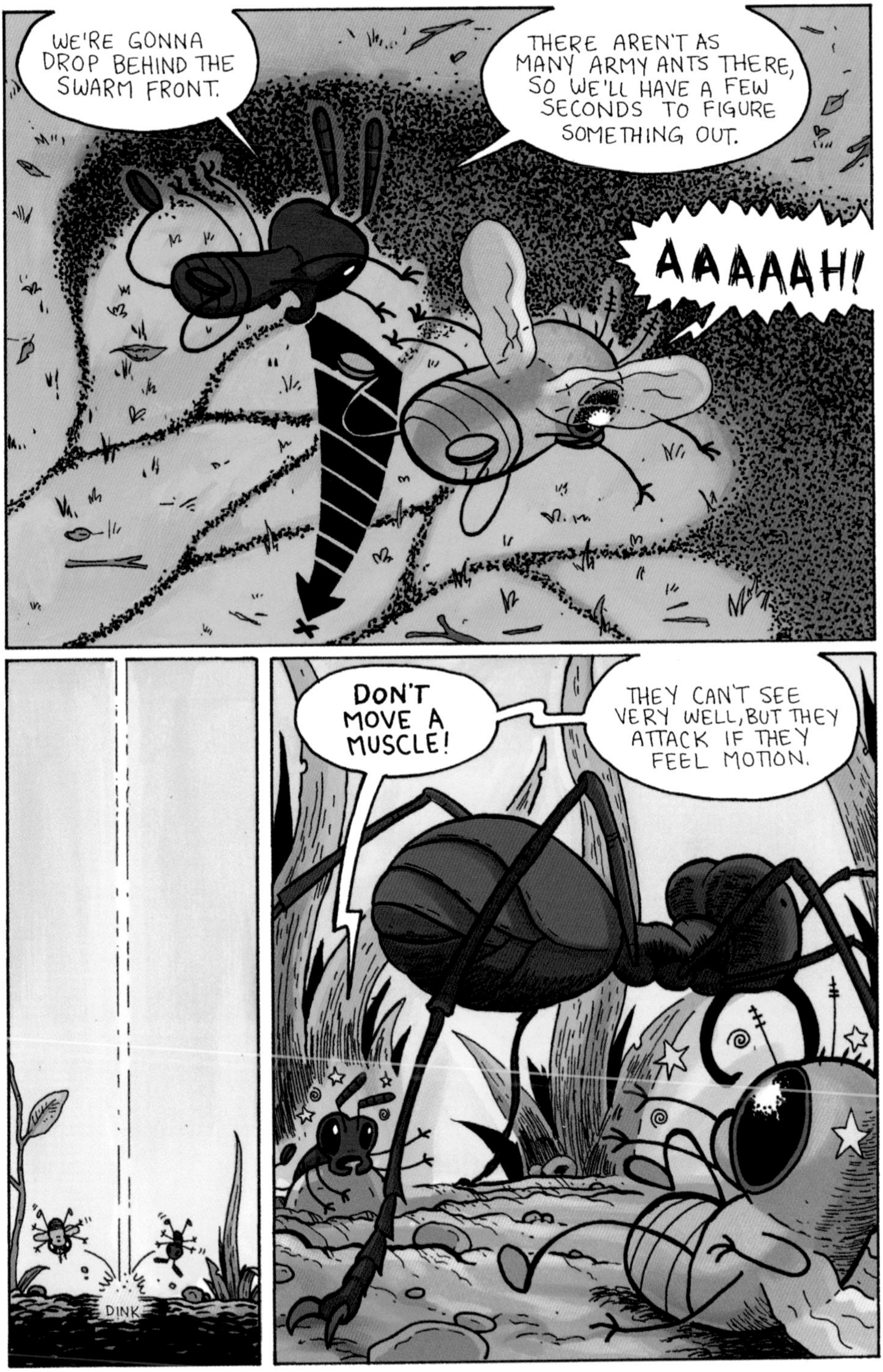
WE'RE GONNA DROP BEHIND THE SWARM FRONT.
THERE AREN'T AS MANY ARMY ANTS THERE, SO WE'LL HAVE A FEW SECONDS TO FIGURE SOMETHING OUT.
AAAAAH!
DINK
DON'T MOVE A MUSCLE!
THEY CAN'T SEE VERY WELL, BUT THEY ATTACK IF THEY FEEL MOTION.

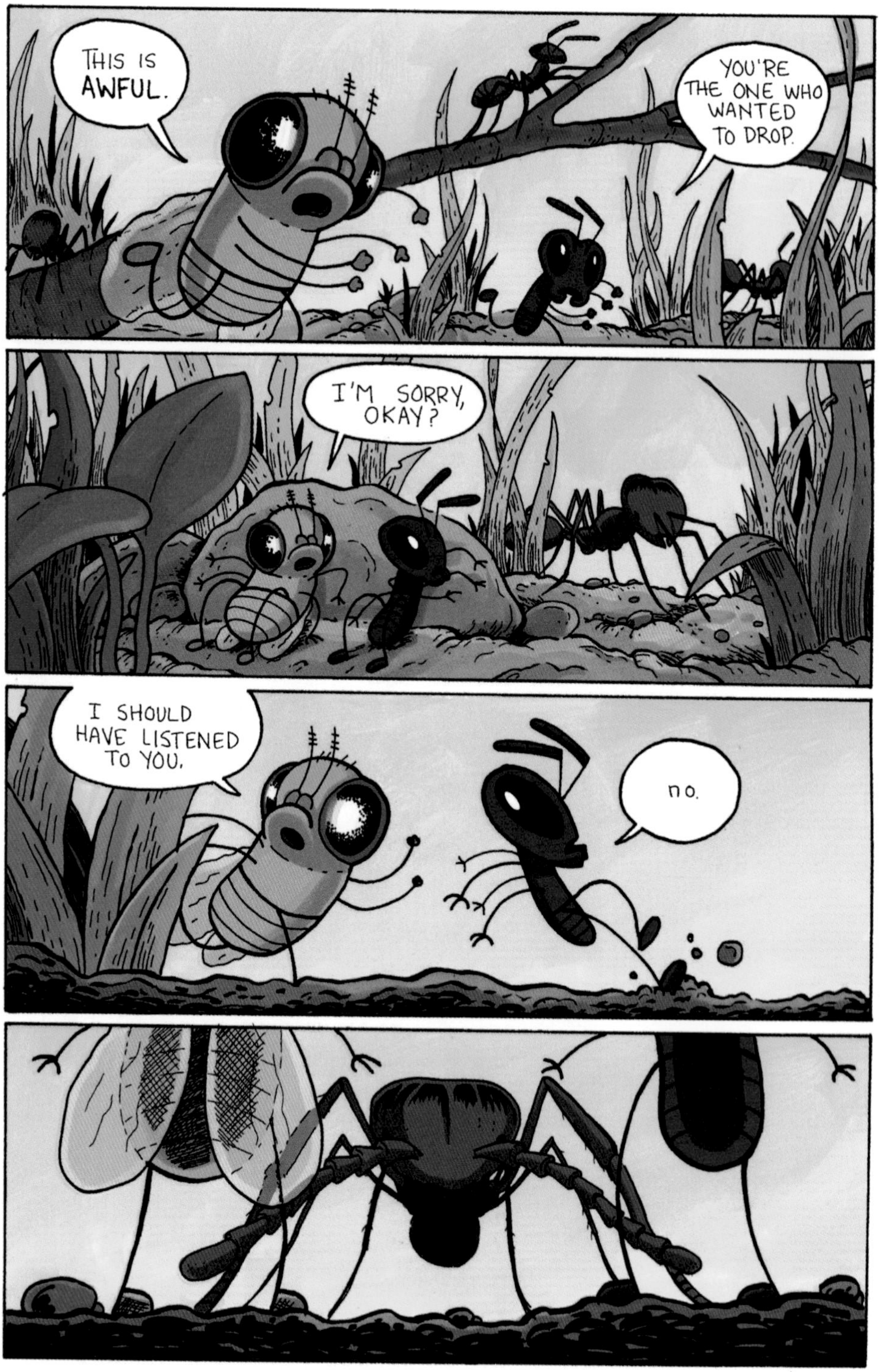
THIS IS AWFUL.
YOU'RE THE ONE WHO WANTED TO DROP.
I'M SORRY, OKAY?
I SHOULD HAVE LISTENED TO YOU.
no.

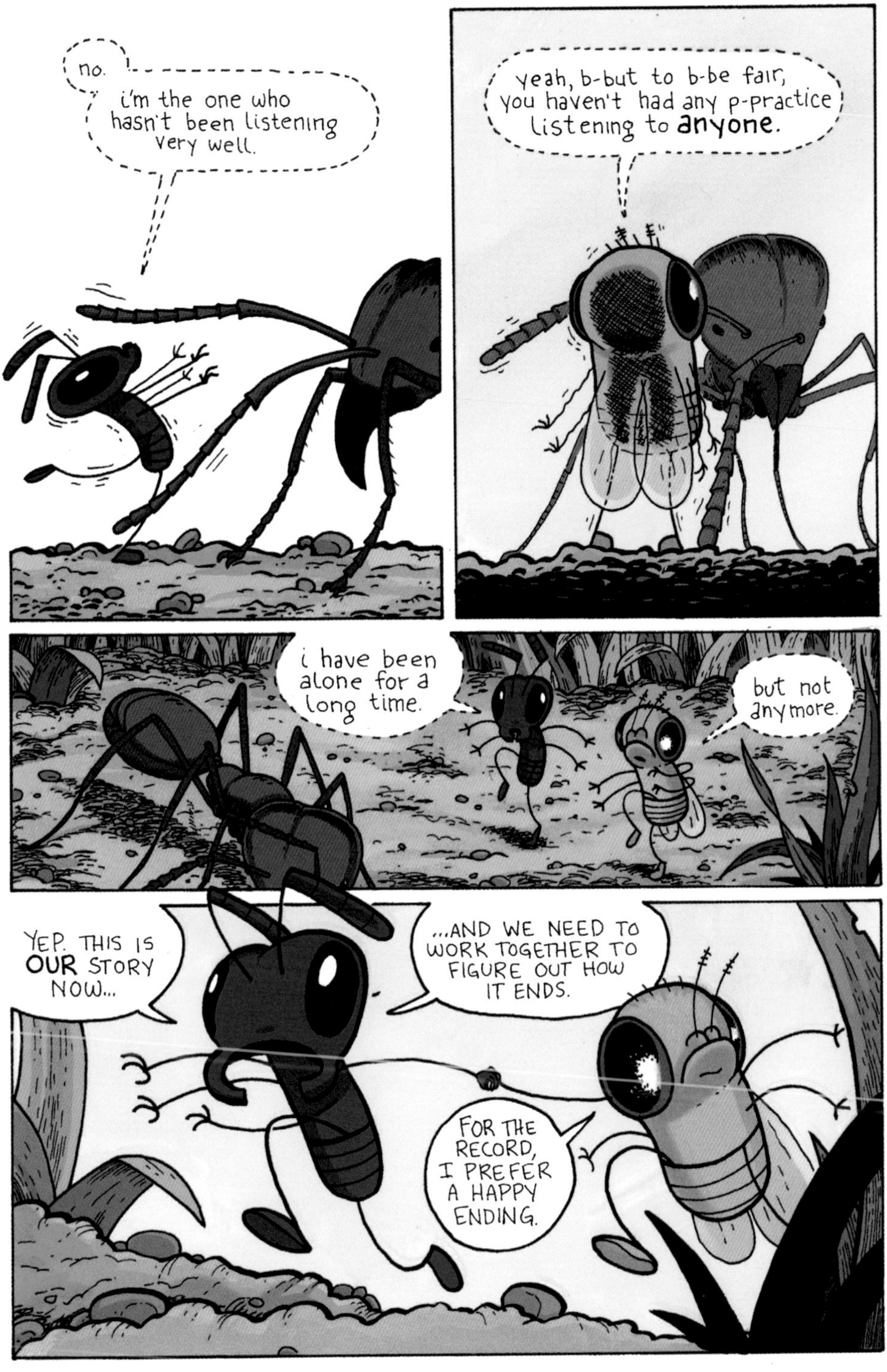
no.
i'm the one who hasn't been listening very well.
yeah, b-but to b-be fair, you haven't had any p-practice listening to **anyone**.
i have been alone for a long time.
but not anymore.
YEP. THIS IS **OUR** STORY NOW...
...AND WE NEED TO WORK TOGETHER TO FIGURE OUT HOW IT ENDS.
FOR THE RECORD, I PREFER A HAPPY ENDING.

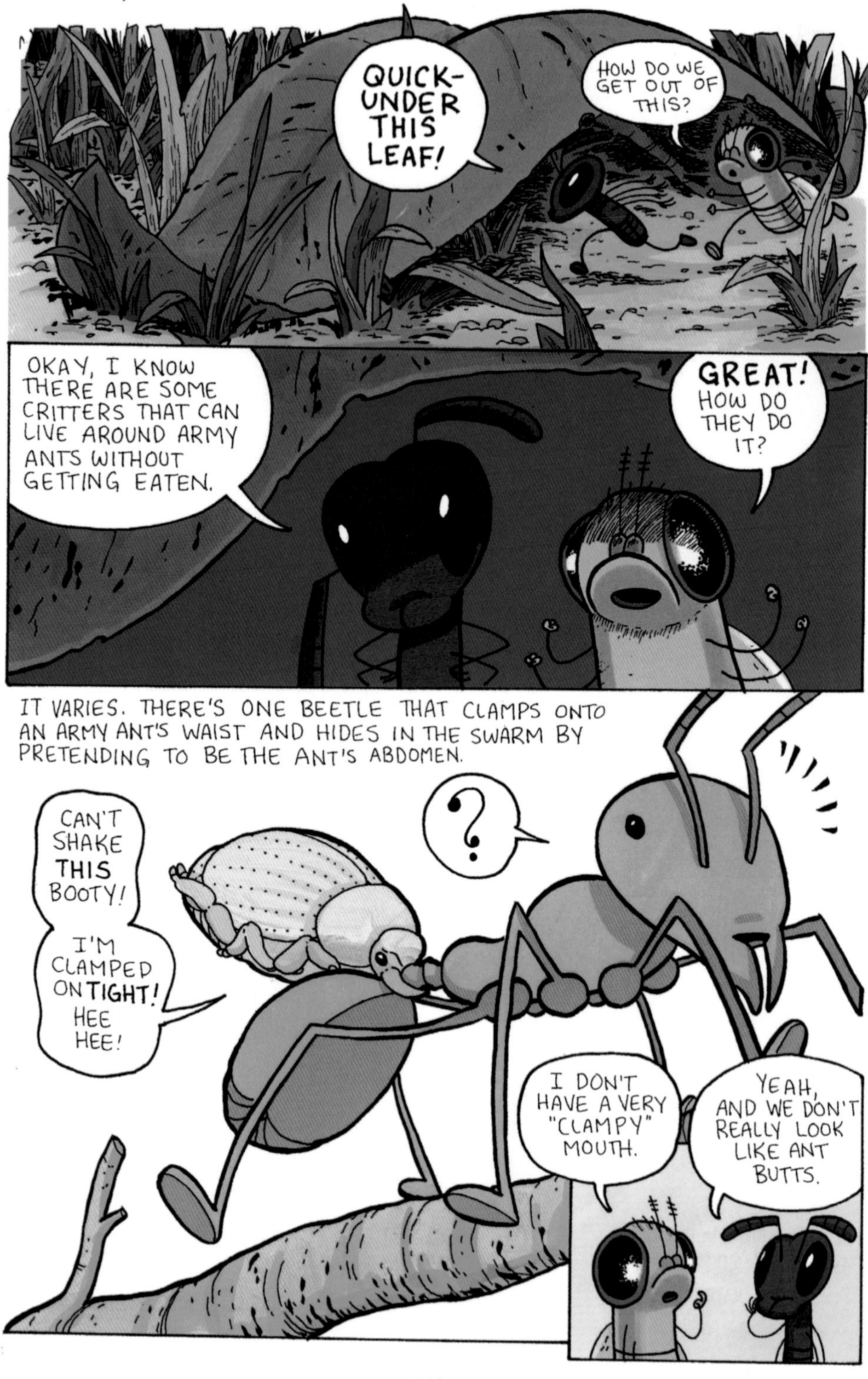
QUICK- UNDER THIS LEAF!
HOW DO WE GET OUT OF THIS?
OKAY, I KNOW THERE ARE SOME CRITTERS THAT CAN LIVE AROUND ARMY ANTS WITHOUT GETTING EATEN.
GREAT! HOW DO THEY DO IT?
IT VARIES. THERE'S ONE BEETLE THAT CLAMPS ONTO AN ARMY ANT'S WAIST AND HIDES IN THE SWARM BY PRETENDING TO BE THE ANT'S ABDOMEN.
CAN'T SHAKE THIS BOOTY!
I'M CLAMPED ON TIGHT! HEE HEE!
?
I DON'T HAVE A VERY "CLAMPY" MOUTH.
YEAH, AND WE DON'T REALLY LOOK LIKE ANT BUTTS.

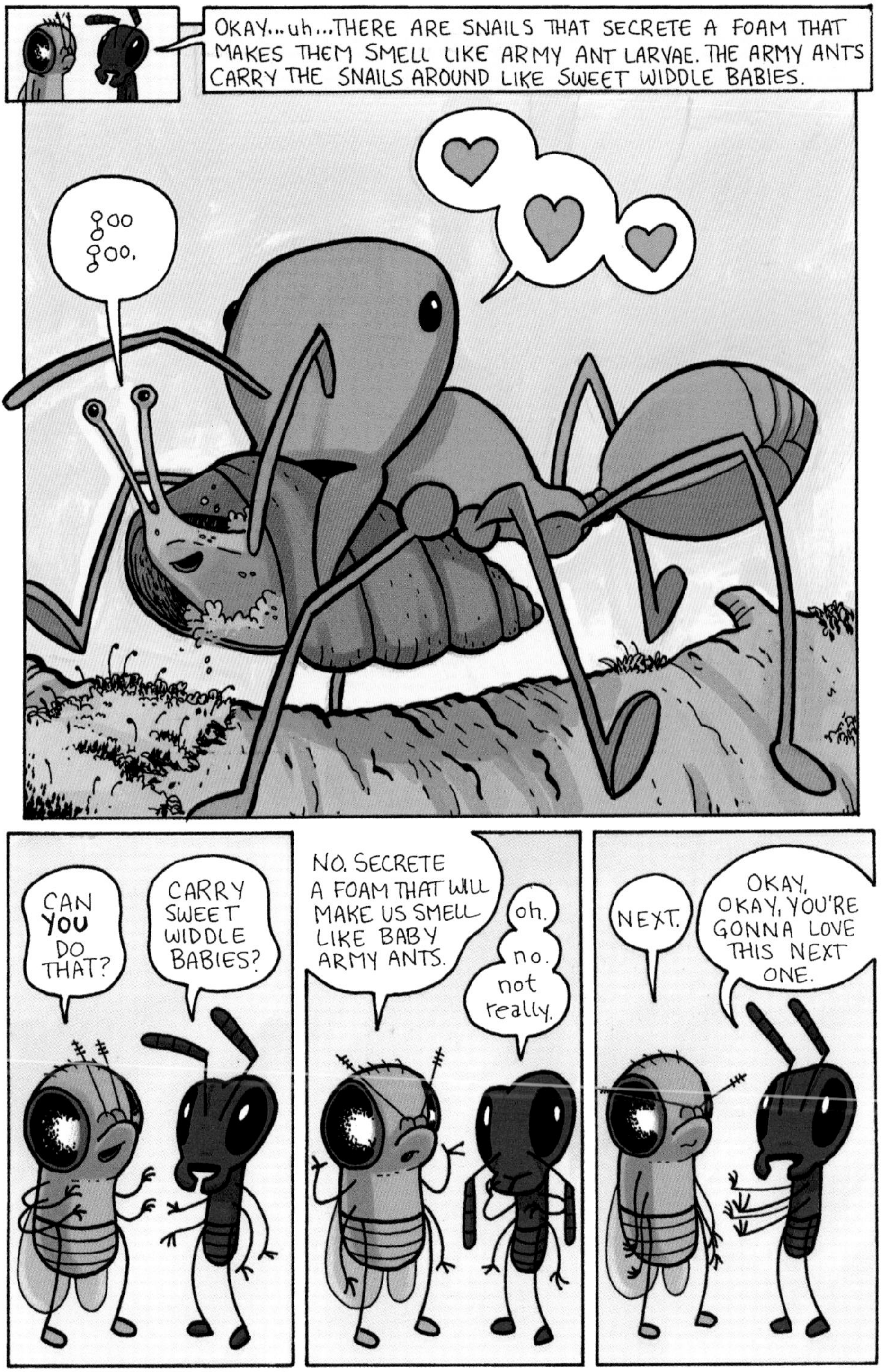
OKAY...uh...THERE ARE SNAILS THAT SECRETE A FOAM THAT MAKES THEM SMELL LIKE ARMY ANT LARVAE. THE ARMY ANTS CARRY THE SNAILS AROUND LIKE SWEET WIDDLE BABIES.
goo goo.
CAN YOU DO THAT?
CARRY SWEET WIDDLE BABIES?
NO. SECRETE A FOAM THAT WILL MAKE US SMELL LIKE BABY ARMY ANTS.
oh.
no. not really.
NEXT.
OKAY, OKAY, YOU'RE GONNA LOVE THIS NEXT ONE.

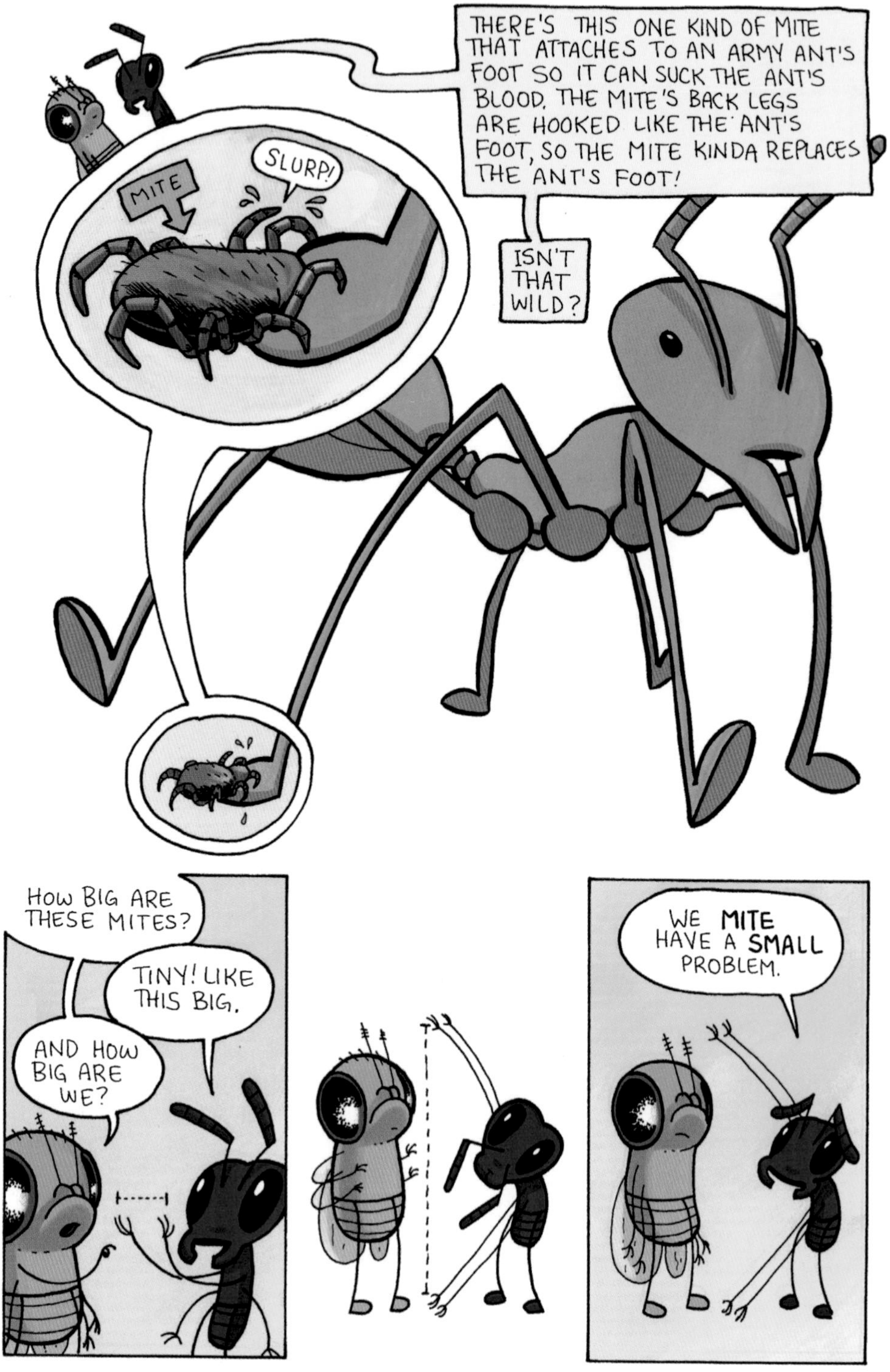
THERE'S THIS ONE KIND OF MITE THAT ATTACHES TO AN ARMY ANT'S FOOT SO IT CAN SUCK THE ANT'S BLOOD. THE MITE'S BACK LEGS ARE HOOKED LIKE THE ANT'S FOOT, SO THE MITE KINDA REPLACES THE ANT'S FOOT!
ISN'T THAT WILD?
MITE
SLURP!
HOW BIG ARE THESE MITES?
TINY! LIKE THIS BIG.
AND HOW BIG ARE WE?
WE **MITE** HAVE A **SMALL** PROBLEM.

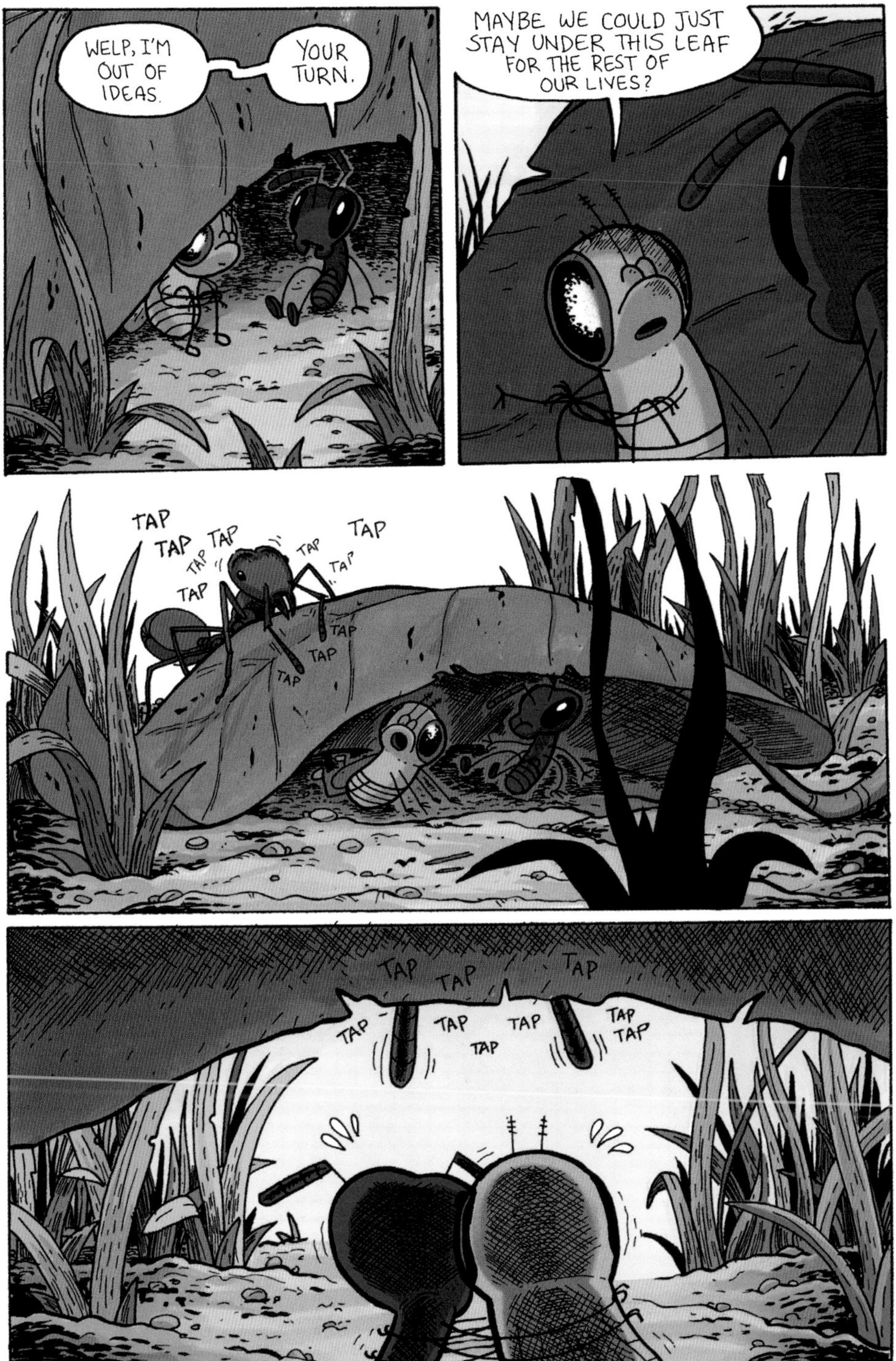
WELP, I'M OUT OF IDEAS.
YOUR TURN.
MAYBE WE COULD JUST STAY UNDER THIS LEAF FOR THE REST OF OUR LIVES?
TAP TAP TAP TAP TAP TAP TAP TAP TAP TAP TAP
TAP TAP TAP
TAP TAP TAP TAP TAP TAP

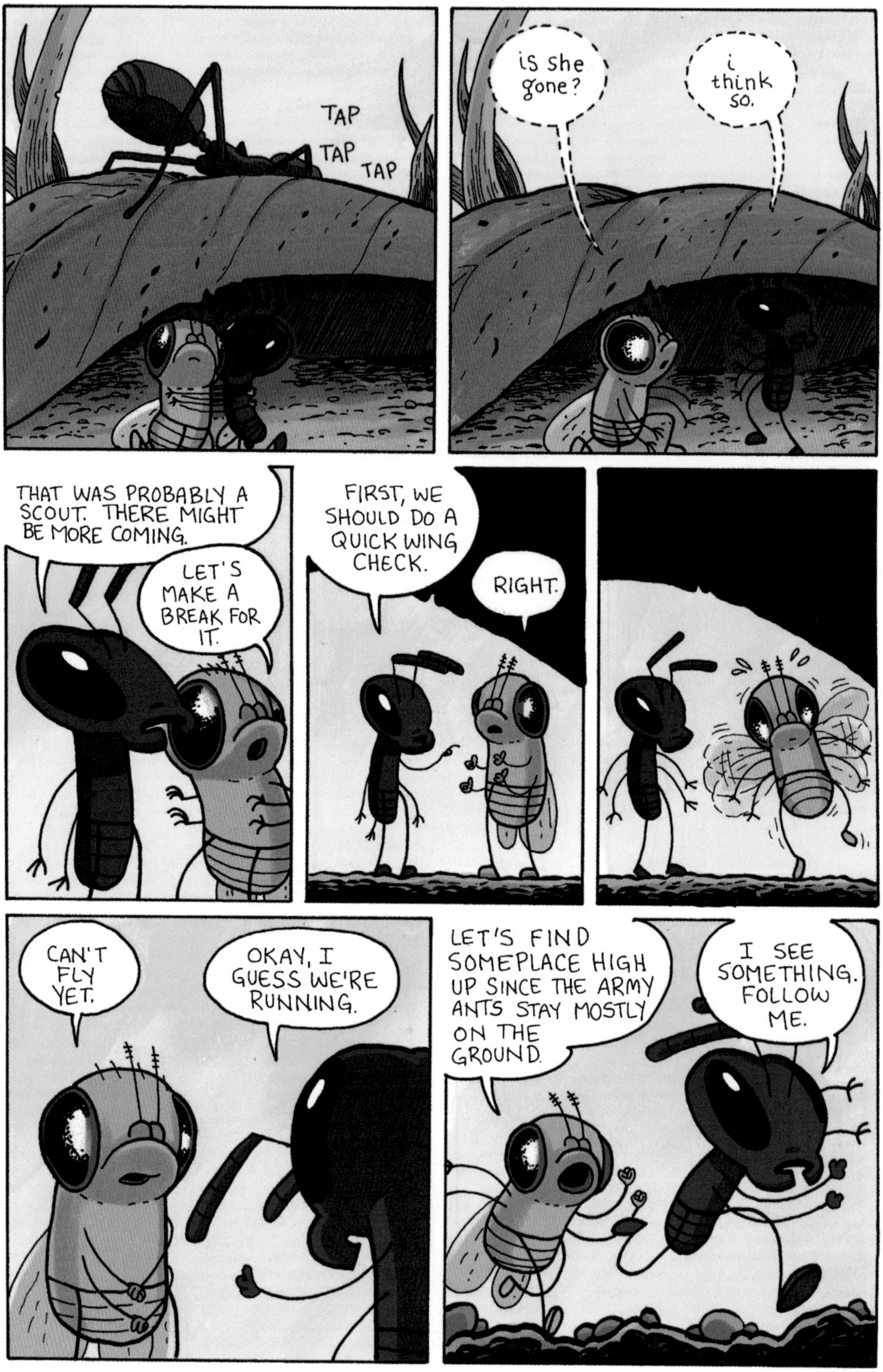
TAP
TAP
TAP
is she gone?
i think so.
THAT WAS PROBABLY A SCOUT. THERE MIGHT BE MORE COMING.
LET'S MAKE A BREAK FOR IT.
FIRST, WE SHOULD DO A QUICK WING CHECK.
RIGHT.
CAN'T FLY YET.
OKAY, I GUESS WE'RE RUNNING.
LET'S FIND SOMEPLACE HIGH UP SINCE THE ARMY ANTS STAY MOSTLY ON THE GROUND.
I SEE SOMETHING. FOLLOW ME.

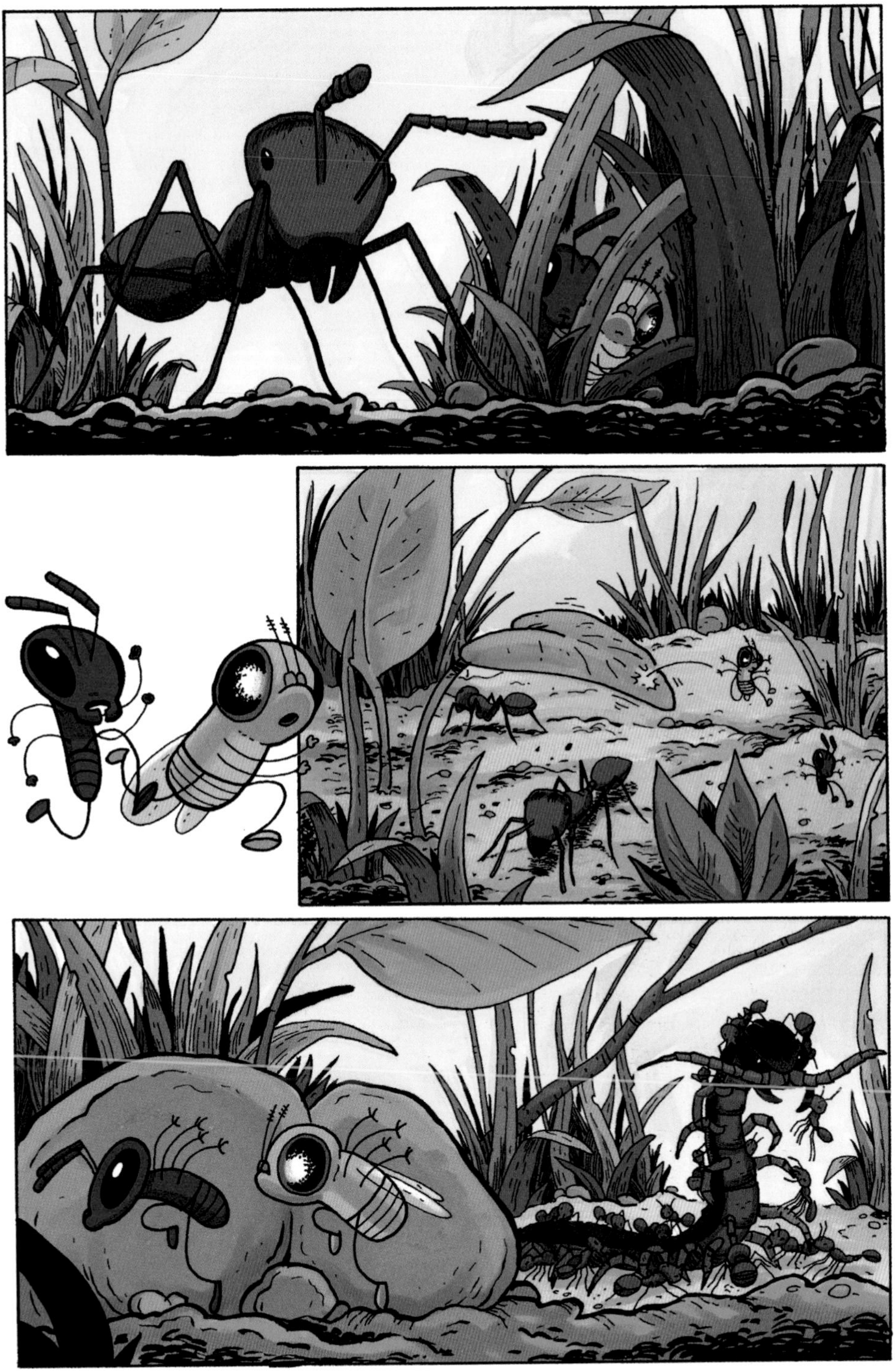

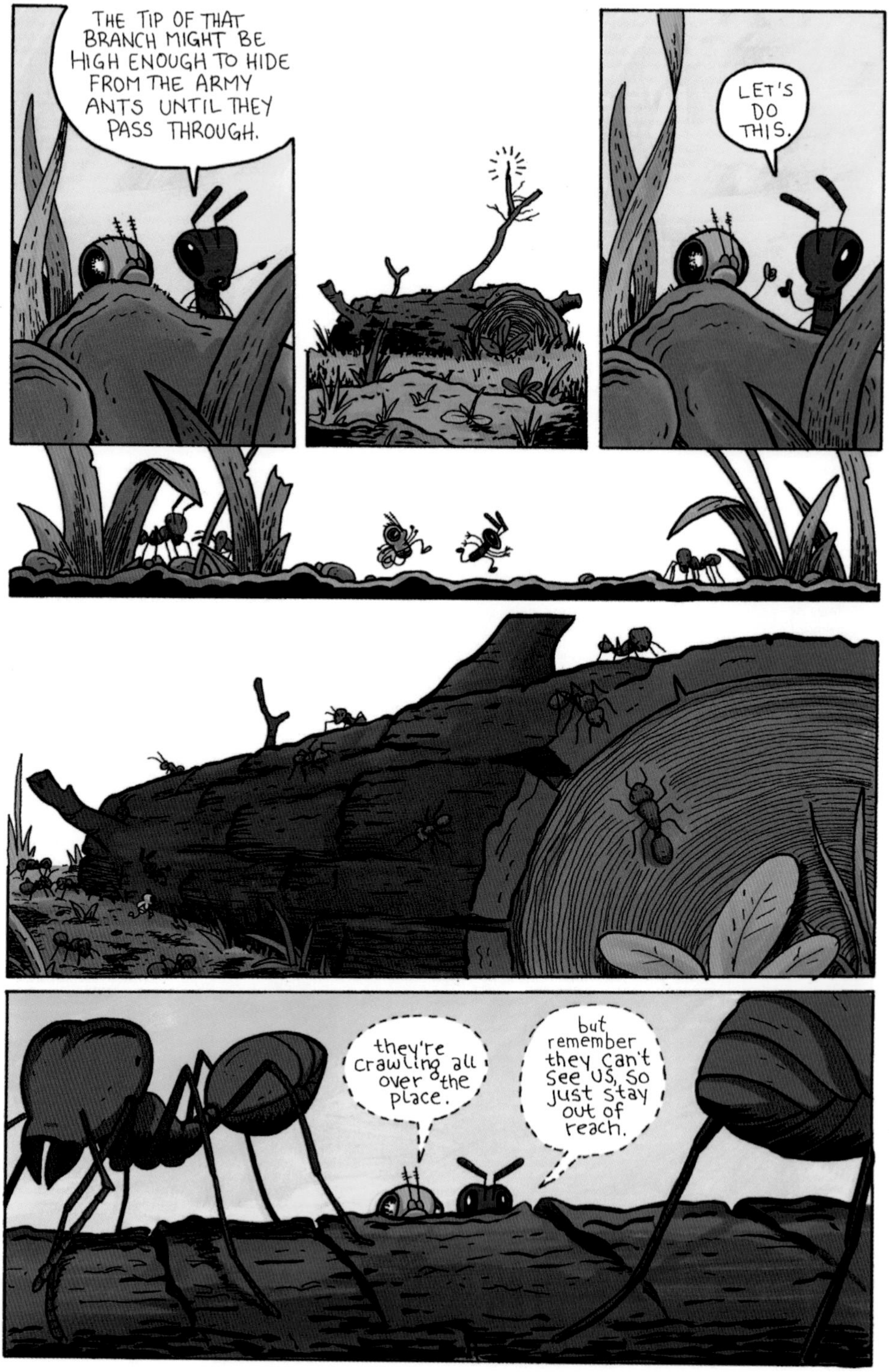
THE TIP OF THAT BRANCH MIGHT BE HIGH ENOUGH TO HIDE FROM THE ARMY ANTS UNTIL THEY PASS THROUGH.
LET'S DO THIS.
they're crawling all over the place.
but remember they can't see us, so just stay out of reach.

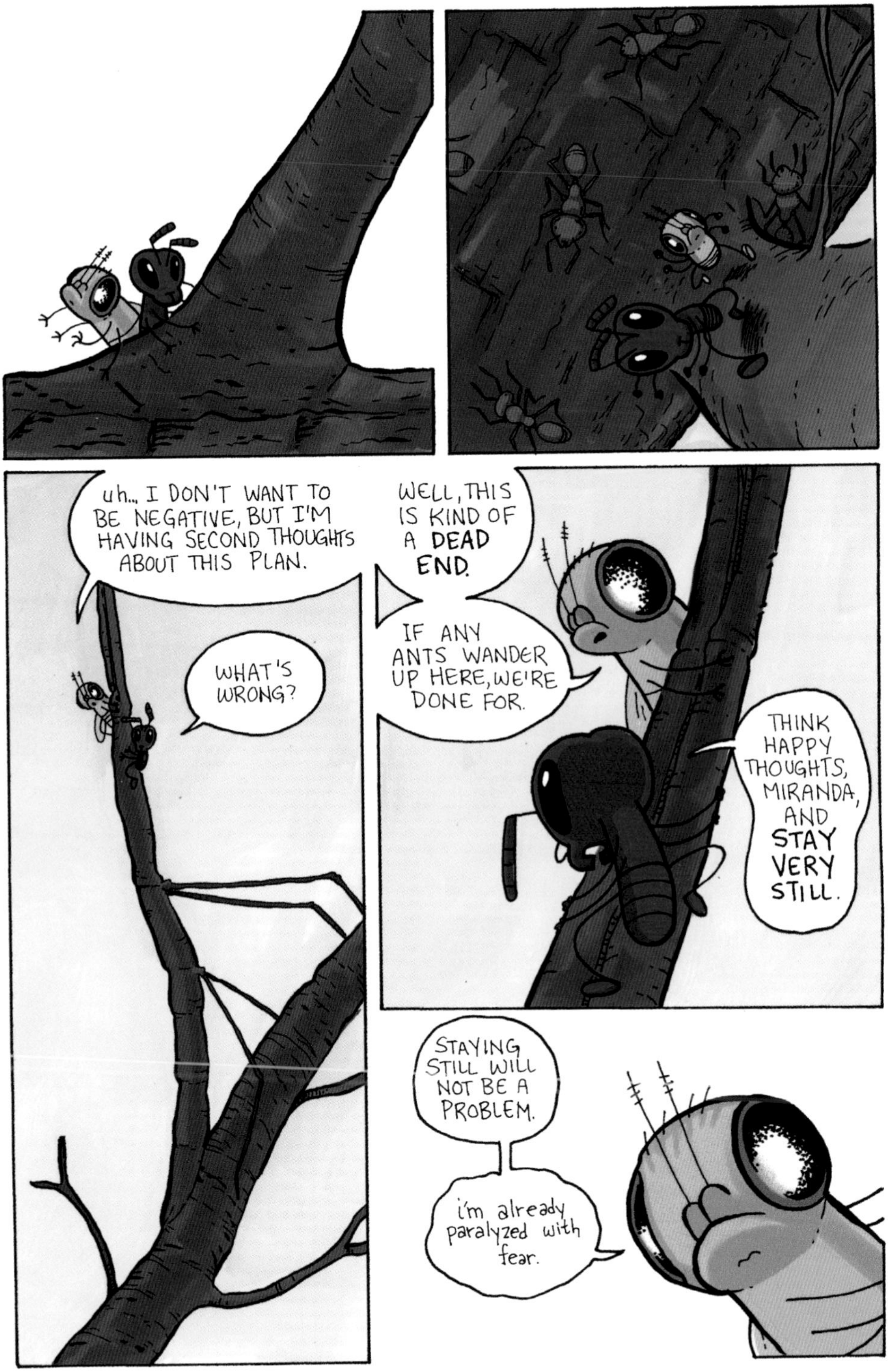
uh... I DON'T WANT TO BE NEGATIVE, BUT I'M HAVING SECOND THOUGHTS ABOUT THIS PLAN.
WHAT'S WRONG?
WELL, THIS IS KIND OF A DEAD END.
IF ANY ANTS WANDER UP HERE, WE'RE DONE FOR.
THINK HAPPY THOUGHTS, MIRANDA, AND STAY VERY STILL.
STAYING STILL WILL NOT BE A PROBLEM.
i'm already paralyzed with fear.

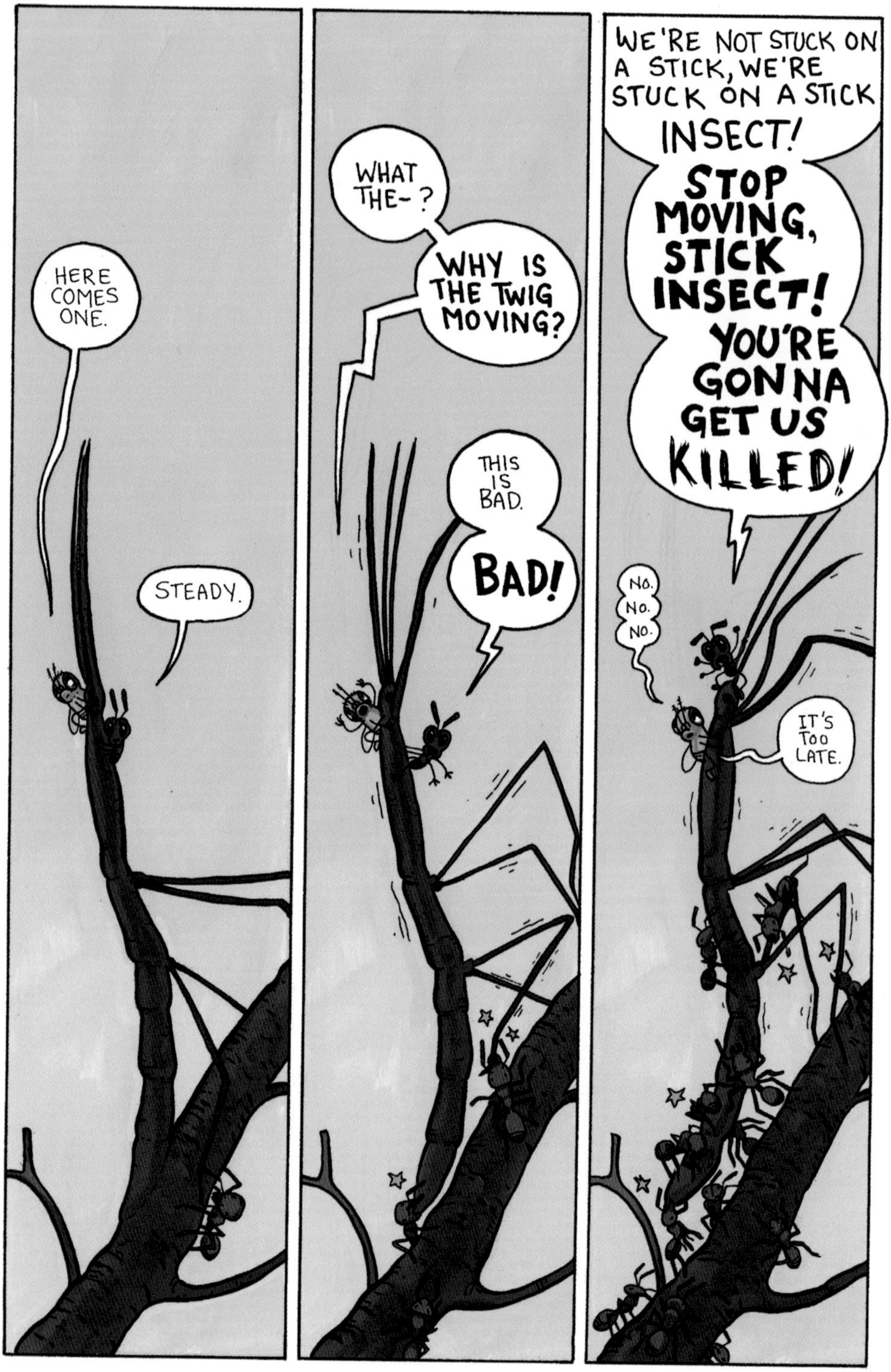
HERE COMES ONE.
STEADY.
WHAT THE- ?
WHY IS THE TWIG MOVING?
THIS IS BAD.
BAD!
WE'RE NOT STUCK ON A STICK, WE'RE STUCK ON A STICK INSECT!
STOP MOVING, STICK INSECT!
YOU'RE GONNA GET US KILLED!
NO. NO. NO.
IT'S TOO LATE.

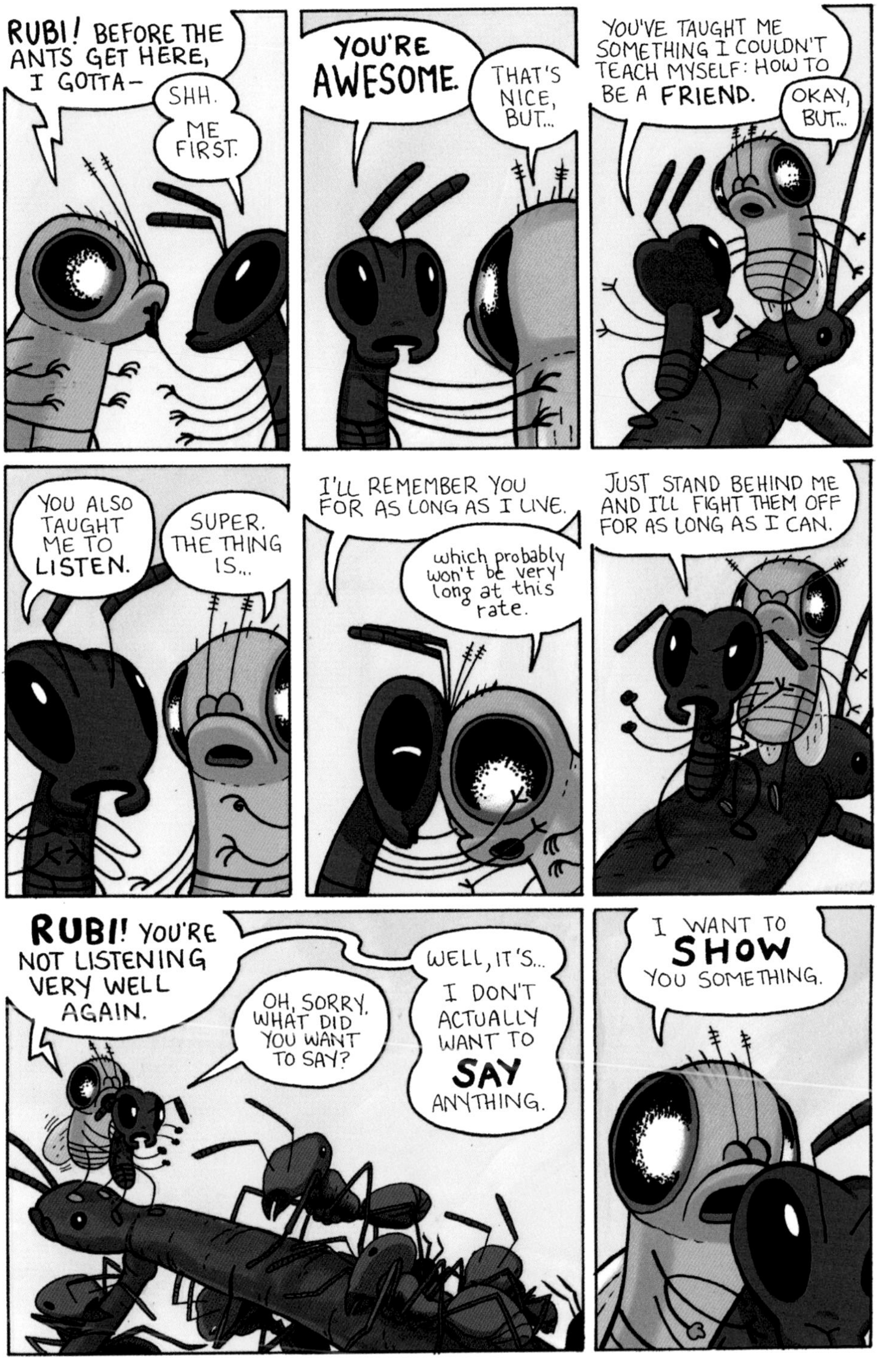
RUBI! BEFORE THE ANTS GET HERE, I GOTTA–
SHH. ME FIRST.
YOU'RE AWESOME.
THAT'S NICE, BUT...
YOU'VE TAUGHT ME SOMETHING I COULDN'T TEACH MYSELF: HOW TO BE A FRIEND.
OKAY, BUT...
YOU ALSO TAUGHT ME TO LISTEN.
SUPER. THE THING IS...
I'LL REMEMBER YOU FOR AS LONG AS I LIVE.
which probably won't be very long at this rate.
JUST STAND BEHIND ME AND I'LL FIGHT THEM OFF FOR AS LONG AS I CAN.
RUBI! YOU'RE NOT LISTENING VERY WELL AGAIN.
OH, SORRY. WHAT DID YOU WANT TO SAY?
WELL, IT'S...
I DON'T ACTUALLY WANT TO SAY ANYTHING.
I WANT TO SHOW YOU SOMETHING.

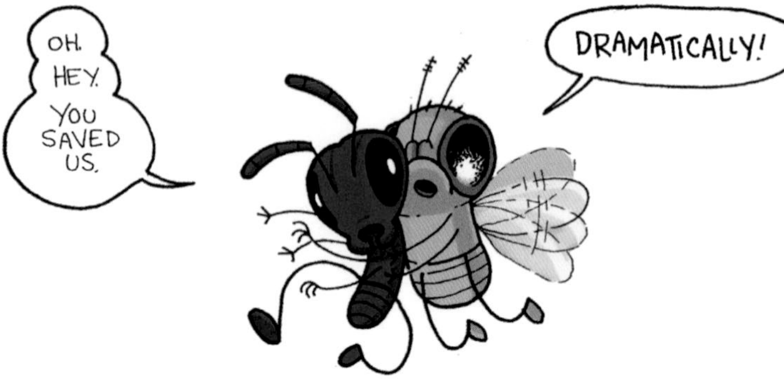
OH. HEY. YOU SAVED US.
DRAMATICALLY!

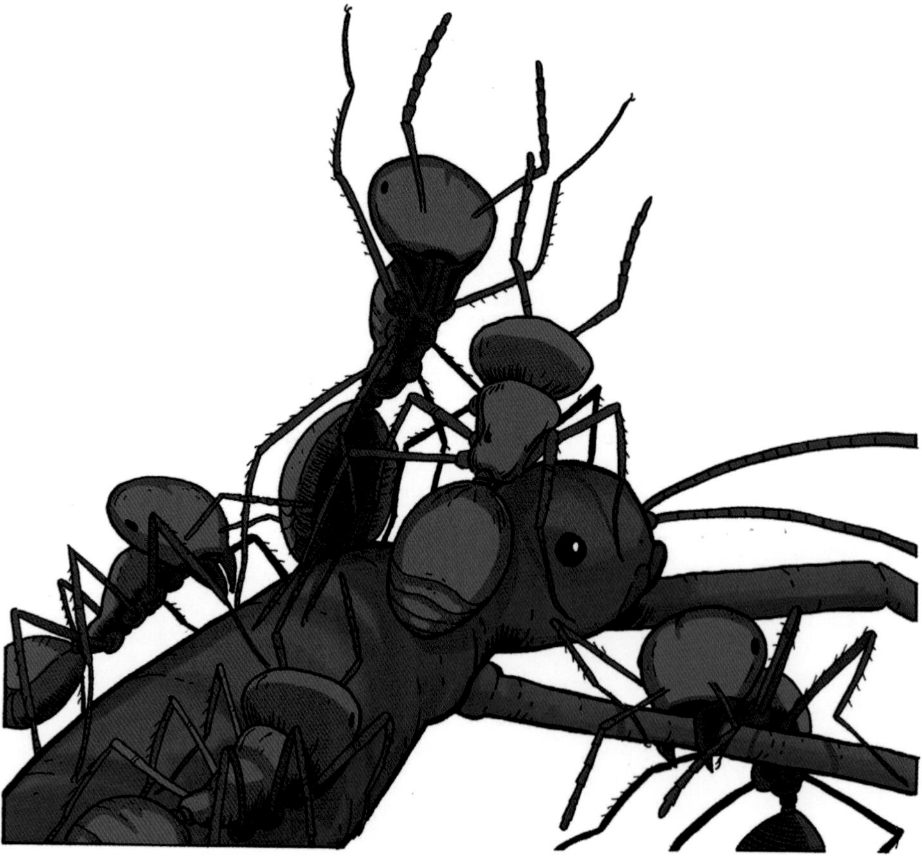

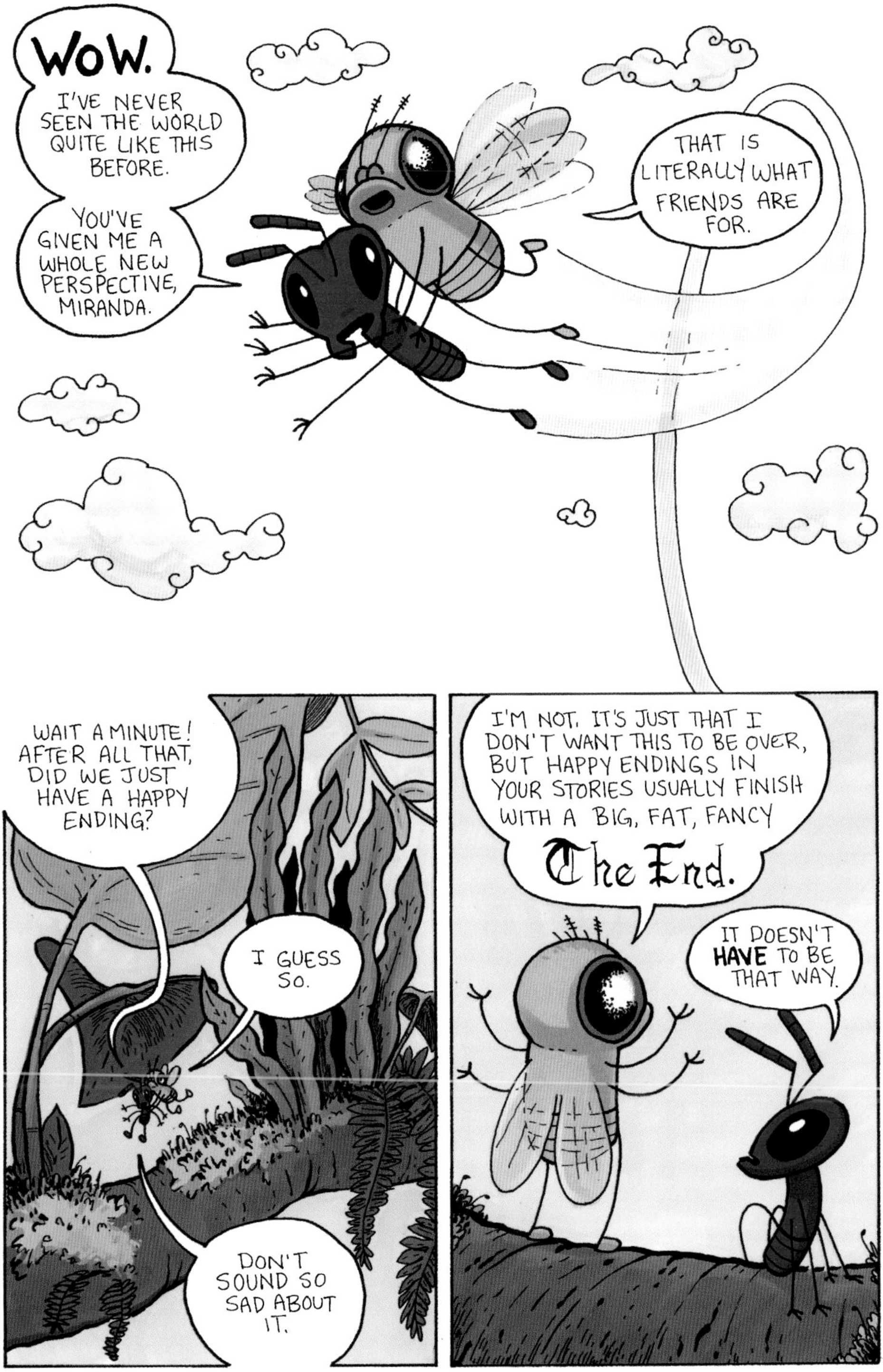
WOW.
I'VE NEVER SEEN THE WORLD QUITE LIKE THIS BEFORE.
YOU'VE GIVEN ME A WHOLE NEW PERSPECTIVE, MIRANDA.
THAT IS LITERALLY WHAT FRIENDS ARE FOR.
WAIT A MINUTE! AFTER ALL THAT, DID WE JUST HAVE A HAPPY ENDING?
I GUESS SO.
DON'T SOUND SO SAD ABOUT IT.
I'M NOT. IT'S JUST THAT I DON'T WANT THIS TO BE OVER, BUT HAPPY ENDINGS IN YOUR STORIES USUALLY FINISH WITH A BIG, FAT, FANCY
The End.
IT DOESN'T **HAVE** TO BE THAT WAY.

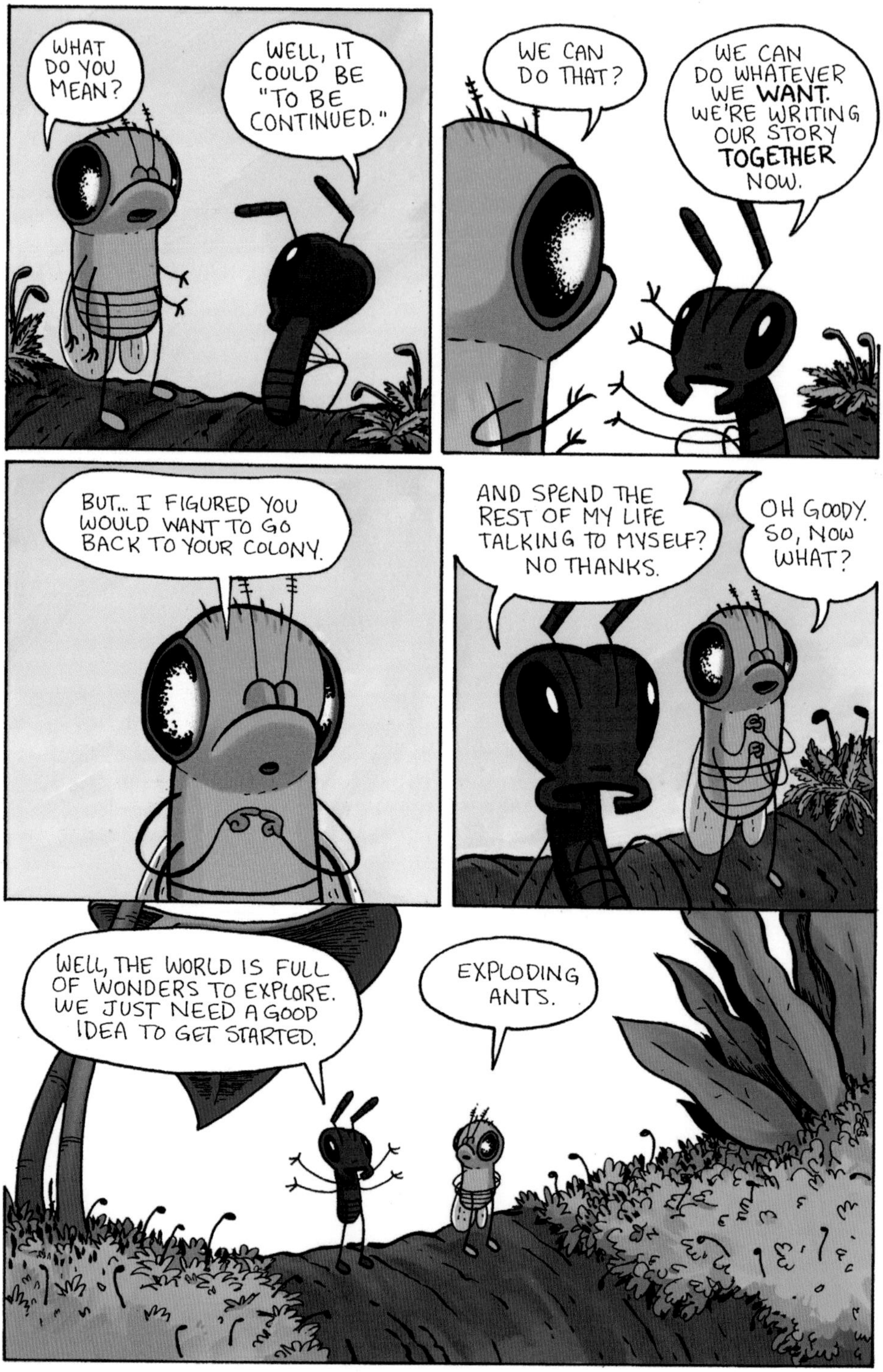
WHAT DO YOU MEAN?
WELL, IT COULD BE "TO BE CONTINUED."
WE CAN DO THAT?
WE CAN DO WHATEVER WE **WANT**. WE'RE WRITING OUR STORY **TOGETHER** NOW.
BUT... I FIGURED YOU WOULD WANT TO GO BACK TO YOUR COLONY.
AND SPEND THE REST OF MY LIFE TALKING TO MYSELF? NO THANKS.
OH GOODY. SO, NOW WHAT?
WELL, THE WORLD IS FULL OF WONDERS TO EXPLORE. WE JUST NEED A GOOD IDEA TO GET STARTED.
EXPLODING ANTS.

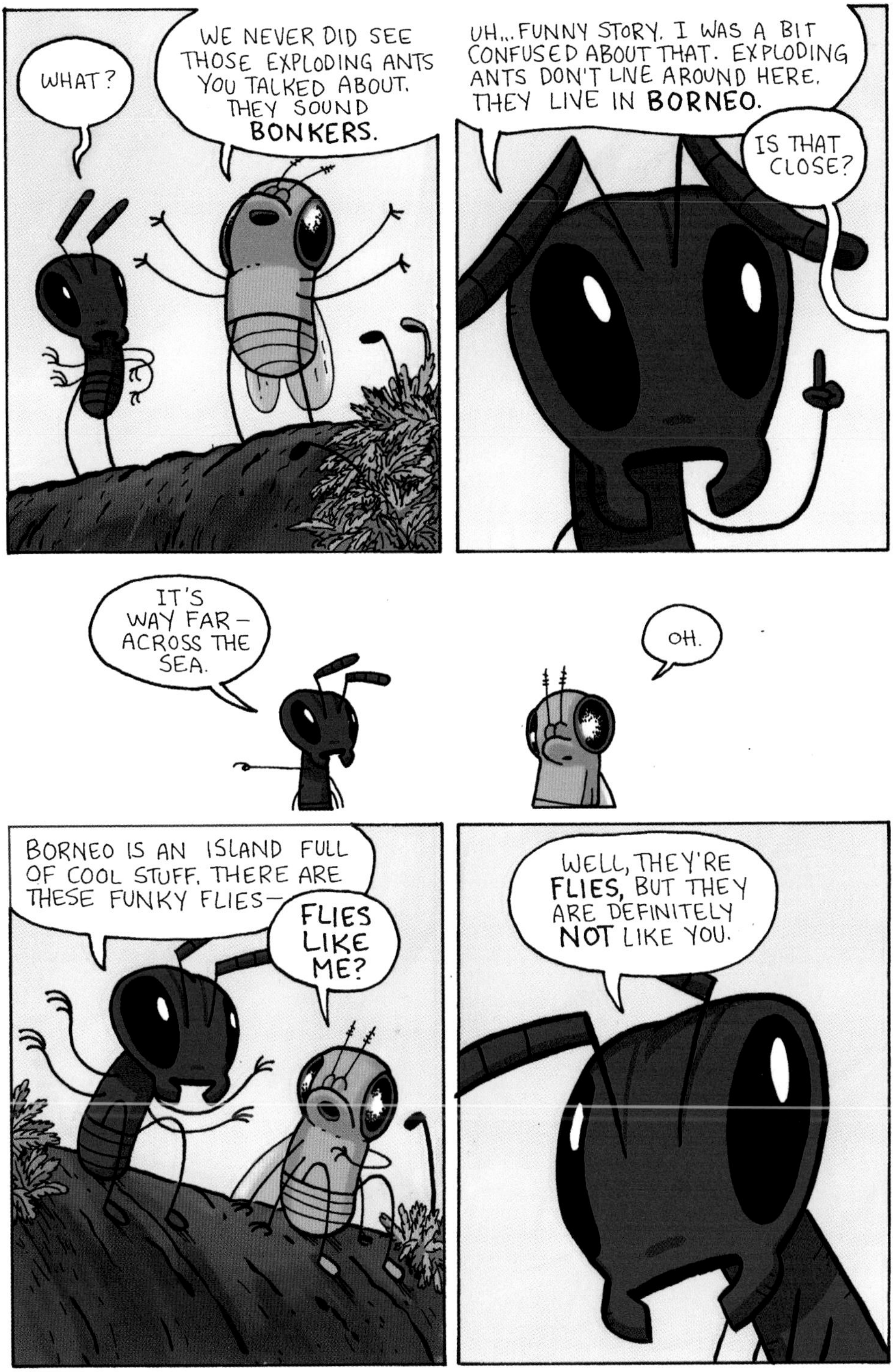
WHAT?
WE NEVER DID SEE THOSE EXPLODING ANTS YOU TALKED ABOUT. THEY SOUND BONKERS.
UH... FUNNY STORY. I WAS A BIT CONFUSED ABOUT THAT. EXPLODING ANTS DON'T LIVE AROUND HERE. THEY LIVE IN BORNEO.
IS THAT CLOSE?
IT'S WAY FAR— ACROSS THE SEA.
OH.
BORNEO IS AN ISLAND FULL OF COOL STUFF. THERE ARE THESE FUNKY FLIES—
FLIES LIKE ME?
WELL, THEY'RE FLIES, BUT THEY ARE DEFINITELY NOT LIKE YOU.

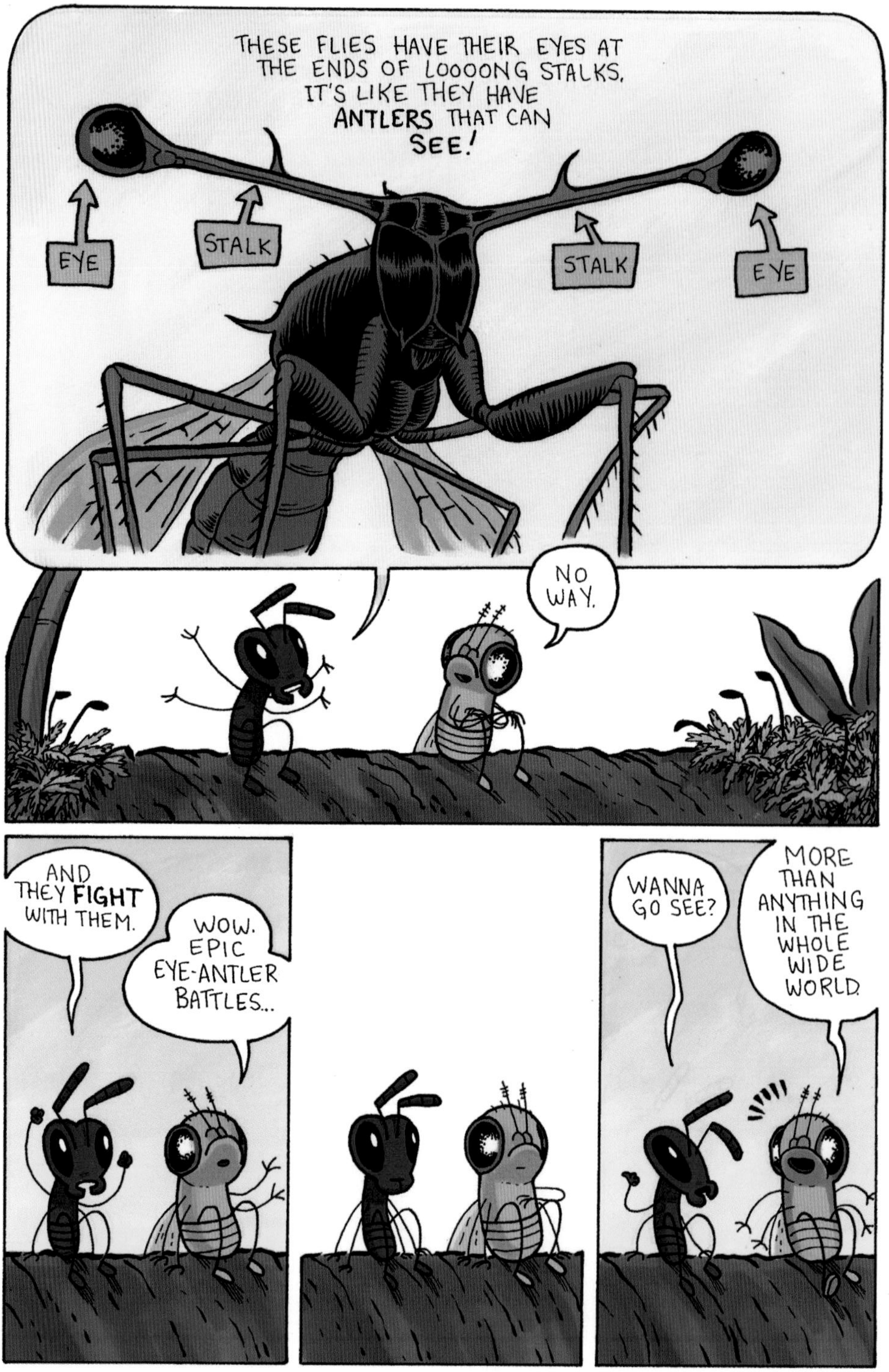

THESE FLIES HAVE THEIR EYES AT THE ENDS OF LOOOONG STALKS. IT'S LIKE THEY HAVE **ANTLERS** THAT CAN **SEE!**
EYE
STALK
STALK
EYE
NO WAY.
AND THEY **FIGHT** WITH THEM.
WOW. EPIC EYE-ANTLER BATTLES...
WANNA GO SEE?
MORE THAN ANYTHING IN THE WHOLE WIDE WORLD.

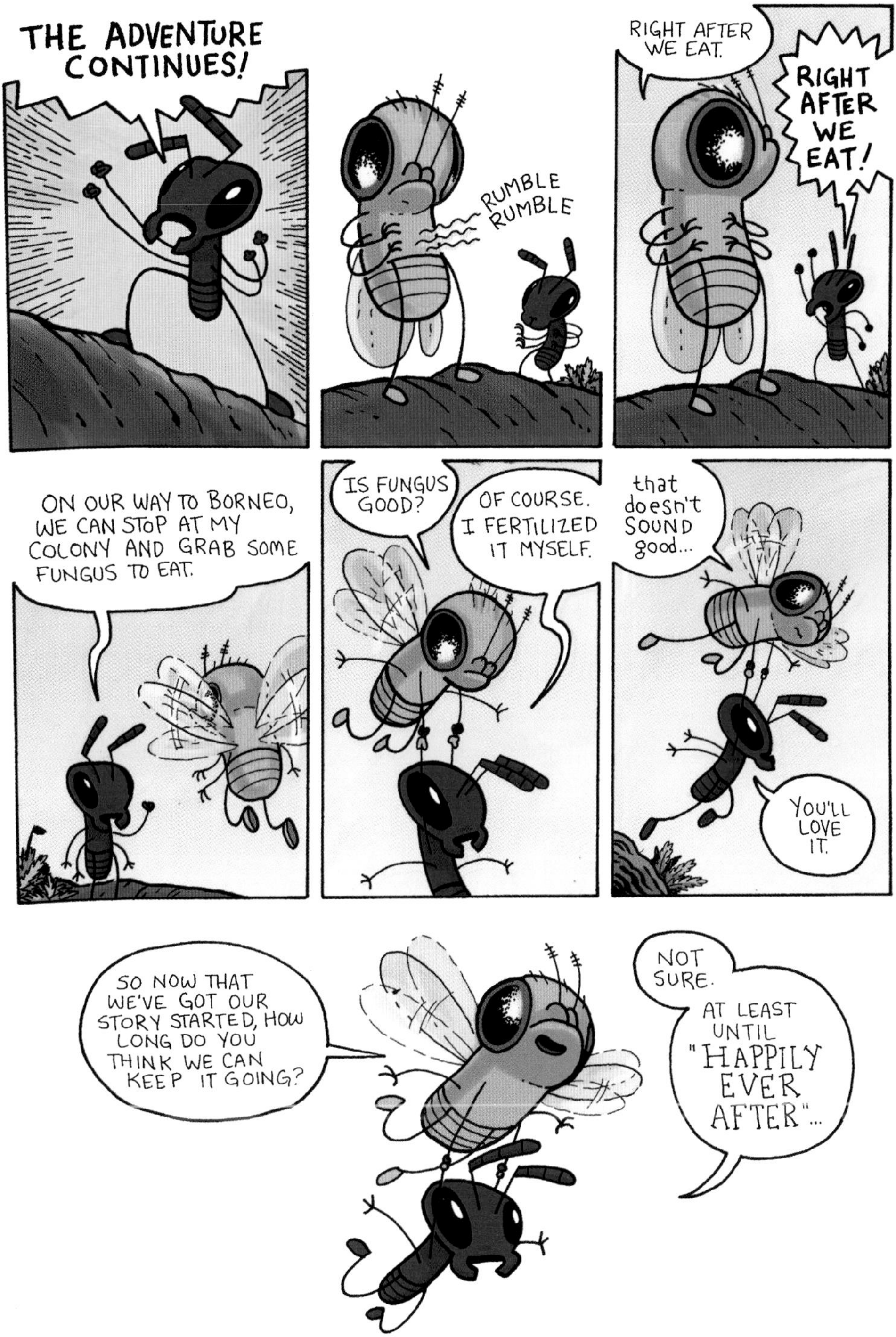
THE ADVENTURE CONTINUES!
RUMBLE RUMBLE
RIGHT AFTER WE EAT.
RIGHT AFTER WE EAT!
ON OUR WAY TO BORNEO, WE CAN STOP AT MY COLONY AND GRAB SOME FUNGUS TO EAT.
IS FUNGUS GOOD?
OF COURSE. I FERTILIZED IT MYSELF.
that doesn't SOUND good...
YOU'LL LOVE IT.
SO NOW THAT WE'VE GOT OUR STORY STARTED, HOW LONG DO YOU THINK WE CAN KEEP IT GOING?
NOT SURE.
AT LEAST UNTIL "HAPPILY EVER AFTER"...

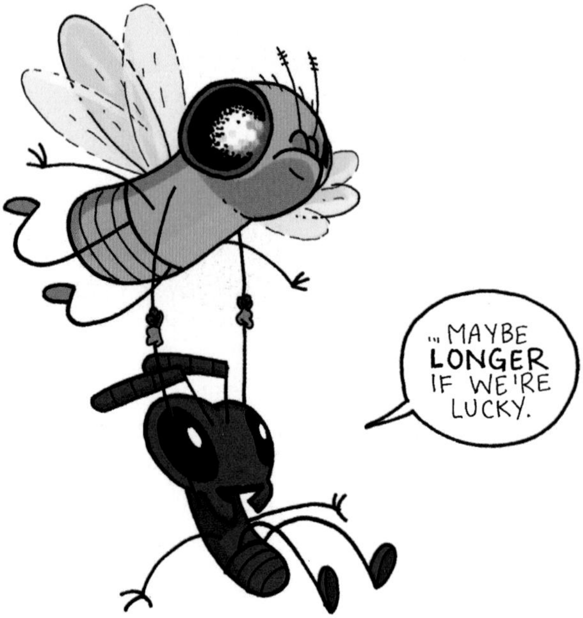
...MAYBE **LONGER** IF WE'RE LUCKY.